EARTH

The Lightwielder Chronicles

Volume One

When Darkness falls without reprieve
and the Hearts of good men quail.
When Nightmare walks the Ways at will,
Courage and Hope will fail.

From out the Wood where Light endures
Will come the One at need.
On Razer's edge will Deeds be judged
and the Fate of all Decreed.

DEDICATION

To three incredible women ...

Marion, my partner in life, thanks for your unwavering smile, love and companionship in all things. Without you, the world in which Alaena and her companions live and breathe would never have made it to paper.

***

Ann my mum who, aside from promising to read the whole series despite the fact that fantasy fiction is not her cup of tea, has constantly supported and encouraged me to bring the Lightwielder Chronicles to life.

***

Jayne, my brilliant daughter who has a PhD in English Literature, for all your thoughts and comments on the 2nd round, end to end edit of Earth. I wonder, my darling girl, if this is the first book ever to have the final edit done while the editor was breastfeeding?

Contents

Prologue

Deep in the mountain, they faced each other.

Tears left white trails down the face of Simcha, last matriarch of the Temple of Light, washing away soot and grime in their passage. The visage of Hor'yn, Arch-Mage of the Order of Earth, once proud and adamant, was a landscape of loss and despair.

In their eyes, reflections sparkled from the swirling lines of Light rotating before them. Cradled in black, smoking gut rock, the Holding sustained itself. Forming a perfect sphere, the vortex of Light measured twelve feet from side to side of bristling, curling, crackling energy. Sparks of silver-blue luminescence sizzled across the surface, linking, feeding and sustaining each other. The charged air in the closed space smelled of ozone.

The Demon Prince, bound within the construct, shrieked curses at those who had imprisoned him. With shocking virulence, the creature hurled rancid, red-hued bolts of power against the inner walls of the Holding, battering the foundations of the spell with a violence born of bloodlust and bitter, twisted hate.

Turning his head to assess the beast in the cacophony that surrounded them, Hor'yn measured the wards, feeling his own Spirit buffeted with each frenzied attack from within as the Demon bent all its mind and terrifying capacity for destruction to breaking free from the structures of Light that held it at bay. Turning back, Hor'yn locked eyes with Simcha once more. Each knew they could brook no further delay.

Nodding with resignation, Simcha took a long, slow breath. Composing herself, she returned her gaze to the stone beneath her feet. Concentrating carefully, she spoke a Word of change. The granite answered, acknowledging her Power. Writhing out of the scarred floor, the age-old rock flowed up like a living thing to form a gnarled pedestal between them. At waist height, the stone solidified once more, twisting and tapering up to spill out flat, forming a wide polished surface before them.

"Come!" Hor'yn called over the screams of the Demon and the blistering, buffeted whine of the Holding. "It is time!" At his command, a shadow detached itself from the walls. Al'tahal, Sword Master of the Northern Palace, limped forward. Exhaustion dripped from his battered, beaten frame. As he approached, the glare from the fractured lightning of the Holding highlighted his pale face. Livid burns glared blood in the staccato light.

"My Lord," Al'tahal croaked, kneeling slowly to one knee and bowing his head.

Leaning close to be heard in the din, Hor'yn rested a black-scarred hand on Al'tahal's shoulder. "Thank you, my friend," he said, in a weary voice that cracked with fatigue. "The world outside will need time to regrow from the seeds we sow today."

Gathering himself, Al'tahal grated to his feet. He kissed the hand of his Lord one final time with blood-flecked lips then, wincing from the pain it caused him, turned to the woman. Al'tahal wanted to speak but no words came readily to his choked, dry throat. Instead, he hobbled forward one more step and, taking Simcha's bruised and bloodied hands in his, lifted them to his parched lips and kissed them tenderly. "Simcha, my love," he rasped at last over the cacophony of the Holding which howled at his back. "Until we meet again." he said simply as he watched another tear spill down her face. Holding hands for a precious second more, Simcha's fingers finally fell away as Al'tahal released them. Bowing his farewell, he turned to the pedestal and drew free his sword with stiff, reluctant fingers. Kissing the hilt to honour the service it had done him, Al'tahal laid the weapon gently on the granite pedestal before looking soberly up at the two again as he placed his hands on the pedestal before them also, palm facing upwards.

Trembling and mentally steeling herself, Simcha took another deep breath that sounded like a sob. Pulling her eyes from Al'tahal, she transferred her focus to the pedestal as Hor'yn stepped forward to place his hands upwards on the surface next to Al'tahal's. Suppressing a need to scream over the screech of the Holding and the Demon held within, Simcha gritted her teeth and focused her mind. Putting all but the weapon and two pairs of bloodied, tattered hands resting on her pedestal in the whirling, writhing light, she pulled up the sleeve of her tattered robe, grasping the bracelet she wore on her wrist with shaking fingers. It came free with difficulty. Symbol of her Order, Simcha clearly remembered the day many years before when she had created it as token and proof of her Mastery. For a fleeting moment, she wondered if she would ever have the chance to see it again, or if today would be the beginning of the end of everything.

Trembling from more than mere exhaustion, Simcha pushed such thoughts from her mind and held the bracelet up for a moment. Through her tears of loss, Simcha watched the light from the Holding refract through the precious gems set evenly around the golden band. A spray of rainbow colours gyrated across the walls of the cavern around them, imposed upon the reflected white glare of the Holding.

Maintaining calm amidst the maelstrom, Simcha placed the treasure gently beside the sword. The hum in the cavern seemed to swell as power built in their minds and Simcha looked at the two pairs of hands lying before her as if in supplication. At last, she moved to complete the ritual. With light from the Holding flickering madly around them, Simcha placed her right hand down in the upturned hands of Hor'yn. Immediately, Hor'yn grasped hers urgently in return, as if to ensure that now commitment was made, neither could let go. Holding one second more, Simcha could not resist glancing up to Al'tahal one last time. His eyes were locked on hers, full of trust and surety as she placed her left hand in his, completing the triad. With her final vision that of the love in Al'tahal's eyes gazing back at her, Simcha opened her mind to the Lanes and spoke, bringing her towering will to bear to complete the ritual.

The Demons' screams were overwhelmed by the escalating whine of the Holding as their might melded, swelled and ignited. Law overturned under the force of their combined wills. Around them, the cavern ignited with raw, untrammelled power as Simcha exhaled her Word of Command.

The roots of the mountain shuddered with the prodigious force unleashed. Light seared the cavern through clouds of dust and smoke as the Holding transmuted with transferred power. Burning from silver to blue to white gold, the Holding strengthened, steadied and stabilised around the Demon Prince.

When the Light faded at last, Simcha's pedestal stood alone in the cavern beside the Holding. Simcha, Hor'yn and Al'tahal had given their all to secure the Demon's prison. Al'tahal's sword and the Bracelet of the Matriarch were also nowhere to be seen.

In the depths of a Wood that lay some leagues to the north of the mountain, a new Stone, set about with runes of Light came into existence. Hidden deep in the ancient forest, where even the most ardent hunters did not delve, the granite edifice in a certain light looked very much like the gnarled figure of a man standing pensive, waiting for fate.

***

Vetren, the Demon Prince whose hordes were responsible for a rampage of death and the widespread destruction of the earth in the years before his final capture by the Disciples of the Light, howled his wrath. Deep within the mountain, bound by an immutable construct of Law and Light, he vented his anguish into eternity with no one left to hear. Nursing bitter loathing for his captors, the enraged being hurled his odium outward for centuries, yet his prison held secure.

For the first hundred years, Vetren conjured spells and incantations with all the venom that his black soul could muster. Sealed in his tomb of coruscant power, Vetren's consummate hatred was matched in virulence only by the impotence of his rage. Vicious enchantments from the depths of time that eviscerated the very air within his prison collided violently with the shimmering field about him, before melting harmlessly into the lattice of light. Brutal barbs of power fuelled by loathing speared from his taloned claws, smashing with screaming force into the barrier, only to be absorbed and to dissipate harmlessly within white-gold rainbows of colour. Words of Destruction and Desecration spewed from his drooling maw, only to be turned, deflected or slammed back against him as the sphere, held secure by his captors' ultimate sacrifice, stood unyielding against the ravening wrath of the Demon Prince.

For a hundred years more, now aware that brute force would not avail him, the Demon's cunning mind sought freedom through other means. Refining his assault, Vetren forced his anger back and began to study his prison with other weapons in his arcane arsenal. Using incantations that in the past had bared the souls of many hapless victims, Vetren conjured lines of force designed to find flaws in the focus and work destruction. Like festering, demented maggots, spells black with vitriol crawled across the interior of the sphere, seeking footholds and flaws in the conjury. Whenever a tendril of force found a crack and black hope flowered in the Demon's heart, white power conjoined to seal the rift, snuffing the finger of force out as easily as a candle is extinguished with a breath.

Defeated in the end by the ultimate sacrifice of his three most bitter enemies and frustrated by the complete failure of all his long efforts to find release, Vetren's mind eventually skirted insanity. As time continued to pass, his efforts for release became more and more haphazard. Centuries more passed until he collapsed, exhausted and undone at last.

With the last shreds of his coherent mind, Vetren understood that his prison could not be breached from within. Even if they were able to help in some way, without his power and hate compelling them, the armies of minor demons, devils and imps over whom he held command before his imprisonment would have been overcome long ago, so he held no hope for rescue from that quarter. Ultimately, it became clear to him that time was the only thing that would save him. If nothing else, Vetren knew, the mountain would eventually fall. When it did, it would either crush him and end his torment, or wear down with the work of the elements on this planet to set him free. While that might take eons, Vetren consoled himself with his immortality. Time was the one thing he had in endless supply. Where force would not avail him then, patience and passivity would have to do.

So it was that Vetren, Demon Overlord of the Sathka and Guardian of the Second Key sunk to the granite floor, sheathed his claws, folded his red-scaled wings, and entered his own trance within the stasis field of the Holding. Retaining only enough cognisance of the environment around him to wake should anything change, he allowed his body to cool as his metabolism slowed, becoming as still as the rock which surrounded him, setting himself to wait.

His consciousness dimmed to the barest spark of awareness, the passage of time became rrelevant to Vetren. Though he had no way of measuring it, over a thousand years would pass locked away in his coruscant prison before he would wake once more.

Chapter 1 - Gathering

From her perch above the crowd, Alaena gazed over the mass of people that packed the public square. The sun was directly above, though winter made it weak. Hunger for the midday meal was just starting to make itself known. Normally on a Saterdei, with three days without school still to look forward to, her mood would be high. Today, however, was a Gathering Day, which filled her with nervous trepidation.

With a cool breeze blowing, the sea of heads stretched out before her like choppy waves of ruffled hair, hats and scarves. Her own dark hair was held back from her slim, pale face with a simple leather tie. Sitting up high on a set of stairs that overlooked the square, Alaena had a clear view of the enormous podium which had been erected in the centre of the area. Two massive oak beams protruded from it, each the height of a tall man. At the top of each beam, manacles stained black with old blood were affixed and secured with large iron pegs driven deep into the weathered wood.

When first erected, the podium was intended as a place where offenders of the most serious crimes could be publicly punished. Murder. Treason. Witchcraft. Its first use caused outcry throughout the town as a cruel and barbarous display of heavy-handed city justice. A man who protested his innocence until his cries overwhelmed words was flogged to death before a shocked populace. The edifice was removed for a while, but soon enough it was announced that another miscreant had been identified whose crimes warranted similar punishment. This time the victim, as Alaena thought of him, was a younger man who survived the fifty lashes, though he was borne away unconscious by the end. Despite, or perhaps because of, the horror of the first display, even more people attended. Since then, rather than being dismantled once more, the platform had been strengthened. Punishment had become more common even for lesser crimes. Over the past year, they had come to include not only women but children as well. As the Protector was fond of saying: a lesson learned early is a lesson learned well.

Alaena jumped, a sharp nudge in the ribs pulling her mind back from past images of violence and blood to the present.

"Ow!" she cried, giving the boy sitting next to her an elbow back in friendly fashion. "What was that for?"

Rince, a wiry boy about a year older than Alaena with tousled sandy-brown hair that contrasted sharply with his piercing blue eyes, offered a lopsided smile. Alaena felt her own lips tug up in response.

"Nothing, Ala," Rince replied, using the nickname that he seemed to have bestowed upon her of late. "I'm just bored." He glanced back to the crowd, which continued to swell as more people pressed into the square, then up to the enormous clock opposite them on the tower of the Town Hall that overlooked the area. It was ten minutes before the hour, and he sighed restlessly. "I just hate coming here and I don't see the point. Can't we go down to the Fields where they're setting up and see if we can get something to eat while we're there?"

Sitting above the crowds, it was unlikely they would be overheard by anyone nearby. A quick glance around showed the nearest Protectorate Guard a good twenty yards away. Nonetheless, Alaena frowned and directed a disapproving gaze at her friend.

"Rince, you know better than to say things like that out loud!" she said in a low, pointed voice. "What if someone overheard you?" Nodding meaningfully towards the podium as the level of noise from the crowd increased, she continued, "You don't want to end up over there, so you need to be careful about what you say, okay?"

"Yeah, Ala. Sure, I guess." Rince shrugged uncomfortably, looking a little abashed but still clearly preferring to be somewhere else. Picking at a splinter of wood that had chipped away from the rough stairs on which they sat, he lapsed into silence once more.

Alaena kept her attention on Rince a moment more, assuring herself that he had indeed taken her gentle recrimination to heart. *Dear Rince,* she thought as she watched some of his stray hairs tousled by the breeze. *If only the world thought the way you do, perhaps things like this Gathering would never even be.*

There was, however, little time for introspection. Alaena's attention was soon pulled from Rince to the scene around them.

The crowd in the square had swelled appreciably in the past few minutes. Gatherings were always well attended now and this one was no exception, with some two or three hundred people present today. While there were always zealots who supported the Protectorate who were vocal in support of the harsh standards they imposed on the population, the hum of the crowd was usually muted. Today, however, Alaena found herself unsettled and distracted by the noise that seemed to swell from the crowd and surround her. Strangely, the people nearby weren't being particularly loud, and those conversations she could see going on were conducted with heads together so she couldn't hear individual voices. Yet the more Alaena tried to shut out the noise, the more it seemed to impinge on her consciousness.

Closing her eyes, Alaena tried to let her mind drift to lighter matters, feeling the sun on her skin and the breeze on her face. Moments later, however, the intensity of the noise swelled suddenly. Alaena opened her eyes to see the Protector, flanked by two black-robed acolytes, walking solemnly onto the platform to announce the charges against the accused, and the punishment deemed necessary for the crimes announced.

His voice was deep, but rather than making it sonorous, the tone was harsh to Alaena's ears. It never failed to make her wish she was elsewhere.

"Fellow citizens of Morlyn!" The Protector's booming voice carried clearly across the square as he raised his arms, hushing the crowd as all attention focused on the podium. "We bring before you today one who is proven to be in thrall to the Black Arts. An abomination before us, she confesses herself a Witch and a Sorceress both! Showing no remorse, this Handmaiden of Evil warrants the harshest of punishment …"

Letting the words wash past her, Alaena's mind drifted across the square, absently listening to the surrounding noise that didn't seem to be abating even though the Protector was warming to his speech. Alaena shook her head and turned her thoughts inward, trying to understand what was occurring. Concentrating, she realised she could pick out individual conversations from the crowd. A pair of farmers over to her right were talking about going to an inn for an ale when the Gathering was over; a woman further away was chastising her child for unsettled behaviour. Finally, Alaena's mind settled on a man who was close to the podium. A cold sweat broke out on her forehead and dizziness started to set in as she realised this man was talking to no one – and indeed, he was much too far away for Alaena to hear him speaking if he were. Yet she could discern his thoughts clearly. Another shiver went through her as she became aware that he was here to see blood and that if a death followed, then so much the better.

All the while, the Protector's exhortations continued as Alaena gripped the rough railing harder in her struggle to restore some sense and balance to the world and come back to herself.

"And so it is, good citizens, that we bring before you this defiler and blasphemer, that we may purge the corruption from her body! May our Lord take her suffering as due retribution that we, His humble servants, carry out in His Name." He concluded his discourse with arms raised to the skies.

Alaena watched as if from another place while the now jeering crowd parted and a young woman, clad only in a torn and tattered homespun robe, was dragged up to the podium. The woman staggered on the top step, but two burly guards pulled her roughly back to her feet before stretching her arms up and securing her wrists in the manacles attached to each post. The woman herself seemed hardly aware of what was happening, her head lolling side to side and her legs barely supporting her as the guards stepped away when she hung helpless before the mob.

The Protector strode over to her, then took a handful of her filthy hair and pulled her head back for the crowd to see as he tore the sparse covering from her body. A sob escaped her frame as an acolyte unfurled a long leather whip with small balls of lead weighting the ends of each strand, then bowed in reverence as he handed it to the Protector. Swinging the strands and feeling the

14

weight experimentally, sadistic anticipation brought an ugly curl to his lip.

Stung with a deep sense of pity for the woman whose crime was probably no greater than speaking out against the oppression of the Protectorate, or worse, against the Protector himself, Alaena at last pulled her mind clear of the zealot near the podium. Unconsciously, she reached out to soothe the confused and terrified emotions that were streaming uncontained from the woman's mind. Alaena received a picture of a dark, dank place where the woman had been kept for uncounted days, chained, flogged and abused by burly men until her will broke. Unaware of her danger, Alaena's natural reaction to such extreme distress took place. Deepening contact, Alaena reached out to soothe the woman's tortured mind as the Protector's voice rang out above the crowd and cut through her senses.

"ONE!" he shouted with an air of triumph. The sharp crack of the whip against skin was followed by a desperate scream of pain. The first blow bit deep into the woman's flesh and beads of blood started to run in rivulets down her shaking, helpless frame.

Alaena started violently, unexpectedly, as the depth of the woman's pain lanced her own senses. As her mind's imprint of the blow hit her own slender frame, Alaena's head flew back and she bit down hard on her tongue, grunting in pain and shared shock.

Her mind awhirl with terrifying new sensations, Alaena blanched. *What is happening to me?* she thought, even as she tasted blood. Gripping the railing of the stair before her, Alaena fought to regain control of senses that all at once seemed to be her own, yet also belonged to another. She felt like she was floundering in a flood, helpless to resist the torrent that had caught her.

Desperate to bring herself back to her own physical presence, she reached out to her left, managing to clutch feebly at Rince's shoulder even as her mind continued to assimilate the feelings of hate, pain and malice that surrounded her.

***

Rince, his attention focused on the morbid scene before him, jerked around quickly at Alaena's movement, then stared for a moment with his mouth agape. For no reason he could discern, Ala, normally calm and composed, was clearly in distress. Taking in the sheen of sweat on her forehead and a trickle of blood at the corner of her mouth, Rince grabbed Alaena's shoulder, shaking her firmly as her wild, unfocused eyes swivelled to him. He saw terror and pain reflected there.

"Ala? Ala! What's the matter? Ala! Can you hear me?" Rince called urgently, oblivious to the heads nearby that turned curiously to look up at the two children on the steps above them. Concerned with her pallid expression and lack of response, Rince put his hand on her other shoulder as well and dragged her round forcibly to meet his gaze. "Ala! Look at me! What is it?" he repeated with worry lacing his voice.

Friendship had never come easily to Rince. His father believed that the use of a belt was the best way to ensure his only son obeyed his commands immediately and to the letter. His mother, at best, was an example of a woman who responded to the abuse of herself and her slightly built son with an insipid obsequience that was least likely to raise her husband's ire.

As such, Rince spent many of his formative years on the streets of Morlyn relatively isolated from others his age. While his parents still provided for him, and his mother, in her own way, cared for him as best she could, their house lacked colour or laughter or joy. As far as Rince was concerned, this was the way the world was. Friends were discouraged and most certainly visitors were not permitted, even if Rince had any to spend time with.

It wasn't until he met Alaena two years ago in a chance encounter that Rince became aware the world might not be as soulless a place as he had come to understand. Just turning fourteen at the time, Rince had been traversing the main streets of Morlyn. The evening was coming on quickly and he found himself hurrying. He was fully aware that he, and likely his mother as well, would be punished if he returned home a moment after dusk fell.

Anxiously looking at the sky to judge the time he had, Rince had stepped from sidewalk onto the road without paying full attention.

To his surprise, he found himself yanked unceremoniously backward by a hand on his arm as an angry shout came from in front of him. Rince had been about to step out in front of an oxen-drawn cart, which surely would have crushed the life from him.

Even so, Rince's first reaction was to turn on the person who had grabbed his arm and hauled him back, covering his embarrassment with apparent anger. When he turned however, words failed him. A girl, perhaps only a little younger than himself, stood assessing him with an oddly direct smile that entranced him. Above that smile, green eyes sparkled in a soft face that was framed by locks of long dark hair. Captivated, his frown faded and his anger melted away. In the eyes that regarded him, Rince saw nothing but genuine concern flecked by good humour.

"Are you all right?" the girl asked as her hand fell gently away. Rince would never forget the feeling of loss that accompanied the movement.

"Ye-yes," he had stammered. "Thank you," he continued, trying to find words. "I ... I ... I was keen to get home and just wasn't watching my step!"

The girl chuckled lightly. Her voice sounded like harps playing in his head. "Well," she said in a more serious tone while her persistent grin still tickled her lips, "let's not let you be late! Where do you live?"

The exchange had been so simple, yet the young man felt his life had somehow reset in the tantalisingly brief interchange. The girl had accompanied him all the way to his house, chatting as though they were old friends. While Rince stumbled over his words at first, he then found himself talking more to her during their short walk than he had to any other person for years. She had introduced herself as Alaena, an apprentice to the Chandler in the city. Unable to invite her inside once he was home, Rince somehow managed to suggest that they meet up again. He was amazed to find that Alaena, again grinning like she knew him, asked if he'd perhaps like to drop into the Chandler's sometime.

Since that day, there had been few where Rince and Alaena had not been together. He knew her now better than anyone else in the world, and because of this, he knew her panic and concern here on the steps while the Gathering progressed was truly out of character.

For a moment, as he continued to shake her and bring her gaze back to him, Rince thought he was getting through. Alaena's eyes appeared to focus a little at last, and he was about to ask again what was wrong. Then, before he could frame the question, the shout of "TWO!" rolled out across the crowd, followed by another sickening snap of leather against flesh, eliciting another cry of helpless, abject agony from the nameless woman.

Alaena's head wrenched back violently and Rince heaved it forward once more, taking her jaw firmly in his hand and forcing her to focus on him. As Alaena's eyes rolled back, Rince despaired. Then recognition returned and Alaena grabbed for his hand, struggling to rise.

"Rince ... I have to go. Please ... help me," she panted.

Still not comprehending the reason for her distress, Rince supported Alaena as she stumbled to her feet. She would have fallen down the stairs if he had not kept a good hold on her arm until she reached the cobbles below. Holding on to her still, Rince tried to turn her back and understand what was happening.

Alaena just shook her head wildly, tore free of his grasp and took off at a run, away from the horror behind her. Rince watched on, with several other much less concerned though no less curious onlookers, as Alaena bolted unchecked around the nearest building and out of sight, just as "THREE!" echoed off the walls, chasing her as she went.

Chapter 2 - Home

Alaena ran blindly through the streets of Morlyn until her breath was coming in gasps. Her mind at last started to clear. Stumbling to a walk once the echoes of the woman's pain faded with distance, she glanced around nervously to get her bearings. Her worn sandals slapped the ground with a staccato click that echoed sharply off the stone-walled buildings to either side.

On a normal day, the centre of Morlyn would be buzzing with the enticements of merchants proffering their wares to people both eager and reluctant to part with their coin. With many of the shops shut due to the Gathering however, there were few people out today. Those that were scurried from place to place, eager to be indoors and out of sight. Far better that than risk being stopped by one of the Protectorate and questioned as to why they believed their civic duty did not make them feel obliged to hear their leader speak and bear witness to the righteous justice being exercised in the Square.

Eventually stone buildings gave way to rough brick, sloughing off any pretence of prosperity as she entered the Docks district itself. Being a port city, the tang of the sea was always prevalent in the crisp, cool air of Morlyn. This close to the wharves, the salt scent became overlaid with the muggy, cloying smells of fish, livestock and wet rope.

Unlike the more prosperous centre of town, where the bulk of the citizenry attended the Gathering, this was a far more diverse area that still bustled with trade from all parts of the Kingdom. Negotiating the pitted roadway carefully, Alaena walked down the street to one side, staying out of the way of the dust and stench kicked up by the commerce that went to-and-fro along the road. Carts pulled by donkeys, and larger ones hauled by snorting, stamping oxen, vied for space on the street amongst men and women moving about on foot and by horse, depending on their station and their business.

By the time Alaena reached the stores that lined the streets around the docks, she had calmed. As always, the sun warming her face and hair restored her spirits. Finally, she cut sideways into an access lane which led to the rear entrance of the Chandler's shop where she lived and served as an apprentice to the proprietor Wilmen, an unusually tall, middle-aged woman.

The Chandler's rear entrance was halfway down the lane. Skirting around the odd broken crate and discarded machinery that littered the way, Alaena's long fingers trailed along the walls as she moved, absently feeling the rough wood grain as she passed, her troubled thoughts turning to the discomforting experience she had just endured. The intensity of her episode this morning left her trembling and concerned with what was happening to her. This was not the first time this had occurred, though the detail she had been able to discern and tangibly feel this time was greater.

Around this time last year, just before her fifteenth birthday, Alaena had experienced what she described to herself as an 'outside' feeling. She had spent that day with her two best friends, Rince and Hally. They had been watching the tourney preparations in the Fields outside Morlyn. Engrossed by the activity, they had stayed too long, which brought them back to the city after the sun had passed, making way for Luna's trek across the heavens. The docks were not a safe place to be after dark for wayward children. Alaena had been nervous, staying close by Rince and Hally as they made their way back through the narrow, poorly lit alleys. Her senses straining to hear anything that might spell trouble, a tremor had passed through her mind as they approached a corner shrouded in night. Though they were a good fifty paces away, Alaena felt her awareness encompass the presence of four men around the corner ahead of them. Experiencing a wash of malice and discontent flowing from their thoughts brought her to an abrupt halt, grabbing for Rince and Hally's hands as they paused also, looking around to Alaena with questions in their eyes as to why she was stopping them, here of all places. Shaking her head to their querulous looks, she turned quietly and backtracked. pulling them with her. Taking another route home, they arrived safely. Alaena explained it away to Rince and Hally at the time as just a noise she thought she'd heard. Since then, however, Alaena had experienced the sensation a few times, but never as uncontrollably or with the intensity of her experience today.

While before she'd been able to get a general feel of a person's intent or demeanour, today at the Gathering was the first time she'd had a physical reaction to that of another. Maybe it was the intensity of the pain the woman was feeling or maybe Alaena had just let it go too far, but quite apart from the shared agony Alaena had experienced, she could swear she'd felt the blows of each lash as though it had been her own bare skin taking the punishment.

Concern washed over her as she realised for the first time that this ability could get her into deep trouble. Practicing Witchcraft, as all Morlyn knew, was a crime punishable by death. The flogging the woman had received today was only the beginning of what Alaena would experience if others were to learn of what she was beginning to be able to do. A slick, cold sheen of anxious sweat broke out over her body as she thought of how she'd fled the scene when the punishment started. Alaena did not want to think about the consequences if someone had recognised her and thought her reaction or her swift departure strange enough to investigate.

Shaking her head to dispel these dismal thoughts, Alaena stopped before a small green gate set into the wall that lined the alley on the left. Reaching through a hole in the gate to trip the latch on the other side, her features softened to a smile as the gate suddenly rattled and a small set of paws scrabbled excitedly on the other side.

"Shoo, Scruff. Get back!" she called gently as she pushed the gate open and stepped through into the tidy, compact courtyard behind the shop. The small black terrier she'd found as a stray some years ago and had unofficially adopted scampered around her and received a scratch behind the ears for his efforts.

"Been good today, boy? Keeping the place safe for us?" Alaena said, chuckling as she moved her hand around his head to avoid Scruff's searching tongue. "Yes, Scruff. I love you too." Alaena gave him a final pat as she straightened up and started up the small set of wooden stairs that led up to the rear entrance of the shop, Scruff following close on her heels.

Pushing the latch down and pulling the door open with its familiar squeak of unoiled hinges. Alaena shooed Scruff back and closed the door behind her as she walked into the small but serviceable kitchen that occupied the back of the building. To her left, the open pantry would usually be an enticing invitation to snack on some coarse bread and cheese that was kept in the cool box within, but still unsettled from her earlier experience, Alaena took a glazed tankard from a shelf near the window and filled it with cool water. Sipping it gently, she leant against the cupboard to settle herself while looking around the dim interior of the room.

Apart from the rear door she'd entered by, there were two other doors in the kitchen. One to her right as she entered was a simple swing door that could be opened in either direction. It led to a sitting room with a modest couch and a small but formal dining table where Wilmen occasionally entertained guests. That room also led to a stairway that went upward then doubled back on itself to give access to the upper floor living areas and bedrooms.

The other door, directly opposite the rear entrance, was a more solid affair made of oak and with a sturdy lock. It led through Wilmen's open workshop and into the Chandler's shop itself. The workshop was where she and Wilmen made the astonishing array of candles that they sold. Together, the work area and the shop itself occupied the rest of the lower floor of the establishment and fronted the main street. Even now, two years into her apprenticeship, Alaena could recall the first day Wilmen had shown her through the workshop, and the delight she'd had in opening and smelling the many additives used to scent the wares she made. Thick lavender-scented candles purchased for bathhouses, small rose candles dyed pink for the parlours of the more affluent, tall plain beeswax candles for the various churches that burned all night – the variety was as broad as the need.

Alaena could hear voices through the door leading to the shop. Though muffled, she could clearly identify Wilmen's firm, no-nonsense voice talking prices and quantities to a thin male voice she didn't recognise. Some minutes and another mug of water later, footsteps followed by the familiar tinkle of the bell attached to the door at the front of the shop indicated the customer leaving. A few moments later, the door to the kitchen swung open as Wilmen stepped through and stopped in surprise to see Alaena still leaning at the kitchen bench, mug cupped in both hands.

"Alaena, my dear! I thought you'd be gone for most of the day today. What brings you back so soon?" she asked, stepping forward to give her a quick hug.

Though unrelated, Wilmen and Alaena had formed a bond these past few years. More often than not now, Wilmen had started to treat Alaena as Alaena thought her own mother might, had she known who she was. Perhaps brought on by her recent fright, a surprisingly strong feeling of warmth and emotion welled up in Alaena at the brief show of affection and she returned Wilmen's embrace strongly, holding her tight and taking strength from her arms about her.

"There, there, dear. What's the matter now?" Wilmen said soothingly, holding Alaena firmly in return, surprised at the intensity of her embrace. After a few moments, Wilmen pushed Alaena back so she could see her face clearly. Taking in Alaena's unusually distracted expression, Wilmen's brows creased with concern and her tone became serious. "Alaena", Wilmen spoke clearly as she watched Alaena's features carefully. "What's upset you so? Tell me what's wrong, dear."

Pushing down an unexpected urge to cry, Alaena briefly considered telling Wilmen exactly what had happened. Admitting to someone that you'd experienced something that could only amount to Witchcraft, however – even a person as close to her as Wilmen was – was something she could not do. Covering her stumbling words with a confusion and distress that was only part feigned, Alaena came as close to the truth as she could while Wilmen watched her face with concern.

"Oh … Wilmen. There was a Gathering today. This poor woman was chained up. There was blood and everyone started screaming for more and … and …" The words began to tumble together as Alaena started sobbing in delayed reaction to her experience. "… and I felt so ill, Wilmen. Dizzy and so sick. I just couldn't stand being there any longer, so I ran. I didn't know what else to do!"

Lifting her eyes as another sob escaped, Alaena saw worry and disquiet reflected in Wilmen's gaze. Knowing Wilmen would want to understand more, Alaena made an effort to explain, but gave Wilmen little more information in the end. She tried to frame more words to explain what she'd experienced, but her head felt like cotton wool and a headache that had formed at the base of her skull started to creep up over her head. After a while she gave up, and when she had finally calmed, Alaena just sat staring stupidly at her hands in her lap.

"I'm sorry, Wilmen," Alaena muttered eventually. "I don't know what came over me, but I'll be more careful in future so I don't create a fuss."

For her part, Wilmen could see that Alaena's upset was very real. She had never seen Alaena so out of sorts before, and it worried her considerably. Something significant must have happened to cause this normally calm, controlled girl such distress.

For a moment, she considered pressing the point to find out exactly what had happened, as there was clearly more to know. But looking down at Alaena's tear-stained face, she realised there was little more to be gained from questions now. It would be better to ask later, when Alaena's experience had faded somewhat. Normalcy was likely what would get Alaena back to herself, so that's what she would provide.

Leaning forward, Wilmen held Alaena tight for a moment before she gave her a final comforting squeeze. Adopting a matter-of-fact tone, she said, "All right, dear. Let's put this behind us for now, get you something to eat, and you can help me in the workshop this afternoon. I have a new order for Ilsun at the Good Knight that we need to get to him in the next week in time for the tourney."

Alaena nodded numbly. As Wilmen bustled about the kitchen preparing a light meal, she slouched at the bench and finished sipping her water. Considering it was not yet midday and the fact that she had eaten breakfast only a few hours ago, Alaena was surprised at how hungry she was. While she would normally help Wilmen prepare the food, Alaena also felt her headache building, so instead of jumping up to help, she leaned forward tiredly with elbows on the bench and put her head in her slender hands, massaging her temples until Wilmen placed a roll filled with cold meats before her, which Alaena proceeded to devour like she hadn't eaten for a week.

Despite the growing headache, Alaena felt a thrill of excitement surge as they discussed the upcoming festival between mouthfuls. She had already talked about the tourney with Rince and agreed that as they both loved it so much last year, they'd attend most of the archery events again this year. Buoyed by the discussion and sated somewhat by the food, Alaena helped clear up, then moved to the workshop with Wilmen as the conversation turned to more practical matters of the candles they needed to produce by the following week.

The first task at hand was to start the order for Ilsun. His order was a large one, as Wilmen had indicated. The twelve dozen tall candles would probably last him a month, given his inn had ten rooms to light that would be fully occupied throughout the week of the tourney at least. Each candle had to be thick to ensure it would last a full day per stick, so they used the largest moulds they had. The process was simple enough, but time-consuming. The moulds were simply hollow cylinders with open tops through which wicks were inserted. When the desired number of moulds and wicks were in place, tallow was heated until molten, then poured into the mould around the wick. From there, it was simply left to cool before removing the mould and trimming the wick to finish the candle. Scents and colour could be added as well if desired.

Apprenticed to Wilmen for over two years now, Alaena understood the processes well. She normally would have managed to start a batch of candles such as Ilsun needed without difficulty. Even the simple process of tying the wicks to the broach, however, proved difficult today. Focusing on the knot sent her vision spinning and made her head pound.

Wilmen, sitting at the shop counter and working out her inventory for new orders that would soon be needed with business thriving, watched Alaena's struggles with an ever-deepening frown creasing her brow. By the time Alaena had finished pouring the last mould and sagged back in her seat with a dazed expression, Wilmen had made her decision. Closing her books with a snap that Alaena barely seemed to register, Wilmen gently took her by the arm, led her unresisting back through the kitchen, left into the sitting room and upstairs to her bed. Moving gently but quickly, for Alaena appeared almost asleep on her feet, Wilmen removed Alaena's apron and clothes, slipping her into a comfortable nightshirt. While smoothing her hair back with one hand, Wilmen laid Alaena back on the bed with the other, then watched with careful concern in her sharp gaze as Alaena slid quickly into a heavy sleep.

Waiting long enough to ensure Alaena was well into her slumber, Wilmen left the room, being careful to close the door quietly to ensure Alaena remained undisturbed. Unable to sort hope from fear in her mind as she considered what little she knew of the day's events, Wilmen quickly moved to her own bedroom upstairs, down the hall from Alaena's own room.

Closing this door behind her as well, Wilmen stood a few moments, listening intently. The noise of commerce drifted up from the street, muffled through the thick glass and heavy material of the blinds. A light breeze played fitfully through the eaves and across the roof of the dwelling.

Satisfied that there was nothing unusual happening and that she was secure for the moment at least, Wilmen moved purposefully towards the small nightstand that stood against the wall on the opposite side of the bed. In the dim light, her reflection in the mirror affixed to the top of the nightstand looked haunted. She dismissed the image from her mind, avoiding distraction and unwarranted additional concern. Bending to one knee before the old, battered piece of furniture, Wilmen reached under, her fingers questing carefully for a cunningly concealed latch under the front drawer.

In a practiced motion, Wilmen depressed the latch with the fingers of her right hand as she lifted the draw with her left, causing a panel hidden within to drop down about the span of her hand before coming to a stop. In the small space the panel concealed sat a silver ring, in which was set a small, golden-hued stone. Next to the ring sat a small box made of a dark, dense material.

Ignoring the box for now, Wilmen reached for the ring. It was heavy considering its delicate look, as though the fine metal strands spun to give it an undulating surface contained something more than mere earthly constructs.

Taking a deep breath to calm the whirlwind of her thoughts, Wilmen positioned herself comfortably on the edge of her bed, closed her eyes and concentrated. For a few moments, her mind remained clouded. Slowly, though, the feel of the silver on her finger focused her mind and the fog began to recede. In the clear space that appeared, lines of Light began to take shape. As always, the beauty of the lattices enthralled her; Wilmen had many times wished desperately that she had the talent or training – or perhaps both were required – to do more.

On this occasion, however, her need and talent were aligned. Reaching through the silver on her hand and the Light in her mind, she framed a picture of a man dressed in a soft leather coat, tunic and boots. His secretive eyes were dark, his stance balanced.

"Talgard!" she breathed into the void. "Talgard Pretau!" she called again, louder. Her mind pushed force into the words as the lattices of Light in her mind sparkled in response.

As she had guessed, she did not have to wait long for a response.

"Sister!" came the abrupt reply. The voice in her mind mingled implications of a reprimand. "I trust the need is great, my friend," came next, the tone softening, "for these trinkets are not to be used lightly!" A picture came briefly to her mind with the words of a ring matching her own sitting comfortably on a slim, scarred hand.

As always, Tag's dry and oft inappropriate sense of humour bothered Wilmen. This time, however, her need took precedence over all else. Wilmen wasted no time getting to the point.

"Tag," she started simply. "Please, come see me as soon as you can. A matter has arisen for the Council, and I would have your advice before we discuss it with them."

"Of course, Sister," Tag responded immediately. "For a matter of such import I will come as soon as I can. I should be able to be there shortly after sunup tomorrow, if that would suit?

"Yes, Tag. That would work perfectly, thank you."

"Till the morning, then, Sister," Tag closed formally before Wilmen felt him leave the link.

Not for the first time in her life, Wilmen felt gratitude for both Tag's brevity and trust. He had not wasted time with banter, nor had he done her the disservice of pointless questions. She had said it was important and he had accepted it as such, and could be counted on to be there as promised.

With some reluctance, Wilmen took one last look at the lines of Light and then stepped back in her mind, pulling the ring from her finger as she did so. As always when using the Power like this, Wilmen felt immediate fatigue when she disengaged.

Pleased she was already on her bed, she kept the ring held tightly in her fist as she laid her head back on her pillow to recover. Sleep would not come, for her mind remained in turmoil as to what to do about Alaena. At least, she consoled herself, she would tell Tag what she felt in the morning and he would hopefully agree to support her representation to the Council soon after.

Eventually, slumber took Wilmen. Her dreams were filled with Earth, Fire and Light.

Chapter 3 - Stranger

Alaena woke slowly, blinking to clear the haze in her mind as she realised she was in her room. Momentarily confused, Alaena laid her head back and thought about how she made it upstairs and into bed. The last thing she clearly remembered was being in the workshop and having to concentrate hard on pouring the wax for the last of the candles she was making before an overwhelming headache engulfed her. Fuzzy recollections of Wilmen helping her up from the workbench came back to her briefly, before she realised it must indeed be late in the morning, for the bleak sun washing in her window shone directly on her in bed.

Forcing herself into motion, Alaena pushed back the covers and swung her long, lanky legs down to the floor. Enjoying the cool wooden floorboards under her bare feet, Alaena padded across the room to her wardrobe, pulling her nightshirt over her head as she moved. Plainly finished but of solid construction, the wardrobe had drawers on the right and a large door on the left into which was set a full-length mirror.

Shaking her hair free, Alaena paused to study herself in the mirror. Her granite-grey eyes, so close to colourless that they sometimes resembled shards of glass, looked back impassively. Dangling from her long slender fingers, the nightdress trailed lightly onto the floor.

Alaena's introspection and contentment faded quickly, however, as the events of and following the Gathering came back to her mind. Focusing on the day to come to push them back from her mind, Alaena put her nightdress away in one drawer and from another shook free her comfortable work clothes. She anticipated a morning at the bench completing the work she and Wilmen had begun yesterday, before hopefully joining Rince to while away the afternoon in the fields, where preparations were underway for the Tourney. It was due to start the following week, only eight days from now, Alaena recalled with a thrill of anticipation. Her feet now feeling the cold from the floor, Alaena decided to wear her light boots rather than the sandals she normally wore. Pushing aside the long cloak that impeded her as she reached to the back of the cupboard to retrieve her boots, Alaena felt a small, hard object within.

She reached into the pocket of the coat. Her eyebrows arched in recognition as her hand closed over the object and pulled free a small knife. Yellowed and discoloured with age, the smooth ivory handle was only as long as her middle finger and had a slim cavity along one side into which the blade folded when not in use. This was Rince's favourite whittling knife that he'd bemoaned the loss of at length last year and that they'd assumed was lost forever. Alaena smiled as she slipped it down into the side of her boot, anticipating the moment she would produce it with a flourish and how pleased Rince would be to see it once more.

Alaena hoped she would have time to find him and see what had happened yesterday after she fled, but first she needed to talk to Wilmen. Making her way downstairs, Alaena was surprised to hear voices in the kitchen Though feeling a little guilty for eavesdropping, she stopped quietly with one hand on the door, listening.

There were two voices she could make out, both speaking in low tones. One was Wilmen's firm voice. Usually confident and cogent, Wilmen's tone conveyed a worrying tension through the thin door that Alaena wasn't used to hearing from her guardian. The other, a deep male voice with an unusually nasal accent, seemed to be trying, unsuccessfully, to make a point.

"Yes, Wilmen, that is true, but we have had no word of this through our contacts. If it were noticed, there would already be word out and we would indeed have cause to fear. But no news is good news in this case, do you not agree?"

"Perhaps so, my friend," responded Wilmen, "but I seek surety on this, rather than assumption. The prize is too important and the price too high if our reasoning is flawed. Surely we are all agreed on this, also?"

"We do not speak for each other, as you well know, Wilmen," the unknown voice chided gently. "Be assured, however, that we are all too aware of what is at stake here. We have not endured in secret for all these years without learning, shall we say, a prudent approach to pragmatism."

There was a pause in the conversation and a clink of crockery from beyond. Alaena placed her hand gently on the handle of the door, ready to push it open and make her presence known, when Wilmen gave a heavy sigh and continued. Her words froze Alaena in place.

"In this, I am unsure, Tag. We have discussed that Alaena is young still and the time for her testing is not yet upon us. I know everyone believes it too early and too dangerous to try." Wilmen sounded to Alaena like she was trying to convince herself of this, yet tension continued to taint her voice. "I understand all this, my friend, but Ala's young friend Rince came by this morning to see how she was. I questioned him closely and what he had to say filled me with both a hope I cannot disregard and a fear that I cannot shed. Alaena didn't just wander from the Gathering after finding it distasteful. According to Rince, she ran from the crowd 'like a demon was on her tail'. I can only think, Tag, that there is more to this than we know. We cannot ignore the fact that it could be a sign that Alaena's Talent is indeed maturing!"

Another heavy pause followed, but the mysterious gentleman either had nothing to say or could think of no response to that. With a sense of trepidation bordering on fear, Alaena carefully took her hand off the handle, absently wiping sweat that had built up on her palm on her clothes as she stepped back soundlessly. Wishing in part that she had just stayed in bed and not overheard this uncomfortable conversation, Alaena held her breath, trembling a little as Wilmen continued with gravity in her tone.

"I want to test her, Tag," she said abruptly, eliciting a sharp intake of breath from her companion. "I know," Wilmen continued quickly, not giving her companion the chance to object. "This is a treacherous road to take. If we do so and if we rouse her before she's ready, then we risk losing all as she'll be exposed like never before. If we don't, however, and she really is coming into her Gift, then it will be only a matter of time before she is discovered in any case. I wish we could still wait and let things happen as we'd planned, but I can feel a storm coming that may overwhelm us all. Without this hope, what more do we have?"

"I hear you, Wilmen, though my heart wishes it were otherwise. Surely there is another answer, but for my life I cannot see it. Let us meet as planned tonight. I will not gainsay you when you speak, but neither will I support you in this. If the Light wills and your hopes or your fears prevail, then let it be done."

Alaena started at the sound of chairs scraping and farewells being said as footfalls made their way across the kitchen. Backing away quietly, she retreated to the stairs, her mind whirling with questions. Who was Wilmen talking to? What was Wilmen so concerned about that clearly implied a danger to Alaena herself? What had Rince said to Wilmen, and who was it that she and the mysterious stranger were going to meet with tomorrow, to apparently decide Alaena's fate? Indeed, what fate of Alaena's was it they were even talking about?

Not knowing whether to cry, or to shout, or just bowl through the door and demand answers from Wilmen for the lie that appeared to have underlined her life, Alaena dallied for a moment in anguished indecision. It wasn't until she heard the bell at the front of the shop chime that she leapt into action. Taking the stairs two at a time, she raced up to her bedroom and across to the window, tripping the latch and throwing it wide to lean out and give herself a good view of the street.

In the press of the mid-morning commerce, however, there were people everywhere. After some time fruitlessly scanning the crowd, she finally stepped back, pulled the window down and relocked the catch, no wiser as to the identity of the man who she had never met but who seemed to be deeply entwined in her affairs.

Chapter 4 - Excursion

Cursing lightly, Alaena returned to the bed to sit and think, her long fingers toying absently with the sheet, still unmade and crumpled from her long slumber. Awhirl with the implications of what she'd just heard, Alaena's mind groped for understanding. The sanctuary of her bedroom, normally so comforting, gave little sense of security. Every loud noise from the street outside made her start.

Closest to her heart and the cause of most hurt, Alaena's perception of her world was rocked as she realised Wilmen clearly had secrets that were not only relevant to Alaena, but were possibly a danger to her as well. Since Alaena was old enough to understand that her own parents had cast her aside, Wilmen had been the closest thing to a mother that she had. Until now, Alaena had trusted her unconditionally.

Taking a deep breath, Alaena sought to calm herself. *This is not the way to deal with this,* she told herself. What was it Wilmen had said to the stranger called Tag? *"If we rouse her before she's ready, then we risk losing all ..."* Rouse her? In what way? Lose all? Lose what?

Belatedly, Alaena realised that while she had lived with Wilmen for years now, she actually knew very little about her. Wilmen did spend some nights out late and Alaena did not know where. There were also times when Wilmen was away for longer periods, leaving the shop to Alaena to look after. Usually these absences were only for a few days, but they sometimes stretched out longer. Ostensibly, Wilmen was out purchasing stock and trading her own wares, but now Alaena started to wonder just how much of Wilmen's excursions related to her business interests, and how much related instead to Alaena.

The first thing she needed was information. Clearly, she could not turn to Wilmen for explanations. Her ignorance of the situation being complete, Alaena was also in no position to assess or predict Wilmen's response were Alaena to challenge her. Turning to other options, Alaena sat bolt upright as it came to her. Rince. Wilmen had said that Rince came by to see her this morning and that she had questioned him closely about what had happened the day before. Sure of him as a friend at least, Alaena jumped up from the bed, determined to find Rince as soon as she could and ask him their conversation.

Rather than arouse suspicion, Alaena went downstairs as normal. After a quick snack to break her fast, she joined Wilmen in the workroom as though this was just another day. Assuring Wilmen she was fine after her long rest, as indeed she was, Alaena found she could dodge Wilmen's questions well enough if she immersed herself in her work and ignored the sidelong glances Wilmen directed at her on regular occasions throughout the morning.

Though patient enough while waiting, Alaena jumped up quickly at the distant sound of the bell in the docks area tolling midday.

Wilmen gave Alaena a considered look when she asked if she might join Rince at the Fields in the afternoon. Wiping her pen clean and stoppering the ink bottle so it wouldn't dry out, Wilmen came over and took Alaena's fidgeting hands in her own.

"Ala, my dear," she began, "it would be good for you to get out of the house and have some air but be back well before dark." Wilmen's voice echoed gravely as she adopted a more serious tone. "I think that business at the Gathering yesterday is behind us, Ala, but there's no point tempting the fates. Stretch your legs and have a look around, but stay clear of trouble and make sure that Rince does too!" The smile Wilmen gave her contradicted the concern in her eyes, but that passed quickly as the smile broadened and she reached into her pocket to pull a few coppers free. "Here, Ala. Get yourselves a treat and bring something back for us to have with our meal tonight."

Closing her fingers on the coin, grateful that Wilmen was not pursuing less comfortable topics, Alaena gave her a perfunctory hug, telling Wilmen not to worry and that she'd just be a few hours. With the spring air still cool at times, particularly down on the open fields on the other side of town, Alaena dashed upstairs quickly to change her top and retrieve a short woollen jacket from her wardrobe that would keep the worst of the wind out. Wilmen was not in the kitchen when she came back down, sparing Alaena the effort of maintaining her air of nonchalance when underneath, her troubled heart thumped in her chest.

It was a relief when Alaena at last stepped out the Chandler's back door, pulling it shut quietly behind her. Scruff, seeing his mistress emerge at last, loosed his bottled-up excitement and accosted her wildly. Unable to make up his mind as to whether he should jump on her or scamper around in excitement, Scruff tumbled around her giving little happy barks as she bent down to catch his bouncing head in her hands and smile fondly at him. "Sure, Scruff. Calm down, boy!" Still trembling with pent up energy, Scruff succumbed to a moment of peace as Alaena scratched lightly behind his ear. "That's it, Scruff, let's go for a walk and give you a bit of a run if we can, eh?" Alaena said, standing once more and giving a laugh as Scruff bounded down the steps and stood barking up at her as if a moment's further delay was simply impossible.

Some few minutes and much licking and laughter later, Alaena had Scruff secured by a short length of twine and was stepping out into the alley once more to go find Rince. Scruff treated any excursion outside the yard as a wonderful adventure, and Alaena could only continue to smile fondly as he pulled her this way and that on the lead, investigating every spot and every smell within range of his twitching, inquisitive nose.

"Come on, boy. This way," said Alaena, turning left down the alley and pulling Scruff along behind her. "Let's go find Rince!"

Finding her friend proved little obstacle. Assuming Rince would be near the town square where they normally met, Alaena pushed down the queasy nervousness that the prospect of returning there evoked, steeling her jaw and making her way to the main road. She turned right onto the road and stayed to one side, keeping Scruff's lead short and out of the way of the early afternoon press of trade and traffic as he trotted along beside her. After only a few minutes' walk, she was pleasantly startled from her sombre thoughts by a shout from Rince, who was weaving his way through the crowd towards her.

"Ala!" Rince cried, drawing a disapproving stare from more than one passer-by. "Ala, you're well, then!" he called before finally reaching her and wrapping his arms around her in a hug.

Given his wiry frame, Alaena was surprised at the strength of the embrace. She let herself enjoy being held for a moment before struggling to extricate herself from Rince's crushing enthusiasm.

Rince let go quickly and covered a quick blush with a pat for Scruff, who had no such inhibitions about enthusiastic displays of affection and was scampering excitedly about the two of them.

After freeing her legs from the tangle of twine that Scruff had wrapped her in, Alaena looked up at Rince. His expression of joy in seeing her was quickly transforming into a look of genuine concern, accompanied by a breathless burst of questions that tumbled one after another with no pause for answer.

"Ala, it really is good to see you! I was just coming back to see if you were all right, but Wilmen said you were ill and needed rest, so I didn't know if you'd be up yet. Are you well? What was wrong yesterday and why'd you run like that? You know it's a dangerous thing to do! Wilmen asked me question after question when I came around earlier ..."

Trying to get a word in, Alaena finally grabbed Rince and gave his shoulder a friendly shake. "Rince!" she said. "I'm fine! Really! I think it was just a passing ague, but I've slept well, and guess what?" Pulling out the coins Wilmen had given her and holding them out in her hand, she grinned at Rince's expression. "Wilmen's asked me to get her something, and we can get something for ourselves at the Fields!" Knowing the answer just by the look in his eyes, Alaena nevertheless pursued the question, "What do you think?"

Regaining some of his good humour, Rince stepped back and gave a formal bow, as though he were standing before no less than a Queen herself in court. "It would be a pleasure to accompany my lady to the Fields," he said with an exaggerated flourish and a lordly lilt to his voice. "Let us do so and sample some of the baker's craft, to ensure we bring the best back with us!"

Alaena chuckled, falling happily into her part. "Indeed, m'lord, I could think of nothing I would enjoy more!" she exclaimed. Linking her arm in his as though in grand procession, they turned and proceeded in step together along the path as if walking toward waiting thrones.

Their banter remained light for a while and Alaena, feeling comfort in the reliable support of her friend, kept her arm linked with Rince's as they walked. She was immensely pleased when she felt Rince settle his arm more comfortably with hers, a small smile playing on his lips as they proceeded arm in arm, Scruff trotting happily alongside.

Even the warmth Rince felt in the moment though couldn't stop the chill that travelled down his spine when Alaena, after a few minutes of companionable silence, broke the mood.

"Rince," she asked simply, "what did Wilmen ask you about me and the Gathering?"

The question was innocent enough, yet Alaena felt Rince tense a little. "You know, Ala," he responded after a moment, "it was really odd. I thought she was going to ask me what happened at the Gathering to make you run away like that, but her questions weren't about that. Rather than ask me about what had happened or who might have seen it that we should worry about, she only asked me about you. What you'd said. How you looked. She asked me about your eyes, Ala, and if anything else had happened that I thought was unusual, as if the whole thing wasn't unusual enough by itself!"

Nervously, Alaena pursued the question, for she had pondered the meaning of such questions herself this past day. "How do you mean 'anything else', Rince? What did she mean by that?"

"I thought the same, Ala, and again, it seemed very odd." Taking a breath, Rince continued. "She asked me if it was windy in the square, or if a breeze had come up while it all happened. She asked me if I'd seen your eyes and if they were focused or unfocused. She asked if there were any other strange things I

37

noticed, like if any other people reacted like you or anything like that."

"Honestly, Ala," Rince concluded, "I didn't get the point, but I told her there was nothing else and no one else I saw of concern. She seemed happy with this but I could tell there was a lot more worrying her than what she'd talked about. Why do you think she was asking things like that?" he queried gently.

At that, Alaena baulked. She trusted Rince more than anyone else in her life, but she still had to think about Wilmen, the man who had visited called Tag and what that all meant before she was ready to share it further with her friend. Thinking it was best to change the topic of conversation before they delved too close to those subjects, Alaena decided brevity was the best course of action for now.

"I don't know, Rince," she said lightly, burying her concerns deep for the moment. "Perhaps she was just more concerned than we thought and wanted to know if others had noticed me run. Either way," Alaena concluded, detaching her arm at last as they reached the outskirts of Morlyn where the Tourney Fields started, "let's get ourselves something to eat and worry about this another day, shall we?"

Rince, too familiar with Alaena's ways to be fooled by the uncharacteristic flippancy of her response, let it drop regardless. There would be other opportunities to discuss it and Rince could see she didn't want to be pressed on the matter now.

Either way, he wanted nothing more than to have Alaena's warm arm linked into his again as they moved on.

Chapter 5 – Awakening

Set at the start of the great grass plains bordering Morlyn to the west, which the nomadic tribes of the Tunyae Horsemen called home, the Fields were buzzing with activity. With all this going on about them, it took Rince and Alaena very little time to forget their concerns, for a time at least.

In greatest abundance by far, there were merchants' stalls for the commoner and tents for the more discerning customer, or for those who preferred their business conducted in private. In amongst the press of commerce, jugglers vied for a place against the rickety stages of puppet masters and magicians whose prestidigitation drew many a curious and awed audience.

Great tents and multicoloured pavilions dotted the grassland well into the distance. Servants, runners and officious city administrators alike dashed to-and-fro with harried expressions, creating a riot of chaotic colour amongst the bewildering array of dress and style Alaena could see before her. Keeping Scruff on a shorter lead, Alaena shared a delighted grin and a nod with Rince as they moved into the press and excitement.

Heading first to the southern end of the area where the competitors for swordsmanship events were practicing, Alaena and Rince stopped along the way and purchased some warm freshly baked tarts from a rotund woman who Alaena suspected consumed as much of her comestibles as she sold to the public.

Taking a bite of the crisp, jam-filled treat, Alaena grabbed Rince's hand and pulled him along. "Oh, these are wonderful, Rince! Let's go down to the practice fields and watch while we eat. Fastest there starts first!"

Rince, about to take a bite of his own, saw the sparkling glint in her eye and took the bait wholeheartedly. "I'll be finished before you even get there, Ala!" he shouted and took off into the crowd, one hand curled protectively around his precious and quickly cooling tart. Scruff, watching him dart away from them and sensing the mood, if not understanding the joke, barked excitedly and tugged at his lead.

"Okay, okay, Scruff," said Alaena. "Let's catch him, then!"

Having attended the Tourney before, both Rince and Alaena knew generally where the fencing and swordplay events would be held, and thus the general location of the practice areas, which were always nearby. Rince dashed ahead and started to dodge his way between people and carts down the main thoroughfare, which ran though the centre of the Tourney. Knowing she'd never catch him weaving through the crowd, particularly with Scruff in tow and getting tangled in people's feet, Alaena figured her best chance of beating him was to dodge off the main way and behind the first row of tents and stalls. It would be a longer route, but there would be no people in the way there, so she might be able to run freely and take the lead.

Moving swiftly, for Rince had already disappeared into the crowd ahead, Alaena swivelled and took off sideways, heading for a small gap between two stalls to her left that seemed to have clearer space beyond them. In her enthusiasm to catch Rince, however, Alaena's abrupt action had calamitous results. Unnoticed until she dived sideways, a roan stallion baulked at her sudden move and reared in surprise, eliciting a startled shout from the green-liveried man atop the beast and toppling him from the saddle. He landed with a dusty thump on the hard-packed road. While Alaena jumped backward as the horse reared above her and the man fell sideways, Scruff instead chose the moment to surge forward, barking at the panicked beast and jerking the lead from Alaena's hand. Too late to grab it again and haul him back, Alaena watched the front legs of the startled horse fall like hammers back to the ground, directly onto Scruff.

Horrified and helpless, Alaena watched as Scruff's tiny body was crushed between hoof and the hard-packed earth. The sound of his ribs and back snapping was strangely distinct to her ears above the noise of the crowd about her as blood gushed over his broken body.

"No!" Alaena cried desperately, jumping forward with a shriek of anguish and pushing the horse back forcibly.

The incensed rider, wobblingly regaining his feet, found his voice far faster and began to hurl abuse at her even as he stood. "Foolish girl! Look what you've done," he shrilled, dusting himself down and staring, mortified, at a small tear in his jacket. "Have you no sense?"

Heads turned at the sound of the raised voice as people, always far too inquisitive regarding the troubles of others, started to gather around them on the road. His words faded as he watched Alaena, sobbing piteously, pick Scruff's broken body from the ground.

His head lolled loosely over Alaena's left arm, eyes unseeing. For a moment, Alaena just stood and stared at the lifeless body in her arms, unable to accept that he could, but for her own heedlessness, be taken away from her so quickly and pointlessly.

Pushing her way through the people starting to crowd around, Alaena gathered Scruff to her chest, unaware the commotion had attracted the attention of the Protectorate Guard, who were making their way through the crowd to investigate the disturbance.

Blinking her eyes clear and thinking no further, Alaena continued on her original path, making her way behind the stalls and out of the main thoroughfare. Walking away from the Fields and into the grasslands, Alaena left the noise behind her. Head bowed in mourning, Alaena quietly sang a bedtime prayer as she moved, tears falling freely as she bid gentle farewell to her friend:

Lord, we thank You for this day,
And friends we met along the way.
Thank You for Your love and care,
And thank You for Your Word to share.

Now to bed and sleep we go,
Protect our dreams so we might know,
When we wake, You're with us still
Our Hearts to mend, our Souls to fill.

After a while, Alaena came to a small area where a flat grey rock flecked through with gleaming strands of creamy quartz formed a small, rounded oasis in the sea of waving grasses about her.

Laying Scruff's body down gently, Alaena sat slowly and sadly before him. The warmth radiating from the sun-drenched stone under her brought forth a new gush of tears as she realised that Scruff would never be really warm again. The floodgate of her emotions opened and Alaena gave herself over to them, bracing her hands on the stone beside her. Closing her eyes, she let the grief flow through her as Scruff's blood pooled and soaked slowly into the age-old granite beneath them.

Her parents having died or left her well before she was old enough to understand the loss, Alaena had no personal experience of death or true sorrow in her young life. She had seen death, of course, and the atrocites brought to the Gatherings by the Protector made her no stranger to violence and pain. To this point, however, barring and perhaps in some part because of her inexplicably personal reaction to events at the Gathering yesterday, Alaena was unprepared to cope with the grief which now consumed her.

Glancing from thought to thought, like sunlight shredded by the spokes of a spinning wheel, Alaena's mind was unable to fix on anything solid. Behind the dark curtain of her closed eyes, Alaena's lamentation turned inwards as she tried to find her way past her sorrow. The things and people that made up her day-to-day life seemed to fade to insignificance. Seeking surety to counterbalance the pressing weight of her distress with the reality of the world, Alaena pressed her long fingers down hard on the stone beneath her, using the unforgiving surface to stabilise her tumultuous emotions.

Warmed by the rock below her and the sun above, the breeze tugging at her hair like a playful imp, Alaena slowly closed the rest of the world off and began to let the initial shock of Scuff's death subside. The muddled noise from the merchants in the distance and, further away still, the echo of hammering as stands and seating were constructed, faded away until the only sound that impinged upon her mind was the sighing, sibilant whispers of the wind through the grassland that surrounded her. Allowing her mind to follow the path of calm that beckoned enticingly, Alaena felt a detached shiver of trepidation run down her spine. Her fingers, pressed hard to the reassuring stone below, began to tingle. Alaena felt transition, as though she were floating over the grasses, whose sumptuous, surreptitious whispers seemed to form words on the edge of her hearing. Soothing, sympathetic syllables stroked her senses, coaxing and hinting of healing and rest.

Cradled by the call of the voices, it would have been so easy to capitulate. Worn by grief and with little desire to do anything else, it began to feel pointless to resist the gentle, insidious urging. That detached part of Alaena's mind, however, pricked her consciousness with cold barbs of rational concern, a sense of urgency edging closer, starting to encroach upon her lassitude. Unsettled, Alaena resisted the pull and pressed her palms down harder, using the stone as her anchor, lest she become completely unmoored.

As if sensing her resistance, Alaena felt the forces around her palpably shift. Coiling, they coalesced, gaining substance as if to strike. Her throat closed and breath became difficult as she tried unsuccessfully to open her eyes and rid herself of what must surely be a grief inspired nightmare. Sudden, visceral fear clenched that part of her consciousness that remained apart. Feeling bands of power forming around her mind, Alaena sought escape by the only available route. She threw her consciousness downward, into the eternal granite beneath her burning palms.

As if merely awaiting her summons, the Earth beneath her beleaguered body bequeathed its strength.

Alaena gasped as power coursed up her arms and cascaded through her being. Hands melded to the earth, she felt one with the stone. Her eyes flew open as the net endeavouring to ensnare her washed away, like drops of blood let fall in a fast-running river. Free again and her frame tingling with power, Alaena looked about her in wonder. With vision that seemed magnified a thousand-fold, Alaena saw every blade and bud of grass and seed in minute detail about her. Despite her desire to gaze on the incredible intricacy of life around her, her attention was drawn downwards to gaze upon the stone below. Within each of the fine cracks in the weathered rock, tiny motes of light pulsed through quartz veins buried within. Moving in steady, fiery trails, each incandescent glow snaked through the crystal towards her. Underneath her hands themselves, the lines of power converged. With wonder, Alaena watched them flow into her fingers and palms, felt them imbue her being with strength, fortifying her will with the ageless, obdurate strength of Stone.

Her spirit singing, Alaena raised her head to savour the unfamiliar sensation of power in her hands, too overwhelmed with the experience to wonder what it meant and what she might do with it.

As she started to gaze through the haze of light that now surrounded her, a dark shape stepped forward, blocking out the sun. It took a moment to adjust her befuddled senses to the immediate world and focus on the object before her. In the same second she realised she was looking at the black leather jerkin of a Protectorate Guard.

Someone screamed "Sorcery!" from what seemed a thousand miles away, and the butt-end of a spear slammed squarely into her forehead, plucking the Light away, putting out the stars and plunging her into illimitable darkness.

Chapter 6 - Vetren

Even for one who has seen millennia pass, the spark of awareness that remained of Vetren's somnambulant mind understood considerable time had passed. Rousing his body proved difficult after such an extended hibernation, but as Vetren was aware, need was as powerful a motivator as hate. The Demon Prince lacked neither.

So it was that for the first time in almost a thousand years, Vetren's eyelids cracked open and he gazed once more at his prison from within.

Squinting as his eyes adjusted to light once more, Vetren was at first at a loss to understand what had roused him from his long slumber. Around him, the white-gold shimmer of the Holding appeared intact and unchanged. Shaking off the weary lassitude of his limbs, he unfolded with a scaly hiss and carefully stood to survey his prison once more, sure in the knowledge that *something* must have changed for his senses to rouse him.

He turned around slowly, reacquainting his body with motion, and also to ensure his inspection overlooked nothing. Taking his time in this fashion, Vetren began to examine every inch of the sphere about him, looking for anomalies or changes that would tell him why he had been roused. At first, nothing seemed apparent. Leaning close to the outer walls, he saw that the sphere's defences coalesced as always, raising white-light shadows that reflected eerily on his red-scaled skin. He held one hand up and let the light play over it, pushing away the disappointment he felt with a guttural growl. Even the reflections seemed unchanged. There was nothing to indicate that any difference existed at all. It wasn't until he looked down at his feet that he gave a hiss of satisfaction. Dropping quickly to one knee, Vetren extended his long dormant senses to examine the floor beneath him.

A small circular section of black granite, some five feet in diameter, lay beneath him within the confines of the Holding, pitted and scorched from both his battle with the Sorcerers and from his frantic attempts to free himself since. Other than bearing these scars, the stone had been unremarkable to date. Not so now.

Circling and dancing within the fine cracks and substance of the granite itself, tiny motes of light were pulsing through the stone. On all fours, Vetren glanced quickly to the side, looking through the glare of the Holding to the stone outside his prison. It took only a moment to verify that this phenomenon was limited to *within* the sphere, rather than affecting all stone within the cavern. In some way, then, this strange display was related to the Holding itself.

Aware that any change represented an opportunity, Vetren cautioned himself. It would do no good to rush too fast and risk severing the link to whatever will or power was causing this. By the same token, he had no idea how long it might last or how long it might take to understand how to take advantage of it, so speed with care was called for here. Vetren took a deep breath and calmed himself before extending one hand and placing it on the stone, talons clicking as they came to rest of the obdurate surface as he focused his will into the rock below.

The response was immediate.

As Vetren exerted his will into the stone, the tiny lights within began to writhe away from his touch and a slight nausea touched his mind, making him recoil and almost lose the tenuous contact he had initiated. *Old magic!* he realised with shock, throwing his head back with a howl. Primal feelings of lust and ancient hate threatened to overwhelm his focus before he steadied himself and concentrated once more. Crouched on the stone still, he sought to calm his trembling limbs while his mind raced. This wasn't possible, yet the evidence was before him. He could never forget that oily, tainting touch of the old Earth magic on his mind, yet that power should have been lost with the passing of his captors.

Now wasn't the time to ponder such mysteries, however. Abhorrent though it was, Vetren knew he needed to embrace the magic before him to understand the spell being cast and how the sorcerer could make itself materialise *within* the Holding. Most importantly, he had to see if he could use it to break himself free.

With patience that only an immortal can command, Vetren again settled back, looked down to the stone and delicately cast his mind forth. Probing carefully, for he expected defences to be in place, Vetren began to gently tap into the lines of power visible

46

within the stone. Putting aside the nausea that ate at his concentration, Vetren became more and more confused – more and more cautious. That this was old magic, there could be no doubt, but whenever he tried to trace the lines of the spell back to the caster, he failed to uncover the structure that should be there. When altering his senses slightly to visualise the resonant web that all power projects, he could see the aura emanating from within the rock. But again, the lines of force that should be the focal point of the spell were nowhere to be seen.

More concerning than that, though his mind delved ever deeper into the stone beneath him, he was unable to discern any trick or trap to this, which surely awaited him. No sane sorcerer would ever open a portal to power such as this without wards to defend against intruders. Even as his mind went further in, Vetren slowed and began extending his senses about him more, anticipating and fearing attack, yet entirely unable to discern any threat as he searched fruitlessly for the spell construct that he could use to trace back to the caster.

Finally, Vetren came to the inescapable conclusion that no caster existed here. He must be feeling the resonance of an artifact or other power source of Old Magic. If that was the case, it would be easy enough to confirm, giving him his first step on the road to freedom and vengeance.

Once again, he applied his awareness to the bedrock below him to test his theory. This time, however, working in concert with the stone rather than trying to see a lattice of power within it. Again, the nausea threatened to unbalance him but he put it aside and focused on the rock itself, linking his mind to the flow of power in and about it. Even here Vetren retained caution, for any object of power could be protected from outside influence as much as a spell could be conjured within a lattice of deadly wards to protect from tampering.

Again, strangely, no defences impeded his progress. No barbs of enchantment lashed back against his intrusion to bar his path or hinder his exploration. Within moments, Vetren had linked with the stone and with a hiss of satisfaction, discerned tenuous but unmistakable lines of power tracing back to the grounded source that was generating the sympathetic reaction within his own prison.

Carefully, carefully, lest any haste shatter the connection, Vetren worked his way back across the resonance of power. Abruptly, a breath of fresh breeze and the smell of wild grasses danced across his awareness. Almost swooning with longing, his need for stealth and care warring brutally with his desire to rend and tear his way past all obstacles, Vetren at last completed his link.

Projecting his consciousness through to the power source proved difficult, and the risk of shattering the link remained at the forefront of his thoughts. It was immediately apparent that the power source was woefully insufficient for transference to be an option. This Vetren had expected, and while disappointed, he was not surprised. Continuing to tentatively explore the link, however, did give him another result that he had *not* anticipated. This phenomenon was not the result of an object of power activating or being activated. The aura of whatever power maintained the link was too fluid for it to be an inanimate object. Too alive for it to be anything but an intelligence of some type.

Maintaining his presence in the power flow but withdrawing a little as this realisation hit him, Vetren again paused to take stock. Whatever intelligence was driving this, it's objectives were a mystery to him. Why create lanes of power that had no protection for themselves or the caster? Was the sorcerer so powerful that such wards were actually unnecessary? If so, Vetren needed to be cautious indeed, as detection could spell disaster for him. That made little sense, however. If the sorcerer were indeed that powerful, then he would be aware there were many powers in the world and in the under-dimensions that only a fool would ignore, at their own peril. In Vetren's experience, intelligences that low rarely survived to become as powerful as he assumed this one was, so again, this made frustratingly little sense.

Carefully then, his caution warring constantly with his natural and long-fostered predilection to rend and tear, Vetren extended his mind into the aura of power. Whispering quiet words into the spell, soothing and smoothing his transition into the other entity's construct, Vetren's nervousness increased as his progression continued without impediment or apparent resistance.

As Vetren moved on, his mind felt other paths and nodes that, like the one that had responded to this power within his own Holding, were active. A detached part of his mind noted this with interest. So whatever power this was, it was being broadcast widely, rather than targeted at him or at his prison. This meant that he may indeed be able to get close to the source without detection if the spell had no specific focal point related to himself or his location.

Encouraged, he pressed a little harder, and at last began to feel a change in the ambience of the spell. To this point, with such a wide dispersal of power, the spell source and controlling entity had been difficult to trace. Despite his efforts to inject calmness into the construct, whatever entity controlled this had noted his presence, and caution began to resonate back through the link. The power flow remained, however, so there was not enough concern yet to react to him, which left two choices for Vetren: He could back away to present as little threat as possible and not risk the spellcaster end the enchantment, or he could continue on and take his chances.

Even as the options presented themselves to his cunning mind, he knew that he could not back out now. He must not lose or squander the first opportunity for escape presented to him since his imprisonment. To that end, by necessity, he quickly erected a lattice in his own mind of wards to protect against backlash, and prepared to impose himself forcefully on the link to wrest control of it from whatever entity held it open.

Hasty preparations made, Vetren committed himself to the link and began to push his consciousness to the source, either to take control or quite possibly be destroyed trying. The response was immediate. For the merest moment, Vetren broke through and perceived the origin of the enchantment, which rendered him momentarily bewildered.

He did not see others of his own kind wielding Fire and Light in one of the nether dimensions. He did not see creatures in deep forests or crystal glades conjuring the powers from Earth, Tree and Stone. Nor did he see sorcerers in temples or mages in towers wielding staves and artifacts to raise elemental magic of old.

To his utter astonishment, the only thing he perceived was a small human female sitting cross-legged on a circle of stone, surrounded by a field of wildflowers. The stone on which she was sitting and on which her hands were pressed was aglow and sang with power.

If his surprise had not been so complete, he may, perhaps, have reacted faster. In the moments he took to assimilate this unexpected vision, however, he saw the human child's eye's fly open, registering danger Fear flooded the link as she cried out, responding with terror-inspired instinct to the demonic visage that appeared before her.

Raw, untrammelled energy of frightening force geysered into the Lane, overwhelming Vetren instantly, blinding him with its potency. Howling in frustration and terror, Vetren realised he had gone too far. In the precious moments he had left before obliteration came, for even at the height of his strength he knew was unlikely to have been able to withstand such elemental might, he mentally scrambled backwards, attempting to close his mind and deflect at least some of the damage that such an unrestrained onslaught would surely wreak.

The anticipated evisceration never came. Riding with the power that washed in astonishing waves from this unlikely creature, Vetren scrambled to the protection of his woefully inadequate shields, realising with nervous awe as he did that the power flowed by and around him rather than directly, ruinously, at him. On an island kept above the ocean of force that flooded around him by desperate act of will, Vetren watched with disbelief as he saw his shields, because they were not directly assaulted, withstand the barrage Slowly, his visceral fear receded, evaporating first into wisps of hope, then elation consumed him.

"Fool human!" he crowed to himself.

That such a diminutive creature should be able to conjure such power so easily at all was incredible enough, but *she was doing so unshielded!* Here, at last, was the power he needed to be free. To visit revenge on the human race, starting with this human female that he would rend limb from limb to sate his desperate appetite for blood.

Wasting no more time, Vetren exerted his will once more. With ease now, he insinuated himself into the flow of energy that thrummed through his mind. There was little need for care or disguise now. In any case, it was unlikely that the ignorant creature would even perceive his presence until he was upon it and it was too late. Greedily, slavering for release, Vetren abandoned all restraint and threw his mind towards his target, revelling in the raw energy that crackled about him.

With nothing resisting him and no shields to bar his way, Vetren blazed back through the open construct, intent on his prey. Reaching his objective, he once again gazed through the lens of his link at the human child whose aura blazed back at him with staggering intensity. Taking one last moment to ensure all was in place before committing to the transfer, Vetren frowned as the female registered surprise and shied back from something in her own world. A thrill of genuine fear surged through her link, followed by a shock of pain. Then, as if it had never existed, the flow of energy and Vetren's escape route was suddenly, brutally severed.

With no Power supporting Vetren's pathway out now, the law on which the Holding was structured snapped forcefully back into place. Vetren's mind wrenched viciously, slamming back into his physical form lying prone on the cold stone of his prison.

The violence of his return and having freedom snatched from him when so close to release at last almost broke Vetren's mind. With screams of unmitigated hatred, unable to believe that he had lost his chance when *so* close to release, Vetren unleashed the full force of his rage with unchecked violence. Rocking the very foundations of the mountain with virulent assaults of screaming, scathing power, Vetren gave the bottomless pit of his hate and anguish free rein.

Time lost meaning in his black rage, but the violence eventually dimmed as exhaustion overtook him. The Holding, unaffected by the violence visited upon it, blazed on securely around him while

Vetren collapsed to the floor, beaten at last and bereft of conscious thought.

At some point, Vetren awoke once more. It could have been days or years later, he had no way to tell, but his mind was recovered enough to start to weakly wonder: Who was the human child that she commanded such raw Talent? More importantly, how might he ensure, should she open the Lanes once more, that he did not miss another opportunity for escape?

Interlude 1 - The Wytharn Wood

Far to the south of Morlyn, deep in the Old Wood where winter never reached, change touched the still air for the first time in millennia. Here, resting in the shaded twilight of age-old oak and elm, stood a massive stone. Bedded deep, it thrust from the earth to reach twice the height of a man.

The rough, grey-granite surface glistened in the dim light that filtered down through the thick canopy of leaves above them. From a distance, though appearing out of place in the glade, the stone appeared natural and untouched. Up close in slim bands that spiralled in an unbroken line from base to tip, intricate carvings of letters and arcane symbols could be seen.

Untouched by time in the preternatural silence of the glade around them, the stone had sat undisturbed since the last darkness had befallen the Earth.

Without warning or apparent catalyst in the quiet glade, the symbols circling the stone started to warm and, with an earthy, golden-brown light, began to glow. Reaching a steady luminescence, fine cracks appeared over the entirety of the obdurate surface, fanning out from the bands of hieroglyphics. Light spilled from within the widening, ever-increasing faults in the surface, accompanied by the snap and crack of tortured stone, which echoed strangely through the uncommonly still glade.

The violence of the change built and the stars above faded from view. Reaching blazing proportion, Light flooded the glade like sun, until mere granite could no longer contain the force. In a cacophony of brilliance, the stone shattered with concussive force. For some time after, the brisance extinguished light and rendered sound mute.

When normality reasserted itself, a strange creature squatted low in the place where the stone had stood. Mewling softly to itself, the creature's segmented appendages stroked the jagged edges of the remains still buried in the earth, much as a mother would stroke and console a distressed child. Where it touched, sparkling drops of golden light wept from its claws and sank gently into the stone.

In time, the creature's discordant song ended. Its segmented body unfolded to stand strangely upright on its two back legs. The bulbous head roved back and forth as it sniffed the air through tiny gills that lined the midd e section of its chitinous body. Facing directly to the north, the creature gave a small, satisfied chirp.

After sniffing the air once more to be sure, it gave a dexterous shrug, then took off at a run with a long, loping gait.

Interlude 2 - Riders from Ald

Far to the east of Morlyn a tall man, still lanky with youth, sat speechless. His hands hung lax at his side, as though he had forgotten their purpose. In his lap, nestled in the folds of the rough overcoat he wore, a small black box carved from two matching pieces of shale and intricately worked with patterns depicting the five elements lay open.

Within the box, attached to a chain by a loop of crafted gold, lay a topaz stone. Like the box, the gem inside was masterfully worked. It was not the box however, nor the clasp, nor even the stone, that had the man's attention transfixed. Rather, it was the pulsing golden light that washed over his face from within the stone itself that had him entranced.

Not normally a man subject to extremes of feeling, he felt almost lightheaded as cascading emotion washed through him. Excitement and fear warred to overcome him, for the time had come at last. So much was at stake; he felt both humbled and awed that he should be one to live to see such times. Finally, apprehension strove to undo him, for he knew that they were still unready for what was to come.

It was not until it registered that the afternoon shadows had lengthened in his tower room and an evening chill touched his shoulders that he came back to himself fully. Lifting his head to stand and call his aide, the man reluctantly closed the box and focused his thoughts on the wood already set in the hearth of his room, whispering a word as he narrowed his concentration. Tendrils of smoke curled lazily outward as fine kindling blackened beneath the logs of the main fire, then burst abruptly into flame, followed by candles about the room as he waved a hand in their direction.

After a gentle knock at the door, his servant entered just as the man settled himself behind his desk, storing the box and its precious contents in a locked side drawer and hanging the key around his neck under his ruffled shirt.

"Your Highness," the aide said, with a respectful bow at the waist, "how may I serve?"

Wasting no time, the man at the desk spoke quickly and directly. "Fetch me my council and have them meet me in the hall when the evening bell tolls. That done, have riders made ready with the fastest horses we have. Be at the hall for the council yourself too and tell all that there will be little time for sleep this night!"

If his aide thought anything strange in the request, there was nothing in his demeanour to show it. "At once, my Prince", he intoned, moving to the door and bowing once more as he exited to carry out the command.

Many hours later, carrying strict and exigent directives from their Prince, a hand of riders raced from the gates of the Keep of Ald, which stood on the border of the Great Desert. Stretching the horses to a gallop, they raced into the night, leaving dust and thunder in their wake. A league from the gate, the riders paused briefly, pounding fists to chests in the traditional gesture of respect and good will as they contained their impatient mounts beneath them. From there, horses spun under sure hands and were given rein. No longer impeded the beasts surged forward. Each rider stayed low on their backs, revelling in the speed and eager to undertake their missions.

Two took the road south, towards the Great Desert and the sea that lay many days hard travel beyond it. Two continued on to the west, one making for the Great Wood, the other to brave Al'rth's Pass before turning south towards the King's lands.

The fifth and last, a stocky figure with a direct stare that brooked little argument, urged his steed northward, making directly for Morlyn.

Gossip was rife in Ald the following morning, as a curious populace pondered the meaning of riders and the strange lights that shone from the Prince's tower room well until dawn.

Interlude 3 - Demon Dreams

Demons seldom sleep. When they do, they dream even less frequently. Without exception though, the rare dreams they do have are full of hate, violence and blood. They can also be recalled in minute detail at any time after by the dreamer.

Kahu Pyra, Overlord of the Arkris and Guardian of the First Key, was discomforted. The dream he woke from this time was considerably different to other he had experienced.

His talons ticked loudly on the bone armrests of this throne. Underlings cowered before him on the floor, aware and alert to their sovereign's unsettled mood.

For centuries now, Kahu's position had been secure. As the years passed, all contenders to the throne from which he now ruled unchallenged had been eliminated. Many were killed by his own hand, with each death having its own relish to savour. The houses that in the past had vied continually to control the First Key were mere vestiges of their former selves. He hissed and bared his fangs in satisfaction as he pondered this, making the subordinates that tended his throne cringe back momentarily in fear. It would have been easy for Kahu to erase the other houses completely, but it amused him to keep the relics of their descendants alive to watch their petty posturing as they fought each other for his favour and, through that favour, for access to the Key.

Returning to the dream in his mind, Kahu's blood surged as anger rose within him. His scaled skin heated and turned a deeper, blacker red as he pondered its meaning. In the dream, through the power of the First Key, he had conquered yet another world. He sat upon a throne made of the bones of that world and the blood of its original inhabitants ran in great rivers before his feet. Two suns hung heavy in the sky, bleeding deep orange light across the blighted landscape of the ruined world. Throngs of his armies held maimed and dismembered bodies above their heads, howling accolades for their leader while the rest of the world burned and the sky clouded over with the acrid smoke of the world's demise. All, to Kahu's mind, was exactly as it should be.

Then came change. Kahu growled low as he remembered. A great white light had split the sky asunder, blinding him momentarily. A cacophony of thunder rolled across the tortured terrain before him and his throne shuddered in response. The great tumult which revered his name faltered as a shadow fell upon him, and for the first time in many millennia, fear touched his cindered soul.

Out of the light, a scaled face appeared and sped towards him. Raw, untrammelled power burned through its skin and insanity danced in its eyes. At any moment, his dream-self knew, his existence would end as the power that burned through the vision was released. Kahu woke screaming as immolation engulfed him, and the name of his nemesis came to his lips.

As his master strategists would tell him, only a soft-skin would ignore a warning as clear as this, and Kahu was no fool. Already he had set his minions to the task of finding out as much as they could of this potential threat, giving them the name from his dream to work with.

"The name is that of another demon," he told them, "and it is 'Vetren'."

Chapter 7 - Capture

Cradling his warm tart protectively, lest he lose it in his haste, Rince dodged nimbly through the crowd as he raced for his objective. He knew the wager made with Alaena was ridiculously unfair in his favour. There was no way she could beat him to the practice grounds with Scruff in tow and with his head start. That thought only widened the grin already on his face as he weaved past a pair of brightly clothed tinkers pulling a small cart full of wares in the opposite direction. A shout of indignation from the two followed as he jostled his way past. He knew Alaena would be smiling as well and taking it all as the good sport she was. Someday, he thought mischievously, he might even let her win!

Not today, though, he thought with that same wolfish grin. He'd have his pie well and truly eaten by the time she arrived, just to ensure he could tease her about being about as fast as a plough horse race.

Within a minute, he'd made his way out of the main crowds that milled around the tents and stalls in the northern part of the fields to reach the flat, open spaces where the actual competitions would be held. Each area was cordoned off with thick rope slung through iron rings attached to solid posts driven into the ground. These barriers, along with a good contingent of the Protectorate Guard, served to keep spectators back and out of harm's way. Most areas, such as those hosting the swordsmanship competition, would stay that way throughout the weeklong festival. Others, such as the Jousting Lists he passed to his right as he continued his dash towards the practice fields, had carpenters sweating hard in the sun as they laboured to complete viewing stands and seating that the nobles and elite members of the Protectorate would use to watch the competition in comfort.

Wiry, fast and fit as he was, the distance was still considerable. He was puffing a little by the time he reached the practice areas. To his delight, there were already some knights out of their pavilions and readying themselves for the practice rounds. Squires proudly sporting the colours of their houses fastened, tightened, checked and rechecked clasps as one by one mail, cleaves, breastplates and helms encased their champions.

By the time he'd finished his treat, sucking the last of the quickly cooling sauce from his fingers and licking his lips in appreciation, Rince was lost in daydreams of his boyish perceptions of the honour and glory of battle. Leaning over the fence with avid interest, he watched with envy as two combatants went through their forms, the weak sunlight of early spring glinting from polished armour as they circled each other. Their swords clashed in a spray of sparks. It wasn't until they raised their visors and, as custom dictated, saluted each other with closed fists thumping their chests, that Rince realised how much time had passed with Alaena still nowhere to be seen.

Dragging his eyes away from others who were starting to take the field, Rince looked around and back into the hive of activity and colour behind him, searching for Alaena's slim, familiar form. Wondering where she could be and at a loss to understand what might have delayed her, he was touched by mild concern and turned fully to survey the fields more thoroughly. It was some distance from here to where he left her, but she knew as well as he where she was going and it was hardly possible to take a wrong turn between here and there! Perhaps, he thought fleetingly, Scruff had got loose as Alaena had raced him to the practice fields and she had to chase after him? Not likely, but what other reason could there be?

He waited another minute in case she appeared, but everything he could see seemed as normally frenetic as the lead up to the Tourney always was. Taking a last, lingering look at the knights behind him, Rince decided he'd best go find her. After a suitable dressing down for losing her way, he could hopefully bring her back to watch the practice rounds some more. Or perhaps take a look at the archers he could see stringing their bows off in the distance as they loosed a few practice shafts to get used to the winds and terrain they would compete in, just a few days from now.

Heading back to the north, the cool, light sea breeze now at his back, Rince slowly retraced his path, casting his eyes back and forth into the distance on either side. His field of vision regularly obscured by people and tents, stalls and structures, he ducked this way and that to make sure he didn't miss her if she'd strayed off the main path. Eventually, he returned to the point they'd parted company without catching any sign of what might have happened to Alaena or Scruff.

Rince stood in place for a few moments, looking about him and wondering what to do. Asking someone would be pointless. There were far too many people around who were far too busy to think that one girl and a dog in the crowd would have been noticed. If Alaena had found something to catch her attention more than the swordplay they planned to see, she would surely have come to find Rince and bring him along rather than just abandon him, so that possibility he discounted as well.

He was just concluding that something worse than a simple distraction must have happened and that he should perhaps return to the Chandler's to see if she'd gone home when a disturbance off to his left attracted his attention.

Accompanied by strident, authoritative shouts of "Make Way!" with an occasional shove to move an inquisitive or recalcitrant body out of the way, a group of burly Protectorate Guards poured at a half run from a gap between the stalls and fanned out in a defensive circle, swords drawn and blocking the roadway in both directions.

Many heads, Rince's no exception, turned at the commotion to see what could have caused the Protectorate to react with such a display of force. Such exhibitions were not uncommon these days and rarely ended well for the focus of their attention, so people were careful to comply and ensure they did not become embroiled in whatever was going on at the time.

So it was, with the area free of obstructions, that Rince had a clear view of the slim body that appeared last from the tents, draped over the shoulder of a grim-faced guard. The guard headed straight for a horse being held steady for him and his burden in the centre of the steel-delimited formation.

Arms and legs tightly bound, Alaena hung limply across the guard's solid frame, her hair hanging loose down his back as her head lolled back and forth. As his blood turned cold, Rince could see a heavy bruise welling on Alaena's forehead as the guard dumped her senseless form unceremoniously across the front of the saddle and swung himself up onto the beast. Wasting no time, the Guard gave a curt nod to the man holding the horse and shouted to clear his way before spurring his heels into the roan's flanks. The horse, giving a huff of surprise at the unexpected prod, bunched muscles and jumped forward, forcing all and sundry aside as it forced a path through the crowd. Once clear of the crowd, the Guard urged the beast to a run for the town then on towards the Keep.

While the crowd of people broke up and the breeze toyed with the dissipating cloud of dust, Rince remained frozen to the spot, momentarily unable to process what had just happened. He could not imagine how the innocent day's outing had become such a disaster, or what could possibly have happened to have Alaena carted off by the Guard, who were obviously agitated when Alaena was carried past and relieved to see her go. Worriedly he wondered, what could Alaena have done to make the burly men of the Guard shy away as her unconscious form was carried past?

Forcing himself into action, Rince decided to skirt the tent where Alaena had come from and see what he could see on the other side that might explain this impossible event. With the shock passing, Rince found that emotion was setting in as he moved towards the gap in the tent, tears starting to prick at his eyes. He didn't know what Alaena had done, but she would shortly be in the hands of the Protector, and once that happened, he may never see her again. He needed to know what had occurred and, he realised, he had to get back to tell Wilmen as soon as he could.

Keeping his eyes down, lest anyone see the fear that shone there for his friend, Rince made his way across the road. Hands clenched tight with tension, he was unaware that he headed for the gap in the tent that Alaena had walked through only a short time before, sorrowfully nursing Scruff's broken body. He heard heavy footsteps coming his way and a deep voice giving orders. Reacting quickly, for he had long since mastered the art of staying out of the way of the Guard when they were on business, Rince altered course slightly and stepped off the path to the left, out of view up against the weather-stained canvas of the tent.

Four of the Guard passed close by, one of them clutching a bag the size of a large water sack that he held carefully away from his body. As they made their way between the tents, the bag brushed up against one of his companions, eliciting a shout of indignation that, Rince thought, was tinged with more than a little fear.

"Ho! Rahak! Keep that cursed thing away from me, you lummox!" the guard said tersely, arms up and palm facing outward in the common gesture used to ward off evil. "I know it's dead, but if Lauth is right and that little witch was using it to work her magic, then I want nothing to do with it!"

Having heard the normally rough banter that went on between the Guard, Rince expected to hear a rebuff from the guard called Rahak, but things were obviously not normal today. Rahak, who clearly wanted as little as he could to do with it as well, responded soberly and in a low voice as they passed Rince's hiding spot behind the canvas. Rince strained his ears to hear an answer that chilled him to his bones.

"Well, that might be, Pagi, but I'm holding it no closer to me than I have to either. So you just keep back and give me room. I know lots of people wonder about witchcraft and whether or not the Protector is mad, but mark my words. If that girl needs blood to work her craft, then it's magic of the worst kind and evil indeed. Whatever the Protector does to make sure she's put away forever has my blessing a thousand times over."

They continued on, their words lost to Rince's ears as his mind whirled. They could only be talking about Alaena. Imagining how a youthful race for a pie could turn into arrest and imprisonment for witchcraft was beyond him. For a moment, Rince simply stood dumbfounded, unable to assimilate what had happened while a lump of angst built in his throat and tears again welled in his eyes out of fear for Alaena's fate. His naturally sharp mind took over quickly, however, and he shook his head to stir himself, overriding his shock-wrought lethargy with the clear and urgent need for immediate action.

At a dead run, not caring who saw him now, Rince took off for the Chandler's to find Wilmen and tell her what had happened. Somehow, Rince understood that she would know what to do.

After racing back in a fraction of the time it had taken Alaena, Rince and Scruff to get to the fields, Rince's feet hit the veranda of the Chandler's and he burst inside. Such was the force of his entry that the doorbell jangled wildly and almost flew from its moorings. Panting from his sprint, Rince's desperate eyes scanned the room, looking for Wilmen.

She was nowhere to be seen. He took off for the door leading to the kitchen to see if she was there. That same door opened and Wilmen, looking calm and unruffled as always, stepped through to see what all the commotion was about.

Rince pulled up halfway across the floor before the front counter of the shop. "Wilmen," he panted desperately, not sure now where or how to start. "Wilmen," he repeated, as if saying it again would allow the rest of the words to flow.

Wilmen's eyes took in Rince at a glance, then widened and darted to the door, seeking Alaena's presence. She advanced a step further, her calm demeanour slipping a notch, and fixed her gaze back on Rince.

Stepping around the counter in a few quick steps, Wilmen grabbed Rince's shoulders as if ready to shake the words out of him.

"Rince," she said steadily, though her voice was laced with concern and he could feel her fingers trembling through the thin cloth of his shirt. "What's happened? Where's Alaena?"

Chapter 8 - Wilmen

Rince's words almost made Wilmen's knees buckle. Employing all of her considerable self-control, she held herself firm as she watched Rince's eyes widen and a sob escape his lips.

"They took her, Wilmen! The Guard took her!" he stammered. "I … I don't know why. I wasn't with her to see what happened!"

Wilmen kept one hand on Rince's shoulder, as much to hold herself up as to keep him talking while she prompted him for every detail of the story. Her other hand she held clenched tight by her side. It took some time, but finally Wilmen extracted where he had last seen Alaena, what her condition was, where she'd been taken and what the guard had said that Rince had overheard. Wilmen insisted on every detail he knew before she permitted him to move on to the next part of the tale.

As she dragged the detail from Rince, Wilmen's first reaction was akin to panic inside. Had they waited too long? Had Alaena revealed herself, or would she in the hands of the Protector? Either way, as Rince described the limp form of Alaena's unconscious body draped over a guard's horse as they rode for the Keep, Wilmen knew that fate was now forcing her hand. Even as she realised this, her hand steadied on Rince's shoulder. Options formed in her mind and she mulled through them as Rince answered the last of her questions. Finally, her eyes darkened as her path from here became clear. Had Rince raised his head to look at Wilmen when their words ran out, he would have seen strength and determination in her eyes. Not only did Wilmen have a plan in mind, but she'd actually been aware such a day might come and – to some degree, at least – was prepared for it.

Wasting no more time, for every moment now was critical for Alaena, Wilmen thanked Rince perfunctorily and ushered him in no uncertain terms out the front door. Voicing mute objection by setting his body against Wilmen's push and resisting her firm guidance towards the door earned him only stiff rebuke and a harder shove.

"Rince. Don't fight me," Wilmen said in a tone that brooked no argument. "I have to think about what to do, and for you to be involved is dangerous for all of us." Her left hand opened the door as the right stayed on his shoulder, propelling him through unceremoniously as she closed the conversation down. "Go home. Stay indoors and don't say anything to anyone about this, lest others get involved and complicate matters further. Understood?"

Wilmen spared one more glance for Rince, feeling sorry for the boy who understood so little of what was actually happening here, but filled with concern for Alaena and unable to give him any more thought. Without waiting for an answer, she gave Rince a firm nod as he stood alone and forlorn outside the shop, then swung the door shut firmly before him and locked it. She swivelled back and headed for the kitchen without so much as a glance behind her, Rince already gone from her mind.

Stopping only for a moment in the kitchen to slam the door shut, Wilmen took the unusual step of throwing the bolt on the door as well, ensuring she wouldn't be interrupted by unwanted visitors.

That done, Wilmen hurried through to the parlour and up the stairs to her own room, feeling a dangerous tug of despair as she passed and slowed outside Alaena's door. Forcing her emotions down with steel resolve, Wilmen continued on to her own room, moving directly to the window to close and lock the shutters before pulling heavy blinds into place, plunging the room into shadow.

As she had done only yesterday, she reached under her battered nightstand to open the panel underneath. The silver ring sat safely where she had placed it back after summoning Tag. Next to it sat the small dark box that both scared and elated her with the possibilities it presented.

After lifting both free, Wilmen pushed the panel shut, taking care to ensure the compartment was secure. That done, she moved carefully over to the bed, slipping the ring absently onto her finger once more. This time, however, the ring was of little importance. All the while, her eyes remained riveted to the box in her other hand as if she could see through it to what lay within, or as if she was scared as to what she might actually find inside.

In the dim room, feeling desperately alone at this point, Wilmen was aware that what she found within may very wel reshape the rest of her life. Sitting on the firm mattress, she gently placed the box next to her and stared at it for one moment longer.

Carved from two matching pieces of shale, the small box was a miniature work of art in itself. Only as high as her index finger and three times that across, it was so perfectly made that the line between lid and base couldn't even be seen in this light. The polished black stone was intricately carved all about with elemental images of Earth, Water, Fire and Wind, contrived to seem as though they cavorted with each other, complementing each other's strengths yet remaining powers within their own right, as Wilmen knew they were.

Sighing, as she knew she couldn't put this off any longer, Wilmen again picked up the box and held it flat on the palm of her left hand, placing her right on the top and gently lifting the lid.

Already beating quickly, her heart leapt in her chest and a hiss of suppressed breath escaped her lips as soon as the lid cracked open a fraction and a muted glow of light pulsed from within. Many times in past years, Wilmen had sat shuttered in this room, running her hands over the box and the treasure that lay within. Each time she had checked, the object within had laid dormant, dark and quiescent, eliciting only a sigh from Wilmen as she gently closed the lid and ran her hands lovingly over the engraved surface, feeling the bumps and curves of the maker's artistry, then returned it to its place, secreted safe within her room.

This time, however, as the lid slowly lifted, light continued to spill out in an ever-increasing arc, lighting her hands, then chest, then neck and finally her face as she pushed the cover all the way open. Gold-yellow light raised sparkles of reflection from the bittersweet tears of joy and anguish that filled her eyes.

Nestled snugly in soft material to protect it lay a golden topaz about the size of a sparrow's egg. The stone was perfectly formed and shaped into the likeness of a water drop, rounded at one end and tapering to a point at the other. A fine silver chain with a clasp shaped like a swirling wind was affixed to the upper end.

A bright ball of golden Light burned steadily in the heart of the gem.

Taking the chain slowly, needlessly holding her breath lest she disturb the fire within, Wilmen lifted her arm high. The gem swung from the chain before her face as she stared transfixed at the Light blazing within.

So, thought Wilmen as she allowed herself to breathe once more, *the Light reveals itself at last.*

Dropping her hand to her lap, absently noting the lack of heat as she closed her fist about the stone, Wilmen sat quietly for a moment as the enormity of the situation came home to her. *Oh, Ala. What have you done, my dear? Should we now shout out the celebration of our salvation, or bow our heads in sorrow that our final doom is at hand?*

Trembling with emotion, Wilmen voiced her worst fear to the empty room as she gripped the blazing gem like a lifeline. "Have we gone for so long only for me to let you down at the last, daughter?" Finally, Wilmen bowed her head and allowed tears to stain her cheeks for a while as her heart ached for Alaena's fate, and for all the pain the world might be about to endure if she, Wilmen, had failed them all.

All the while, the Light blazed steadfast, shining free and clear through the flawless facets of the gem, caring nothing at all for the world or its woes.

Chapter 9 - Egan

Soon after, her sorrow exhausted itself. At last Wilmen wiped her eyes and shook her head to clear her introspection. "Fool woman," she chided herself gently. "Sorrow and despair are for those already lost!"

Opening her hand once more to gaze upon the Light of the gem, Wilmen's jaw firmed and eyes narrowed as her resolve returned. "And we who have a Light to show the way can hardly be lost," she stated firmly as she put her fears away and pushed herself into motion.

Reverently, Wilmen returned the stone to its container and secreted it away once more, for a short while at least.

She considered replacing the ring too, but decided to keep it with her now, though there was danger in wearing it publicly. The symbol of white staves embossed on black might be noticed by unfriendly eyes and cause trouble she did not need. Equally, however, it might bring help from unexpected quarters should those who understood its meaning and supported her cause notice it. At the present time, Wilmen needed help more than anything else and if obtaining that help came with risk, then so be it. With Alaena captured, caution was no longer a luxury they could afford.

That decision made and the pendant again securely stored away, Wilmen opened the blinds and shutters of her room once more, checking the sky and estimating at least another two hours of light left in the day. Frowning for the time she had wasted, Wilmen took a light but long cloak from her wardrobe and tossed it across her shoulders before moving quickly back downstairs to the kitchen, where she added another item to her inventory. Pulling the drawer where she kept her carving tools open all the way until it reached the end of its run, she lifted the front slightly, clearing a block inside that allowed the draw to roll out a few inches further than normal. From a compartment revealed at the back, Wilmen retrieved a slim, beautifully wrought dagger and a knife belt made of supple leather that she strapped quickly round her waist, well concealed by her cloak. Taking a moment to check the blade, she pulled it free and expertly flipped it in her hand, watching it spin end over end in the air, spraying rainbow reflections of afternoon light through the kitchen from the highly polished, wickedly honed blade. Completing its arc, the weapon returned to Wilmen's hand, the handle landing squarely back in her palm with a satisfying smack. A glow of white light pulsed from a small crystal embedded in the handle as Wilmen wrapped her hand tightly around the hilt.

For the first time in hours, a smile touched Wilmen's lips. While circumstances seemed determined to conspire against her, she still had the element of surprise on her enemies and while she had that, she would use it to the greatest possible advantage. *Try, you bastards,* she thought, twirling the knife back through her fingers with practiced ease. *Just try and take my Ala away from me.*

Only one task remained before Wilmen locked up the shop and left. For as long as she and Alaena had lived in Morlyn, Wilmen had kept candles in the window as a display of her wares to entice customers in. Over the years, she had placed candles of all shapes and sizes in the window, and of all hues bar one. As she left today, with great deliberation, Wilmen extracted a thick gold candle from the back of her stores and placed it prominently in the window.

Then, satisfied that those who watched for such signs would see, she pocketed several coins in the folds of her cloak and departed quickly, locking the door securely behind her.

Despite her heightened sense of urgency and awareness of momentous events gathering around her, everything seemed preternaturally calm and normal once Wilmen stepped outside. Carts were trundling along the street, their straining oxen urged on by swarthy, sweating men, and the general press of commerce flowed back and forth before her. The sounds of hammering and the shouts of workers and sail-hands floated on the air from the docks, competing with the cries of gulls in their eternal squabbles for the scraps that the harbour always provided. Some children played nearby, alternately shouting in delight or frustration as the game shifted to and against them. In short, life carried on, blissfully unaware of the doom which threatened it all.

For the next hour, Wilmen made her way back and forth through the streets of Morlyn, stopping briefly at a number of establishments. An observer, other than perhaps thinking it strange that Wilmen did little or no business at any of the places she visited, would have seen no connection between each. A run-down inn in the poorer quarter of the docks area she paused at only briefly, exchanging quick words with the burly, heavyset innkeeper before moving on. A seamstresses shop in the more affluent northern quarter of Morlyn received the same attention, though the proprietor of this establishment was noticeably more ruffled after Wilmen's visit and closed her shop almost as soon as Wilmen's heel had left the doorstep. Indeed, the only place where money would have been seen to change hands was at the stables on the edge of town near the Fields, where Wilmen negotiated the hire of two horses and saddles for a week, paid for by coin in advance and including a bond for their return. One horse was an enormous stallion over twenty-hands high, the other a smaller mare that didn't look as fast, but appeared solid and reliable.

Clucking absently to the horses as she led them away, Wilmen made her way back towards the centre of town where a small abbey fronted one side of the main square. Skirting to the side, she entered an alley that led to the rear of the unimposing structure. The metal-on-stone sound of hooves on cobbles as she led them down was loud and distinct, echoing off the walls that towered up on either side and pressed in on her, creating an uncomfortably enclosed space.

Reaching her final objective at last, Wilmen pulled on a slim rope that hung near a wide and well-kept wooden gate. As she did, a bell pealed quietly inside the building on the other side of the fence. She heard a door open and close, then padded footsteps made their way down the path and a small peephole opened in the gate. A quiet male voice greeted her formally.

"Welcome to the Abbey, Sister. Set disquiet and worldly concerns aside and you may enter. Do you so wish it?"

"Thank you, Brother. I give myself unto solace and wish it to be so," Wilmen responded in kind, very aware of the fact that the pursuit of peaceful solace and avoidance of worldly concerns were the furthest things from her mind at the present time. "May I enter?" she finished the ritual phrase.

The man on the other side said no more as the peephole cover slid back into place, followed by the sound of the heavy bar that Wilmen knew was on the other side of the gate being lifted away. The gate swung open and a monk that Wilmen didn't recognise, dressed in a sky-blue habit with a hood covering much of his head and face, stepped to one side to allow Wilmen through. Invitingly, he extended a soft, pale hand towards the bridles of the horses.

"Welcome once more, Sister. I am Brother Ulma. Allow me to tend your beasts so I may see them watered and stabled while you remain with us," he continued as Wilmen handed the horses over to his care. "May I know the purpose of your visit? Is there anything further I may do to assist you?"

"I am here to see Father Egan, Brother Ulma, to discuss a matter which is personal to us both. Would you please tell him that Tria is here to see him and seeks his wisdom as soon as is convenient?"

Though his face was shadowed by the hood, Wilmen could see the quizzical look that crossed his brow, perhaps wondering what personal business this woman could have with the Abbot, though he accepted the request in his stride.

"Certainly, Sister Tria," he responded after the merest hint of a pause. "Please wait a moment while I have the horses tended to, then I will take you inside and seek out the Abbot."

Though familiar with the layout of the Abbey from past visits, Wilmen resisted the urge to rush Ulma in his duties as, with a shake of the reins, he clicked the horses into motion and padded quietly off to the left, towards the Abbey's small stable yard.

The rear of the Abbey where she now stood was a walled oasis of peace inside the city that few knew existed. Wilmen took the moment to gather herself, allowing the peaceful ambience of the place to wash through her. From where she stood at the gate to the back entrance of the Abbey itself, a path wound lazily amidst a lush forest of vegetation that the Abbey monks maintained with vigilance. All the flora within produced fruit or other edible produce, allowing the small Abbey to be largely self-sufficient in its needs in this respect. Even now, another monk in the brown robe of a Novitiate moved up and down rows of pots along the far-right wall, pruning what looked like apple trees back for the winter so they were ready to sprout again for the spring.

Even as the thought crossed her mind, Wilmen felt discomforted. Peaceful moments like this were likely to be few and far apart in coming months. If all failed and the worst came to be, there may not even be a spring to come. As if the very elements were matching the sombre twist of her thoughts, the wind chose that moment to drift cloud across the sun, plunging the courtyard into shadow and sending a shiver down her spine.

Given the turn of her mind, it was with pleasure that Wilmen saw Ulma returning. With a nod, he indicated she should follow him inside.

As Wilmen expected, Ulma conducted her to a small sitting room near Father Egan's chambers. Two chairs, comfortable enough though utilitarian as befitted the Abbey's character, sat by a low stone table on which were two cups and a jug of water. Seeing Wilmen settled, Ulma left to locate the Abbot. Though he indicated that might take some time, Wilmen barely had time to pour herself a cup or water before the door reopened and Egan entered the room.

As befitted his rank at the Abbey, Father Egan wore white, though his robes bore no emblems, reflecting his order's belief that worldly trappings and physical symbols of rank were of little value compared to the sanctity and purity of the soul. A tall, powerfully built man with strong clean lines to his features, Egan hardly looked the part of the spiritual leader of a modest Abbey in a small city far from the central politics and religion of the Southern Realms. Wryly and entirely to herself, Wilmen once again pondered the fact that Egan would look far better garbed with armour and sword than robes and sandals.

After checking the corridor carefully, Egan pulled the door closed quietly behind him. Turning then, he studied Wilmen for a moment as she studied him. Though alone, both stayed silent a moment more, unsure how to begin. With a sigh, Egan broke the silence and stepped towards Wilmen. Inclining his head respectfully, he reached to take her left hand in his, then held it up for them both to see.

Egan eyed the silver ring on her hand with a look of both trepidation and anticipation before locking his gaze on Wilmen herself and letting her hand drop. "So, Wilmen," he said as he moved to the other seat, gathered his robes around him and sat down heavily. "This is not a social visit, then."

Wilmen paused. The words were difficult to find. Impatient, Egan leaned forward and came directly to the point. "Come, old friend," he implored. "What brings you here, and what brings your ring out of hiding after all these years? This is not something I know you would have done lightly!"

At last, Wilmen decided the best course here was direct to the point.

"As you surmise, Egan, we have a significant problem. It's Alaena. She's been taken by the Protector." Almost as an afterthought, Wilmen said, "And the Star is afire."

Eyes widening, Egan appeared to struggle to absorb this momentarily. He abruptly surged to his feet, unable to string words together coherently for a moment. Had Wilmen not been so concerned, she may have smiled as she watched Egan's reaction.

"What?" he cried. Consternation, fear, confusion and hope warred across his features as he tried, unsuccessfully for the moment, to assimilate her news. "How, Wilmen? The Protector? Is she at the Keep, then? What of the Star?"

Apparently realising he was standing and shouting in the small room and that this was hardly the time to attract attention, Egan cut his questions short and composed himself. He sat once more, pulling his robes more tightly about him as if that small security could help shield him against the news that Wilmen bore.

"Tell me, Wilmen. Tell me all," he said at last.

Wilmen nodded, pausing for a moment to order her thoughts, then gave Egan all she knew, starting with Alaena's return from the Gathering and her understanding of Alaena's experience there, then on to all the events that followed up to Rince informing

Wilmen of her capture. Egan absorbed the information thoughtfully, continuing to nod as Wilmen finished relating Rince's panicked visit and his summary of Alaena's reaction.

"I met with Tag too, Egan. I suggested that Ala be tested soon, as she obviously experienced something more than just physical revulsion for the Gathering." Now it was Wilmen's turn to get to her feet and pace. "Damn, Egan. If only I'd insisted, I may never have let her go to the Fields and she'd still be safe with us!" She shook her head. "Tag's advice seemed sound, however, and as you know, he's hard to convince otherwise once he's made up his mind."

At this, Egan grunted once, punctuating his point. "Well, Wilmen, it's always easier to say what should have been done once the outcome is known, but that's not what is important at the moment. Go on. I gather Tag didn't agree to the testing, then?"

"No," Wilmen replied shortly, "he didn't. But he agreed not to argue against me if I put it to the council."

She sighed heavily, frustrated that she lacked detailed knowledge of what had actually transpired that afternoon.

"In any case, that point's moot now. Alaena went to the Fields with Rince today and somehow found trouble. I don't know the detail though, as I only have Rince's update to go on and he only saw her being taken away to the Keep, not why the Guard took her in the first place. All I know for sure is that after I sent Rince away, I checked the Star – as I did last night and every night since Alaena was entrusted to me as a child. Until today, it has always been dark, but it is no more!" Wilmen fixed her gaze on Egan with wonder in her eyes. "The fire inside burns cold but true in the heart of the gem, Egan! There can be no mistake. Whether or not it was Alaena – and I believe it too much of a coincidence to think otherwise – one born to Mastery of the Old Magic walks amongst us once more!"

Wilmen could see Egan processing this information slowly, deliberately. Like her, she guessed that Egan suspected there was more to this than either of them knew. She waited a moment to see if he had any direct questions. After a few moments, she took Egan's silence as an indication to proceed.

"In any case," Wilmen continued, "I've been to see Rogan and asked him to listen at his bar for any news of what might have happened at the fields today. I've also sent Yeta to the Fields themselves, ostensibly to measure the stands for material. Perhaps she can find out about what happened if she's actually there. They've both seen the ring and agreed to meet tonight to tell us what they've found, after which we can decide what to do based on any new information we have. I've also secured two horses should we need them. They're in your stables."

Concern clouded Egan's sea-green eyes. In a grave, low voice, he said, "Good, Wilmen. We may indeed need them, as I don't think we'll have much choice as to what we must do. Clearly, we must get Alaena out of the Keep and away from the city as soon as we can." Egan gave a resigned sighed. They were both aware that the shroud of secrecy that had helped protect them until now was about to be torn away.

He nodded towards Wilmen. "Your actions, however, are wise, Wilmen, as always. The more information we have about what happened, the better prepared we are to gauge the defences in place around her and what we might have to do to get her out of there."

A longer stay might raise unwanted questions, so Egan suggested they close the conversation now and meet back for council with Tag, Rogan and Yeta later in the evening to pool knowledge and act.

Standing to part, Wilmen bowed to Egan and intoned, "Farewell, Egan. Be safe in the Light."

Egan returned the bow and completed the ritual phrasing. "Farewell, Wilmen. May your steps never stray from the Path."

With that, Egan stepped over to the door and tugged gently on a small rope concealed by the doorframe. Without another word, they waited a short interval, after which footsteps sounded outside and the placid face of Brother Ulma reappeared as the door swung open.

"Brother Ulma," Egan greeted him with a nod. "Please escort Sister Tria to the gate once more and see her away. Her beasts will lodge with us until she returns for them."

And with that, Egan nodded once more to Wilmen and moved off. Shortly after, Wilmen was once more in the alley, turning with a nervous step to make her way back to the Chandler's, aware that this might be the last time she would or could visit there.

Chapter 10 - Dungeon

The first thing Alaena became aware of was the smell. A rank odour of old blood and decay hung fetid in the air, offending her senses. Disoriented, Alaena vaguely wondered what could make her room smell like this. Wrinkling her nose in distaste, her eyes fluttered open and consciousness returned.

Blinking a few times in the dim, smoky environment, Alaena shook her head to clear her vision, trying to understand what she was seeing. With the movement, wracking pain shot up through her arms and across her shoulders, snapping her back to the present as memory returned and fear settled deep in her gut.

Hanging by her arms in a large, rectangular room walled with black stone blocks, Alaena's boots dangled loose on the filthy, straw-matted floor beneath her. Heavy iron manacles encased her wrists, and new pain shot through her frame as she struggled to stand and take the weight of her body off her agonised arms. Blood leaked from her wrists and trickled warm rivulets down her arms as she flexed her hands, skin breaking and tearing away on the manacles from which she'd hung prostrate for however long she'd been here. Her ankles were also bound with short chains that kept her from moving more than a few inches from the wall.

Illuminated only by a few sputtering torches in black iron sconces that cast more shadow than light, the room radiated threat. Alaena's stomach turned and her trepidation increased as she surveyed her surroundings and her last memory surfaced of the Protectorate guard who had clubbed her down. *"Sorcery!"* he had screamed, while impossible lights danced around her and power coursed in her veins. Ethereal presences had whispered to her, tempted her, before all had gone black.

The chamber had no windows, so Alaena had no way to tell how long she had been here. An oppressive, heavy feel to the air indicated she was below ground, though it was impossible to tell how far. She could see only one door, midway down the long wall on her left, about ten paces from where she was chained. Various devices, all solidly constructed of stained oak and iron, were dotted about the room. Many were affixed to the walls by metal pegs driven deep into the stone, as were several more sets of iron chains and manacles, such as the ones that held her arms securely at present. Some stood free, such as the enormous rack that dominated the centre of the room. Others had no function she could understand, but dreadfully, all had a number of things in common. Each had cruelly pointed and barbed implements attached to them, or standing close by. Each was deeply stained by years of violent use. And each stood in the same cell as herself, where their purposes would very likely become terribly clear all too soon.

Tears welled in Alaena's eyes as she realised that between now and the end – which would probably be on the very podium she had run screaming away from only a day or two before – there would only be pain. Though unaware of her exact location, Alaena guessed she was in the dungeons of the Protector's Keep. She had no doubt at all that wherever she actually was, she was in the hands of the Protector and that with him as her judge, her life was forfeit.

Minutes or hours more passed as Alaena favoured one foot then the other to help relieve her muscles, but with nothing to measure the passing of time, Alaena didn't know how long she remained there, helpless. At intervals, she thought she heard footsteps in the distance, and at one point, she was startled by a long, drawn-out wail, which cut out abruptly as a door slammed shut somewhere outside. The door to her own chamber looked thick and tightly fit, so little noise intruded to interrupt her terrified musings on what was to happen to her. She didn't doubt for a moment that there was no one to hear her own sobbing as her legs started to cramp from the prolonged incarceration, though that was nothing compared to the pain she experienced if she tried to ease their load on her own up-stretched arms and already lacerated wrists.

During this indeterminate period, her world shrank to a tortured existence of suffering, where memory started to fail. Her home and those she held dear seemed distant, untouchable memories. Bouts of shivering overtook her, and at one point her legs gave out completely, driving her weight down on her arms once more and tearing a shrieking, anguished cry from her wracked frame as new blood coated the dark stains down her arms, soaking further into her sweat-drenched shirt.

Parched from lack of water and dizzy with prolonged distress, it was almost with relief that, through the woe-filled haze that her world had become, she registered the latch on the door click. Lifting her lolling head, she saw the heavy door of her cell swing ponderously open.

Somehow, he seemed smaller than she expected. Used to seeing him at Gatherings or at the occasional function he presided over on behalf of the city, Alaena had only ever seen the Protector in official garb. She was strangely surprised to see him otherwise.

Wearing solid black boots, black trousers and a dark blue coif, the only signs of his position were the ring on his finger and the medallion of office around his neck. Struggling to keep her head up now, Alaena tracked him with her eyes as the Protector sauntered into the room as though unaware that Alaena was even there. Closing the door behind him with a solid thump, the Protector looked around as if somehow dissatisfied, glancing around the walls as if to check all the equipment was in place and all in order as it should be. His eyes grazed by Alaena as if she was as unimportant as the various implements he surveyed, continuing on around the walls, then moving to the various contraptions set on the floor.

His gaze finally alighted on the rack dominating the centre of the room. He considered that for a moment, glanced back to Alaena, then back to the rack again, letting out a small, malice-filled chuckle.

Footsteps muted on the straw covering, he advanced into the room, pausing to run his hands over the chains that hung from the massive, spoked wheel of the rack. The iron links clanked as he measured their weight, as if considering how much stress they could take, before looking up directly at Alaena and fixing her with a predatory stare that made her stomach turn.

"So, little witch. It appears we have a problem, do we not?" the Protector said in a conversational tone as he let the chains drop and sauntered towards her. "Here we are, in a land in which witchcraft is categorically prohibited on pain of death. Only three days ago, in fact, another woman only a little older than yourself by the looks of you, was publicly executed for this very crime! You may only recall the start of the proceedings, actually, as some of my friends tell me that you were the one who fled the celebration before it was done, yes?" The smile he gave as he related this news did not touch his cold, grey eyes.

Confused, disoriented, Alaena tried to focus on what he was saying. He already knew she was the one who fled? And was it really three days ago? Wasn't it only yesterday that the flogging took place? She shook her head, tried to talk, say this was all a mistake and that she'd done nothing wrong, but all that came out was a dry croak past parched and cracked lips as the Protector came to a halt before her.

Lifting her chin with one leather-gloved hand, he used the other in a strangely personal gesture to stroke her hair back from her clammy forehead. Turning Alaena's head this way and that, the Protector examined her as critically as a wolf might paw at a small animal it had trapped, before deciding which part to consume first. He continued in the same disconcertingly conversational manner.

"You know, she lasted quite some time after you left. Sadly, she died before the full fifty was done. You're younger than her, though," he said in a matter-of-fact tone. "I'm sure you'll last longer and give the crowd a better show. It's difficult to tell in this light, though, isn't it, so let's get a better look at you ..."

Still holding her chin firmly in one hand, the Protector turned his head slightly, his eyes glazing strangely as he gestured with an outstretched palm towards the brazier that stood in the corner to Alaena's left.

A strange hum sounded in Alaena's mind at the edge of her hearing, but lasted only a moment. Her befuddled mind couldn't latch onto it before the brazier to her left burst into flame, heat washing across her chilled frame. Gesturing in the same manner to his left, the brazier there likewise ignited by itself. The Protector turned his chill gaze back to Alaena. The same superior, humourless smile touched his thin lips as Alaena's eyes widened in sudden understanding.

81

"Yes, my dear," he said laconically, laughing at her shattered ignorance. "We have something in common now, don't we? We both know something of the Dark Art, it appears!" Clearly delighting in her distress, the Protector held her chin tighter and stared directly into her eyes. "The only difference is, girl, that I use it to improve my lot, whereas for you it promises only your demise." Almost as an afterthought, he added with a malicious sneer, "but not before a great deal of unpleasantness for you, and a great deal of pleasure for me!"

Leaning forward, he grasped the collar of her shirt and in a quick motion, tugged it hard. The top button flew clear and disappeared into the straw on the floor as Alaena pressed herself back against the wall, muscles protesting in pain at the renewed activity. Still smiling in that unnerving way, the Protector pushed the top of the shirt open, exposing Alaena's neck and the top of her chest to air that was quickly becoming warmer than was comfortable. Again she tried to protest her innocence, but the hot air only made it harder to speak, and all that came forth was a dry, rasping whimper.

"So. Let's find out just how pleasurable you're going to make this for me. We'll start with the simple things and work up from there, yes?" The Protector's predatory gaze locked onto the fear in Alaena's eyes. "What is your name, my dear, and where do you come from?"

Desperately, Alaena tried to speak but her mouth was too parched, her vocal cords too dry to enunciate even a letter. Gaping and gasping as she hung from her tethers and the Protector watched in amusement, she forced her aching throat to work.

"No!" she gasped. "Not me!" Chewing her tongue, which felt swollen and twenty sizes too large for her mouth, she tried to force moisture into her throat and started again to protest her innocence. "I ..."

Too fast to register, her words were cut off by a backhanded blow across her jaw that cannoned her head sideways and smashed it brutally against the stone wall behind her. Stars filled her vision and blood filled her mouth as her teeth ripped deep into her tongue. Before her lolling head had righted itself, the Protector's powerful grip clamped again onto her jaw and forced it back to face him.

"Wrong answer, my dear, though I must say I would have been disappointed if you'd made it that easy." He tugged again at her shirt, sending another button flying and pushing the garment, now peppered with drops of blood spattering down from her chin, further open to expose the upper curves of her budding breasts.

"Let's try that again" he drawled, running one finger down her chest to hook it behind the next button, which still held her a step short of bare chested. Pulling her forward by her shirt until both arms and legs strained harshly against the metal bonds and a sob of pained anguish escaped her, the Protector leaned in close and stared into her terrified eyes. "What is your name, witch?"

Holding back a scream of torment as her back arched painfully, Alaena swallowed her own blood and almost retched in the face of the Protector. Vile though it was, the blood moistened her throat enough to string words together again. Despite her extreme distress, Alaena found that the strange compartment in her mind that had opened to her in the field and allowed her to think as though detached from the immediate present, was still with her. In that logical, detached place, her mind screamed at her that if she gave her name up now, it wouldn't be long before Wilmen and, yes, even dear Rince, might end up here with her. So she did what was possibly the bravest thing she'd done in her life to date.

She lied into the Protector's face.

"Elena, sir!" she gushed with her newfound voice, stressed with pain. "My name is Elena! I'm just a street urchin, sir. I live down by the docks. Please don't hurt me – I'll tell you anything you want – but I'm not a witch, sir, really I'm not. I don't know anything at all about magic!"

"Lying wretch!" the Protector responded with vitriol. Grasping her shirt in one hand, he ripped it towards him viciously, the muscles in his arm rippling with the effort, tearing her shirt off her body and leaving her upper torso entirely naked. The action elicited a scream of pain from Alaena as both wrists and ankles snapped tight in the manacles and tore fresh strips of skin from both before the shirt gave way.

Flourishing the ruined cloth before her eyes, he raged, "Do you think *urchin's* wear clothes like *these*, you stupid, ignorant wretch? Do you think you can *lie* to me without consequence?" Throwing the cloth aside, he leaned in close, tracing a calloused finger casually around her pale breasts, leering with pleasure as his words and touch had their desired effect.

"First I will take your body, then I will take your mind, little witch, and you *will* tell me everything I need to know before the end."

His dark eyes seemed to tilt, and terror took hold of Alaena. A black wind seemed to rush through her senses, violating her mind. The room seemed to dim as the fires took on a deeper, redder glow. Twisted desire radiated from his eyes and it was then that Alaena, in the detached, calm section of her mind, realised she was the prisoner of something much darker than just a power-crazed lunatic.

Abruptly, the feeling of defiling intrusion passed. Alaena tried to clear her mind, and a whimper of fear escaped her lips as the Protector stood straighter and looked her up and down. Almost casually, he stated "You see, little witch, you will tell me everything I want to know. Before I am done with your body, you'll ache for the Gathering so your pain can end."

With that, he leant back and put his body into the blow, thundering a fist into Alaena's unprotected abdomen. The breath blew out of her body and new pain screamed from a myriad of sources as she was crushed back flat against the wall. Sharp, jagged pain pierced her insides.

As Alaena struggled to recover from a depth of pain and torment completely outside her experience, the Protector stepped back and eyed her thoughtfully. Wiping spit from his chin and smoothing down his clothes, his gaze slid over her body, pausing on her bare, heaving chest before taking in her slim waist and her lower body.

"Well, Elena, or whatever you want to call yourself for now. A lie is a demonstration of will and I commend you for it, though it will not avail you in the end." With a sweeping motion, he gestured broadly around the chamber. "As you can see, I have a variety of tools with which the truth can be obtained. My personal favourite is the rack. Do you know how talkative a woman can get when her limbs pop from their sockets, or as her nipples are burned from her breasts?"

Stepping to one side, he picked up a poker. He brandished it so Alaena could see it clearly, then pushed it into the brazier on that side, its pointed tip buried deep in red-hot coal and flame. He continued as though giving a lesson to a small child. "I had originally thought the screams that particular activity brought forth were the pinnacle of what the female throat could utter, but listening to them when one of these"—he tapped the end of the heating poker—"takes her womanhood away, is particularly satisfying ..." With a lascivious grin, he leered at her. "But then, you're going to have the chance to find that out shortly yourself, witch. Then we'll see what you know and who your associates are!"

He waved his hand and that strange rush sounded again in Alaena's shocked mind. Without warning, the pins holding the manacles locked at her wrists and ankles flew clear. With a scream of anguish and a sob of terror for the fate that awaited her, Alaena's body crumpled to the floor like a rag doll, face buried in the filthy straw at the feet of the Protector.

Alaena lay gasping, sprawled out on the floor. Had the Protector stood over her with a stake to drive through her heart, she doubted she would have been able to move. Indeed, she likely would have welcomed it rather than endure what was to come from this man, who she now understood relished the pain he could cause others. Knowing now that this was only the beginning and that there would be no respite until she betrayed everyone she loved and sought release in death, she started to cry. Her tears dripped onto the straw beneath her and mingled with her blood.

***

The Protector, relishing the prospect of an evening teaching this young thing to understand what pain and torment really meant, allowed the girl a few moments respite as he stood over her and watched her sob, gloating quietly to himself. He would have preferred she was a little older – a little more developed – to really enjoy ruining her body and mind before having her beaten to death. Still, he consoled himself as he ran his eyes over the flawless skin of her back, there was a unique pleasure to be taken in the destruction of innocence. Her skin looked soft and smooth. It would mark well with a whip and perhaps later with a brand or two before he started on her chest and between her legs. The names and information he wanted from her were really secondary at this point. She would give them up before her mind broke anyway. For now, he licked his lips in anticipation as his groin began to stir, knowing he had the entire night ahead of him to enjoy.

"Enough! Get up, you insect!" he shouted. Though the girl tried to comply, her trembling limbs gave out under her.

Unimpressed with the effort, the Protector yelled at her again and lashed out viciously with one booted heel, eliciting a very satisfactory scream as a deep bruise welled immediately beneath her rib cage. Her body convulsed with the shock and she rolled to one side, obviously desperate to avoid another bruising kick.

"Do you need more encouragement, little witch?" he hollered down at her, moving around and pummelling another kick into her midsection. The skin broke, blood welling from the wound as the girl struggled to stand, making it only to her hands and knees on shaking limbs.

Much as he enjoyed watching her struggle beneath him, the Protector was even more eager to see her naked body stretched almost to breaking point on the rack so he could start on the finer, and ever so much more delectably intimate, stage of her subjugation.

Standing in front of her, the Protector reached down and grasped a swathe of hair at the back of her neck tightly in his left fist. Pulling her up roughly to her knees, he started slowly but surely forcing her head back, bending her neck viciously so her face tilted upward and his maddened visage stared directly down into her terrified eyes. Unable to resist against the weight of his body and the strength of his grip, the girl had no defence. A low moan escaped her lips, scaling up to a wail of anguish as her back bent backward and her arms, hanging loose, dragged on the ground behind her as her neck strained further and further back.

"This is your last chance, witch," he said in a low voice that brimmed with threat. With a brief tilt of his head, his eyes not leaving the girl's for a moment, he continued. "When I let go, you *will* stand up, or I will drag you across the floor and push your face into that brazier to get some life into you. You'll still be able to talk and tell me what I need to know, but no one will ever want to look on your face again."

***

Alaena tried desperately to gather her wits. The base of her spine felt like it was going to snap, and her insides were afire from where she had been punched and kicked. Her arms and shoulders were just a dull aching throb from where she had hung, and her lacerated wrists and ankles burned with every small movement.

All this was nothing to the threat just delivered, however. She could feel the heat washing from the braziers on each side, and nothing he had said so far terrified Alaena as much as having her head forced into the hot coals, burning out her eyes and face. She had to be ready to stand after this, for anything to come later could not be as bad as that immediate and terrifying peril.

As he continued to rant and press down on her and as she desperately tried to rally her resources to be ready to meet this need, the fingers of her right hand brushed the top of her boot. In an oddly detached manner, she felt a strange bump next to her ankle as her fingers slid inside to close on the foreign object. Recognition came to her.

Rince's knife.

Forgotten until now, it had slipped right down into her boot where it wouldn't have been seen by whoever manacled her to the wall. Alaena hadn't had the chance to give it back to Rince, and probably never would now, but her heart leapt in her tortured chest as her fingertips closed on the smooth, worn handle. Abruptly, the Protector released her hair and watched as she collapsed once more to the ground, gasping. Fighting pain from every part of her body as she crashed to the floor, Alaena used the motion to pull the knife from boot to hand, concealing it in her fist.

The Protector leaned over her once more, his breath hot on Alaena's face. "Now, stand up, little witch, so you can tell me all your secrets. Or do you prefer the alternative?"

It was probably the bravest and most difficult thing Alaena had to do, but need is a powerful motivator and never before had her situation been more dire. If she didn't act now, there would probably never be another chance.

With a groan as bone and muscle protested every move, she heaved herself to hands and knees once more, letting her right hand slip under the straw to disguise the movement as she depressed the small catch halfway up the smooth bone handle and felt the honed steel blade spring free. The Protector, completely absorbed in her struggle to stand, continued to hover over her, taunting her with the consequences should she not be on her feet in moments. Preoccupied as he was with her body and with her pain, the slight movement under the straw completely escaped his notice.

He smiled cruelly as he watched her struggle to stand. "This pain is nothing compared to what is to come, little witch."

Alaena, committed to either action or an inevitable death to follow, gritted her teeth. Lost in thoughts of lust and torment as he was, the Protector was completely unprepared for what followed. Ignoring the screaming objections from her body, Alaena surged up from her knees, ramming her fist into the Protector's gloating face.

The blade was small, but Rince had always kept it viciously sharp. Driven by desperation, it found its mark. Moving in an upward slant, the slim blade caught one nostril, slicing it open as it continued its upward path into the Protector's left eye.

Stopping only when the hilt hit bone and it would travel no further, Alaena twisted the blade as it dug deep behind the eye, severing muscle and sinew in its path. Bright red blood gushed from the Protector's face. With a scream of pain and surprise, he fell backwards onto the floor, clawing at the bone handle, which had ripped from Alaena's grasp as he gyrated back. With a groan of visceral anguish, he pulled it free with a jerky movement. The eyeball itself, spitted deep, ripped from its socket as he pulled the blade free, leaving a raw, red gaping hole behind.

Still with blade in hand – made grotesque by the eyeball, which wobbled like jelly as his shaking hand raised it – his good eye stared in disbelief. He scrabbled to rise, screaming vile obscenities as he gained his feet.

Still on hands and knees and aching immensely, Alaena had watched the Protector fall back with blood fountaining from his face. As he grabbed at the blade though, she knew the wound was not mortal and that she had to finish it before he gained his feet, or all was lost.

Forcing herself up with a visceral groan, Alaena reached for the nearest weapon she could find. Taking a few tottering steps to the side, she grabbed the end of the heavy poker, which stuck out from the top of the brazier, and turned back to the Protector as he struggled to stand. The tip glowed hellishly hot as, with both arms and the last of her strength, Alaena swung the heavy implement with all the force she could muster at his ruined face as he lifted his grotesque visage to look for her.

The iron rod caught him square across the forehead, bludgeoning him brutally and burning a deep furrow of seared flesh across his brow. Her arms shrieking from the violence of the impact, Alaena watched as her tormentor cart-wheeled backwards and crashed, unconscious, to the floor.

Still holding the poker before her in both hands, gasping from her exertions, Alaena stood for a few moments in a daze. The tip of the poker cooled enough and lost the last of its glow as her fuzzy mind sought to work out what she should do now. The Protector lay on his back a few feet away from her, his face a landscape of ruined flesh and oozing wounds. Not sure if he was dead or not,

Alaena considered using the poker again to make sure of the job. Even as she contemplated it though, she knew she was no killer. To do so would make her as bad as the monster lying before her, and regardless of his crimes, she could not and would not make herself his executioner if he wasn't already dead.

The poker landed with a dull, heavy thud on the floor as Alaena finally let it slip from her fingers. Exhausted, she wanted nothing more than to curl up somewhere in the sun and give herself time to heal. Her body called stridently for rest and the chance to recuperate. In her mind, however, she knew that escape was paramount and that she must brook no delay, regardless of the condition of her body.

Pushing her battered frame into motion, she took a few difficult steps, then painfully knelt to retrieve her ruined shirt from the floor. Tracing a wide circle around the Protector's prone body, Alaena struggled to stay on her feet as she moved towards the door. Laying a shaking hand on the catch, Alaena pushed it downwards, where it released with the slightest of clicks. A cool breath of air slid through the opening to caress her face as she put her ear to the crack, verifying that there was no noise in the immediate vicinity. Peering through as she inched the door open, a dim passageway with another door similar to the one of her own cell came into view. Opening the door wider and poking her head out, Alaena could see that doors lined the corridor on both sides.

With a last glance behind at the supine body of the Protector, she straightened her torn shirt over her shoulders and across her chest as best she could, then stepped carefully out into the corridor while pulling the door gently closed behind her.

Even as the latch clicked shut and Alaena's thoughts turned to the possibility of freedom, her worn body froze in fear as muffled shouts were raised in the distance. The strident peal of an alarm bell echoing down through the Keep rang like doom in her ears.

Chapter 11 - Rince

After being summarily dismissed by Wilmen, Rince wandered the streets aimlessly, his mind awhirl. Avoiding the areas where his other friends would be so he wouldn't have to talk to anyone, he kicked at stones, glared at anyone who was in his way and was generally at odds with the world. Angry at being treated as though he had nothing to offer to help the situation and upset with the uncomfortable feeling that this may actually be true, he drifted along without considering a destination as the afternoon sun sank slowly and shadows lengthened in the streets. Foremost in his mind, and the real cause of his deep concern, was Alaena.

Wilmen obviously had her own plans, but he was unwilling to risk Alaena on the chandler. A strong woman she might be, but as far as Rince knew, Wilmen had few paths to use to contend with the Keep, so perhaps he could figure out something himself.

His sharp mind working overtime on the problem, Rince sorted and discarded options. All came with some degree of danger, but compared to the need to have Alaena freed, any risk seemed a secondary concern. None were anything he thought likely to succeed.

It wasn't until late afternoon, when shadows on the ground stretched long and there was perhaps an hour of light left to the day, that an audacious thought occurred to him, freezing him in his tracks. The risk it entailed was frightful, but it was by far the most promising option he could see. Failing a rich benefactor coming to the rescue – which was about as likely as the Protector admitting a mistake and releasing Alaena with a full apology to boot – any action to secure Alaena's freedom would have to be done with inside help. To his knowledge, Wilmen had no links within the Keep to achieve such an end but he, Rince, did.

There was a girl that sat near him in lessons during the week and who, mostly when Alaena wasn't around, seemed remarkably adept at finding reasons to speak with Rince and ask him questions. At first he'd found this a little uncomfortable, and didn't know what to say to her in return. But she'd persisted, and over the past months they'd started to talk more and more about things other than their letters and numbers to find out more about each other's lives.

Her name was Talia. The corner of his mouth crinkled into a smile as he pictured her grey-green eyes that always seemed to be searching his face as he spoke. Most importantly at this moment, however, he recalled that her parents had found her work as a chambermaid in the Protectorate Keep at night. She'd been excited about getting the job and had even told Rince about some of the rooms she'd been in throughout the Keep and how sumptuous some of them were. *She has the run of the Keep,* Rince thought. If she krew where the bedrooms were and had keys to get around, then perhaps she also knew where they kept those who were being questioned and how one might get to them too!

Having walked home with her a couple of times now, Rince knew where she lived, so it would be no problem to find her. The difficulty was, though, that he didn't know what time she left to go to the Keep, or how he might broach the subject of going there with her, or, for that matter, what reason he might give her for even suggesting it. There were also his own parents to consider, for dinner would be on the table soon and they'd already be wondering where he was. What he had in mind, assuming he was successful, could take most of the night so he needed to clear that first, then deal with Talia.

It was fortunate for Rince that he thought quickly rather than deeply, for the momentum of the decision carried him through the next hour or so, when a more considered evaluation of the potential perils may just have caused the whole idea to stop in its tracks.

Running the short distance home first, he found, to his relief, that his father wasn't there. He had sent word to his mother that he was going to be home late due to some sort of stock catastrophe at the warehouse he managed. Rince wasn't squeamish about the odd white lie to his parents, but he didn't particularly relish any detailed questioning by his father, who would see through any subterfuge he might stage quickly and with unpleasant consequence for Rince.

Over a rushed dinner, his mother couldn't help but comment on Rince's state of agitation. In rushed words, he explained that Talia had asked if he could see her tonight to help her with some errands at her house. Feeling more and more guilty as he delved deeper and deeper into the lie to answer his mother's questions, and more so when she praised him for being kind (and handsome!) enough for a girl to ask him to help, Rince at last helped finish clear away and dashed out the door, saying he didn't want to be late.

The lamplighters were already doing their rounds when Rince skidded to a halt in front of Talia's house. The streetlamps in this area were already alight, bathing the cobbles beneath them in warm and welcome light, but relegated the upper halves of the terraced houses that lined the street to an even deeper darkness, pockmarked here and there by smaller pimples of light, where candles had already been lit in upper rooms. Now he was here, his body itched for further action to match his racing mind. He didn't knock immediately and thought he'd wait to see her leave, particularly as he didn't want to explain any of this to her parents as well.

Some time passed and at last the door to her home creaked open, allowing a wash of warm light out onto the street. Talia emerged from the house wearing a traditional skirt and slim fitting vest, giving a backward wave to whoever was in the room before closing the door behind her and stepping out into the street. She turned left, as Rince had known she would, towards the Keep.

"Hi, Talia, how's things?" Rince asked, stepping out from the shadows on the other side of the street.

The startled surprise on Talia's face transformed to a shine of sheer pleasure as she realised it was Rince that hailed her up. "Rince! You startled me so!" she said, placing a lingering touch on his arm, as taking a moment to prove he was actually there, then launched into a breathless sequence of excited questioning. "What on earth are you doing here? Is everything okay? I have to get up to the Keep. Will you walk with me aways?"

Even as she spoke, Talia's eyes started searching his face in that way Rince found disconcertingly fascinating. Her hand hooked itself comfortably into the crook of his arm, and she started to lead the way even as Rince endeavoured to frame his reply.

"Sure, Talia. Of course! I'd love to walk you there." He felt a flush of shame seeing the shining response in Talia's face while she pulled him close, so they brushed together as they walked. He knew she liked him and, f truth was told, he thought he liked her too, but he was using that affection to let her get him close to Alaena. Even without a great deal of worldly experience, Rince knew deep down that this wasn't the right thing to do. Alaena's need outweighed all other concerns however and, though he wasn't sure, he suspected that Talia would be unimpressed to know he was walking with her only to help Alaena.

On this basis, Rince continued the pretence of this being a chance meeting, chatting amiably with Talia as they made their way east and north through the town, working steadily closer to the Keep. Discussing the tourney and other general gossip first, Rince eventually brought the conversation around to Talia's work at the Keep.

"Do you like working there, Talia? What's it like inside? Is everyone really as scared of the Protector as rumours say? I'm not sure I'd like to be making his bed or anything in case I did something wrong!"

Talia gave a light laugh. 'Oh no! It's nothing like that, though I've never met the Protector himself, of course! His rooms are higher up on the north side of the Keep, looking out over the Fields, and I never get up that way. I work mostly in the lower areas, cleaning dining rooms and kitchens. It's all pretty easy, really."

"Well … nothing wrong with that," Rince responded kindly. "At least you get to see what it's like inside! I'd love to see the guard room and the swords they have there. Are they anything like the ones the knights use in the tourney?"

Furrowing her brow as she considered Rince's question seriously, Talia gave small shake of her head. "I haven't ever seen where they have their weapons. I think there's a store somewhere deeper in the Keep where they're kept safe. You know, though," she continued as she looked up at Rince with a smile, "there are suits of armour in some of the corridors that are pretty amazing! We clean them once a month with oil and special cloths to make sure they don't get any rust on them." Then, in an almost timid voice, she added, "Would you like to see them?"

Only concern for Alaena stopped Rince from breaking there and then and apologising outright to Talia for using her. Alaena's face was clear in his mind, however, as he responded.

"Wow! That would be great, Talia!" Now it was his turn to turn a furrowed brow on his companion. "But how is that possible? The gates are always guarded, and I certainly don't have any reason to be allowed in."

"No, Rince," she responded with a smile tickling the sides of her lips. "The *front* gates are always guarded. The servants have their own gate around the side of the Keep that we come and go by pretty freely. There'll be one of the Guard there too, of course, but it'll be someone who knows me and it won't be a problem getting you in. After all, who would want to break into the Keep? No thief in their right mind would try his hand at anything the Protector owns!"

Uneasy now that it was happening so easily, Rince gave a short, nervous laugh at her small joke. Little did she realise how close she was to the very reason that Rince wanted to get into the Keep. "I guess not, Talia!" he said, glad the early evening darkness covered the flush he was sure was on his face.

Before he could say more, Talia surprised him with a squeeze on the arm. "You know though, Rince, that if I'm doing a favour for you, then you have to do one for me too!"

Unsure what she meant and with his mind already running ahead to think about what he might do once he was actually inside, Rince didn't catch the suggestion in her voice or the sidelong glance she gave him as she said it.

"Sure," he responded in a distracted manner before realising he wasn't positive what he was promising. "Anything you like, Talia!"

With a satisfied nod and brazenly leaning her head onto his shoulder for a few brief moments, Talia sealed what she obviously thought was a deal. "Right then! Let's get inside and I'll show you around."

It was more of a walk than Rince expected to reach the Keep. It sat atop a small hill at the northernmost point of Morlyn, high enough to look over the entirety of the town and probably to remind those that lived there that they were always being watched. The road to the front gate ran in a gentle slope upward for almost a league. Each occupied with their own thoughts, they maintained a comfortable silence as they walked. If either had any inkling of what the other was thinking, however, they would each have been considerably shocked.

Rince's first view of the Keep from up this close was daunting, and almost made him back out of his plan there and then. From afar, it looked impressive and could be considered without too much trepidation, notwithstanding the fact that its primary occupant was universally viewed in Morlyn as a man not to be crossed for any reason. Up this close though, darkening as it was in the fading light, it was imposing. Great hand-hewn blocks of granite, black with age and fitted together with remarkable skill, comprised the majority of the four-storey building. The occasional guard could be seen moving along the upper walls, with crenelations along the outer walls permitting staccato views out across the township. Small towers reaching an extra storey above the walls dominated each corner of the squat, square structure, three of the four with a warm glow of light coming from within through thin, glassless, arrow-slit windows. Overall, the impression was of security, authority and muted threat. Just the impression the Protector would want to give, Rince thought nervously, starting to realise just how unrealistic it was to expect one young boy to be able to rescue his friend from the locked and probably well-guarded dungeons of this place.

Talia, however, had no such concern and, indeed, seemed eager to get inside rather than loiter outside the front gate. "Come on, laggard!" she joked, disengaging his arm and moving left onto a thin, well-trod path that snaked away to the left of the main road. With the evening well set in and the path hugging the wall of the Keep after a few footsteps, they would have been in darkness were it not for torches set atop iron stakes burning fitfully at even distances along the way.

Walking carefully, they made their way around the left corner of the keep. Rince trailed his hand across the rough stone surface, still warm from the sun that the dark stones had absorbed during the day, but quickly cooling as the evening breeze danced fitfully across the face of the blunt structure.

Rince was starting to wonder if the servants' entrance was actually at the back of the Keep itself, as Talia, keeping one eye on the uneven and poorly lit path at all times, continued almost all the way along the eastern side to the far corner before cucking to the right through an archway that was almost invisible in the black wall, Rince following obediently.

Their footing immediately improved as they stepped from the sodden, unpaved track and their feet found solid flagstones beneath them. From what Rince could see in the dim light, they were made of the same stone as the walls, but polished flat rather than left rough from the chisel marks of the stonemasons, or more likely slaves, who hewed them out of the earth. *However they came to be here,* Rince thought to himself sardonically, *the person who built this in the first place certainly liked black!*

Only a moment was permitted for this introspection, however, and Rince's head came up from his study of the masonry with a start. His heart felt like it lodged in his throat as he heard the clink of metal on metal up ahead. His tongue felt like fur as, with visions of walking into a dozen drawn swords and arrest for conspiracy to free prisoners from the Keep's dungeons, he watched them stop before a tall, iron gate set firmly into the wall. Behind the gate was a small open area where a table and small bench sat, behind which another gate, similarly solid and set into the wall, gave way to what looked like a small courtyard beyond.

Rince almost passed out with relief as Talia, completely unaware of his trepidation, stopped and exchanged easy words with the guard, who was putting down a beaten metal jug of water he'd just refilled his goblet with. He reached for a set of keys as he glanced briefly up and down at Rince, evaluating him.

"Hi, Findaril," Talia said easily, drawing his eyes back to her. "How's the family?"

"Talia," Findaril responded with a nod. "All's well there, thanks for asking, though the young'n has a cough that we'll have to get looked at if it gets any worse."

He stood, keys now in hand, and moved towards them. Glancing around, the Guard appeared to satisfy himself that they were indeed alone before fitting a key to the gate and ushering them through. Rince noticed uncomfortably that a sword swung easily from a well-worn scabbard about his waist and scars that crisscrossed his face gleamed evilly in the torchlight. Had he been able, Rince might just have turned and bolted right there and then, but he had come too far now. He stepped past the threshold with Talia, then stood and waited while the guard swung the gate shut and relocked it. The heavy clang as the gate was secured echoed in Rince's ears like the sound of his doom.

His task done, the guard turned, towering over them both. "Who's your friend?" he asked brusquely, inclining his head towards Rince and looking down on them both with a worrying sense of authority. Rince couldn't have answered if his life depended on it and was immensely relieved when Talia responded readily.

"This is Rince, Findaril," she said with a strange look at Rince as though she'd just seen the terror on his face. "We're running low on wood for the fires and he's going to do a few hours' chopping for us so we can fill the store a bit more."

"Hoo! Is he now?" Findaril chuckled. A huge smile split his features, stretching scar tissue into spider-web patterns, and he took one of Rince's arms into his massive fist. The fingers closed around it like a vice, reaching easily around Rince's slender arms, uncomfortably suggesting iron bands to Rince's overactive imagination. "Well ... looks to me like he's done more thinking than fighting, and I think the axe will do him more damage than he'll do the wood, but there's no harm in building up, eh, boy?" Findaril said as he leaned down close to Rince's face. "How'll you ever swing a sword if you don't get some muscle on those scrawny arms of yours, eh?"

Rince gave a sickly smile as Findaril straightened and freed his arm. He selected another key from the set and gave Talia a wink as he swivelled on one heel towards the inner gate. "Well … just make sure you look after him, won't you, Talia? He's just as likely to split his foot open as split the logs by the look of him!"

Findaril continued to chuckle as he slid the key home and the gate, like the first, swung smoothly open. This time, Rince almost shoved Talia through in his eagerness to get out of the gaze of this guard who so unnerved him. It wasn't until he heard the gate lock behind him that he started to breathe again and pay attention to his surroundings and the fact that Talia was speaking to him again.

They had stepped through to a small rectangular courtyard and behind them now, the inner wall of the keep scaled upwards. Braziers set around the edges, supplemented by torches set in wall sconces, gave ample light to see by, though little of the warmth the braziers gave out was retained as the area was open to the sky. Rince turned once to glance back, realising the area they'd just come through was actually under and within the wall itself, which made the wall some twelve feet thick! It was probably honeycombed, Rince thought, with rooms and passages just like the guard station they'd just passed through. He wondered briefly what other secrets the walls of the Keep contained before Talia again captured his attention.

"Now, Rince," Talia was saying in a low voice, as though sharing a secret with a child. "You're going to have to stop worrying so! This is the Protectorate Keep and you'll meet a lot of the Guard here. None of them will bother you, though, and the ones I've met are actually really nice! If you look as terrified as you did with Findaril, someone is going to ask you what the matter is and then we might have a problem. So stop worrying so, okay?"

Listening to Talia dress him down like his mother might, much of Rince's concern evaporated. Of course, he'd done nothing wrong so far other than be here without actual permission, but Talia's excuse for him to be here was obviously more than sufficient for the guard and, at least for the moment, he had nothing to worry about. At least she had had her wits about her and had clearly thought this through before turning up at the gate of the Keep asking to come in just because he wanted to!

Rince shook his head at himself. Sometimes his naivety was truly appalling.

"Sorry, Talia. I just realised that I hadn't thought about a reason for me to be here, and when I saw that guard, I – well, I just froze up!" He gave a little shiver to illustrate the feeling and a stronger grin to assure her that he was back in control of himself now. "Good thing you'd thought it through!"

Tilting her head to the side, Talia adopted a serious expression. "Well ... it wasn't all bluff, you know! I have promised to show you around and I will, but I did need a good reason for you to be here and I have to get inside to see what chores are to be done tonight. So ..." she said suggestively. A hint of a smile tugged one side of her mouth again as she tossed her head to the left and indicated with her thumb.

Rince followed her direction and looked over to the other side of the courtyard, diagonally opposite to the gate by which they'd entered. There, in a tangled mess, lay piles of branches and boughs of trees – some thin enough to snap with his hands, others as thick as his torso. Next to them, a large chopping block was set in the ground, an axe with a leather blade guard affixed resting beside the block. Next to that again, a large wooden trolley with a flat base and worn iron wheels sat, on which a substantial amount of wood was already stacked.

Clearly, one picked up the wood on the right, chopped it on the block, then loaded up the trolley on the left with the trimmed wood, then wheeled it to wherever it was required. Rince, who had never lifted an axe in his life, looked back to Talia as understanding dawned that he was here to actually chop firewood. Wearing a grin that stretched from ear to ear, she continued as though he wasn't looking at her in complete disbelief. "So. You get on with that and get as much wood as you can done before I get back in about an hour. Then we can take all that's there into the Keep and I can show you around while we stock a few fireplaces with fresh wood. Okay?"

Still a little surprised, Rince couldn't help but appreciate the fact that Talia's plan not only got him in the gate, it also gave a good reason for them to be wandering through the Keep. Rince's natural humour resurfaced as she turned and made her way to a few small steps and opened one of the heavy wooden doors set in the wall nearby. Light flooded out, accompanied by the tantalising smells of roasting meat and herbs, shimmering on long, red-brown locks of hair as Talia moved.

"Okay!" he called as she stepped through. "I'll chop your wood for you, but you'll be the one looking after me if Findaril is right and I lop off a leg rather than lop off a log!" he said with a laugh, then turned back to contemplate the woodpile and the axe.

With a fond smile of her own, Talia gently shut the door behind her, eyes riveted to Rince until the moment the door blocked him from view.

Chapter 12 - Council

Wilmen sat alone in a dim room, awaiting her companions. Her hands clasped tightly in her lap, she used the quiet time she had until the others arrived to run over events and plans in her mind.

She had made good use of her afternoon, gathering spare clothes for both herself and Alaena, a slim rope, flint and steel, some hard bread, dried fruit and other necessities for the road in a large sack. Returning to the Abbey briefly, Wilmen entrusted the sack to Brother Ulma, who, with the exception of a raised eyebrow or two, asked no questions as he took the bag from her and promised to keep it safe with her saddlebags as long as she required.

Back at the Chandler's once more, she had reverently retrieved the topaz pendant from its hiding place and reassured herself that it remained active, allowing the light from the gem to again wash over her face in wonder. Not long did she dally here, however. Assuming Alaena was the cause of the Star coming to life, of which Wilmen had no doubt, the light meant not only that Alaena's powers were active but, more importantly at this juncture, that she was still alive. Sitting and gazing at the gem, no matter how fascinating it was or what that shining stone promised for the future, it would do nothing to ensure that situation would remain the same.

Lastly, Wilmen changed into a light long-sleeved shirt, with a worn but well-made skirt that would be suitable for travelling and sturdy boots that had plenty of wear left in them should she need to leave the horses and take to any roads by foot. Discarding the light cloak she'd worn earlier that day, she flung a long, dark hooded robe of much finer weave across her shoulders that would protect her from all but the worst weather outside, then secreted within the slim box containing the Star, along with a small bag of coin and other valuables that might be useful on the road.

Finally, after locking the Chandler's and taking a lingering look back at the shop that she believed she would probably never see again, Wilmen turned and made her way purposefully towards the docks and the agreed meeting place.

As she had a dozen times in the short while she'd been here, Wilmen stayed in her seat and resisted the urge to pace. The others would be here soon, and when they arrived, they needed to see her calm and in control, not circling the room like some madwoman. So she sat, outwardly composed, suppressing the urgent panic she felt coiled within. Wilmen's only concession to her inner turmoil was her hands that fidgeted incessantly, restive fingers clenching and unclenching and touching the ring on her left hand, thoughtfully tracing the staves embossed on the surface.

The room in which she sat was a small cellar below one of the many warehouses that Tag managed in the docks districts of Morlyn. It felt damp and smelled of mould, wrinkling Wilmen's nose with its stale odour. She could understand why the room wasn't used as a store anymore. Unless impervious to damp, anything kept here would quickly be ruined. All that occupied the room now was an old wooden table that had seen many years of wear, around which sat a half dozen chairs which remained sturdy, though in various states of disrepair. A single candle from Wilmen's stock bathed the table and immediate surrounds in a dim, flickering glow that barely reached the walls. Noting this sardonically, Wilmen couldn't help visualising the disturbing metaphor of her present situation where she sat alone, aware of a single source of light in the world, while all around darkness closed in. With this in mind and with Alaena in the hands of the Protector, Wilmen brooded. It was difficult to shift her mind to a more positive frame and while she continued to wait, Wilmen pondered futures that were a great deal darker than the walls around her now.

At last, Wilmen heard a door up above open and close quietly, then soft footfalls on the stairs that led down to the cellar itself. *Tag,* Wilmen thought, reminded that his occupation overseeing warehouse stock on the docks was secondary to his prowess with a blade. For Talgard Pretau, trained by the Sword Masters of Ald, walking down the stairs so quietly was simply an inherent outcome of the balance in his movements and lightness of his step.

Shortly he appeared, sombrely attired as always in a short brown coat with leather trim that sat comfortably on his slim shoulders over a dark tunic and trousers with tight fitting cuffs over the soft leather boots. As was his habit, Tag scanned the room quickly with eyes that missed little detail. He fixed his gaze on Wilmen.

"I have not changed my mind, Wilmen, in case you were wondering," Tag began without preamble, taking a chair opposite her and folding his lanky frame smoothly into it. He looked expectantly at Wilmen, obviously anticipating a response. Tag was a man of few words.

Wilmen paused, briefly unsure about what he was referring to, before she recalled her conversation earlier that day with Tag. She'd been pressing for his support to test Alaena, and while he had not agreed in full, he had promised not to argue against her as she spoke her case to the Council. If the situation not become as dire as it had since this morning, Wilmen might have laughed. Had it only been this morning that they'd been discussing whether or not to open the subject to Alaena and test her for Talent? At least this question was no longer moot, though Tag was the only one of the council that remained unaware of the fact.

"I understand, Tag, but things have progressed far more quickly than we expected, and our hand is now forced. I have made the others aware, but you need to know. Something happened at the Fields today with Alaena.'

Tag leaned forward with interest. In that position, candlelight highlighted the long features of his face, but the rest of his body remained in shadow, making his head appear to float disturbingly across the table as though disembodied.

Wilmen continued with a frown, putting the discomforting impression aside but keeping her eyes on his face to gauge his reactions to her news.

"We don't know exactly what happened yet. Yeta was going to see what she could find out this afternoon and will tell us what she discovered when she arrives. Only two things we know for sure, and I warn you that both will come as a shock. Firstly, and the cause of most concern, Alaena has been taken by the Guard and we believe is being held at the Keep."

In all the years that Wilmen had known Tag, she had never seen him agitated or observe him lose control of his emotions. It was one of the reasons, if reputation were to be believed, that he was such a deadly opponent when battle became earnest and blades were unsheathed. This time, however, she truly appreciated how much self-control Tag possessed. Rogan's anger had been evident and Yeta's fear palpable when she had informed them of Alaena's incarceration. Even Egan had surged to his feet in consternation when she delivered the news. Tag, however, seemed only to tense, much as a snake might before striking. Physically, there appeared to be no change in his expression, yet Wilmen suppressed a shiver as somehow his demeanour changed from focused interest to coiled menace. *Yes,* Wilmen thought to herself as she recognised the contained violence in his eyes and unconsciously pressed her arm against her thigh to check her dagger was still in place. *This is not a man I would want as an enemy.*

After a moment, Tag shifted minutely and his hand closed slowly on the table, as if seeking a weapon. "You have a penchant for understatement, then, Wilmen, for that piece of news is far more than just 'things progressing quickly'! Tell me everything, Wilmen, and leave out no detail, including why you're wearing your ring openly now."

Wilmen, stressing again that little information was available, conveyed what she knew thus far in a few concise minutes. Tag listened intently, asking Wilmen to repeat what Rince had told her to make sure he understood it all. To Wilmen's surprise, Tag seemed unconcerned that the Star had woken and she questioned him about that, given his reluctance to support her testing earlier in the day.

"It is not that I didn't believe she had Talent, Wilmen. I merely believed the test was too early rather than not needed at all! There is as much danger in waking such powers too early as there is in leaving them untrained for too long and, like a good blade, the balance must be right."

Tag took a breath to continue but was interrupted by the sound of the door at the top of the stairs opening then closing and heavy feet on the stairs.

"It appears Rogan has arrived," Wilmen commented unnecessarily, his heavy footfall unmistakable.

To her surprise, Tag added, "And Yeta too, actually," which was proven correct a few moments later as the slight woman appeared at the bottom of the stairs first, her light footfalls camouflaged by Rogan's heavier ones.

Skirting the room, Yeta nodded to both Wilmen and Tag before taking a chair on Wilmen's left while Rogan took a larger chair to her right, which creaked alarmingly as his bulk settled into it. Rogan nodded respectfully to each of his colleagues, then looked back towards the doorway as another set of feet padded down the stairs.

Egan looked harried. Instead of the homespun robes he wore about the Abbey, he was attired in much finer vestments that he normally kept for more formal occasions. The deep green robe, which covered a matching tunic and hose, often gave Egan a regal bearing, picking up the both the lighter green of his eyes and the more vibrant green of the emerald set in the centre of the pendant that announced his office. In the dim room, however, the robe looked black and his eyes a little washed, as if worry had bled the colour from them. He took his seat quickly, sitting on the edge and leaning forward, elbows on the table before him as he scanned the faces of his colleagues as if searching for comfort there.

"Well, my friends," Egan began. "We knew they would come, and we hoped not this soon, but the days we feared are upon us." Silence laid heavy on the air as he pondered his next words. "Wilmen, let the Council first look to hope before we consider the worst. It has been a long wait and it would be good for us all to remember why we are here. Would you show us what you have brought?"

Understanding immediately that Egan referred to the Star, Wilmen nodded and reached deep into her cloak, pulling free the small bag in which she'd placed the box containing the gem. A brief reluctance came over her as she withdrew the intricately carved container and placed it on the table before her. Wilmen had been

106

guardian of the gem for over ten years now, and in all that time no one else had laid eyes on it. Indeed, most of the people who even knew of its existence now sat in this room with her. Wilmen found it more difficult than she'd anticipated to overcome her possessive and protective feelings and unveil the gem to anyone other than herself, even those she trusted as completely as she did the people around her now.

Shrugging off her unwarranted reticence, Wilmen swivelled the box so it would face the room rather than herself as she opened it. Unconsciously holding her breath as she watched the others lean forward in anticipation, she gently lifted the lid back towards her.

As it had in her own room earlier that day, warm, welcoming light spilled out as soon as the lid cracked open. Brighter and steadier than the flickering candlelight, the light continued to expand until the lid was open all the way, golden light bathing the astounded faces of those around her. Rogan, usually the quiet one of the group, was first to break the silence.

"So there is no doubt, then," Rogan said, his deep voice tinged with resignation and rugged face full of concern. His eyes glinted with reflections from the Star as he glanced around the rest of the group, most of whom were still transfixed by the gem. "It is hard to have our long-awaited sign come to us when circumstances are most dire."

"That it is, Rogan," Egan replied, "but we are not yet undone, and this light before us shines hope rather than despair into my heart!" Gesturing to the Star with one hand, his voice filled with passion as he embraced their shared destiny. "Here, at last, we have proof that our struggle was not in vain, my friends! More so, it is proof that the reason we formed this council – to bring magic back into the world and end the threat of demon kind against Man forever – is alive and well. Not shall the sacrifices of so many since the Fall be in vain!"

Egan waited a moment for his message to sink in, watching each in turn as they considered his words. They were at the crux, and all present knew none would hesitate to give whatever was required to meet their collective goal.

"Thank you, Wilmen," he continued, shifting focus, "but let us put the Star away now, lest its light distract us from the work we must do tonight."

As Wilmen complied and relative darkness seemed to close in on the room while eyes readjusted to the meagre candlelight, Egan suggested Wilmen take up the story at the beginning so they could make plans on common understanding.

Though she had related parts of the story to each of the people present, Wilmen had not given any of them the full background, so she started back with Alaena's strange reaction to the Gathering and gave a detailed account of all that had happened since, including her discussions with Tag about her desire to test Alaena and to discuss the proposal with the Council. Concluding with her visits to Rogan, Yeta and Egan following Rince's distraught appearance at her shop, Wilmen brought her tale to an end, after which an ominous silence filled the room until Egan spoke once more.

"Thank you, Wilmen, though I know your news gives us all little comfort. I have news also, but I think it best we hear from Yeta now. While I don't doubt Rince's word, for he has been a stoic companion to Alaena for some time and I suspect would not leave her in danger to run to Wilmen's side if there was another option, I would like corroboration of the facts before we consider a rescue from the dungeons of the Protector's Keep!"

Turning to his right, Egan looked at Yeta who, like Wilmen, nodded slightly before taking up her part of the tale. Yeta, though her voice was soft, spoke in concise, clipped sentences. A lilting accent rounded her speech, reminiscent of the language of her homeland far to the north of Morlyn. Round, owl-like eyes flicked quickly from person to person as she related her findings.

"As Wilmen said, she visited me this afternoon. Told me of her fears and asked me to investigate, which I did immediately given the importance of the news. What I found, it was not final, but neither was it comforting."

Yeta paused, ordering her thoughts before relating her findings. As Wilmen had requested, she went to the Fields. There, she found that a dark-haired girl had indeed been taken by the Guard and that witchcraft was rumoured to be involved. Some stories told that the girl had killed a dog to be used in her sorceries, but this was difficult to be sure of, as yet others said a dog had been killed and a girl matching Alaena's general description had been involved, but that it was an accident rather than the result of black sorcery. Yeta folded her hands and frowned as she concluded. "So, you see. I cannot say. That a girl was taken to the Keep, there seems no doubt. That a dog was involved somehow it appears yes, but why and how remains unclear. I cannot, however, say with assurance whether or not Alaena is the one in question who was taken!

Large eyes glowing eerily in the candlelight as she finished her topic, Yeta leaned forward to make her final point.

"I am reluctant to speak my next thoughts. In my land, I would be chastised for saying without the facts to stand beside me. My feeling, however, is that there is too much coincidence here. Alaena is missing. We have the word and worry of her friend Rince to view and consider. Most importantly also, on the evidence of the Star, is the belief that Alaena somehow came into her Gift this afternoon and that, woe betide us all, the Protector has her and is even now putting her to the question!"

Slapping an open palm on the table to drive home her final point, Yeta blinked owlishly and concluded, "For my say, though I cannot prove beyond doubt, I believe Alaena is at the Keep and our duty is clear. We must move now, while surprise is with us, to effect her rescue."

Before anyone else could respond, Rogan slammed a heavy fist to the table, making the candle and everyone else in the room jump in surprise. "Damn, Yeta," he pronounced roundly. "I've said it before and I'll probably say it again. You don't say much, but when you do, it's always right in my book!"

He looked around while Yeta, self-conscious as always, covered a smile with her hand.

"After Wilmen visited me this afternoon, I kept my ear to the ground also, for loose tongues and tales are perfect companions to a tankard of ale! I also heard rumour of a dark-haired girl being taken at the Fields." He shook his head briefly as he talked. "Though whether she burnt down a tent or whether she summoned the Dark One himself, I couldn't make out from the variety of tales being told."

He frowned, making his bushy black eyebrows appear to fold into one across his broad brow. "To my mind, though I need less fact than Yeta to be comforted, I'm convinced. We take the Keep and we take it tonight, lest any delay on our part gives opportunity for Alaena to come to harm!"

Egan looked to Tag and Wilmen for confirmation, though it was already clear that they were all of one mind. Tag merely deigned to lift one hand, palm raised while he cocked an eyebrow, stating clearer than words that his opinion was "What else is there to be said?" Wilmen, remaining composed, merely nodded.

Egan drew a breath, which was heavy with the knowledge that everything was about to change. "So we are decided, my friends. We infiltrate the Keep for Alaena and bring her out before harm can befall her. From there we must still decide, but Wilmen has already made preparations for further flight. Sadly, after this, their lives in Morlyn are ended and they must start anew, elsewhere." Egan paused before adding with a tinge of regret colouring his voice, "Which may be something we all must think about soon."

Keeping their voices low and careful to maintain vigil on the stair to ensure no one overheard, the five leant in close. Over a pitted table in a dim cellar lit by meagre candlelight, they laid plans for the evening that ultimately could change the fate of the world.

The candle had burnt noticeably lower by the time they were done and ready to move. While all had skills that would contribute to the success of their endeavour, it was agreed the party would remain small to avoid unwanted attention and, once they were inside, to facilitate movement through the Keep without questions. Egan had valid reasons to enter to the Keep on Abbey business, so he would be one to go. Wilmen would accompany him ostensibly as his assistant, but primarily because of them all, Wilmen was the only face familiar to Alaena and would need to be there for her when she was found.

Of the others, Tag was most adept at being present without being seen, so would be stationed near the entry gate to help if required when they emerged with Alaena. Yeta would craft notes to be sent out by pigeon to those who might help on the road, that they would be aware of travellers coming and watch and help in need. Rogan would await them in the Abbey to ensure the safety of the horses and that they were ready as required.

Within the hour of the final decisions made, Egan and Wilmen approached the gates of the Keep, dark walls making a blank, black hole in the night before them. From this distance, glimpses of the lanterns carried by the Guard who patrolled the walls looked like fairy lights, sparkling yellow against the whiter backdrop of stars that dotted the night sky behind them. A small detour to the Abbey had Egan attired in the deep blue robes befitting the head of his order on official business to the Keep, and Wilmen robed in the lighter blue of a functionary of the Abbey. Tag had melted into the night before coming within sight of the Keep and all was ready.

As they approached the gates, however, the strident peal of an alarm bell tolled, and sounds of running and shouting echoed from within the Keep.

Chapter 13 – Subterfuge

Night had fallen by the time Talia returned. She carried a small lantern that illuminated her face but was insufficient to cast more than a paltry glow on the walls about them. A chill had settled in the air with the departure of the sun, reminder that warmer days were on the wane and that winter's hand would soon reach out to grasp the land. Particularly here, in the deep shadows cast by the walls of the Keep around him, the cold settled quickly on Rince's sweat-slicked skin. As Talia approached, Rince considered the several varieties of equally painful blisters that he now sported on each hand. Slim shoulders aching from the unaccustomed activity, he was reasonably sure that he'd come up with some curses in the past hour or so that no one had ever heard before. While the blisters were something he wasn't pleased with, he couldn't help but notice with some pride that the pile of wood on the ground was now considerably diminished and the wood on the cart itself was noticeably higher.

He would have liked to just stop right there to enjoy the achievement, along with the praise he expected it would bring from Talia. As Talia's slim form crossed the courtyard, however, silhouetted by the light streaming through the open door behind her, his thoughts turned immediately to Alaena and what he must do from here.

Putting on his best smile, Rince turned towards Talia as she approached. Careful of his stinging palms, he started to place the axe down, intending to lean it against the chopping block. Talia stepped forward quickly and took it from his hands before he could do so.

"Silly!" she said as she bent close to retrieve the axe. Her hair, Rince noticed, smelled wonderful. Complementing the pervading smell of freshly cut wood, it was dusted with the scent of rose, or lavender perhaps. "That's no way to store a blade, for it will rust and lose its edge!" She exclaimed with a smile, handing it back to him.

Suppressing a wince, Rince reluctantly took hold of the haft once more and looked expectantly at Talia, trying not to think of her hair, or her hips, or the fact that he was about to betray her trust terribly.

Unaware of his disquiet thoughts, she gestured with a delicate hand. "Drive it into the block there so the blade is buried and it doesn't rust, then let's get inside and out of this chill."

Rince couldn't help but let out a gasp as his blistered hands protested at the jarring stop of the axe biting into the block, and he let go gingerly and gratefully as Talia stepped close once more, taking his hands in her soft palms and turning them over carefully. A smell like spring wafted around Rince as she moved next to him.

Dumbly aware that he was out of his depth and that Talia seemed remarkably adept at finding reasons to stand so close, Rince stood stupidly in the failing light as she ran her fingers gently over his throbbing hands. "Oh, Rince! You poor thing!" she exclaimed, as the not-altogether-unpleasant tingling from her touch ran up his arms. "I didn't realise your hands were suffering so, or I would have come for you earlier! Let's go inside where we can see these better and you can wash up, then we can attend to the wood." Not waiting for his response, she turned without letting go of his hand and made for the door from which she'd come, chatting happily as she guided him up the short pair of stairs and into the kitchen.

Warmth and wonderfully fresh smells wrapped around Rince's senses as Talia closed the door gently behind him, keeping one of his hands in hers at all times, ostensibly protecting it from further damage. They were in a small, square entryway about five paces long on each side, which opened out into the wider kitchen area before him. Lanterns were hung at regular intervals around the walls but only every few were lit, illuminating the area dimly but sufficiently to see. If Talia's ministrations were not enough to stop him in his tracks, the kitchen itself was. He had seen the kitchens of inns and taverns aplenty, but never had Rince seen such an enormous place dedicated solely to the preparation of food as the kitchen of the Protectorate Keep. Two massive iron stoves, fires banked for the evening, stood squarely against the wall furthest from him, soot-black flues snaking up from above the cooking surfaces and disappearing into the wall behind them. His view of the heavy beams that supported the roof was obscured by a plethora of hanging pots, pans, ladles, knives and all manner of cooking paraphernalia suspended on hooks above an enormous table whose surface was pitted, scarred and stained with use. Further to the right sat a fireplace with a bakery oven built into the structure of the wall, along with a massive copper cauldron on a tripod with a hinged arm, allowing the pot to be shifted closer to or further from the flames as required. The kitchen extended to the right and Rince was about to step forward to see how much further it continued before Talia nudged him to the left of the small alcove, directing his attention to where a small basin sat atop a low cupboard, accompanied by a round sand soap and a towel.

Gently, Talia guided Rince's hands to the basin and turned them over carefully until his palms were facing upwards. Lifting an earthenware jug with one hand while holding his hands steady with her other, she gently poured cool water over his palms, washing away the dirt and grime before patting them dry with a cloth that hung nearby. All the while she worked, Talia chatted aimlessly and appeared to take every opportunity she could to touch and brush up against Rince. He thought he saw frustration on her face every now and then as opportunity for him to return the innocent contact passed without action, but she persisted admirably before announcing his hands clean and dry with no lasting damage.

"I think you'll survive now, Rince," she said with a smile as she stood before him and gave his hands one final inspection. "I do think, though, that I'm going to have to get you in here a lot more for practice to build up those hands and arms of yours, you know! How will you tend your business and look after your wife in a few years if she has to bathe your hands every time you chop wood for the fire!" Giving him a mischievous smile that brought up small dimples on her cheeks, she took Rince by surprise, leaning forward quickly and going up on her toes to give him a quick kiss on the cheek.

With a self-satisfied giggle and giving Rince no chance to respond, Talia retreated back through the door they'd entered and back into the night, beckoning Rince to follow. In the dark, the muddy ground was more difficult to negotiate, so they picked their way carefully back to the wood-laden trolley guided again by Talia's little lantern. Talia wrapped her arms about her chest for warmth and indicated the other door in the area with a nod of her head.

Her cheeks were a little flushed with the cold and her dark eyes were even deeper in the half-light as she spoke.

"Okay, Rince, you bring the trolley over to the door and we'll get this all inside as soon as we can. I'll meet you inside."

Not waiting for a response, Talia turned and made her way across to the other door in the courtyard – the only one they hadn't been through yet. She stepped up the one stone step, then lifted the latch and pushed the door inwards. Brushing her skirt quickly to remove any clinging dirt and flashing Rince a quick smile, she stepped through into what looked like a corridor beyond. Leaving the door open and the lantern on the step below the door, she disappeared from sight into the Keep itself.

Not quite sure what happened from here, Rince shook his head and decided to just follow this through as it looked like he was finally going to be able to enter the Keep proper. Dutifully, he leant down and grasped the wide iron handle that was attached by a hinged bolt to the front of the trolley. His mind occupied with thoughts of what he might do once inside, he didn't stop to consider his hands as he took the weight and started to lift it from the ground. The rough, cold metal bit immediately into his blistered hands and with a small yelp, which was as much surprise as pain, he let go quickly and jumped back, mud spattering his front as the bar fell with a heavy plop back onto the ground.

Standing for a moment as he blew on his palms, Rince cursed the world in general as he waited for the new throbbing in his hands to subside. Casting his gaze about the dim area, Rince looked in vain for a cloth or something he might wrap around the handle to help lift it without removing more layers of skin. Seeing nothing that might help, he briefly considered taking off his shirt and using that to hold on to, but somehow the prospect of standing in this cold, rapidly darkening corner with the Protectorate Keep looming up all around him while only half clothed wasn't a comforting one.

Resigned to the task and having no other options, Rince collected some stringy pieces of bark from the ground and laid them in his palms as best he could before grasping the handle once more. It still stung and he grit his teeth as he took the weight in full, but the bark softened the grip and took the cold sting from the metal, so he persevered. Ignoring the discomfort as much as he could, he manhandled the trolley over to the doorway that stood open. The uneven ground didn't help, but at least the wheels rolled smoothly under the weight of the wood. *Someone probably has to do this every day,* Rince thought sourly as sweat broke out on his brow once more with the effort. *No wonder they keep the bloody wheels oiled!*

Tugging the load the last few feet, Rince gave a groan as he reached the step and dropped the trolley handle with relief. He had dragged it across with his feet set on the ground and his back to his destination, so he hadn't noticed that Talia had arrived back at the door. His nerves jangling from stress, he almost jumped with fright as a low chuckle sounded behind him.

He swivelled quickly, his burning palms momentarily forgotten, then felt his face flush red as he realised Talia was trying not to laugh. His mortified look quelled Talia's amusement somewhat and she calmed herself, though her smile remained.

"Oh, Rince. I'm sorry, but I think I got the easier job of the two of us here!" She pushed the door open wider and Rince could see a small wooden hand cart sitting on the flat stone floor of the corridor beside her. Big enough to hold sufficient wood to stock a fireplace, but small enough to be manhandled through the corridors of the keep, Rince didn't need Talia's explanation to get what happened next. Clearly, they would make several trips, loading the smaller cart up at this point from the trolley, then wheeling it through the Keep to each fireplace, where it would be unloaded and the process repeated until all were fully stocked. The wooden cart fit snugly through the doorway here, as it presumably would through every other door in the Keep, so it was no trouble to manoeuvre it halfway out the door, right next to the iron cart outside. From there, it was a simple matter to fill the first load, and at last they were inside.

Rince's pulse quickened as Talia shut the door behind them. Against all expectation, he was here, in the Keep itself, and as yet unchallenged. Alaena was close, and now he just had to keep his courage up enough to see the rest of it through. Looking around, he began to assess his surroundings.

Rince's first impression of the Keep's interior had been the kitchen area, which had dwarfed his expectations. That massive room had been bigger than anything he'd seen before, so he had presumed that the rest of the Keep would follow the same theme. Not so, at least in this case. The corridor they'd entered was just wide enough for the two of them to stand side by side behind the trolley and push it along. Had he tried, Rince could probably have touched both sides of the corridor at the same time with his arms outstretched. Closely fitted stone blocks combined with a low roof supported by stout wooden beams added to the closed in feeling, and the small oil lanterns set at intervals along the corridor, which provided meagre illumination at best, completed the claustrophobic effect. They had entered at the far end of the corridor, and Rince could see several small doors set into the wall at intervals down the right-hand side. On the opposite side, only one door, slightly larger than the others and about halfway down the corridor from where they stood, broke the continuous run of stone. There were no windows anywhere to lift the sense of entrapment that Rince felt.

Keeping her voice low, which just seemed natural in this compressed environment, Talia explained what they would do from here as she helped Rince push the cart along the corridor. The floor was smooth and the wooden wheels moved easily over them with minimal noise, so he had no difficulty hearing.

"This corridor and most of the rooms on this side," she said, waving her hand negligently at the doors on the right, "are for the household staff. They don't have fireplaces, so we don't need to go in there." With a small grimace, she added, "Actually, like me, many prefer to live in the town rather than stay in the Keep anyway these days, so they're not used much."

Now that *I can understand*, Rince thought to himself as Talia continued quietly. *If I had to work in this gloomy place during the day, the last thing I'd want to do is sleep here all night as well!*

"Through there, Rince," she said, indicating the heavier door they were approaching in the corridor to their left, "we enter the main Keep. Other than a few of the Guard, there won't be many people around at this time of night."

Stopping before the door, she fixed him with a serious stare while resting a slim hand on the handle. "Now this is important, Rince, so don't forget unless you want to spend a night in the dungeons! Don't talk to anyone while we're in there. The Protector has made it clear that servants and staff in the Keep are not to disturb those whose business brings them here, or those of greater station than themselves. So we go in, we remain polite, we do our jobs and we leave. Is that clear?"

Surprised at her tone, Rince nodded carefully. "Sure, Talia. I get it. No talking to anyone and keep out of the way, right?"

Talia laughed and closed the subject as she used both hands on the door to heave it open. "That's about it, Rince, but they take these things very seriously so, unless you want to be on the wrong side of the Protector, make sure you remember it!"

Though the door was heavy, it opened smoothly. Light flooded out and voices could be heard in the distance. As they went through, pushing the cart before them, a hallway five paces wide and easily ten times as long opened up before them.

Like the corridor they had just left and the main structure of the Keep itself, the walls, floor and roof, supported by thick wooden beams, were composed of large stone blocks that fit snugly together, leaving only a few fine cracks to be seen where the stones met. There, however, all comparison ended. Large lanterns were spaced regularly along both walls, their light supplemented considerably by two braziers that burned a deep red on either side of the massive double doorways with stone trellises that commanded the centre of each wall. To the right the doors were shut tight, but the ones on the left stood open. It was from that area that the sound of voices drifted out. Two great tapestries adorned the walls to the left, one depicting battle scenes with such vivid lustre that Rince had to tear his eyes from it to take in the rest. The other, further down the corridor, appeared to be a religious scene with the Creator the central figure looking down upon Man with both love and regret in his eyes. Rince had never understood or followed religion much but had sometimes wondered why something that many people appeared to think so highly of had so much to do with regret, loss and the need for compassion.

For a moment, Rince's attention was captured completely. Clearly this hall was designed to impress, and at least to Rince's mind, it achieved that end. It took only a few more moments, however, for Rince to become aware of the final details. At each end of the hallway, stairs were set, surrounded by exquisitely carved balustrades of a wood stained almost as dark as the stone into which they were set. The stairs immediately next to him as they pushed the cart through the door went down to lower levels of the Keep, while the one at the farther end of the hall gave access to the upper levels.

Rince felt his hands go clammy and his throat constrict as he peered, trying to look nonchalant, over the railing and down the stairs next to him. It was entirely possible these led down to the dungeons eventually, and if so, then Alaena might just be within earshot were he to call out her name.

Much as he would have loved to give her this hope and, against all expectation, hear her voice respond, the suicidal aspect of that idea was immediately apparent. Instead, he tightened his grip on the handle of the cart and tried to keep his voice even as he asked Talia about the hall, including an innocent query as to where each set of stairs might lead.

"Impressive, isn't it?" Talia responded with hushed enthusiasm, oblivious to the uneven tremor in Rince's voice. "This is the Entry Hall of the Protectorate Keep. Those doors on the right lead out to the courtyard and the front gates. The Protector stands there with the doors swung wide when his Guard are gathering so he can make speeches. I heard him speak once only a little while ago, and it was an inspiration!"

For the first time, it occurred to Rince that Talia, rather than believing the worst of the Protector as everyone else seemed to, appeared to hold him in fairly high esteem. The very idea shocked him and made his plan even more dangerous, for he hadn't anticipated that Talia might actually try to stop what he intended, should she become aware. Looking sideways at her, he saw nothing but her eyes shining as she glanced up at the tapestries on the wall to their left. She continued gushing, not noticing his querulous look. "The Mistress told me that these tapestries were created by master craftsmen in the employ of the King himself, sent here over the mountains as a gift for the Protector when appointed to his position! Aren't they wonderful?"

Talia looked back to Rince, obviously expecting him to be equally enamoured by the imposing space, and he did his best to put on a suitable face. Her smile fell, however, and her eyes looked puzzled, so he changed the topic quickly, hoping he could distract her and keep the momentum of information flow going.

"It's an amazing place, Talia, and yes, those tapestries are incredible!" Almost nonchalantly, he peered over the balustrade to his left and down the stone stairs. "So where do these lead?" As if sharing a secret, he leaned closer to her. "Is that where the dungeons are? I've heard the Protector keeps people down there for a very long time sometimes."

Concern touched Talia's brow immediately and her hand went to Rince's arm with a suggestion of alarm. "That's not something we mention, Rince. It's the only area of the Keep that the staff aren't permitted to enter without the express permission of the Protector himself, and even then, only when we're with one of the Guard. I've never been down there, and I hope I never will be!"

With that, Talia became businesslike, lifting her head and shaking it to straighten out her hair. "Anyway," she said, closing the subject down, "we've got several trips to make and the night is moving on! Let's get this load done in the Main Hall first, then I can show you the rest of the place."

Deciding not to press the point further but pleased he now knew his objective, even if he wasn't sure how he might get there just yet, Rince acquiesced. Pushing the trolley before them with no further discussion, they approached the central point of the hallway and turned to the doorway on their left. Unlike those on the opposite side, these doors stood wide open. Their span was enormous and they could probably fit three such trolleys, or two warhorses, through at the same time, Rince thought. Like everything in this area, they were oversized. The room they entered as they passed through was no exception.

The Great Hall of the Keep was a large, rectangular space, as long as the corridor they'd just come in from and half as deep, clearly set for many uses. While large enough to host banquets with hundreds of guests, it was presently set as an eating and meeting hall. Heavy trestle tables ran down the centre of the hall, dominated by a raised podium on the far side at which five large chairs were set overseeing the entire area. Above the centre chair, mounted proudly on the wall, was the royal coat of arms, reminding all who entered that while the Protector was the paramount authority of the Southern Realms, it was the King who ruled all.

At each end of the hall, two massive fireplaces with wide flues for smoke and ash were set deep into the stone walls. One of the fireplaces was unlit, though stacked with wood and ready to be lit when required. The other fireplace burned low but warm, maintaining a bed of glowing coals from the day. At the table closest to this fire, half a dozen of the Guard sat with dice and tankards in hand, cheering each other on as coin clattered on the scarred table and winnings were traded back and forth.

Rince followed Talia's lead and kept his head down as they approached the fire and the Guard, pushing the laden trolley before them. Sure that everyone could hear his heart pounding in his chest, beads of nervous sweat broke out on Rince's brow as one of the Guard glanced their way. For a moment, Rince felt that the only thing stopping him from running screaming from the Hall and from the Keep was his hands clenched around the iron handle of the trolley. The guard seemed to be more interested in the trolley than in who was pushing it, however, and after a moment's consideration, he turned his head back to the game, dismissing them from thought.

It took only a few minutes to unload the trolley and stack the wood next to the fireplace. Glancing surreptitiously at the Guard as he worked, Rince assessed them more calmly as he took most of the load and Talia supervised. Like those he had seen around the city, at Gatherings and in the Fields, these Guard were swarthy men, heavyset and with an unpleasantly superior air about them that Rince recognised from bullies of his own age group. The very fact that they were ignoring Talia and Rince so completely was a clear indication they viewed servants with the same disdain that upper classes usually reserved for beggars on the streets. They had no swords with them, which was a surprise as Rince thought they carried them everywhere. Clearly in the Keep itself they didn't feel the need to carry them, though each had a long dagger tucked into sheaths at their belts with worn handles that spoke of regular use.

Disappointed that their coarse discussion didn't touch on matters related to the Keep or the events of the day in the Fields, but revolved instead round mead, money and women, Rince finally moved the last of the wood over. Now much easier to move, he and Talia swivelled the trolley around as quickly as polite haste would allow, then headed back for the door, still apparently beneath the notice of the Guard, who paid as little attention to their departure as they did to their arrival.

It took them only a few minutes to go back to the servants' entrance and restock the small trolley with wood. Much to Rince's relief, they didn't need to go back into the Great Hall. Talia, while Rince marvelled at her ability to keep an apparently continuous flow of conversation going as she went about her work, directed them towards the door at the far end, next to stairs there that led to the upper levels.

As they proceeded about their tasks, Rince's nervousness increased apace. From what Talia had told him about the Keep and where they were going, there was a library somewhere ahead that sounded just right for what he planned to do. As the laden trolley trundled across the floor before them and Talia reached to open the door so he could push it through, Rince once more suppressed an urge to turn and flee as quickly as he could, putting this whole experience and ludicrous idea well and truly behind him.

Each time the feeling rose, however, the last image he had of Alaena appeared in his mind. She was standing on the path in the Fields, holding her tart carefully and smiling at him fondly as he took off into the crowd. Emotion surged up in his chest unexpectedly as he thought that even now she might be beneath his feet and desperately in need of his help, for there was no one else here other than him that would do so. *No,* he thought to himself. *This does not end here.*

Lost in his thoughts, it wasn't until Talia touched his arm lightly that he realised she was saying something to him. Quelling the trembling he felt, he tried to look unconcerned as he wrenched his attention back to her, but he knew that in the reflected lantern light in the hallway, his eyes were betraying him.

"Rince," Talia asked gently, "is something wrong?"

Rince watched her push the door closed behind them as she stepped closer, only then realising they'd moved into another corridor, running in the same direction as the one that led to the servant entrance on the other side of the Entry Hall. Looking around without acknowledging her concern, Rince noticed distractedly that the doors here were sturdier and of much better quality than the others he'd seen. Recalling Talia's earlier description, he realised they must now be outside the guest rooms of the Keep, which meant the library wasn't far from here – which meant that the time to act was near.

Shaking himself free of lethargic reluctance, Rince formed a half smile for Talia to indicate he was fine, hoping it was convincing enough to allay any concerns she had. The last thing he needed at the moment was for her to decide he needed more attention. Rince breathed a quiet sigh of relief as Talia seemed to accept his apparent recovery with only a sidelong look, then proceeded to fill a brief and slightly uncomfortable silence with more information about the Keep and the section they were in as they moved further down the corridor. These were, as Rince had surmised, the guest rooms. Four doors, each ten paces apart, lined the right-hand wall. The corridor was adequately illuminated by small hand lanterns next to each door, for use by the occupant as required. An absence of the lantern, Talia explained, usually meant that the room was in use, so this confirmed for her that all the rooms here were presently unoccupied.

As they walked and Talia talked, Rince found his nerves calming and his thoughts clearing. Focused by the immediacy of his objective, he started paying more attention to his surroundings and began finalising options in his mind. A little over halfway down, the corridor branched to the left. By the time they were manoeuvring the trolley around this corner, Rince felt back in control of himself. His knack for measuring distances and rarely losing his sense of direction, even in the dark, served him well here as he realised that they had just walked the depth of the Great Hall and were probably now walking along the wall behind it.

This was the shortest corridor Rince had seen in the Keep thus far. Perhaps fifteen paces long, a solid door of the same construction as those of the guest rooms stood open at the end, beyond which Rince could see books and bookcases covering the far wall. Rince noted another door set in the wall to the right as they moved down towards the open door, but Talia didn't choose to explain what lay beyond that portal and Rince was far too preoccupied with his own thoughts to ask. The squeaking wheels of the cart echoed off the walls as Rince pushed it along, amplifying the silence between them.

The library of the Protectorate Keep, which opened up to their right as they stepped through the doorway, was well lit. In addition to the now familiar oil lanterns that hung on iron stands around the room, large candleholders squatted on the two heavy oak tables that dominated the centre of the room. The dozen thick white candles in each, all about the girth of Rince's neck, burned low with steady flames. Bookcases lined most walls from floor to ceiling, the only exception being around and above the fireplace on the far wall, where the black granite blocks which made up the Keep could be seen. While he had had enough learning to be able to read and write, books were a fairly unfamiliar part of Rince's life to date. Even if this wasn't the case though, Rince suspected that he would still be awed. There were hundreds of books here. Some with thick leather spines and gold lettering down the side looked like they might be valuable. Others were more mundane but each, Rince thought with relish, were perfect to help carry out his plan. Now he was here, a thrill of trepidation ran down his spine, warring with outright fear at the audacity of what he planned.

***

Rince had stopped dead at the entrance, staring around the room as if the books entranced him. Gratefully, Talia stopped pushing as the trolley came to an abrupt halt, then watched him for a moment, enjoying the way the light played on his face, softening his features and making his eyes glow. She listened for a moment, aware that the footsteps of anyone coming down the hall echoed clearly into the library. Faintly in the distance, she could hear the banter of the Guard back in the Great Hall, but other than that no sound disturbed the silent, patient weight of the Keep. Convinced at last that she had him to herself and that this was going to be her best chance to tell him how she felt, Talia gathered her courage, lifted herself up on her toes to reach his height, lent forward and gently brushed his cheek with her lips.

Rince's reaction was a far cry from that which her hopes or dreams had anticipated. Starting as violently as if she had jabbed thorns to his cheek rather than caressed it with a kiss, Rince let out a strangled yelp of surprise. Jerking backwards, his movement took him a step away from Talia. At the same time, his hand flew up to his cheek as if to assess the damage her lips may have done to his skin. His eyes, that only moments ago seemed a million miles away, were focused on her now, but they were most certainly not filled with the passion she had hoped for. Instead, they were wide and staring, as if she had just laid a mortal curse on his soul for which there was no redemption.

Keeping her head up as her eyes welled with tears, Talia ached to understand through her hurt. With a gentle and resigned sigh, she finally lowered her gaze to avoid the rejection in his gaze and pensively asked the question she didn't want answered.

"Don't you like me, Rince? Am I not comely enough, or do you have eyes for another after all this?" Gathering herself once more, determined to keep her voice steady though her knees felt like they were about to buckle, she looked back once more and opened a little more of her heart to him. "Tell me, please, so I know what it is you want?"

Rince seemed unable to meet the gentle hurt in Talia's eyes. His gaze roamed the books that loomed all around, as if the knowledge they contained could give him the answer that she needed.

Finally, his expression calmed and he reached a hand out to gently place on her arm. She felt him trembling.

"I'm so sorry, Talia. I don't know what's come over me," he said sheepishly. "I just feel so lightheaded tonight. Maybe chopping all that wood was too much for me. Serves me right for trying to impress you!"

"Oh, Rince," Talia fluttered, while her mind savoured his words. At last, here was an indication that she meant something to him. With returning confidence, she placed one arm around his waist and led him away from the trolley. Pulling a chair free with one hand while she continued to support him with the other, Talia urged him to sit. Then, with wretched predictability, she asked what any kind soul would ask in the situation. "Would you like some water, or some mulled wine perhaps? There are barrels in the kitchen stores, and no one would miss a mug or two …"

"Yes, Talia, that would help, I think," Rince responded in a small voice. "Maybe you and I could share a taste?"

She nodded slowly, checking his face as if to assure herself that this was the correct thing to do. One hand on her hip, she made her decision, patting his hand while she continued to assure him that all was well.

"Of course, Rince," she said, smiling. "You rest here while I get something to drink, then when you're feeling better, we can see."

***

Talia had left the sentence hanging as to what they might actually 'see', but Rince got the drift. They were never going to get to that point, of course, so he smiled back for her sake, then placed his head back in his hands to ensure he looked suitably dizzy as she made her way out to the kitchen.

Rince stayed in that position until he heard her footsteps fade down the corridor. When it was clear she had gone, Rince lifted his head, checking that he was indeed alone at last. Knowing what corridors she had to traverse to get back to the kitchen, Rince knew he had very little time to act. Aware that this was his best opportunity, he sprang into action, all disappointment and lethargy erased.

Only a few feet from the table where Talia had positioned him, an iron stand with ornately decorated legs stood near the bookcase immediately to his right. Around the room, positioned at points which ensured each rack of books was adequately illuminated, stood more lamps. There were eight in total, and as long as they were well stocked with oil, they would be more than adequate for the task.

Keeping his steps as light as he could to avoid unwanted noise, Rince moved to the first lantern and lifted it gently from the hook on which it rested, extinguishing the flame easily with a quick breath. After unstopping the cap, a smoke trail drifting lazily from the wick as it cooled, Rince stepped to the nearest bookcase. Pausing only a moment, aware that this was the point of no return, he upended the lantern across the row of books directly before him, letting the oil flow out freely. The dark, viscous liquid stained and soaked into the covers immediately, spattered onto the pages and dripped down the heavy wood shelves. For an eerie moment, glancing at his handiwork as he placed the empty lantern back on the stand, Rince thought the oil looked like black blood dripping from the books themselves.

By the time he reached the next set of shelves, Rince realised he had to hurry. Talia would not tarry to get back here, and he needed to be done and gone well before she returned.

Doubling his pace, Rince no longer took care to pour the contents of each lantern on the books individually. Instead, while listening intently for sounds from the corridor that might spell his doom, Rince simply pulled the wicks free on the remaining lanterns and shoved them upside down into the shelves wherever there was space, allowing the oil to run free while he dashed to the next, and the next, and the next. Barely a minute had passed before he realised he was done and stood, panting, in the centre of the library while the rising stench of oil-soaked parchment permeated his senses.

For one more moment he tottered on the brink, almost stepping back. Were he to continue, he would be ensuring his own death if captured for this crime. In that brief moment, however, a vision came to him of Alaena. She was in a dark place, leaning against a stone wall for support. She looked beaten, bruised and was crying, bereft of friends or support, her shirt hanging in tatters from her shoulders.

As if she knew he was watching her, Alaena's head came up, and in the dim light an ugly gash showed across the right side of her face. The glimpse he had was so real that his breath caught in his throat. Love was a concept Rince was yet to understand fully, but in that moment an absolute certainty took him. He would never allow Alaena to come to harm if any breath remained in him to prevent it.

Chapter 14 - Burn

Those who grew up with Rince would not have recognised the man that stood in the centre of the keep's library. His face hardened, and the muscles of his jaw stood forth firmly, a premonition of the man he might become. His eyes, normally jovial above a mouth that was made to smile, shone more grey than blue now. Intent was written across his brow.

In one precise motion, as if indecision had and would never trouble him, Rince stepped back to the table once more, wrested a large candle free of the candelabra there, then stepped back to the nearest set of books and held the flame to the oil-soaked bindings.

He watched with detached calm, holding his body away from the flame, expecting a conflagration to erupt immediately. The fuel was a viscous substance, however, designed to burn slow and long. A few nerve-racking moments passed while Rince held the flame directly to the oil that dripped languidly down the books and across the shelves, waiting for it to catch. Finally, to his immense relief, a blue flame snapped to life on the surface of the liquid as the oil ignited.

Once alight, however, without the lamp collar to arrest it, the flame travelled quickly. Leaping upward, the spines of the first books to feel the heat started to blacken and peel as the fire took hold. At the same time, blue and yellow flames danced quickly across the flat surface of the shelves to the next reservoir, where they again ignited before spreading rapidly upward and outward.

By the time Rince had repeated the process with another candle on the bookshelves on the other side of the library, the heat emanating from the first was already becoming uncomfortable. He could see the shelves themselves blistering and starting to burn through a wave of heat pouring towards him as the fire escalated toward an inferno.

With one last look around to confirm that the other side of the library had caught properly too, squinting against the smoke that was starting to choke up the room, Rince nodded to himself with grim satisfaction. Heat bathed his face, and he could see that the library would soon be engulfed. Earlier in the day when thinking about how to cause a distraction, he had considered the kitchen the most likely place to start a fire. When he saw it with his own eyes though, he realised the kitchen was too far from the living areas of the Keep to be sure it would distract those inside enough to give him a chance to rescue Alaena. The library, however, was immediately behind the Great Hall and directly below what Talia had described as the main living quarters of the Keep. Perhaps, Rince thought with a briefly malicious smile, it might even be right under the Protector's quarters. As it was constructed largely of stone, Rince doubted the fire would actually destroy the Keep. This room though, consisting mainly of paper and wood, would be more than enough to stir up a hornet's nest of activity and distraction.

With that, he delayed no more. The whole process had taken no more than a minute or two. Talia had probably reached the kitchen by now and was pouring out their mead, so would soon be on her way back. He had no desire at all for her to run back to him with all the flames of Hell licking at his back.

Taking off down the corridor, praying his luck would hold, he skidded at the first corner, then proceeded at a run down the longer corridor which gave access to the guest rooms. Screaming "Fire!" at the top of his voice and banging on the doors as he passed to make all the noise he could, he reached the far end and heaved the heavy door there open. Air that felt bitterly cold after the heat of the library rushed in as smoke and increasing heat poured out and upward to the soaring roof of the Entry Hall. Behind him a glow of light was increasing as the flame built in the contained area of the library. With nowhere else to go, the fire began to billow out into the corridor, hungrily searching for something else to incinerate. The crackling roar of the fire behind him competed enthusiastically with his strident cries of alarm.

Leaving the door ajar to keep the flames fed, Rince bolted first for the massive doors to the Great Hall. Stopping at the entry way, he peered inside to find the four Guard who were there before looking about them in a state of alarm. Either they had heard his earlier cries, or could smell the smoke that was starting to permeate the Keep, but either way he had their attention.

"Fire!" he yelled once more, riveting their attention to him. "Help! The library is on fire!" he screamed, putting all the panic he could into his voice.

The Guard took off at a run towards him, leaving their game and not bothering to retrieve their belongings from the table in their rush. His heart beating madly and with sweat on his brow from heat, excitement and nerves, Rince didn't wait to give them time to cover the distance to the doorway of the Hall. Instead, his lithe form bolted once more. Rather than heading back towards the fire, however, he sprinted straight for the stairs leading downward that he and Talia had passed only a short while ago when they first entered the Entry Hall. Not pausing to think, he plunged down the stairs two at a time. By the time the Guard emerged from the Great Hall to deal with the emergency, Rince was nowhere to be seen.

While shouts of alarm became increasingly strident up above, it was relatively quiet and the air was still cool down here. The stairway opened up into a small, square chamber, about five paces across on each side. A weapons rack sat against the far wall and to the right, a single solid door secured with thick iron bands was set imposingly into the wall. Within easy reach of the weapons rack a small table was set with one chair. The guard who occupied it, wearing a long black coat to keep warm, was already on his feet and appeared agitated by the time Rince arrived.

Wasting no time with civility, even had he been inclined, the guard came straight to the point. "You, boy," he stated in a clipped, demanding tone. This was a voice that expected to be obeyed. "What's going on up there? What's all the commotion?"

Adopting an expression that he hoped portrayed him as beneath both suspicion and notice, Rince stammered out a response that he expected would send the guard dashing up the stairs to help manage the problem or to run for his life. "Sir! The Keep's afire! There's smoke and flame everywhere! The Keep is burning down, sir! Everyone has to get out!"

As if to validate his point, the clamorous peal of an alarm bell began sounding above, echoing eerily down the stairs and around the oppressive stone chamber. More running feet could be heard, along with shouting that seemed to be increasing, competing with the persistent tolling of the bell.

"Burn me!" the guard swore vehemently. "The Protector'll chew rock when he hears about this!" In a fluid motion, he pulled a set of keys from a clip on his wide leather belt and sprang into action.

Rince stepped back from the stairs, expecting the guard to dash upwards. To his surprise, the man moved quickly over to the other door in the chamber, fitted a key into the lock, which turned smoothly, then wrenched it open violently. The heavy door swung back with a crash against the wall, revealing a long corridor made of the same stone as the rest of the Keep. Without pause, the guard took off into the corridor at a run.

Still standing back in the entryway, Rince took only a moment to shake his head in disbelief at either his stupidity or his luck. He wasn't sure which it was, but there was no doubt that, had the guard run up the stairs immediately as Rince had hoped, he would have taken those keys with him. Rince would have had no way to actually get into the cells to look for Alaena, no matter how much time the distraction of the fire afforded him.

Shaking himself from his reverie, Rince focused back on the guard. He had covered about thirty paces at a run, stopping before one of the doors halfway down on the left-hand side of the corridor. There were no windows down here and the place had a stale, musty smell about it that turned Rince's nose up, though the smell of fresh smoke was beginning to insinuate itself on his senses. The walls were made of the same dark stone as the corridors up above, but were far more dimly lit by the handful of lanterns that leaked light from low cut wicks. Spaced out some distance from each other, they left dark spaces between them, where the meagre illumination struggled to reach.

At this distance and with the dim environment, it was hard to make out the face of the guard. His calls echoed clearly down the hall, however, and his shouts sent a chill through Rince's soul.

"My Lord!" the guard bellowed urgently. "Protector!" he repeated, accompanying the appeal with heavy thumps of his fist. "There's fire in the Keep and you're needed!"

Rince's guts turned to water and his knees almost folded there and then. It simply hadn't occurred to him that he might run into the Protector himself in the Keep, let alone down here in the dungeons. Moments later, a wave of nausea turned his stomach as he realised that not only was the Protector here, but it was very likely that the Protector was with Alaena herself!

When more pounding and shouting failed to raise a response from within, the guard let loose a string of creative expletives, obviously unsure how to proceed. Perhaps the Protector had left orders not to be disturbed, or it may just have been standard practice that he be left alone while interrogating a prisoner. Either way, as much as Rince could tell from here, the guard was reluctant to intrude on the Protector and his work without an invitation to enter.

Competing with the noise of the guard shouting and pounding on the door and the booming echoes that accompanied it in the confined space, the noise level upstairs seemed to be increasing. Rince felt like he was standing in the eye of a storm. Heavy-booted footsteps stampeded back and forth above him, and the shouts he could hear seemed to be increasing in urgency. Above all, the shrill clangour of the alarm bell continued to ring out clear and strong.

Standing in the middle of all this, Rince put his hands to his ears and attempted to block out the din so he could think. He had not thought this through. The situation was quickly spiralling out of control. Alaena was probably behind the door down the corridor. Between himself and Alaena, however, stood one of the Guard in the cell corridor and the Protector himself in the room, both of whom were obstacles he knew he could not overcome. Indeed, if he were not careful, Rince might find himself in one of the cells down here very soon and no one, he realised belatedly, knew where he was or what he was doing. Truly frightened as he thought through the implications of his brash actions, Rince realised he'd been a fool and that he may never again see the light of day.

The guard took that moment to overcome his reluctance. As he opened the door a crack, light spilled out, etching his craggy, concerned features in an expanding yellow line. Rooted to the spot, Rince watched as if his doom were being played out. The guard disappeared from view as he stepped into the room, and

Rince turned to run. If he could make it to the top of the stairs, he could very likely escape in the confusion still. Much as he wanted to help Alaena, he knew that his efforts tonight had failed. Perhaps they had even made her plight worse. Either way, he knew it was better to leave and try another means than find himself in a cell, sharing her fate.

Rince had covered only a step before another, entirely unexpected, cry arrested his flight. "Boy! Come here! Quickly!"

The guard's voice sounded strained, but the command it carried brought Rince's escape to a reluctant halt. Hesitating, Rince glanced up the stairway, considering freedom. That freedom would doubtless come at the cost of losing Alaena, however, and he had come so close. With Alaena at the forefront of his mind, another shout from the guard found Rince turning once more. With each step possibly taking him closer to his doom, he moved down the corridor towards the doorway that still gaped open, spilling a square of yellow light onto the other side of the corridor where another door stood.

In the moments before he crossed the threshold, Rince's worst fear – that he'd find Alaena dead on a spike, or worse – crossed his mind. Perhaps the guard was calling him because there was blood everywhere and he thought Rince could clean up. The reality that greeted him as he stepped past the lintel was quite the opposite.

The room smelt of burning and blood. Dominated by a large oak rack in the centre, the room was rectangular, the walls comprised entirely of black stone blocks, with the exception of the door by which he entered. A few torches sputtered in sconces on the walls, but most illumination in the room came from a pair of deep, round iron braziers at the end of the room to Rince's right that burned bright, casting ruddy, red-black reflections from the wall behind them. Amongst a staggering array of heavy wooden and steel equipment that bristled with spikes and fetters, Rince couldn't see the guard who had called him until he'd taken a few steps into the room.

From that position, Rince's eyes were drawn to the floor, where the Guard was leaning over a heavyset figure lying prone on the straw. By the look of the black leather boots Rince could see, the figure over which the Guard leant was male. A creeping feeling of terrible trepidation mounted in Rince as the Guard stood and turned, concern mingled with fear etched in every line of his face.

Taking a step towards Rince, still blocking a full view of the body on the ground, the Guard pronounced in a shaky voice quite unlike his commanding tone earlier, "Boy. Stay here and watch over him." Obviously, this man assumed Rince knew exactly who it was on the floor. "I'll fetch the healer and be back with help." With that, Rince watched him dash and disappear back through the door once more, urgency driving him to a run without further thought.

The thump of the Guard's feet retreated quickly, though Rince thought that his heart thumping in his chest was just as loud. Dumbly, Rince just stood for a moment, as if absorbing the outcome of his actions thus far. The echoed din of shouting and running of booted feet continued in the distance, but down here in the cells a surreal silence pervaded. A moment more passed before Rince shook himself to a start with a curse. Here he was, in the dungeons of the Protectorate Keep as he had wanted to be, and like an idiot, he could do no more than stare at an empty doorway! In the chaos Rince had instigated above, it might take the Guard a while to track down the healer, but track him down he would. The time he had gained was there but was brief, and Rince knew he'd best make the most of it.

Spinning on one heel, thick straw rustling beneath his feet, Rince paused to take in the figure on the floor. Even if he didn't have the Guard's reaction to go by, Rince would not have mistaken the bulky build of the Protector lying a few feet away him now that he could see him without obstruction. Whether or not the Protector was going to live to wreak greater grief on the citizens of Morlyn, or even whether he was still alive now, was a question Rince couldn't answer. His face was all but unrecognizable even at this distance, though both fear and revulsion kept Rince from moving any closer than he presently was.

Blood covered the entire left side of the Protector's face and a black hole stared from where his left eye had once been. The eyelids hung grotesquely loose without an orb to cover, and dribbles of blood still seeped from the gaping socket. Further, as if the violation of his features wasn't sufficient with the absence of his eye, a deep gash tracked right across his forehead. The skin

135

had been ripped open and torn back across the front of his head, where Rince could clearly see bone showing through the bloodied mess of ruptured tissue.

Tearing his gaze from the repulsive sight before him, Rince's eyes tracked left and his mind again started to work. Beside the Protector on the ground lay a heavy iron poker. Skirting the body on the floor, Rince moved towards it, noting what appeared to be pieces of flesh stuck to it towards the end. It took little imagination to conclude that this was the cause of the gash across the Protector's forehead, though who would have done this to him was a mystery still. Surely slim and fragile Alaena, if she had been in this terrible place with him, could not have overcome a man of the stature and sheer wilful force of the Protector? Rince wasn't sure Alaena could even lift the heavy iron bar without considerable effort, whereas the Protector could probably bend it with his bare hands if he chose to. Shaking his head unconsciously, for this made no sense so far, Rince continued to scan the floor, trying to piece together the puzzle. He was considering the possibility of an altercation with another of the Protectorate in which the Protector had come off second best. While it didn't fit with his understanding of the Protector as the sole and undisputed Lord whose word was law within the confines of the Keep, as well as within Morlyn and its surrounds, Rince was unable to come up with an alternate hypothesis for the moment.

In the brief moments Rince took to survey the area and consider this, his nerves calmed and he began to wonder if he should look elsewhere for Alaena while the chance remained. Suddenly, Rince's bowels knotted and sweat broke out across his brow.

There, lying partially obscured on the ground, was the ivory handle of a small pocketknife, yellow and discoloured with age, protruding from the straw.

Shaking, he knelt and delicately, almost disbelievingly, wrapped his fingers around the all too familiar handle to draw it free from the straw. The slim blade was covered in blood and gore, and Rince's stomach turned as he glanced back briefly to the ruined face of the Protector still lying so close, unmoving. Still on one knee, unwilling to trust his legs while his sharp but shocked mind put the pieces together, Rince thought frantically. There could be no doubt that the weapon in his hand – the blade that had clearly been used to assault the Protector – was his own knife, loaned to Alaena some time ago and long thought lost. That meant that Alaena was indeed here at some point and, against all odds, had overcome the Protector, for who else would have his knife at hand in need?

As he realised this, the sense of resolve that had driven Rince to start the fire upstairs in the first place began to return. Wiping the blade clean on the straw, he took another look at the Protector with harder eyes. Whatever extreme had driven Alaena to do this, this man was the source and was therefore deserving of the outcome. "Evil gets as Evil does," his mother was fond of saying. Well, in this case Rince couldn't argue the logic.

With a swift motion now, Rince gained his feet. Sheathing the blade and pocketing the knife, his thoughts turned fully to Alaena. How exactly this had come to be was secondary to finding her now, for she may herself be wounded if she had fought the Protector for her freedom. Clarity of thought returning, Rince calculated. The Guard would easily be upstairs now, searching for the healer. He might even tell others to search and then return himself, in which case Rince may have only moments left to find Alaena.

Moving to the door, Rince looked carefully up and down the corridor to orient himself and decide what to do next.

To the north, about fifty paces away, the door to the Guardroom was open. Though dim inside, Rince could see it was still unoccupied. Looking up and down the corridor, he counted at least twenty other doors set in the walls on both sides.

He hesitated, despairing. Alaena must have been here, but it appeared the Guardroom was always occupied, so his logical mind told him she must still be down here. Thus, she must be in one of the other cells, either held there against her will, or having fled there if she had, against all hope, escaped the clutches of the Protector. He could hardly run down the corridor checking each door as he went, for surely a Guard would appear at any moment. The sight of a lanky boy running madly through the Keep's dungeon, bashing on cell doors as he went, would most surely raise questions he certainly did not want to answer.

Vital seconds passed as Rince wracked his brain for an answer. He needed so desperately to know where Alaena was that she was all he could think of yet he knew he didn't have the time it would take to check each cell in this horrible place. An image of her smiling at him in the Fields before he had lost her came to mind so strongly he had to grasp the doorframe for support lest his knees buckle. Gently but quickly, like a soft curtain drawn back to reveal a pristine sunrise, clarity dawned. Without being aware of how it happened and barely even recognising that it had, there was no longer any question in his mind. He knew where she was.

Spinning on his heel, Rince took off up the corridor in the direction of the Guardroom, running at full pace. Past one set of doors on either side, then a second set, Rince didn't pause. As he approached the third set, which was the last before the Guardroom door itself, he skidded to a halt. Utterly confident, he put a hand to the cell door to his left and shoved, knowing it would open before him. The door swung back, the old hinges giving a creaking resistance as they grudgingly gave way. There was little illumination within, making it difficult to tell what the musty room contained. What small amount of light that fell inside through the open door showed a bare stone floor that was stained with age and too much sorrow. Again, without hesitation, Rince stepped through and firmly pushed the door shut again from within. The door closed against a small ridge of stone set in the floor, cutting off the meagre light outside completely.

In the utter dark, Rince shook his head, the lucidity of thought falling away from him like a stone dropped from a ledge. Hand still on the door, Rince only had long enough to wonder what had possessed him to run to this door and to come into this cell before an achingly familiar voice floated weakly to him from the darkness within.

"Rince. I'm here. Help me!"

Chapter 15 - Reunion

Startled, excitement surged through Rince as he spun to face the room, eyes searching the dark for his friend.

"Ala?" he whispered tentatively, almost timidly, to the darkness, afraid he had imagined the quiet plea. "Where are you?"

The strangeness of the situation stabbed at Rince, and he wondered if this was some kind of trick or trap. But a gentle sob came from the far side of the room, driving doubt once again from his mind and mixing hope into his emotions.

"Walk straight ahead, away from the door about ten paces. I'm here," Alaena's voice repeated, wavering slightly as if speaking was an effort.

Obediently, Rince paced tentatively forwards, arms outstretched lest he walk into an object shrouded in the dark. Feeling his way with his feet, Rince covered the area using the voice as a compass, slowly crossing the gap between them. After what seemed an eternity, his hands touched the cold stone of the far wall of the cell. As his eyes adjusted to the environment, Rince could see shapes in the room now, though it was still much too dark to make out detail. Below him to his right, however, he could make out a huddled shape on the floor. His heart leapt in his chest as he saw Alaena looking up at him in the gloom. Her knees were hunched up, her arms wrapped around them cuddling them to her chest, but as Rince leaned towards her, Alaena freed one arm and reached for him out of the shadow.

Gratefully, Rince grabbed at the offered hand and wrapped his other hand around Alaena's wrist. "Come, Ala. Let's get you out of here," he whispered as he started to pull her up from the floor. Unexpectedly, he found Alaena's wrist sticky, and his touch elicited a hiss of pain. He quickly disengaged, concern again overriding his thoughts. "Ala – what's wrong? Are you all right? What can I do?"

The flurry of questions was answered after a moment with a gentle pat on the hand that still held hers in his. "Don't worry, Rince. I'll tell you all about it later."

Her grip tightened and urgency tinged her voice as she continued. "We have to leave here as fast as we can, though. What I've done is something that will never be forgiven and cannot be undone, so somehow – wait!"

Alaena broke off abruptly, her hand stilling on Rince's. Leaning closer, she whispered, "Hush, Rince. They're coming back!" Rince strained his ears, but it was a few moments more before he could hear feet tramping down the stairs in the Guardroom through the thick cell door. To his surprise, Alaena continued in hushed tones. "There are three of them. Two Guards and a healer, I think."

Rince turned to face her in the dark, though he doubted she could see the surprise on his face. He was able to discern shapes in the room now his eyes had adjusted, and he could make out Alaena's face framed by her dark hair, but the light was just too meagre to allow him to make out her expressions. How in the world Alaena knew there were three of them coming was beyond him, let alone knowing anything more! Questions piled up in his mind, but all talk ended and they held each other tight as the men stepped into the corridor and heavy, steel-shod boots chimed urgent intent on the stonework of the corridor outside. Words drifted through the thick wood as they passed by the door to the cell in which Rince and Alaena huddled. He cou dn't make out specifics, but the voices were deep and rough, and they were not pleased.

As soon as they passed, Alaena clasped Rince's hand urgently and spoke in a low voice that brooked no argument. "Rince. We must leave. Now." Alaena, obviously in some pain, started to struggle to her feet, leaning on Rince for support. "Don't ask me how I know, but they're going to lock the door to the room where the Guard sits soon and will probably search the cells thoroughly after that. We don't want to be here when they do that!" Alaena moved across the room and grabbed at the door, clearly convinced that haste rather than caution was called for here.

Following Ala's lead, Rince tugged the door open a little and peered out carefully to confirm the corridor was clear, expecting at any moment to see the fearful, black-cloaked form of a Guard approaching him, sword drawn to skewer them both. While he could hear voices in the room down the corridor where the Protector lay bleeding, no one was to be seen. Holding his breath and hoping their luck held, Rince pulled the door open all the way.

He quickly put an arm about Alaena's waist to support her and helped her out into the corridor with him.

This was the first clear view Rince had of Alaena since finding her, and her condition shocked him. Around both her wrists and ankles, torn skin hung from angry welts. While she held her shirt around her shoulders with her spare hand, it was ripped to pieces, and where it hung loose, Rince could see deep bruising and welling wounds on her once soft and flawless skin. Now was not the time to ask. Alaena's face was a mask of concentration and determination as she summoned the strength to continue to move, but the sight of her centred his resolve. If he had to carry her all the way and fight through the Guard themselves, Rince would either see Alaena clear of the Keep tonight and into safe hands or die in the attempt.

To his complete surprise, even as he thought this and half-carried her down the corridor towards the Guardroom, Alaena stopped for a moment and gave Rince the strangest, staring look. Holding his gaze for precious seconds, a smile curved her lips and she lifted her spare hand to stroke his cheek tenderly. "Thank you, Rince," she whispered quietly, and brushed his cheek with a kiss before turning back to the task of clearing the corridor.

Glad she wasn't looking at him anymore, for Rince's face had gone as red as a spring beet, Rince put his arm more firmly around Alaena and together they stepped out of the corridor and into the Guardroom itself.

Alaena, focused on her struggle to stay upright and still leaning heavily on Rince for support, seemed to pay scant attention to the room, other than contemplating the stairs before them and, in her weakened state, probably wondering how she was going to reach the top, let alone escape the Keep itself.

Despite his concern for Alaena screaming at him to be away from this place as soon as possible, Rince took a moment to catch his breath and recognise a change since he last came through the room. Unlike before, the alarm bell was no longer pealing upstairs, though the thump of boots and urgent shouts continued to reverberate down the stairs from above. Clearly the fire was still doing its work, so with some luck they might still escape through the chaos above, if they could make it there. Even as the possibility of escape entered his mind, the far more likely outcome of a prolonged and painful death for his activities tonight sent a tingling shiver of fear down his spine. Wishing Alaena could move faster while avoiding a pace that would cause her more pain, Rince glanced back towards the corridor to ensure their escape continued to be unnoticed. As he did so, two things captured Rince's attention immediately.

The first turned his guts to water.

About thirty paces away down the corridor, a Guard had stepped from the cell where the Protector lay and halted in shock for a moment, staring towards them as he registered the presence of the two struggling children in the Guardroom beyond the dimness of the corridor. Though difficult to be sure underneath the black polished armour, Rince thought it looked like the same Guard that had summoned him to the cell earlier. Only a moment passed before the Guard mastered his surprise. With a bellowed cry of rage echoing down the corridor before him and steel scraping as he tugged his sword free in a fluid motion, the Guard took off at a run towards Rince and Alaena with death in his eyes.

The second thing Rince noticed, just as the Guard took off in full flight towards them, was the set of keys to the door that separated the Guardroom from the corridor. Forgotten by the Guard in his earlier haste to warn the Protector that there was fire in the Keep, the keys still hung where he had left them, in the lock on this side of the door.

Precious seconds passed while Rince stood frozen by indecision, his predicament overwhelming him. Alaena, hanging from his shoulder, was clearly in no condition to run anywhere. Rather than abating, the noise upstairs seemed to be increasing. The smell of smoke and fire continued to build in the Guardroom. Overall, however, Rince's gaze remained transfixed on the Guard that had covered half the distance between them, and the point of his sword, which preceded him by a good four feet and was aimed squarely at Rince.

At the last possible moment, Rince's paralysis left him. The Guard was close enough now that the murderous intent on his face was clearly visible. Leaping to the door, still only a few steps from him, Rince grabbed it with both arms and with all his might, swung it shut, throwing his weight against it as it gathered speed and crashed with resounding force against the heavy steel frame set into the rock. A split second later, the key turned smoothly in the lock and Rince, heart pounding, put his chest to the aged oak, spreading his arms against the pitted wood and hoping against hope that it was solid enough to hold the Guard out and keep them safe for the moment.

Behind Rince, suddenly left bereft of support, Alaena's legs gave way and she crumpled to the floor with a small squeak of surprise and pain.

On the other side, Rince heard the pounding of the Guard's boots on the stone floor increase in pace and volume as he charged towards the door.

The crash that had boomed in the enclosed space as the door had slammed shut moments before was nothing compared to the thunderous impact of the burly Guard's body as he threw his armoured bulk against it. The entire door and the frame in which it was set shuddered under the impact. Puffs of dust punched out of the old walls and roof above it, spitting then spiralling lazily into the air with the violence of the assault. Pressed up against the other side, the far more diminutive Rince took the impact to his chest. With the wind knocked out of him, Rince was thrown back forcibly from the door as if struck by a hammer. Flying through the air past Alaena's dazed and disbelieving face as she struggled to her knees, Rince crashed on the ground some feet back from the door, jarring himself from head to toe and struggling for air.

Sucking in dust kicked up from the floor as he caught his breath, Rince pushed himself up on one arm, half expecting to see the crazed Guard halfway through the door already and poised to end Rince once and for all. Instead, a frenzied and frustrated pounding began on the other side, accompanied by oaths and expletives, many of which were new even to the street wise ears of Rince. Built of white oak, bound with iron straps and secured with iron pins, this door and the stone frame in which it sat was built to withstand a concerted force and ensure that escaping prisoners were unlikely to ever find freedom. While it continued to jump and shudder from the assault on the other side, it quickly became clear to Rince that one man, no matter how large or how enraged, would defeat it quickly.

Realising they had gained space and fervently hoping their luck would hold, Rince at last sucked in a clear breath as he slowly gained his feet, exchanging glances as he did with Alaena, who was tentatively sitting upright and seemed to be regaining her balance and some of her spirit.

"Well, Rince," Alaena said tiredly, raising her voice to compete with the din from the other side of the door and the crescendo of noise that was now pouring down the stairway. "Now you've dealt with the Guard, do you have any more surprises for me to get us out of this place?" As she spoke, a weary smile touched her lips and she stretched out a hand towards him.

Holding back a stress-induced chuckle that would have sounded entirely out of place, Rince responded in kind. "Maybe one or two, Ala, but let's get you up the stairs first and see what happens from there." Taking her hand, Rince helped Alaena to her feet and held her steady with one arm while she gained her balance.

More confident now, Alaena nodded as if to say, "Yes, I'm ready." With her arm once more around Rince's shoulder and his arm once more around her waist, they turned their back on the shuddering door and the irate Guard behind it, heading for the stairs.

***

As soon as they set foot on the stairs and started to ascend, Rince knew something was wrong. While a considerable amount of smoke was billowing around the top and rolling down the stairway now, it was the heat that really made him worry. Only halfway up, Rince could already feel hot, dry heat bathing his face from above. The shouts and running they had heard earlier were a great deal louder here, and as they reached the top of the stairs, they paused beside the stone railing to take stock. Alaena sat heavily on a stair near the top, leaning her back to the wall and keeping out of sight while recovering from the climb. Rince crouched on the top step, staying low behind the railing to avoid notice while staring out in disbelief at the scene before him.

Grey smoke filled the entire area before him and an intense heat, emanating from the corridor that led to the library, bathed the incredulous expression on his face. The doors to the Great Hall

144

stood open to his left, difficult to make out properly through the haze. To his right, across the main hall, the massive doors to the courtyard also stood open. Though only a dozen paces from him, Rince could only just make out the figures that were running back and forth through these doors at frequent intervals. It took a moment to understand that both Guard and those who worked at the Keep were dashing back and forth with buckets of water, presumably filled from a well in the courtyard outside, to attempt to douse the flames that were clearly getting out of control.

A small cough from behind startled Rince from his reverie. Alaena, resting on the stair, was sitting with her eyes closed and head leaned back against the stone, clearing her throat against the sting of the smoke. Through eyes that were starting to weep from the smoke, Rince thought how vulnerable Alaena looked, even as it occurred to him that there would probably never be a better time than now to get her out of here.

He nudged her gently. Alaena opened her eyes tiredly then turned her head towards Rince, nodding in understanding. It was time to go. Taking her hand once more in his, Rince levered them both up to their knees. Motioning to Alaena with his free hand, Rince crooked a finger and indicated a path around the railing and back away from the main doors and the fire. Once more, Alaena nodded. Shrouded by smoke and camouflaged by the chaos that Rince had caused, the pair quickly cleared the top stair, skirted the railing and headed towards the door to the servants' quarters.

It was the longest ten paces of Rince's life. At any moment, he expected to hear a shout of challenge or an order to halt, or more likely, to feel an arrow or crossbow bolt take his back and end this ill-conceived escape. Breathing shallowly to take in as little smoke as possible while keeping a firm grip on Alaena's right hand, they made it to the door without incident, and it turned easily under his hand. Not even risking a glance backward, Rince slipped through into the corridor beyond, pulling Alaena after him. With enormous relief, he pushed the door closed behind them both.

Alaena seemed content, or perhaps just too tired, to question where they were or where Rince was taking them. This corridor was quiet compared with the clamour outside, though strident yells and the noise of stomping feet still came strongly through the door. More importantly, the corridor was relatively free of smoke, and both Rince and Alaena found themselves taking deep breaths of clean air here in relief.

Eager not to lose their advantage, Rince once again led the way. Alaena followed without question. With fatigue and shock taking their toll, she seemed to register little of their surroundings as Rince led her hopefully to freedom. Bypassing the doors that punctuated the walls at regular intervals on their left, Rince made for the door at the end of the passageway, encouraging Alaena as they moved. More and more nervous as the moments passed, Rince was positive that the cell door downstairs could not stand up to the Guard's rage for long.

The commotion engulfing the Keep was more than enough noise to cover their movements. Rince barely paused as he grasped the handle carefully and gently tugged the door open. Outside, the small courtyard was unoccupied. Obviously, anyone hale enough to do so was already at the main door to the Keep, carting water to bring this blaze under control. The cart Rince had filled with wood still stood waiting nearby. Something seemed different, but he couldn't place the change. A small thrill of excitement thrummed through Rince, and for the first time, he allowed himself to hope that they may actually escape alive.

Again, urgency drove his movements. Taking Alaena's hand in his own once more, oblivious to the blisters and sores he had given himself in this very place only a short while ago, Rince tugged her forward. Taking the two small steps quickly down, Rince and Alaena stepped onto the still soggy ground. Indicating quiet with a finger to his lips, Rince led them across the small courtyard, picking his way carefully between soggy patches and watching their shadows move as they walked.

Suddenly, the change he had noted a few moments before finally registered with him: he could see. The ground beneath him and the walls of the courtyard around him were quite visible. It wasn't bright, but the light had been failing when he was last here with Talia and it had already been getting difficult to see. Surely the few torches on the walls here weren't sufficient to cast this much light?

Realising their shadows were before him, Rince glanced over his shoulder to track the source of the illumination. The sight that met his eyes arrested his step in mid-stride. As his shoes sunk into the

146

mud and small pools of water gathered at his soles, he stared in disbelief at the upper levels of the Keep. Past the walls of the courtyard where he stood and easily the length of the Great Hall away, flames poured from the windows of the southwest tower of the Keep. Burning fiercely, the fire was still far enough away that the heat didn't touch them where they stood, but it was terribly bright against the night sky. Both stars and moon above were blotted out completely by the deep orange intensity of the blaze. Alaena, realising through her fog that Rince had stopped moving and searching his face for the reason, followed his line of sight, her mouth falling open.

Shocked out of her trauma-induced lassitude by the scale of what Rince had done to secure her freedom, Alaena turned and reached a slightly shaking hand up to his chin, dragging his dumbfounded expression to her face. The flames high above reflected eerily in her eyes. "Rince," she said firmly, engaging his stare and speaking directly into his face with conviction. "Let's worry about this later, if there is one. It's time to go!"

Rince nodded numbly, his gaze flicking back to the burning heavens as if to validate the unbelievable sight before turning his back on the inferno and forcing himself into action again.

Veering left, dragging Alaena with him now, Rince made a beeline for the iron gate set in the wall in the corner of the courtyard. His mind a muddle of noise, urgency and fear, it wasn't until he had covered several paces and it was too late to turn back that Rince realised, after getting so close, that he had forgotten one very important aspect of this escape. There, on the other side of the imposing gate, stood the same Guard that had let Rince through with Talia only a few hours before. The red light bathing the area giving his swarthy face a demonic cast, he was looking with disbelief towards the flames leaping from the top of the Keep as he registered Rince and Alaena's presence struggling across the courtyard towards him. Eyes narrowing and suspicion settling immediately on his face, the Guard called out, reaching for the keys at his side.

"You, boy! What in the seventh hell is going on in there?" he growled as he fitted a key to the inner gate. "What are you doing there and who is this?" he continued, gesturing at the dishevelled figure of Alaena struggling through the mud beside him.

147

Turning the key quickly, the Guard threw the gate open and stepped through with an aggressive set to his features. Taking no time for niceties, he wrapped a vicelike hand around their arms and dragged them both forwards, into the gatehouse where a small lantern hung to light the area. Throwing them in before him, he repeated his question more forcefully, taking in Alaena's torn clothing and battered frame with a frown. Leaning towards Rince, he grasped his shirt and dragged him closer, yelling into his face as Alaena collapsed to her knees on the ground beside them. "Who the hell is this, and where do you think you're going as the Keep burns, boy?"

Rince, worn and tired and unable to think fast enough this time, shook his head in mute denial. *I'm just saving my friend,* he thought to himself simply, but no words came to his lips as the Guard used his free hand to draw a black-handled dagger from his belt as an evil grimace pulled his lips back from his teeth.

"By hell, boy, you'll tell me what I want to know, or you'll wish you died inside than face what's coming to you!"

Getting a tighter grip on Rince's shirt, the Guard brought the blade up to rest against his neck, red light glinting off the honed metal, a precursor to the stain of blood which soon would give it a brighter, wetter hue. His breath in Rince's face, the Guard's eyes locked on Rince's terrified gaze as he delivered his ultimatum. "Last chance, boy. Let's start with who this is with you, or I slit your worthless throat now then start on her anyway."

His mind failing him, Rince ran out of options. The world seemed to stand still and he licked dry lips, realising that luck had finally deserted him and that at last he'd reached the end.

Even as he started to form the words that would seal both his and Alaena's fate however, something strange seemed to happen. Suddenly, the Guard stiffened and his eyes widened, whites showing clearly. His face took on a blankly puzzled expression. For a moment he held this rictus pose, then the knife tumbled from his grip and he started to fall forward towards Rince. Tearing his shirt from the weakening grip of his captor, Rince dodged to one side as the Guard tumbled slackly to the ground, falling face first next to Alaena, who, other than pulling her legs back to stay away from his body, barely reacted to what was going on around her.

Stunned and cautious lest this be some ruse, Rince looked down to the Guard. The red glare reflecting off all surfaces made the scene surreal. Somewhere nearby Rince thought he could hear a roar of sound, but he wasn't sure if it was the blood pounding through his veins or the fire announcing its final possession of the Keep. Glancing at Alaena still on the ground next to the Guard, Rince saw her looking at him with a dazed expression. Following her gaze, Rince turned his head and saw something that didn't register at first. Screwing his fists into his tired eyes to clear them, Rince looked again, making a closer examination in the dim light. There, at the small gap where his helmet ended and his armour began, a small stick with feathers on the end protruded from the Guard's neck. It took Rince a moment to realise that he was actually looking at the fletching of a small crossbow bolt lodged in the back of the man's head.

Before they could even start to understand how this could be, both children jumped in startled fear as a voice behind them floated out of the dark. "Well?" it queried with impatience. "Do you plan to stand there staring, or would you rather get out of here?"

Rince spun quickly from his uncomprehending examination of the crossbow quarrel protruding from the Guard's neck as the calm voice, so out of place against the turmoil in his mind, spoke. Alaena, still on the dirt floor staring in worn shock at the body next to her, dragged her eyes from the corpse to the outer gate. Suspicion narrowed her weary gaze.

"You're Tag," she grated wearily. It wasn't a question; it was an accusation.

If he was surprised Alaena knew him and knew his name, it didn't touch Tag's intense features. As though it was the most natural and logical thing in the world, he ignored Alaena's comment and looked to Rince. His low voice thrummed with competence, cutting through their concern, though not diminishing their distrust. "Come, boy. If you don't want to be caught with this"—he indicated the Guard on the floor with a jerk of his chiselled chin—"or tied up with any of that"—he glanced up to the ever-increasing blaze over the wall behind the courtyard—"then you need to pick up those keys and get this gate unlocked right now."

Rince didn't know how Alaena knew him, and now wasn't the time to ask. Whether or not he could trust this "Tag" he wasn't sure, but the man had erased their last obstacle to freedom, and if he wasn't sure of anything else, Rince was certain that it would be better to be on that side of the gate than this one!

Driven to action and feeling the heat of the blaze more keenly as it gained intensity, Rince wasted no more time. The keys had dropped from the guard's hand as he fell and lay only a few steps away in the dirt. Rince knelt to pick them up, then tossed them the short distance to Tag, who reached between the bars and caught them deftly before fitting them to the lock.

By the time Tag had turned the key and swung the gate to the outside world open, Rince had gone to Alaena. With his right arm about her waist and her left across his shoulder, he helped her to her feet and together they limped towards the opening. Tag moved forward quickly and Rince started, fearful that all this was just a ploy to allow Tag to get to them after all. Without words, however, Tag stepped lithely to the other side and placed Alaena's other arm about his own shoulder.

So arranged with Alaena strung between them, Rince and Tag stepped out of the Keep. Rather than turning to follow the uneven path that ran along the western side of the Keep as Rince expected, however, Tag carried them forward into the thick stand of beech trees that bordered the Keep on this side and where they quickly disappeared from sight.

Though the crackling roar of the flames as they consumed the Keep continued to chase them as they fled, the red hue of the flames behind them mercifully disappeared quickly as they moved deeper into the trees.

The main road by which Rince and Talia had originally approached the Keep sloped gradually upward to reach the plateau where the edifice stood, commanding a view of all the surrounding lands. The ground on this side sloped away at a much steeper grade, made even more treacherous for footing by the tangled weave of shallow roots that caught their ankles at every opportunity. In the darkness and in their worn state, Rince and Alaena were bruised and sore from many trips and stumbles on stray rocks, roots and limbs that seemed to loom out of the dark for no other purpose than to tear at their clothes and skin. Tag, who seemed to glide over the terrain as he moved despite the numerous obstacles, fared considerably better. His attention was focused ahead, however, so he did little to help other than supporting Alaena enough to stop her tumbling headfirst downhill.

Rince found himself looking at the man more than once in the red-shadowed light, wondering if he and Alaena were just replacing one problem with another. It took only a moment to think of the Protector's ruined face lying before him on the floor of the Keep's dungeons to dispel such thoughts and call himself an idiot. No matter who this Tag was or what he wanted, Rince thought to himself, they were better being with him than back in the Keep!

The slope, while steep, was relatively short. Scratched, sore and bleeding but otherwise in one piece, the trio emerged abruptly from the tree line, where the ground flattened suddenly and the main road to the north out of Morlyn ran directly across their path.

Before stepping onto the road, Tag held them back within the shadows of the tree line, staring and listening intently, though what he hoped to hear above the roar of the inferno Rince couldn't tell. Despite the hour, the blaze they could still hear above them tearing through the structure of the Keep cast an eerie red haze over the landscape all around. The road itself, tinged flickering sienna, was easy to see and appeared clear in either direction. Alaena, leaning more and more heavily on his shoulder, appeared unaware of anything going on around her. Glancing sideways and hefting her up to support her better, Rince could see that she had little strength left to stand, let alone run if they needed to.

Through lips that felt as parched as they would having walked the Sandwaste for a week, the great desert that lay far to the west of Morlyn, Rince tried to whisper his concern across Alaena's vacuous expression to Tag. A mere croak emerged before Tag's head spun. His eyes, dark in their deep sockets, fixed on Rince with purpose. His voice cut across the fire-tinged air, stifling further debate. "Hush, boy," he hissed. "Now is not the time for debate." He indicated the road with a nod of his head, not taking his eyes from Rince. "We will attempt the road to put some distance between ourselves and this, then look to rest. Come."

With little option other than to collapse where they stood and wait to be discovered, Rince urged Alaena to her feet once more. Groaning with the effort, Alaena complied, staring into the night as if expecting the red hue to fade and day to dawn bright and clear as it had only this morning. Rince shook his head as he wrapped one arm around her familiar frame to take as much of her weight as he could, and together they put one foot in front of the other and pursued the shadowy silhouette of Tag's back into the gloom. Somehow, Rince just could not bring himself to believe that his luck was going to hold and that they were going to see the night out alive.

Step by dragging step, holding each other like kin returning from war, Alaena and Rince disappeared into the night, leaving the inferno on the hill behind them. Before them, Tag floated like a wraith in the dark, his silence drawing them inexorably on to whatever fate had in store for them now.

Interlude 4 - Creation

The creature continued north at a steady pace. Ageless, it had no need of haste. Tireless, it had no need of rest. Its quarry had been clear since a time now forgotten in this land, as was its purpose. Its creators had made it understand, however, that the path was often obscure and human behaviour rarely predictable.

Brushing boughs, caressing trunks and stroking foliage as it passed, the unlikely creature communed with the forest as an old friend while it moved, gradually gaining an understanding of the world as it stood now. As always, the trees cared little of the outside world and were slow to share their thoughts. Eventually though, with patient touch and trilling tones, it coaxed from them a picture of the world, and with each message shared, sent thanks and blessing back to the wood and earth. In this way, moving steadily north all the while, the creature learned of wars, waste and of the human need to consume. Sorrow shaded with anger coloured its thoughts. It appeared that man had changed little in the past few millennia while it slept.

Undeterred, for its work would brook no impediment, the creature bent lower and increased pace, sending the desire for a clear path through its touch on the earth beneath its crooked appendages.

Obediently, boughs and limbs swayed back to provide unhindered passage, straight as an arrow, north to Morlyn.

Interlude 5 - Rider of Ald

Of the five riders that had set out from Ald at their Prince's behest, Darven Ross was the one tasked to make his way to Morlyn. Of them all, the Warrior-Smith would be the first to concede that he was the one least prone to conjecture and flights of fancy. In the hours he had ridden already, however, he could not count the times he had hoped to be the one to find the Appointed and return him in shackles to Ald, accompanied by accolades of praise and glory.

All males in Ald, from the time they became men at thirteen, were taught the sword and apprenticed to a secondary trade for which they were named. In addition to their craft, all were taught of the Art that had long since passed from the world. The Art was a gift of the Gods that, according to prophecy, would one day come again to save the world from the next Cataclysm, as it had saved them from the last. The Prophets of Ald had long since foretold of the Appointed, who would appear at the next time of crisis to bring an end to the danger once and for all. They could not tell how this would occur, but that was not for the mortals of Ald to understand. They knew merely that, when called, they would answer and give their all to find and obey the Appointed in whatever way they could and in whatever way was required. For this to occur in his time was the dearest wish of every man of Ald. Darven himself, a Smith counted as one of the finest workers of metal in the city of Ald, could barely contain his pride to be selected as one of the first riders to respond to the call that had long been prophesied.

The Prince had spoken with them and revealed that the Light had awoken in the gem. Darven Ross could still see his grim features, far too young to have such age etched into them, reflected in the light of the gem he brought forth for all present to see, shining like the sun in Orindum's hand. As one, in reverent tones, they shared with their Prince the words of the Keziah Codex, scribed by a prophet now dead hundreds of years and recalled only in name, but recited daily and kept alive by all the men and spiritual teachers in Ald:

That day will come
When Prince's Stone
Awakes and calls out bright.

Man's peril now
Awakes in step
And Power returns to sight.

Come forth, stout men
And heed the call
Look North and South and East.

The Appointed One,
Whose hand will heal,
Must never heed the Beast.

With a fervour he had difficulty restraining, the Warrior-Smith pressed his steed as much as he dared. It was a fine animal, bred for such a ride as this, but clouds hung low this night, consigning the landscape to gloom and forcing him to make his way carefully. The road from Ald to Morlyn was not frequently used and, as Darven knew from the few times he himself had made the trip, was in poor condition in a number of areas along the route. A thrown shoe or worse could be ruinous if it meant delaying his mission. So it was that Darven followed the road north with as much cautious haste as he dared, his trepidation heightened by the need to maintain a watchful eye on the dark bulk of the Swampwood that loomed along his path for a while, respectful of stories that told of bandits and worse that made a home of the Drowned Wood, as he had heard the Elders of Ald refer to it on occasion.

Breathing a sigh of relief as he rode into clearer country without incident some hours later, Darven took a moment to study the night sky. He had travelled only a fraction of his journey, yet hours had passed as he picked his way along the pitted road in the shadows of the trees under the shrouded sky. Darven clenched his teeth at the delay and, cursing quietly, urged his steed to a cautious canter. At least now the clouds were clearing and he could make up lost time.

Watching the road as it bent east towards Morlyn, he calculated quickly. He could cover several leagues in the hours before dawn. With no trouble on the road and as long as his horse held out, he could eat in the saddle and perhaps make Morlyn by midday. Leaning forward, he patted the neck of his horse, whispering encouragement to the beast as its hooves beat a lonely rhythm of urgency into the night.

Interlude 6 – Kahu Pyra

Kahu Pyra, Overlord of the Arkris and Guardian of the First Key, sat comfortably on his throne, smugly contemplating his next move as minions dotted around the massive room awaited his pleasure.

Well aware that knowledge, in addition to fear and subjugation, was a crucial aspect of hegemony, Kahu Pyra considered himself a master of the latter two. Knowledge, however, was something external that he had worked hard to gather and retain. Based on the power of the First Key, Kahu Pyra had a network of informants in place that spanned his domain of worlds. The few that now stood tall enough to perhaps pose a threat to him one day not only did not match but could not match such a resource. The secret of the First Key, which was the only way such a network could even exist, let alone function, was something he guarded zealously and with absolute control.

It was this network that Kahu Pyra had engaged after his first dream. He had shared that dream with his closest advisors, seeking their opinion. All had agreed that this 'Vetren' represented a threat. Clear action was required to find out who this potential usurper was so he could be dealt with before he became a danger.

Few references were found at first, and a number of underlings had lost their lives reporting back that there was no information to be found. As always, this had the effect of motivating others to search harder and, finally, an answer was found – though it was a strange one.

It appeared that a Prince of one of the houses some two centuries ago, before Kahu Pyra had taken possession of the First Key, had disappeared. His name was Vetren. No one knew what had become of him, though it was known he had been using the First Key to seek out new worlds to conquer. It was believed he had found one so rich in resource that he had set off personally to investigate. Unfortunately for Kahu Pyra's minions, Vetren had been cautious. There was no record of where that world was, or what resources it might contain, or even if Vetren had made it there. It was only known that, wherever he went, he had not returned and he had not been heard from again.

Vetren's House had collapsed when he disappeared and ultimately the First Key had fallen into Kahu Pyra's possession, but relatives of the fallen Prince still lived. Mind interrogations had shown that Vetren's face was the face in Kahu Pyra's dream.

Though his absence for so long was a mystery yet to be solved, Kahu Pyra had to assume from his dream that this Vetren still lived. He set his spies to watch, and finally word had come that Vetren's mind-signature had been detected, though strangely subdued, in the Lanes of a distant world.

Now Kahu Pyra had a place to start, he had a dozen minions doing nothing but searching for Vetren's presence to reappear so he could narrow down his location. When he was found, Kahu Pyra would track him through the Lanes to the world he was on. Once Kahu Pyra uncovered that piece of information, he would act immediately to ensure that the threat in the dream was never realised.

If the world Vetren had found was as rich in food and resource as the stories said, then, well, that would just make its devastation that much more pleasurable.

Chapter 16 – Aftermath

By the time dawn came to Morlyn, there were few save heavy sleepers or drunkards in the city that were unaware of the events at the Protectorate Keep during the night. As the sun greeted a crisp and clear sky in the southernmost realm of the Kingdom, even the most disinterested observer could not fail to stop and stare for a moment as the extent of the disaster became evident.

Once both a proud and forbidding edifice that overlooked Morlyn with a black, disapproving frown, the Keep today drew stares of shock and disbelief rather than glances of trepidation or apprehension. A testament to the efforts of both Guard and conscripted citizens who happened to be unfortunate enough to be in the vicinity when the blaze broke out, over half the structure still stood. The entire eastern side, where those familiar with the layout of the Keep knew the kitchens and servants' quarters were located, were largely intact and undamaged. The northernmost walls of the Keep also stood, behind which the courtyard, stables and armoury appeared, at least from the vantage point of those in the city, unharmed. There was no mistaking the black pall of smoke that still rose from the rear of the building. Those who had worked through the night to save what they could and those brave but inquisitive souls whose curiosity outweighed their trepidation at approaching the feared Keep could see that the entire southwest corner of the Keep had been all but destroyed by the conflagration. Hot enough to burn out supporting beams, the blaze had collapsed the roof in places, destroying not only the guest rooms and library that occupied that section of the Keep, but also much of the Protector's quarters that occupied the upper floor on that side.

The Protector himself was somehow still clinging to life, though none who had seen his wounds expected him to last much longer. He had been moved to private quarters in the city to be tended to by healers for as long as his body held breath, while those who usually bowed to the overarching superiority of the Protector took charge in the Keep.

There was talk of a servant girl with red locks who was questioned by Uré Etowin, the House Master of the Keep. Before she died under questioning, for Uré was second only to the Protector in his love of cruelty, she had spoken of a sandy-haired boy that was in the Keep with her when the fire broke out. He could not be found, but his parents were subsequently brought to the Keep. Unfortunately, before they also bled out, they could shed no light on where this boy might be found or whether he had something to do with all this.

Then, of course, there was the mystery of the girl the Protector was questioning and how, if it was even possible, she had bested him, let alone arrange her escape. The crossbow bolt found buried in the neck of the Guard at the servants' gate gave Uré some insight here. The bolt was finely made and fired with remarkable accuracy, so he could be sure there was more to this than met the eye.

Every avenue of investigation from there, however, ran dry. The boy could not be found. The prisoner had escaped. There was no way to know who had killed the guard or even to be sure who set the fire.

In the end, Uré sent his spies out into the town and surrounds to unearth what they could without much hope of success. The culprits were away and he had work to do while he waited for the Protector to die.

Chapter 17 – Helpless

Wilmen had spent the previous night waiting and worrying, followed by most of this morning fretting.

She had gone to the Keep with Egan as darkness set in the previous evening to attempt to gain entry under the authority of the Abbey, ostensibly to minister to and receive the prayers of the faithful there who might like to pay homage to the spirits who created and still watched over the world and the creatures that inhabited it.

Egan was one of those faithful. He carried out his role well as Abbot of the Morlyn Abbey, and Wilmen did not discount those beliefs, for she saw them merely as an extension of her own. While Egan believed there were many spirits, each overseeing and nurturing their own aspect of the world around them, Wilmen's beliefs were rooted in much older lore, based on the existence of but three supreme deities who, together, governed all creation through the aspects of Earth, Fire and Light.

As Head of the Abbey in his official robes and with Wilmen posing as an acolyte in lighter blue robes, they had expected no obstacle to entry, though the hour was late. Before they were in sight of the main gate, Tag had melted into the darkness to attempt other, less conventional, means of entry if he could find them. Calming herself with a ritual verse that grounded and settled her mind, Wilmen secreted her ring in a deep pocket and checked the knife at her waist, well concealed by her robe, before nodding to Egan to proceed. *One way or another,* Wilmen thought with a grim set to her chin as they approached the gates, *I will not leave this place without Alaena safe in my arms.*

As was customary, the heavy doors of the Keep were closed and secured at dusk, though this was done more as usual practice now than out of a real defensive need. It was many years since the King's forces had crossed the mountains to secure this coastal region, after which he had expanded his empire to neighbouring lands via the iron grip of the Guard and his Protectors.

Some way before Egan and Wilmen reached the gate and hailed the guard on watch to request entry, however, Wilmen jumped to the sudden peal of bells sounding across the commons from within the Keep itself.

Concerned and unsure, Wilmen put a hand to Egan's arm to stay his step, peering around in the darkness to try to ascertain the nature of the threat, to no avail. The night was still and nothing seemed amiss around her. As shouts and commotion began to stir within and quickly gain volume, Wilmen realised with dismay that the alarm had been raised due to some threat from within the Keep itself. Cursing herself for letting Egan convince her to leave the Star at the Abbey, Wilmen felt momentarily adrift. The light within the gem could not tell her if Alaena was involved in whatever was going on within the Keep, but its very radiance would assure her that Alaena was indeed still alive. Until and unless it went dark, Wilmen would know Alaena's heart still beat and that her infinitely precious gift was intact.

Moments later, Wilmen's heart sank and her hand dropped from Egan's arm in defeat, for the Guard at the gate had responded to the alarm as they had been trained to do. Wilmen could hear the clanking of chains and metal as the iron portcullis was lowered behind the wooden doors, sealing the Keep off from all passage. Though they might pound on the gates until their knuckles were raw and scream until they were hoarse now, Wilmen knew the gates would not open until such time as the Keep was declared safe and secure again by the Protector himself.

Aware that simply waiting by the gate was a fruitless and probably dangerous exercise, the pair retreated back down the road towards Morlyn as the night deepened, and considered their next steps. Taking up a position some few hundred paces away, ensuring the Keep remained in view so they could move swiftly when the gates opened once more, they kept their voices low, though the clanging of the bells carried clearly through the night and would likely cover their conversation from anyone close by even if they were shouting.

Pulling her cloak closer about her, for the night was cooling quickly and a light breeze was chilling her skin, Wilmen ordered her thoughts while Egan stared back towards the Keep, one slim hand absently toying with the circular medallion hanging around his neck, as if it could supply the answers they required.

Most of all, Wilmen wished Tag was with them, for she knew him to be a cunning and deadly opponent. In past years, Wilmen had witnessed him emerge alive, if not unscathed, from situations where other men would most certainly have perished. It was not for protection and security she wished to have him with her at this time, though. She needed the Star and, other than Egan, did not trust anyone else to retrieve and return it safely to her. Wilmen had no desire to stand on this lonely hill in the dark as alarm bells pealed out from the Keep while Egan returned to the Abbey for the Star. Likewise, she desperately wanted to stay nearby in case the gates should open again, lest she miss an opportunity to enter and search for Alaena.

As Wilmen twisted her hands in frustrated angst, glancing from the Keep to Morlyn and back again, Egan found his voice first.

"Spirits help us, Wilmen!" he said, having difficulty holding his voice to a frustrated whisper. "This throws all our plans into disarray!" He paused, then voiced Wilmen's concern directly. "This cannot be coincidence, surely! The Star awakes and Alaena is taken, only to have alarms sound from the Keep that same night?"

Wilmen picked up the conversation as Egan paused in bewildered concern.

"Indeed, Abbot," she responded, reverting to Egan's formal title in the stress of the moment. "Our plans are disrupted, but we must not lose hope. I do not think it coincidence at all, but I am equally at a loss for what this could mean." Seeing the dim shape of Egan's head nodding in the dark, she continued. "We still do not know what has raised the alarm within the Keep. Tag is also still out there and may find opportunity to help Alaena where we may not. I suggest we hold ourselves here awhile. We need to know what has happened in the Keep and perhaps Tag will return shortly, for he must also have heard the alarms and may have his own story to tell."

"What you say has merit, Wilmen," Egan replied. "Though should an hour pass with no further news, I would return to the Abbey to retrieve the Star, for I would dearly like to be comforted in the knowledge that Alaena is still with us."

They continued to discuss the situation without further resolution for a short while, and soon saw torches ascending the hill from Morlyn. Clearly the bells had raised the interest of the curious in the city and people were coming to investigate. Onlookers continued to arrive for some time after the bells had stopped pealing. By the time the reason for the alarm was evident as the first flames started licking out of the roof to the rear of the structure and the smell of smoke saturated the air, there were some thirty people standing witness outside to the burning of the Keep.

Entranced by the sight of the hated edifice in flames, Wilmen and Egan started to feel heat on their faces as they moved closer with the crowd and the flames licked higher into the sky, lighting the landscape around them now with dancing, dark red shadows.

Fixated by the growing inferno, Wilmen almost missed the movement at the gate nearby. In the shadow of the wall against the glare of the flames above, one of the massive gates had opened and the other side was now swinging back as well to make way for a horse pulling an open cart to emerge, accompanied by a small contingent of Guard. Each held a torch high in their left hands, shedding a circle of light for several paces around and in front of the wagon to light the way. Their right hands sat competently on the hilts of swords buckled around their waists.

Barking an urgent call to Egan to follow, Wilmen gathered up her robes and made a dash towards the group. On approach, they could see the driver at the front and two men atop the rear of the cart, leaning down and tending another. Weapons slid clear of scabbards in practiced defence as they neared. The Guard were obviously allowing no one to come near, but bathed by the growing glow of flames from the Keep, Egan's sharp eyes recognised both the men on the cart and he shouted out immediately to attract their attention.

"Halar!" he called, smoke making his voice sound thick. "What goes within and who do you have there? Can the Abbey help?"

Halar squinted past the ring of torches that surrounded him into the relative dark beyond as Egan and Wilmen approached. His face creased into a smile as he recognised the medallion glinting in the torchlight, then put name to face. The Abbey in the city was of little interest to the Keep as a general rule, but Hatar knew them

163

as a place of rest and healing, and it was the latter skills he urgently needed now.

"Abbot! You are welcome indeed!" Waving impatiently to the Guard to allow them to pass, he urged Egan to approach. "Come," he beckoned. "The Protector has been harmed in the blaze and we are taking him to Penther for care. Come and tend to him as we travel, as I fear he may not survive even this short journey!"

Though stated as more order than request, Egan appeared to falter at the name of the Protector. A staunch believer in the sanctity of life as Egan was, the Protector was one person who continually challenged his rectitude in this respect. Wilmen was pleased his hesitation was only momentary; she knew he was not foolish enough to believe that standing before the gates of the burning Keep surrounded by armed Guard was the time to debate such issues with himself.

Wilmen followed in his wake as Egan moved to the back of the cart, keeping her head bowed and sheltered by her hood. It was unlikely she would be recognised by either of these men as the chandler in the city rather than an acolyte of the Abbey, as she tended to deal with functionaries of the Keep rather than those higher up, but it never hurt to keep one's profile low.

Halar and the other man, whom Wilmen recognised as Uré, the House Master of the Protectorate Keep, leaned down to help Egan as he struggled in his robes to board the wagon, which had cleared the gate now and continued to move at a gently consistent pace down the road, away from the Keep.

Wilmen glanced back at the gate, one side of which had already closed behind the departing wagon. The other was swinging ponderously as well and shortly she would lose her opportunity to enter.

Egan, now aboard the wagon, was ahead of her. As Halar and Uré dropped his arms and started to turn back to the Protector, Egan quickly interjected. "Halar – my Acolyte will do no good here. May she enter the Keep to tend to any other wounded there?"

"Abbot," Halar snapped, disinterested in anything other than the Protector himself. "I care not for the Keep and its occupants at the present time – let your woman do what she will. For now, our priority must be the care of the Protector!" Kneeling back to the Protector, Halar grabbed Egan's robes to pull him down next to him and tend to the wounded man.

Wilmen watched as Egan went to one knee and his eyes widened with shock at whatever he saw there. He waved a hand at Wilmen, directing her away from the wagon and towards the Keep.

Wilmen needed no further urging and dashed away towards the closing gates, fighting an unbecoming urge to rejoice inside.

***

Surrounded by a ring of torchlight as they moved, Egan could see that the Protector had indeed suffered grievous wounds. The left side of his face was covered in blood. At first glance, Egan assumed the wound to his head on that side was responsible for the massive blood loss, but by the time they reached the sloped road down to the city, Egan had realised that the mutilation was much more severe and that a blood and gore filled socket was all that remained of his left eye. Though he made no mention of it, Egan was immediately sure that this had nothing to do with fire, no matter what Halar said.

With a guilty sense of relief, Egan realised that the Protector was likely to die regardless of what he did. The wound was mortal. At least to that end, Egan was able to put aside his animosity for the man and his many crimes against the Spirit and tend to him in what Egan believed would be his last hours.

Egan stayed tending to the Protector until Halar and Uré had him settled as comfortably as they could at the Healer's in Morlyn, after which he excused himself, citing a need to gather the resources of the Abbey to help those who would need it at the Keep. He need hardly have bothered with the excuse. Halar's attention was focused solely on the Protector and the ministrations of the Healer who, with a very grim face, was gently cleaning the Protector's wounds and examining him to fully understand the extent of his injuries. Uré was standing back somewhat, appearing a little distracted, but waved Egan away as soon as he voiced an intent to leave, as if the House Master cared not whether Egan stayed or otherwise.

With that, Egan dashed away to the Abbey as quickly as he could to retrieve the Star and, against all hope, discover whether or not Alaena still lived.

***

The Keep had reopened its gates not long after first light, and shortly after that Wilmen returned to the Abbey, where Egan conveyed the wonderful news that the Star still shone bright.

As the mid-morning bell tolled out across the city, Egan and Wilmen took the opportunity to update each other with events since they had parted. They talked in Egan's private chambers with the Star nestled in its ornate box on the table before them. White rays shone steadily and brightly from within, contrasting starkly with their own darker deliberations.

Wilmen, like Egan, could not bring herself to feel any sorrow about the extent of the Protector's injuries, nor the fact that Egan believed he was unlikely to wake at all and had probably already passed. The injuries themselves they discussed for some time, though the only thing they decided was that they were probably unrelated to Alaena. The Protector was a powerfully built man. To deliver wounds so serious, the Protector's adversary must have been formidable indeed. Between them, Egan and Wilmen could think of a number of people who would have both the desire and motivation to do this, but within the Keep itself who would have the opportunity and capacity to actually succeed in delivering such a blow?

Realising soon that the attempt to identify a likely culprit was becoming an exercise in useless conjecture, as neither had any insight as to who might really have been capable of this, Wilmen and Egan turned to the subject of the fire itself.

As succinctly as possible, Wilmen described her search within the Keep for Alaena, or at least for information about her.

The Guard attending the gate as it closed had seen Wilmen leave the cart carrying the Protector, the House Master and the Master of Arms and dash in his direction. Assuming this figure racing for the gates, blue robes flapping madly in the red light, had important business, he had signalled those working the winches to hold for a

166

moment, allowing Wilmen entry before sealing them shut behind her.

With the authority having come from such company and with her robes identifying her as an acolyte of the Abbey, Wilmen had no difficulty convincing the Guard to allow her to help before she was able to turn her attention to the main bulk of the Keep and the noise and chaos within.

The first thing to hit her was the heat. On the other side of the gate, shielded to a large extent by the massive stone walls of the structure itself, Wilmen had not appreciated the size and ferocity of the blaze. Here, standing behind the gate with the courtyard before her, the scale of the disaster became apparent.

Scorching, ravenous flames leapt uncontrolled from the roof, bathing the entire area in bright, hellish, red-stained heat. A handful of people were standing off to her right near the stables, some holding hands and arms up to shield their faces and eyes from the conflagration. Others, less entranced, simply faced away from it. Some appeared injured and some were sobbing. Wilmen spared them little attention for the moment, as Alaena was clearly not with them and they were simply staying as far away as they could get from the fire and the Keep itself while they nursed their respective wounds.

Across the courtyard, frenetic activity was taking place to attempt to stem the conflagration under the stern eye of one of the captains, who was bellowing orders that carried over the roar and crackling cacophony of the blaze. Under his direction, a line of Guard and others in various stages of dress that had obviously been conscripted to assist ran some thirty paces from the stone-walled well, across the courtyard, up the stairs and through the main door of the Keep, passing buckets and containers of all types full of water into those fighting the fire inside and back out again to be refilled once more.

Becoming more desperate by the moment, Wilmen contemplated crossing the courtyard and pressing the Guard Captain himself for information. Perhaps if he was too occupied with directing efforts to quell the blaze to spare her any attention, Wilmen might even slip by and conduct a search of those parts of the interior she could reach herself to find Alaena. Steeling herself for a probable confrontation, as she deemed it unlikely the captain would miss her approach or consider letting anyone for any reason enter the Keep while the fire raged, Wilmen had squared her shoulders and stepped forward.

Before she had taken a dozen steps, the beams supporting the roof where the fire raged finally gave way. With a resounding crash that rolled all the way down the hill to Morlyn, the roof to the rear of the building gave way, taking what remained of the internal floor in that section of the Keep with it. Sparks, embers and flame spewed skyward, etching scarlet trails high into the night sky as the heat of the blaze found full release. Simultaneously, a choking plume of dust and smoke billowed out of the main door, eclipsing the captain and all those near the door from view until, some moments later, they ran from the cloud, coughing and hacking as they gulped clear air into their lungs once more.

Backing away, Wilmen was forced to bide her time as the plume thinned and spread through the area. The Captain moved everyone back then, realising that the situation was beyond them for the moment. For that short while, before the Captain gathered those who could lug water back to the well to finally subdue the fire, Guard, civilian and servants huddled back away from the main structure, giving Wilmen an opportunity to learn what she could of the events that had transpired inside this evening.

One Guard, Wilmen informed Egan, knew the Protector had cleared the cells that afternoon to make way for the questioning of a particularly dangerous prisoner that night. Another had captured Wilmen's interest when he made mention of a sandy-haired boy he'd seen in the Keep helping one of the maids stock the fireplaces with wood before the fire broke out. Hopeful that this maid might furnish more information, Wilmen learned her name was Talia but nothing more, as the maid was nowhere to be found and hadn't been seen since the fire broke out.

No further information came to light for some hours. It wasn't until the first hint of dawn touched the sky that the fire was at last brought under control and Wilmen was able to approach the Keep. Scanning the place to pick her best opportunity, Wilmen plucked a waterskin from where it hung near the well and headed purposefully towards the main entry to the Keep. Passing by exhausted Guard who milled around aimlessly or sat wearily on upturned buckets, heads lolling sleepily, Wilmen moved up the steps towards the main door. There, a Guard blinked at her momentarily as if unable to fathom her intent, then gathered himself to shift across in front of her, barring her way with the spear he was leaning on. The knuckles on his hand that gripped the spear, like his face, were black with soot and grime.

"Are you mad, woman?" he said incredulously, crossing the spear in front of her to bar Wilmen's way. "You can't go in there! The whole place might come down on your head!" Even as he spoke, the Guard regained some of the authority of his position. "Step back now, before you get hurt," he insisted, starting to move towards her to push her back from the step.

Rather than moving back, Wilmen lifted the waterskin in one hand as she placed the other on the hand that held the spear before her. She pressed her advantage as the Guard hesitated, surprised. "Assuredly, sir," Wilmen gushed disarmingly. "I wouldn't dream of entering until such as yourself declared it safe!" Indicating her gown, as if presenting it as her credentials, she continued. "I've come from the Abbey, sent by Abbot Egan himself, to minister to those hurt as best I may." Lifting her hand from his, she unstopped the waterskin and proffered it towards him, sensing the Guard relax as she identified herself as a healer.

"I saw you by the door a while ago as I tended others and you looked weary." Wilmen nodded towards the people dotted around the courtyard without taking her eyes off the Guard. "It's been a long night for the Guard especially, has it not?"

The Guard seemed pleased as much for the distraction as for the water itself. "Indeed, it has!" he confirmed, taking the bladder in his free hand and lifting it to his mouth to drink.

Some minutes later, Wilmen walked back towards the courtyard. Her waterskin empty, she left the Guard significantly cleaner and considerably more refreshed than when she had approached him. Wilmen had been at pains to ensure the Guard was properly cared for. After all, she had assured him, everyone in Morlyn knew that his position was one of great importance and he should be attended to as such! In short order, she had him engaged in easy conversation. Wilmen learned more in those few minutes than she had in the past few hours gossiping with servants in the courtyard.

The Guard, Jarrett by name, didn't know anything about the fire, but knew the Protector had been injured. While Wilmen was already aware of the Protector's injuries, she was surprised to hear Jarrett refer to more than one fight the previous evening. A little prodding uncovered the much more interesting fact that one of the kitchen hands had, in the early hours of the morning, discovered the East Gate open and the Guard within dead in the dirt of the gatehouse, a crossbow bolt in his neck and his sword not even drawn.

Pondering all this, tired but buoyed by the things she had heard, Wilmen departed as morning light crept over the walls, streaked with dark tendrils of smoke that smudged the sky. She had made a few short stops on the way back from the Keep, one at the Chandler's and one at a small shack in the poor quarter, before returning to the Abbey.

Now, washed and refreshed in Egan's private quarters once more, Wilmen leaned forward and concluded her recount of events at the Keep, with her eyes riveted on the Star and her demeanour grim.

Taking a sip from a cup of watered wine before her, Wilmen paused a moment to let Egan absorb her news before continuing. "We have a number of mysteries here, Egan," she began again, breaking the thoughtful silence. "I suspect Rince has outdone himself and been involved with the fire that took half the Keep. Whether that act killed him or not is unclear, but it was a brave deed and may have set the circumstances in place for Alaena to effect her escape."

She shook her head, still unable to credit Rince for the courage it must have taken for him to attempt the feat.

"Either way, I stopped by his home on the way here. He did not return home last night. Where he might be none of his family seem to know. It appears that Alaena has indeed escaped the clutches of the Protector, however, and has been rescued without our help!"

She glanced up to Egan, who was sitting similarly transfixed by the Star and nodding gently, before shifting her gaze back to the golden light swirling slowly within the gem.

"As for the death of the Guard at the gate and the wounding of the Protector, I can only consider that the work of Tag. The Guard certainly sounds like his work, for Tag's prowess with his crossbow is second only to his skill with a knife. Even if he killed the Guard though, how would Tag have unlocked the gate to even make the attempt on the Protector's life? And if it was indeed Tag that brought the Protector down, I cannot help but wonder how it is that the Protector still breathes? I've never known Tag to miss a target and he would have no hesitation in dealing that death blow in particular, for he has often argued the merits of assassination to solve our problems with the Protector, as you well know!"

"Indeed, Wilmen," Egan mused in a thoughtful tone. "Tag is also never careless." Looking up at Wilmen, he nodded in agreement. "The side of the Protector's head was struck rather than cut, and while his eye looked to have been gouged by a blade, Tag would sooner slice his neck and be done with it."

Tired of the guesses and eager for action, Wilmen pushed herself up from her seat.

"The fact remains, Egan, that it appears that Alaena is no longer at the Keep. Further, Tag would have returned here or sent us word by now if he were able. We must therefore assume he is otherwise occupied and, given the events at the Keep and the Star which lays before us, I can only conclude that he has somehow secured Alaena's freedom and is at this very moment fleeing with her to somewhere safe."

A heavy silence followed.

"There, then, lies our predicament, Wilmen," Egan eventually stated in a quiet voice. "There are a number of places we know of – and very likely several we are completely unaware of – that he may decide to take her, depending on their need and the danger that pursues them." He spread his hands on the table, fingers splayed on the cool surface to either side of the gem as if the gesture of supplication could elicit a response from the stone itself. Lifting his gaze and eventually meeting Wilmen's eyes in the absence of a response, he asked, "Where do we look to help them?"

Exhaustion and a feeling of helplessness flooded through Wilmen as she realised she had no answer. Her voice reflected the weary lassitude pressing on her mind.

"I know not, Egan," she stated simply. Waving a hand at the Star shining before them, she concluded, "We really only know that Alaena is alive. We can guess, but first we must rest. We have had little sleep these past two days. I will retire and I suggest you do the same. Perhaps rest will allow us to think more clearly and time will bring new news, in any case."

Not waiting for an answer Wilmen gently closed and gathered up the obsidian box in which the gem and a sign of their hope for the future of the world rested, before leaving to find a bed.

When at last Wilmen lay her head on a pillow, sleep remained elusive as her anguished thoughts turned plans and possibilities for Ala over and over well into the night. Before falling at last into a restless slumber full of fearful dreams, Wilmen had decided. There was little she could do here but fret. At first light, she would set off after Alaena, Rince and Tag herself, and may Hell take the Protector or anyone else who dared stand in her way.

Chapter 18 - Healing

For Rince, the night spent stumbling along the road following Tag's dark shadow was interminable.

Leaving the blazing chaos of their escape from the Protectorate Keep far behind them, Rince and Alaena stumbled blindly along the rough dirt road as the night crept on. Three things dominated Rince's life during those impossible hours.

Firstly, Alaena was draped across his left shoulder as they walked. Intensely aware of her fragility, Rince braced each stumble and guided each of her steps with intimate care, for she seemed barely aware of her surroundings. When they had first set out from the Keep, Rince had taken her left arm over his neck and supported her with his right arm wrapped around her waist. At the first stumble, however, Alaena had gasped with pain as her weight bore down on his arm, which pressed into her ribs on that side. Moments later she had actually cried out as another misstep forced that side to take her weight once more. Avidly hoping to avoid drawing attention to them as they disappeared into the dark, and equally keen to avoid causing her further hurt, Rince had taken time to shift Alaena to his other shoulder. The hours of pressure on that side had gone past pain and now all Rince could feel in that shoulder was a dull numb ache that had settled into his back.

The second thing that dominated his thoughts was his feet. Most of the time he walked with his head bowed, for it seemed too much to summon the strength to lift it. While the moon was dark, stars lit up the night. Like a million distant but distinct lanterns, the pinpoints of light bathed the road and the trees that lined its way with a wash of pale white. In this light, numbed by the repetitive and imperative movement, the time passed for Rince in a hypnotic state as he watched his feet somehow put one shoe in front of the other, one shoe in front of the other, over and over, as the road passed by beneath them.

Lastly, the driving presence of Tag before him occupied his mind. As black as the night around them, Tag's cloak seemed to absorb light and he moved with a fluid grace that appeared, to Rince's numbed perceptions, ghost-like. The night absorbed him as

173

readily as it did the starlight and the dark was clearly his friend. While Tag appeared generally at ease, however, Rince often noticed his head turning back and forth, scanning and sniffing the air as if searching for predators, or perhaps as a predator searching for prey. Either way, as the time wore on, Rince became more and more aware of the coiled violence within the man they followed into the dark, though he had no room in his mind at the moment to question whether or not it was a wise choice to follow this stranger into the unknown.

Rince had no idea how far the stars had turned in the sky or how far they had travelled. Alaena continued to put one dragging foot in front of the other, but had stopped making any noise at all some time back and now blindly stumbled along where he led. Rince had no doubt at all that if he were to walk off a cliff, she would just walk right off it with him.

At some point, whatever time it was or what distance they had now travelled, it appeared that it was deemed sufficient to put them in relative safety for the moment. Tag's purposeful stride slowed as his head turned this way and that, senses alert as he assessed the road and the deep shadows of the wood that now rose thick against the road on either side of them. "Here," he grated levelly, coming to a halt.

To Rince, the word floated from another reality. Blunted senses unable to process the directive, his disconnected body lurched onwards until a firm hand on his shoulder halted his momentum.

Instantly, Rince's world tilted, turned and swirled. As long as he was moving, his mind had been fixed on maintaining that momentum and, for Alaena's sake, moving them further and further from danger. Once halted, the need that drove him fell away and the automatic imperative to continue moving failed him completely. Before Tag's dark, unbending form, Rince's knees buckled and Alaena's weight became unsupportable. Allowing gravity to take them, Rince let himself and Alaena slump heavily towards the ground.

Before his body failed him completely though, Rince was surprised to feel Alaena's weight taken from him and his own body supported by an iron grip.

"There, boy." Tag's voice drifted soothingly from the darkness that clouded his mind. "You've done well and earned a rest. We'll stop here a while and tend to your friend once we're off the road and out of sight. It's only a short way now, so hold up and soon you'll rest. Follow me."

With that, Tag lifted Alaena smoothly into his arms, nodded his head to the left of the road and without further delay stepped into the brush next to them, disappearing from sight. Rince's bemused mind took a moment to realise that he could see more clearly now and that pre-dawn light was seeping into the woods. Forcing his body into motion once more, grimacing as feeling began to flow back into his shoulder, he shoved blindly into the brush, incapable of caring what was on the other side other than knowing Tag had taken Alaena this way.

Once off the road, they were again enveloped by gloom. The trees overhead eclipsed both the last of the starlight that was shining as well as the dawn glow, leaving only vague outlines in the dark to follow. Tag had moved on and would have been difficult to follow, cloaked as he was in the dark itself, but to Rince's numb surprise, the gap in the brush that Tag had pushed through led to a game trail beyond.

Lurching forward, Rince summoned the last of his resources to follow the trail before him, much as he had the road for hours just passed. Soon after, Rince stumbled into an area that widened slightly. His mind registered Alaena lying on the ground with her tattered shirt pulled aside, unresponsive as Tag examined her swelling side carefully with his hands. Somewhere in the distance water bubbled pleasantly, a strangely normal counterpart to the surreal situation he found himself in. Rince's mind dimly continued to process his new environment even as, exhausted by the events of the past day and night, he swooned and fell. His final thought was one of surprise that Tag could move so swiftly as to catch Rince before he hit the ground, then darkness consumed him completely.

Rince woke to a gentle hand shaking his shoulder, rousing him from a deep sleep filled with troubled dreams of pursuit. Opening his eyes a slit, Rince was at first disoriented. Why was there a canopy of leaves far above him, and open sky beyond that? When had the sun come up, for that matter? Moments later, his eyes narrowed their focus and he registered Tag leaning near, urging him to wake. With that, the events of the past night came crashing back to his consciousness. Fear, smoke and their desperate escape crowded his mind for attention, but his first and primary thought was for Alaena. His body jerked automatically as he attempted to jump upright, but with the movement pain lanced his frame from head to toe. Every muscle ached and both his shoulder and back felt like they'd been beaten with heavy sticks.

With a loud groan, Rince sank back to lean on his elbows instead, breathing hard as the initial pain subsided.

"Hush, boy," Tag chided gently, lending a supporting hand to his shoulder. "We are safe for the moment, but let's not attract any unwanted attention, shall we?"

Rince shot a dark look at Tag, still not sure that he should trust this stranger who, for reasons yet unknown, had plucked them from what appeared to be an unescapable situation and now had them at his mercy in the woods. Leaving that issue for the moment, his young body rapidly recovering as he moved to sit upright, Rince glanced about further to take in his surroundings. All other concern washed away as he spied Alaena lying by a tree a short distance away on the other side of the clearing.

Forcing muscles to grudgingly respond, Rince pushed himself to his feet. Fighting down dizziness as he moved, he shambled over to where Alaena lay breathing lightly. Fearing the worst, Rince knelt to the soft earth beside her and checked Alaena for injury or harm. Gingerly pulling her tattered shirt aside, careful not to disturb her rest, Rince was surprised to see a makeshift bandage around her ribs. The many cuts and scrapes he could see on her skin had been cleaned as well and did not appear nearly as severe as they had in the dark of the previous night when flight was all he could think of. While perhaps still a little pale, Alaena appeared much improved and palpable relief washed through him as Rince realised that Alaena had been well tended. Pleased beyond words, Rince simply took Alaena's slim hand in his own as he settled next to her while Tag folded gracefully to the ground on her other side.

Rince started to lean forward to check the swelling on her cheek, but Tag held up a hand long figures gesturing him back. Rince had heard him mutter few words since they had met at the gate of the Keep the previous evening and was surprised to hear a low melodious voice come from his sharp, angular face.

"Leave her be, boy. She's strong and she'll recover. We'll give her a bit longer to rest, then we need to be on our way. You two well and truly kicked a hornet's nest open yesterday and the further we can get from that place today, the better."

Pulling his hand back, as much for Alaena as to comply with Tag's request, Rince returned it to his lap, though he didn't let the gentle grip he had on Alaena's hand with his other release.

"While we wait, boy," the stranger began casually, "tell me about last night. How did the fire start and how did you come to be at the gate with Alaena? It was fortuitous indeed, but I am at a loss to understand how these things came to be."

For the first time since last night, Rince took a really good look at Tag. His blue eyes caught Tag's pale green stare, seeing the coiled danger behind Tag's gaze, but no subterfuge. *Besides,* Rince thought to himself, *if he wanted to kill us, he could have done so a hundred times by now.*

Too tired to think of deception and yearning for someone to trust, Rince held Tag's gaze and spoke simply, deciding to confide in their strange saviour.

"I spoke with Wilmen, who takes care of Alaena, to tell her that Alaena had been taken to the Keep. She said she'd look after things and told me to stay out of it, but I couldn't. After all, what can one woman who makes candles do to sway the will of the Keep?"

Rince paused, licking his lips as he recalled the fear he felt for Alaena after she had been taken. His gaze straying back to Alaena's face, he lost himself in the story.

"So, I used a friend to get myself into the Keep and make my way to the library within. It was late at night and I managed to get alone for long enough to douse as many books as I could with oil from the lanterns there, then set the place aflame."

He did not notice Tag's eyes widen in surprise as the tale unfolded with blunt, swift candour.

"I ran to raise the alarm and then, as the Guard in the main hall were running to the fire, I slipped down into the dungeon to find Alaena."

Rince's eyes narrowed as he recalled what had happened there. He completed the telling in a rush.

"I thought I was lost when I found out the Protector was down there, but he was lying on the floor. There was blood everywhere and one eye …" He shuddered, unable to describe the scene adequately. "Anyway, I think he was dead, or soon was to be if he wasn't already. A Guard found me down near the cells and I thought he was going to skewer me there and then, but then he saw the Protector too and ran to fetch help. After he'd gone I just left the Protector lying there and searched the rest of the cells as quickly as I could for Alaena. I don't really know how but I walked straight to the cell she was hiding in, so I helped her up and took her back out the way I'd come in, through the servants' corridor. People were running and there was smoke everywhere, so it wasn't that hard to slip out unnoticed until we reached the gate near the wood pile, which is where you found us."

Rince's voice faded as his story ended and, for one of the few times in his life, Tag was dumbfounded. Rince seemed unaware of the impact he had had on his companion, falling silent when the tale was told, his eyes returning to Alaena as he stroked her hand gently.

"Do you think she'll be all right?" he asked quietly of Tag as the silence stretched out.

Tag, finally recovering his voice, took a few tries to calm himself. "You … How?" he spluttered a few times before cursing in disbelief. "Spirits burn me, boy, you actually have me at a loss, which I didn't think was possible!" he exclaimed finally, a wholly uncharacteristic grin splitting his features. Leaning across Alaena's still form, Tag clasped Rince firmly on the shoulder to get his full attention. "You tell a hero's tale that's worthy of a bard's song in a few short sentences, then sit there afterwards as if you've just told me that the sun has risen this morning!"

Rince, taken aback by Tag's praise, was unsure how to respond. "Well," he muttered in pleased confusion, even as he winced back from Tag's enthusiastic grasp of his shoulder, which still ached from the efforts of the previous evening. "She's worth it," he finished simply as once more, his gaze went back to Alaena.

Tag dropped his arm from Rince's shoulder, watching him a moment longer and realising that, for Rince, no risk would have been too great to contemplate to ensure Alaena's safety. As it was, Tag agreed that any risk was worth it to save Alaena, though his motives and reasons were entirely different. While Rince would save her for herself, Tag, Wilmen and their companions would save her for the world.

About to frame a response that would let Rince know Tag felt the same way, if not for the same reasons, his words cut short as Alaena stirred on the ground between them.

Rince pulled a quick breath and grasped her hand tighter as Alaena's eyes opened and she slowly took in her surroundings, gaze finally stopping to rest on Rince and Tag as they hovered over her in concern.

"Ala!" Rince exclaimed happily, before muting his voice again in response to a quick hush from Tag. "Oh, Ala," he said more sedately. "I'm so glad you're awake! How do you feel? What did they do to you? Are you okay?" The questions tumbled from him in a rush until Alaena herself quieted him.

"Hush, Rince," she said with a smile. Her granite-grey eyes twinkled with fond affection. "I will be fine if you'll just stop crushing my hand, please!"

***

After giving Rince's hand a squeeze in return to let him know all was well, Alaena, still lying on the ground, reached her arms above her head and stretched luxuriously on the bed of leaves and loam on which she lay, before sitting up in one fluid movement and shaking the leaves from her long, dark hair.

Appearing completely alert as she drew her legs up and clasped her knees with her elbows, Alaena looked about them with interest.

"This is a beautifully peaceful place!" she declared lightly, tilting her head side to side to each of her companions before smiling and pushing herself to her feet in one lithe motion. "Where are we and where is that water I can hear? I'm so very thirsty!" she said, taking a few steps forward.

Still kneeling on the ground, Tag and Rince exchanged a surprised and shocked look. How was it that Alaena was even able to stand, let alone do so as lightly as she had and without any apparent discomfort? Rince, still nursing his injuries from the previous evening, struggled to his feet to follow Alaena, who was moving away from them, towards the sound of the water.

Tag also stood, but remained still for a moment more, staring at the place where Alaena had laid for the past few hours. It had been dark when they had come here, so he had not been able to conduct a thorough examination of the spot, but he was sure he had placed her in a relatively clear area. Now, it appeared that a network of vines and new shoots had sprouted out of nothing, under and around where she had lain. Taking this in, Tag looked back to Alaena, who was stepping lightly over a log at the edge of the clearing to reach the small stream that lay beyond as Rince limped along behind her. A shiver spun down his spine and the words Rince stated only a short while ago floated back to his mind: *"She's worth it."*

Indeed, thought Tag as Alaena disappeared from sight and he took a last, lingering look at the impossible new growth at his feet. *She is worth so much more than you know, boy.*

With that, Tag swiftly regained his feet, checked his weapons and retrieved his cloak as he moved quickly to follow. Behind the clearing ran a small brook, likely sourced from an underground spring nearby. The water moved quickly, running clear and fresh. Alaena and Rince were already lying on rocks that jutted into the water, cupping hands to drink their fill and to wash the grime of their recent ordeal from their faces.

Tag took a moment to share some light rations he had at his belt with the two, who sat up and grabbed at them gratefully, consuming them with ravenous delight, then drank his fill.

Unwilling to break their good mood but aware that pursuit wouldn't be far behind and they had already spent more time than he liked at rest here, Tag stood and pulled his two young charges back into the shadows of the leaves to discuss his plans and emphasise the gravity of the situation they were in.

As Tag outlined his intent, Rince appeared too preoccupied with his joy that Alaena appeared whole and hale to pay too much attention. Alaena, for her part, was much more attentive. Running her hands through her hair to help it dry, she listened carefully as Tag informed them of his intent to continue to travel south towards the mountains until they came to Fyr, hopefully before dark fell if they were not delayed. From there, he told Rince and Alaena that he would arrange to have a message sent to Wilmer to inform her of their situation, though he mentioned nothing of Egan and others with whom he would share the news. While their route would run roughly parallel to the road, they would stay well within the trees to avoid notice by unwanted eyes.

Expecting his stated intent would be accepted without argument, Tag finished and advised the two to fall into line behind him, to step where he stepped and to move as quietly as they could.

Turning to move off, he was surprised when Alaena spoke up quietly but firmly.

"Very well, Tag, we will follow the plan you suggest," she confirmed, then continued in a tone that brooked no argument, "but on the condition that as we travel, you will tell us exactly who Wilmen is, what you have to do with her and how it is that you came to be at the gate just when Rince and I considered our chances of escape ruined."

Looking back over his shoulder, Tag saw Alaena standing with arms crossed as Rince looked from one of them to the other.

Knowing they had no time to argue and aware that Alaena had to find out more about herself soon in any case, Tag capitulated without argument, happy to tell her what she needed to know, if not everything she *wanted* to know, at this stage.

Moving back to the clearing before turning south and making their way into the trees, Tag started to talk in a low voice as they walked. In some strange way, Tag was surprised to realise that he felt honoured to be the first of those that still believed in the return of the Old Ways to truly recognise Alaena for who she was and to be the one to take her through the first awareness of her legacy. He knew now that he must see this precious girl to safety, and that he would gladly give up his life to do so if he must.

Chapter 19 – Lost

Not only did the opportunity for freedom present itself sooner than expected, the nature of the opportunity was, unfortunately, something that Vetren did not anticipate.

Though buried deep under a mountain of rock and imprisoned by the crackling, unassailable force of the Holding, he could nonetheless still feel the path of the pale, yellow sun around which this world circled. He knew that it had passed overhead only twice since he had lost his chance to use the Lane the human sorceress had opened to effect his escape.

Whipping his spiked tail against the Holding in anger, accepting the pain that came from the coruscating backlash of power as his due penance for the lapse, Vetren nursed a coiled and cold hatred for all things human. His centuries of imprisonment had been honed into a violent craving for their destruction with a fervour approaching madness.

For some time after his first failure, Vetren's mind was black with desolate disappointment and an overwhelming and utterly unsated desire for revenge. When he had calmed and come back to himself as much as he could, Vetren replayed the experience in his mind. Even now, just reliving the sheer force of the Power the human female had been able to summon was daunting. Able to isolate that feeling from a cold analysis of the experience now, however, Vetren was able to see where he failed, and hated himself for it even more.

Perhaps his defeat and long imprisonment at the hand of humans before had taken its toll on his spirit. Perhaps it was the fact that another human had appeared without any warning, wielding even greater Power than those who had entrapped him here. Either way, Vetren was forced to face the humiliating fact that he had failed because he had been afraid. His long existence had been threatened with the very real danger of complete immolation and, for the first time since he had fought his way free of his egg, his first instinct had been to back away rather than fight and dominate.

Ashamed, Vetren threw back his scaled head and howled. His forked tongue snaked out in his anguish. Black bile spat from his fangs, sizzling on the walls of the Holding before burning away quickly in sparks of blue flame.

In the past, when worlds had bowed before the armies he commanded, such weakness was never permitted. Rather, with relish, he would have torn the heart from those that displayed such cowardice and sacrificed their tainted carcasses on the fires of the temples he raised to his own name so that the conquered could praise him.

Swearing on the memory of his brood-father, whose blood and life he had consumed to consummate his own ascension to power, with the power of the Holding around him mocking his very desire to be free, Vetren vowed that he would never again show such weakness.

So it was, as he rested on his haunches and chewed on his hate in his cell only two days later, that his hackles rose and he prepared to launch all his resources into the attack. The nature of the Holding around him had changed again and he felt Old Magic active once more in this world. Committed to action, Vetren stood, braced himself and opened his mind wide to accept what would come.

Raising no shield of his own, he risked all to gain everything. If this time, unlike the last, the Power he felt stirring through the Holding was directed at him, his long existence would be instantly extinguished. It would all be over. The deluge of Power he would encounter would burn his mind and his soul away before he even realised it was happening. If his desperate gamble held however, and the young sorceress again laid her talent into the Lanes of this world without first shielding that Power as any apprentice is taught they must, then he would wrest it away from her with ease. Once done, he would obliterate this accursed prison once and for all, then turn this world and all life upon it into the cinder it deserved to be.

The moment he attempted to engage though, he knew something was wrong. As they had been for the centuries he was incarcerated, the Lanes were empty. He could feel them there as always but was unable to manipulate them from within the Holding itself without that external catalyst.

A snarl of rage threatened to spiral out of control as Vetren once more found himself thwarted. Anger built and the impotent desire to rend, tear and destroy almost overwhelmed his mind. With supreme effort, Vetren checked himself. He must not allow his rage and hate free rein now. He had felt the Power and, as he calmed, realised he could still in some fashion feel the flow. This time, the setback was not his doing and he might yet find a way to turn it to his advantage.

Taking a deep breath, the beast folded his tail beneath him, sank back to his haunches and closed his pitch-black eyes as he crouched, concentrating.

The flow he'd felt before was a thriving torrent of active Power. Cascading in blistering waves, it flooded the Lanes with an unfettered, fearful strength. Considering this, Vetren reminded himself the Lanes were simply channels for the Power in and around a planet. They were conduits that allowed the flow of strength, guided by will, to move from source to destination, ultimately manifesting itself as or how the wielder desired.

If the Lanes are empty, Vetren pondered, *then how is it that I can feel the Power flowing?* Forcing back frustration, he pushed further. Never before had he opened himself so completely. The danger both thrilled and terrified his already fractured mind.

The Lanes existed on dimensions parallel to and dependent upon the world on which the Power was being wielded. In the past, his mind had travelled the network of Lanes on many worlds without fear. For regardless of how far his awareness roamed, he knew he could instantly be back in his body at need.

At those times, however, Vetren was his own master. The Power he rode was his own. Here, with the Holding severing his link with his own strength, he was reliant on this strange external force to ride the Lanes. Were it to cut out suddenly, his mind could be cut from his body, never to return. His body would last a while, but eventually die.

Fear once again threatened to overturn Vetren's resolve, but gritting his jaw and pushing his talons hard into the ground, he refused to capitulate.

With the intimate scrutiny of the demented mind, Vetren abandoned all external concern and focused his thoughts on the Power he sensed to track its source. Time passed without result. Far and wide Vetren roamed. He could feel the scourge of humanity around him as he travelled the network of Lanes that surrounded this world, for the veil between dimensions was thin. The temptation to drop out and view the world was strong, but he knew there would be time for that later when he was free. At present, it would only be a diversion, for he had no Power of his own with which to do anything. Once free and Travelling on his own will and strength, not only would he view it but he would luxuriate in its demolition.

Vetren's jaws ground in anticipation of the pleasure he would have taking decades to wreak his revenge when he was free.

It took some time for Vetren to realise he was looking at this the wrong way. He had Travelled far further than was wise, returning to the point from which he began no wiser as to the source of the Power that he could still feel thrumming through the lanes. Finally, it occurred to him that looking wider was not the answer; he had to look deeper!

Altering his approach, Vetren stopped looking for a source, and began to examine the thread of Power itself to see if he could understand its nature.

Immediately, he encountered resistance.

Surprised, for his brief encounter with the girl had certainly indicated no capacity for the creation of such defences, Vetren pushed harder, attempting to find his way in.

Again, he was met with an adamant wall of protection that did not give.

Patience wearing thin, Vetren's anger started to build. He had not come so far and risk so much to be thwarted at this point!

Straining, the Demon Prince summoned all his resources. Driving his will to extremes, Vetren attempted to surround the thread with his own awareness and close his mind upon it, intending to crush it enough to break open a gap wide enough to permit him entry.

Harder and harder he pressed, pushing himself to breaking point as he unfettered his soul and committed it into the link, throwing centuries of unmitigated hate into the fray in an attempt to find entry, for he could bear his imprisonment no longer.

Effortlessly, the Thread resisted his frenzied assault, and ultimately, Vetren's mind broke.

Screaming, shattered, Vetren's pain reverberated through the Lanes as madness took him.

Devoid now of purpose and sanity, his mind retreated back to his body, where his eyes opened to the sight of the Holding. As if he had never tried before, never understood the futility of assault, Vetren threw himself at the Holding anew, venting now mindless rage in unrelenting assault, despite the pain it caused his body as Power responded and threw him violently back time after time. Uncomprehending and devoid of reason now, Vetren's mind remembered and knew only hate.

Interlude 7 - Ancient

Though night had fallen some time ago, the creature moved as easily now as it had when it started its travels the previous day. In the thicker part of the wood where the stars and moon were obscured, it travelled in near blackness on its rear legs, mewling pleasure and communion as segmented limbs touched the foliage it passed. Where it could not see with its round, unblinking gaze, the earth and the trees themselves guided its path so its footing never went astray.

Alert to the voice of the forest, the creature paused for a moment in its relentless, tireless passage north. Something had changed. The creature did not feel human emotion, for it had not been made for such things, though it did experience a sense of completeness as it realised that which it sought had entered the domain of the forest at the northern fringes. Soon, the creature's purpose would be fulfilled. It felt no apprehension at the knowledge that once its purpose was served, it would no longer exist. As it well knew, physical existence was only one form of actuality. Either way, it made no discernible difference to its intent.

Picking up its pace once more, it calculated. The being it tracked was not far now. They would meet before night fell once more on this world. It was not moving, however, so the creature pressed the forest for more information. An undercurrent of pain returned through leaf, bough and root in answer to his question. The being it tracked was injured.

Again, no sorrow or concern touched its consciousness. It merely recognised that this was a situation that needed to be corrected. Pausing once more, the creature pushed its gnarled hands to the ground and dug them in deep, communing with the earth, entreating aid.

For the second time in this world in this past day, after centuries of quiescence, Power responded. This time, the trees themselves answered to light the Lanes, for the creature itself was no sorcerer. To initiate magic required both will and soul, and this creature had neither. Instead, as its creator would have done, it thanked the forest in the old tongue as Power lit the Lanes, directed northward to focus strength and healing at the point where his objective lay.

Satisfied that the being he had waited centuries for would be healed for their encounter, the creature resumed its trek northward, unconcerned that the play of Power in this Lanes of this world was not going unnoticed by others, for that also had nothing to do with its purpose.

Interlude 8 - Priorities

Late in the morning of that same day, as Alaena, Rince and Tag made their way south through the Wytharn Wood and Wilmen and Egan fretted in the Abbey awaiting news of the missing trio, Darven Ross crested a final rise. With great relief, he caught his first glimpse of Morlyn in the distance since he had left Ald the evening before.

Though weary after a hard ride, the sight of Morlyn raised Darven's spirits and his enthusiasm for his quest made him sit straighter in the saddle once more.

His stallion, however, could be pushed no further. Hardy though it was, the beast was slick with sweat, its strength failing. Though every delay grated, Darven had taken the time to rest and water the beast thrice during the ride thus far. Judging the distance a good four or five leagues yet to go, he dismounted and chose to walk awhile. Laying one hand on its trembling withers and taking the reins in the other, he patted it gently and lead the horse awhile, allowing it to rest before a final run to make the city before nightfall, after which he could leave it stabled to recover its strength as he sought news of the One.

Such was his haste, Darven had had little opportunity to talk to fellow travellers on the road, save one merchant. The portly gentleman, ostentatiously garbed despite being on the road, passed by as Darven rested his horse at early light. The man was full of gossip about the burning of the Keep at Morlyn. Suspicious of coincidence, he immediately wondered if this had anything to do with the Prince's stone awakening and asked a number of innocuous questions to elicit more detail. But the man knew little that Darven found of interest, and he eventually went on his way. To all accounts, Darven thought, the Keep had little to do with the more spiritual pursuits of man. Perhaps the two things were unrelated after all.

In any case, he was determined to halt at the Abbey as the Prince had requested, to inform the Abbot that the stone in the Tower of Ald was awake. Though he was unsure what such news had to do with the Morlyn Abbey, the Prince had taken Darven aside before he left and been adamant that this must be his first priority on reaching Morlyn. He intended to see his Prince's wishes done, then pursue the trail of the One as soon as possible. Darven was sure the One would be someone unique, a man who stood out in the crowd, and should be easy to find.

Bringing him to Ald would be an entirely different story; while Darven hoped he would go willingly, go he must and Darven knew he would find a way.

Interlude 9 – Anticipation

The minion cowered low, delivering its report. Mewling pathetically, it spread segmented arms wide and pressed its forehead in obeisance hard against the black, blood-stained throne room floor as Kahu leapt up in gleeful astonishment at the news it delivered.

Kahu took a huge, heavy step forward and reached a massive taloned hand down to the cowering underling. His scaled, elongated digits wrapped easily around the slave's throat, talons digging cruelly into its neck as he stood, effortlessly lifting it from the floor to dangle helplessly before him as he looked straight into its terrified eyes.

Looking deeper, Kahu delved into its mind to understand the information in full as the fiend's life choked away. While it was a far easier and much more accurate way to get the detail, the Demon King also enjoyed feeling the underling die as he did so.

By the time he threw the lifeless husk away, Kahu had all he needed. As the body was taken away to feed the fires, he considered what he had learnt.

The information he had stripped from the underling's mind was surprisingly detailed. Vetren had travelled the Lanes on a planet that was many years travel from Leraje, the Demon home world. At such a distance, even with the power of the First Key behind them, his mystics would usually have had trouble discerning information so accurately. It appeared, however, that Vetren had not only spent a considerable time in the Lanes of that world, he had done so with few if any protections raised.

Kahu paused to shake his head and lean forward as he pondered, his long, barbed tail weaving dangerous patterns in the air behind him. He growled once more, making the few creatures that awaited his orders in the throne room look his way with trepidation, but his thoughts were worlds away.

Without being in physical proximity, his mind could not be read, but without protections in place Kahu Pyra's mystics had been able to discern Vetren's surface thoughts. The gaps were frustratingly delicious. Unconsciously, Kahu's fangs began to release dark drops of venom.

Vetren had been trapped for hundreds of years, but they could not see who had trapped him. He was searching the Lanes for something, something he strove desperately to attain, but without success. They could not tell what it was. He was a Demon Prince of extreme power, yet he did not or could not utilise it to achieve his objective, but they could not tell why.

Importantly, the world was indeed rich. A bead of venom dripped free, rolling over his lips and marking a deeper stain down his dark red jowls. Kahu's genitals hardened beneath their scaled sheath, as they always did when a new prospect appeared. While the detail was not known, Vetren's lust for the abundant flesh and fodder of this world was apparent.

Flicking a clawed finger towards an underling, Kahu ordered a legion commander be found to appear before him immediately so that plans could be made.

This would be a particularly pleasing diversion that Kahu would relish, for he had found both an enemy to be vanquished and world to be conquered!

Chapter 20 - Necromancer

The Protector stirred in his bed.

With the sun approaching its zenith, the day was warming considerably and the room becoming stuffy. Under covers pulled too high, his first thought was of discomfort caused by the heat. Automatically, still slumbering, he lifted his arms to push the cloying covers from his heavy, muscled frame.

With the movement, pain lanced his muddled mind. Bright lights swum in his vision. New torment washed through his soul as he tried to open his eyes and spears of burning hurt radiated from his left eye all around his face. Crying out in shocked agony, the Protector couldn't understand why it felt like he was looking straight into the sun, even though he had his eyes clenched as tightly closed as he could. Shying back into the sweat-matted sheets beneath him, The Protector tried to gather his thoughts and comprehend the source and volume of the pain he was experiencing.

A few moments later, he felt a damp, cool cloth touch his forehead, accompanied by a gentle, soothing voice telling him to rest back and not to worry as all would be well. Relaxing his body slightly as instructed, the pain localising now to a throbbing torture radiating from the left-hand side of his face, the Protector reached up weakly to grasp the hand that tended him. He felt a slim wrist pull back briefly, as if avoiding his touch. The Protector tightened his grip, not aware yet what he needed, only that he didn't want the woman to stop soothing some of the hurt from his face just yet.

"M'lord." The voice spoke again, accompanied by a slight tremble. The Protector could feel her feebly attempting to wrest her wrist away from his grasp. His iron grip didn't shift. "I'm glad you're awake, m'lord," she said from a distant place beyond his pain. "You've been sorely hurt, m'Lord!"

She tugged harder against his grip.

"M'Lord," she implored, "let me fetch the healer for you, m'Lord. He'll know what to do!"

Her tugging was starting to irritate. The Protector had enough hurt inside his head to bring down a mountain, and the last thing he needed was some fool woman rocking him and making the whole thing worse.

With supreme effort, The Protector pulled the resisting woman a little closer to him. "Quiet, woman," he ordered in a harsh, dry whisper.

Immediately, the yammering halted, though he could feel her trembling. Still, he avoided opening his eyes, aware that something was terribly wrong with his left eye and unwilling to subject himself to more pain without being ready for it.

Lying as sill as he could, the Protector marshalled his thoughts and pushed the pain away. He needed to understand what was happening before he could act.

"Tell me what happened," he grunted through his darkness. "Where am I?"

The Protector had her close now, keeping a firm grip on her wrist as she knelt on the floor beside the unfamiliar bed on which he lay. Marginally, he eased the pressure on her slim wrist, allowing her fear to retreat so she might relate her tale.

For the first few moments, the Protector failed to connect her story through his pain. His head throbbed horribly, and he grasped only snippets of detail as she rambled through her tale, trailing to a close with the information that the Keep Healer and Master Hetar had brought him here and left him in her charge, then returned to the Keep where both were needed.

Slowly, he pieced it together. A fire had broken out in the Keep and he had been brought here on a litter. He couldn't remember any fire, though, nor could he recall being brought from the Keep to Morlyn. One thing she made clear though was that his wounds were not the result of the fire. So, how had he been injured?

Memory came suddenly, like a wall giving before a torrent of water. His grip on the woman's arm tightened and she whimpered pathetically as he pulled himself up in the bed, white-hot anger burning past the pain the movement caused him.

That girl. That calculating, conniving, witch of a girl. He had been close to breaking her, and somehow she had turned a knife on him. Bright light had exploded in his vision as a knife took his eye, then all had gone dark as the poker had swung at his head.

While the Protector had many enemies and had taken pleasure in arranging their ruin and demise, this was the first time such hurt had been visited on him by another. The fact that it was merely a girl who had done this to him only increased his anger.

Rage burnt hot in him, and revenge pounded for release behind his ravaged eye. Already he could hear her screams in his mind, and he savoured the pain she would feel as he placed hot coals on her own eyes, burning them slowly from her skull. She would know the pain she had visited on him many times over before she died.

Lost in this fantasy of delicious revenge, allowing it to push back the pain he felt, it took a few moments for the Protector to return to the present where the woman he still held was sobbing and begging, trying to wriggle from his grasp.

"Silence!" he spat towards her as he opened his good eye a crack to get his first glimpse of her. The light pushed another wash of pain across him, but he forced himself to assess her. She wasn't young, which was a shame, but at least she looked healthy. She would do, he thought absently, as he tightened his grip.

Usually, the Protector would gloat over his prey when its time came, but he was too weary and his need too urgent to play out and enjoy the preliminaries this time. His grip secure, the Protector cleared his mind, allowing the pain to drain away as he called up Power.

In the years he had been hunting and cleansing the realm of Witches, the Protector had learnt much. In many instances, the men and women he had captured and accused of sorcery clearly had no power or even knowledge of power to claim. Those he immediately recognised as useless. These who served no purpose were raped or tortured or both, often given as gifts for favoured Guard to enjoy before eventually being executed for the pleasure of the crowd or, for particularly young and attractive boys or girls, kept alive for some time longer for his own private pleasure.

Those few whose capacity for Power had become apparent as the Protector broke mind and spirit, however, he found particularly useful. These he kept for himself and never them wasted on public spectacle.

How ironic, he had often considered, that those executed in the Square for witchcraft were actually the ones who had no talent in the Art at all.

The Protector learnt from his victims before they died, stripping detail from their minds using a dark art long ago mastered. Those that considered their art pure rarely gave him much other than the value of their life force as they perished one way or another. Those that had blacker hearts, however, the Protector had an affinity for and learned much from. One witch, who named herself Onyx after the dark stone of her birth, had delved deeper than many others in the dark arts and taught him one very useful skill before her heart burst in her chest.

Focusing his eye on the woman before him, the Protector wove his mind into hers, pleased for once that this particular woman had no talent and, as such, no means of protecting her mind. In his weakened state, a shielded mind would cause him difficulty. With this woman, it required no effort at all.

"*Moriemini et de anima vestra*," he murmured as he worked. "You must die and give up your soul." The words themselves weren't important; they merely helped him focus. Though with no Art herself, there were no obstacles to overcome. The Protector saw her mind and could feel it shrinking from his as he delved deeper and obliterated her life as he would an insect beneath his foot. Her name was Juli and the fact that her husband and three sons would never see her alive again was of no interest or concern to the Protector at all.

Her struggling stopped as her mind gave out and the Protector took possession of her being. The room grew dark, and strangled whispers flitted amongst the shadows as he worked his Art, channelling Juli's life force into his own body. In minutes, it was done. Through the thick curtains, light reluctantly seeped back into the room as the Protector let his spell fall, lying his head back against the pillow for a moment to recover his composure and let the whispers fade.

As strength returned, the Protector thought back to his youth. Son of a minor noble in the King's court, he had chosen to apprentice with the court magicians. The King had always thought highly of them and their powers. He had been impatient to learn from the outset though, and dismissive of those he deemed too timid to attempt real power. His mentor, an elderly sorcerer in the King's Guild whose name he barely recalled now, taught protection, care and caution as a primary tenet of what he termed the Practice of the Arts.

Dukar, as the Protector had been known in his youth, viewed this approach with both disdain and dislike. Shunning such caution as the legacy of weakness and age, the young Dukar experimented more and more in his private hours with darker paths that promised much greater reward. One night, a spell he had attempted to see if he could influence the minds of those around him almost ended in catastrophe. Having weaved the barest of protections before raising his power, the spell had failed. Frustrated, Dukar had reattempted the incantation immediately, unaware that the inadequate defences he had woven at first had degraded and holes in his shield existed. The moment he committed Power to his second attempt, the voices that usually were mere distractions in the background came howling through to shred his concentration and overwhelm his mind. His spell in tatters, Dukar frantically attempted to disengage, but other minds were already in control of his and would not allow him to let go. Panic took Dukar as an image formed in his mind: a slathering, slavering demonic form, black venom dripping from its elongated jowls, approaching him as it battered his mind with visions of Dukar's imminent evisceration.

Moments before he was consumed, a blinding crack of light had burned through Dukar's mind, severing the connection. A sharp concussive force threw his physical form back through the room to slam against the far wall, where he blacked out for a while. He regained consciousness to the sound of shouting outside and the heavy surge of Power in the air. A few moments later, the door to his room exploded inwards, splinters of wood peppering the room and the terrified Dukar, who thought the demon had returned again to take him. Instead, staves glowing with power, two of his mentor's colleagues leapt into the room, robes flying about them and ready for battle.

There, framed by the rectangular splash of illumination flooding the room through the ruined doorway, lay his mentor. The body was a burnt husk, the robes still smoking. Dukar could only shake his head at the accusing stares levelled at him by the two sorcerers, as he did over the coming weeks to all those who accused him of dabbling in the black arts. Finally, judged by a panel of those he thought beneath him, Dukar was expelled from the Capital to the far flung north. A Keep where he could do no further harm in a backwater called Morlyn.

The Protector chuckled briefly. After that night he had promised himself he would never raise Power again without first setting the appropriate wards in place. Yet here he had done so again in need, albeit briefly, and somehow escaped harm once more. The whispers that usually threaded the blackness behind his spells weren't even there this time, so perhaps the attention of those beings was elsewhere at present. This was something he might ponder later, but for the moment the Protector had more urgent things in the physical world to attend to.

Unclenching his fist at last, he released his hold on the arm of the woman whose life force he had just taken to replenish his own diminished resources. The dry, lifeless limb thudded onto the carpeted floor and the Protector reached up to his face, hands feeling his features. Still closed, his right eye felt whole, as did that side of his face.

The left side was a different matter. While the woman's vitality had sufficed to heal him considerably, the wounds were still tender. His fingers traced scars and twisted skin along a gash across his forehead before gently probing the puckered skin now covering the ruin of his left eye socket. His eye being gouged from his head completely, it could not be healed. Anger returned along with his hate. That girl would pay for this, he promised himself once more.

Completing the cursory examination of his face, the Protector stretched his limbs. As far as he could tell, the rest of his body was fine. It was time to move. Tentatively, the Protector opened his right eye once more. The room was dim, but no longer did the light hurt. Pushing himself up to a sitting position, he gave the room a moment to steady as he regained equilibrium. Moving carefully to get used to his balance with only one eye, he swung his feet off the bed to the floor where the body of the woman lay. Grimacing with distaste, the Protector kicked the corpse out of the way so he could stand slowly, stretching his neck, shoulders and back as he did so to work the blood back into them.

There were no clothes in the room other than those he had been transported here in. His trousers weren't too abhorrent, but his shirt was a mess of dried blood, dirt and straw. A reminder of what he owed the witch when he had her back in his hands. Some minutes later, dressed once more, the Protector surveyed the room and realised he must attend to one more detail before making his way back to the Keep and to find that girl. Glancing at the greying shell of the desiccated corpse, he resisted a sigh. Not yet fully recovered, he had no wish to waste any strength on tasks unrelated to his main priorities, but he was in no mood to answer questions people might ask about the presence or state of a body found in his room following what would doubtless be considered his remarkable recovery. Before he could venture out, then, he would sort out this last detail.

Moving back to the bed, the Protector knelt beside the body. As with others he had drained, it had a dry, grey look to it. The eyes had sunk into the skull, and the skin had the kind of look you'd expect to see in the earth of a dry riverbed that had baked in the sun too long. Cracked, moistureless, lifeless. *Ah, well,* he thought as he bent his head in concentration, then gave her life no more thought.

With practiced ease, the dark space where the Protector worked his Art opened up in his mind's eye as the physical world faded around him. Creased carpet and worn wardrobes dimmed as the Protector thrilled once again at the endless space that opened up in his mind. This place, the Protector firmly believed, promised equally boundless opportunity to the determined soul. Quietly but succinctly pronouncing the words that guided his work, this time he took care in establishing wards around his awareness first, noting again the strange absence of whispers in the void.

"*Primus. Secundus. Tertius. Quartus.*"

Translucent spheres, obsidian black and sparkling with dark energy, formed quickly at four points around his incantation. With a practiced and decisive thought, the Protector completed the ward. Lines of power sprung out from each defensive point to join the others, then arced outwards in each direction to form a sphere of power. Looking about with his mind's eye, the Protector nodded in satisfaction and took a mental breath before the next step. The net of wards formed a perfect sphere about him of hissing, crackling Power. Should any entity outside his ward seek ingress, they would rue the attempt.

Secure in his space, the Protector moved quickly now. This was a spell he knew well and had performed often to rid himself of unwanted baggage, yet he was still relatively weak and well aware his body was kneeling next to a corpse in a room that anyone in the physical world might enter at any moment. For both reasons, he wasted no further time before raising his next incantation.

Pushing the thread of power he maintained to keep the wards intact to the back of his mind, the Protector started to weave another spell. "*Et ecce foramen unum in spatio.*" The words flowed easily, though a bead of sweat traced his brow with the effort. In his mind's eye, within the safety of his sphere, tendrils of force began to coalesce and spin. Coaxing it carefully, the Protector allowed more power to flow from his mind into the construct, kneading and expanding the lines of power. With his own reserves draining quickly, the Protector permitted himself a mental sigh of relief when he was done. In the void, surrounded by his sphere, a ring of force hung, gently spinning in the nothingness, spitting sparks and locked to his Art. With the spell complete, the Protector tied that thread off in his mind, pushing it back so he could focus on the final and most dangerous piece of this particular exercise.

Without letting go of the spells he had wrought, the Protector began to push his mind away from the void. Slowly, his room in Morlyn came into view, dimly seen through the veil of darkness of the void. Balancing his progress carefully, the Protector moved far enough back that he could see the body of the woman lying before him on the carpet as the void surrounded him with his sparkling, circular construct still floating before him. This close to his physical form once more, the Protector almost faltered. His body, pressed by injury and not yet recovered, was exhausted. He could feel that tiredness leech palpably to his mind, already overworked from maintaining two spells in the void and pushing this third onto his final form.

Gritting his teeth mentally as well as physically now, the Protector refused to give into weakness. He had not come so far to be undone by such a simple thing as the disposal of a body. A few determined moments later, the feeling passed. Rallying his resources, the Protector focused on the ring of power he had conjured, turning and twisting it to shape, positioning it directly over the lifeless husk of the woman lying on the floor of his bedchamber. At last, he had it where it needed to be and stabilised the construct. Then, with a final, decisive punch of force, the Protector connected the ring in the void to the physical plane for the briefest time. A rush of air in the room ruffled curtains and candles alike. In that moment, the black of the void consumed the room then vanished as reality snapped back and the Protector gratefully let his threads of power dissipate.

The corpse was gone, as were his spells. A preternatural calm set over the room. Wiping an unsteady hand across his brow, the Protector sat heavily on the bed, gathering his strength for a moment, along with his thoughts.

Wishing he could lie back and rest awhile to fully recover, the Protector prepared to stand once more. The sounds from the street leaked through the drawn curtains. It was hot in the room, and though the curtains were thick, light glowed about the edges. Clearly, he was in Morlyn town. It would likely be early in the afternoon, then, he surmised, with the summer sun near its peak. The sea was a distant smell, and the noises floating up to him were of horses with single riders rather than carts with creaking wheels; he must be somewhere within the upper quarter.

His remaining eye squirted. What had that woman said? Something about a healer? Of course. It had been the middle of the night when that witch whelp had taken his eye and left him for dead. They wouldn't have waited to fetch a healer to the Keep. Hetar, and possibly Uré would have taken him directly to Penther's quarters above his apothecary. He recalled mention of a fire as well, but that would have to wait. For now, he needed to get to the Keep so he could see the fear in the eyes of that girl.

Chapter 21 - Pursuit

Pushing himself to his feet, the Protector took a last moment to steady himself, then strode across the room and flung the door open. Annoyed that he had to hold onto the old handrail as he descended the stairs, he nonetheless made the lower level without incident. From here, his mouth started watering as he smelled fresh bread. Rather than making straight for the street to find a horse and make his way back to the Keep, he walked forward, following the smell into the kitchen of the house.

The kitchen was dominated by a large oak bench in the centre of the room, at which Penther sat, broodily nibbling a slice of bread that had been cut from a new loaf sitting on a platter on the table. He looked up slowly, blinking in surprise at the figure in the doorway. A moment later his chair flew backwards, clattering against a large stove further back against the wall as Penther jumped to his feet, spluttering.

"My ... my Lord," he exclaimed in disbelief, wide eyes scanning the impossibly upright figure before him. Taking a deep breath, Penther took a step towards the Protector. He continued to mouth words that wouldn't come, his hand extended and shaking as if terrified that, should he touch the apparition, it would disappear entirely.

Ignoring his discomfort and wasting no time with pleasantries, the Protector moved into the room and took another stool, sitting heavily and tilting his head towards the bread. "Shut your mouth, Penther, and cut me some of that loaf," he ordered gruffly. "I need to know what's been happening before I head back to the Keep."

Penther, all awry, moved to the table. While his hands reached for the bread, his eyes continued to track the Protector. "My Lord," he queried, taking up a knife to hack off a portion of the loaf before him. "Forgive me, but I am at a loss! Only a short while ago you were dying before me, yet here you stand – and your eye!" Penther licked his lips nervously, as though realising he was approaching dangerous ground but unable to pass it by. "Your eye was a ruin, My Lord, yet the wound now is closed and, dare I say, healed over!" His hands stilled as the knife cut through to the board beneath and he leaned forward to take a closer look. "How is this possible, My Lord?"

Brusquely, uninterested in engaging in conversation with Penther, let alone discussing the apparent miracle of his recovery, the Protector took a moment to tear a chunk of bread from the fresh loaf and savour the taste as he watched the nervous healer with his good eye. Magic always took a great deal of strength, and draining souls, the Protector pondered briefly as he chewed, just did not do the same for the body as the physical act of consuming food.

"So," the Protector growled through his mouthful. Penther started at the staccato syllable. "Clearly my wounds were not as grievous as they first appeared, which is a good thing, do you not agree?"

Penther merely nodded his head while his mind's eye revisited the open wreck of a wound he had examined in detail only a short while ago, pronouncing his opinion that he thought it unlikely the Protector would last to the morning before Hetar made his way back to the Keep.

"Indeed," the Protector muttered, pleased that Penther wasn't going to waste his time with needless questions.

Pulling another chunk from the loaf with thick, scarred fingers, the Protector used the piece of bread to articulate his next point, stabbing it in the air towards Penther to accentuate each word. "Now. Get me some wine and tell me all that's happened since that wench attacked me." Scowling, irritated further by the puckered skin pulling across his left eye as it stretched, the Protector ripped another bite from the bread and added almost as an afterthought, "I want to get back to the Keep and find out just what that witch is hiding from me."

The sound of Penther's sharp inhale pulled the Protector's attention back to the healer. Penther had moved back to fetch a glass and flagon from the cupboard at the far side of the kitchen and now appeared frozen, staring at the Protector as if he had seen another ghost. Face pale, he was staring as if the only thing he wanted to do in the world was run screaming from the room.

Puzzled and still too tired to muster anger, the Protector sighed and took another moment to swallow the last chunk of bread with relish before reaching out a hand.

"Penther," the Protector said with eroding patience. "Wake up, man. Give me that wine and tell me what has you so out of sorts."

The basic request pulled Penther from his trance. With a shaking hand, he finished pouring the goblet and took a few steps towards the Protector, placing it carefully in his outstretched grip before stepping back one pace, then two.

Clutching the edge of the heavy table as though to steady himself, Penther launched into his report. "M'lord. I'm sorry. You don't know, of course." Licking his lips, he took another step back from the Protector. "Last night, m'lord, even as we brought you to safety here in Morlyn, fire all but destroyed the Protectorate Keep!"

The Protector stiffened, the goblet halfway to his lips. The woman had told him of a fire in the Keep, but his single eye widened as Penther's words struck home.

Fearful of the Protector's reaction, Penther finished quickly, even as he took another step backward. "Hetar returned to the Keep when word came in the early hours of the morning. I have not seen it myself, m'lord, as I was here caring for you, but news this morning is that the Keep is all but ruined from the blaze!" He finished in a rush, bumping up against a cupboard, unable to retreat further from the black hate that was twisting the features of the Protector. The puckered flesh on his ruined eye socket was turning a ghastly red, and the veins on his temples were pulsing with anger.

The Protector surged to his feet, the goblet in his hand shattering as he threw it aside and strode around the table towards Penther, blood in his gaze.

As he raised an arm to grasp Penther by the neck and wring the full story from the terrified healer, the Protector stopped, the healer's earlier words seeping through at last. Fire took the keep as the Protector was brought here, which meant that the fire and his injury much also have occurred around the same time. "That girl!" he exclaimed into Penther's blank face. That witch, he thought, more accurately. *She* was doubtless responsible. He had to get back to the Keep.

The Protector whirled and bolted for the door, shoving it savagely and snapping a hinge as he barged through, leaving the door hanging askew after his departure.

Hands shaking, Penther stood for a moment more, holding firm to the staunch solidity of the stove behind him as the sound of crashing doors and furniture unfortunate enough to be between the Protector and the streets of Morlyn moved into the distance. When the sounds finally faded, Penther mustered the courage to let go of the stove and make his way back to the table, where he gathered up the flagon left there. Not bothering with niceties, he put the bottle to his lips and upended it and took a long draft.

In the street, people scattered as the madman with one eye and torn, bloodied clothing broke screaming from the Healer's into the street. They need not have feared, however, for his mind was far from the mundane issues of the citizenry of Morlyn. At a dead run, the man took off across the street to reach a horse tethered nearby, pulling the reins free of the stake and leaping up to the saddle, ignoring the yells of the merchant who came running to accost the thief, to no avail.

Upon the horse, the Protector wrenched the reins, pulling the head of the beast towards the Keep as he dug his heels brutally into the animal's flanks. "Yah!" the Protector screamed, urging the beast to motion. The beast took off at a gallop, bolting for the Keep.

Careering around and through people, wagons and trade alike, the Protector only halted for a moment as he crested the hill and took his first full view of the Keep. One side of the structure was gutted by fire. Curls of smoke still arose from the ruin. Anger gave way to hatred at the sight, and the Protector once again put heel and leather to the horse, pounding towards the gates.

Guard at the gate drew weapons as the madman approached, unaware that the bedraggled figure atop the beast hurtling towards them was indeed their own Protector. Such was the furious force and pace of the whirlwind coming towards them that even with steel drawn, they gave way and gave entrance, lest they be run down themselves by the wild-eyed animal being driven with such fury or madness, they couldn't tell which.

The guards' mouths were open with disbelief as the horse dashed past them without pause, the figure atop looking neither right nor left as he urged it on without surcease. Looking at each other with amazement, the Guard either side of the gates stared at each other for a moment as dust swirled about them, wondering what new madness this was. As one, they turned and bolted into the gates, taking chase to the rider as he careered into the courtyard, towards the ruined remains of the inner Keep.

A cloud of black dust billowed around the madman as he pulled hard on the reins before the steps to the Keep. Startled and snorting in pain as the bit sank deep into its mouth, the terrified animal all but threw the rider from its back as its hooves skidded on the hard ground to halt its forward motion as Guard closed in around the strange rider. Before the beast had steadied itself, the Protector threw the leather aside and leapt to the ground in one fluid movement. The sharp ring of sword points that quickly surrounded the interloper wavered briefly, then were sheathed quickly as the Protector stepped forward, barking with a voice and command that was unmistakable.

"Get me whoever here is in charge and have them meet me in the cells," the Protector ordered to no one in particular as he strode up the stairs to the Keep and into the corridor before the Great Hall. The only indication he'd registered the collapsed corridor to his right at all was a deepening of the frown on his forehead as he spun left to make his way down the stairs to the dungeons.

The anger he felt at the desecration of his Keep was nothing compared to the white-hot hate he felt for the Witch that had harmed him. *Burn the King's palace to the ground for all I care,* he thought to himself as he passed through the guardroom and into the corridor of cells. *Just let me have my hands around her neck so I can pull the soul out of her and make her watch while I do it!*

The Protector came to the cell where he had held the girl such a short, destructive while ago. An oath snapped free from his throat as he grabbed the handle, turned and pushed to no avail. The door was locked. "Damn it all to Hell and back!"

Aware that the guardroom had not been manned as he passed through, the Protector declined to waste further time going to fetch or find keys himself. Raising one hand, he turned back to the door and spoke in a low, guttural tongue. Closing his good eye, he focused his energy on a point before him, settling the focus of his power on the centre of the door. Still not fully recovered, it took him a few moments to concentrate his strength but finally, the torches set in sconces along the wall wavered as the light seemed to drain away from them. Mist touched the Protector's breath as he spoke the last syllable and pushed his hand away from him towards the stout oak door.

The door disintegrated, exploding inwards with concussive force. Splinters of oak and shards of iron went flying across the room to spatter against the far wall and bury themselves deep in the straw covering the floor. Opening his eye, the Protector allowed himself a flicker of a smile as he wiped a slick of sweat from his brow. His lust for violence temporarily was sated. What he'd done to the door would be nothing to what he would do the girl who had somehow contrived to escape his Keep.

Stepping through, the Protector focused his consciousness once more, waving his hand in the dimness. As one, the torches and braziers burst to life, flame washing the room with light and showing that little had changed since he was last here. Dominating the centre of the cell, the rack still sat, mocking him with his failure. Further into the room, the poker she had used to club him down still lay on the floor, taunting him with his failing. The knife though, the instrument of his greatest hurt, remained elusive.

The Protector was still kicking straw aside to find the weapon when Uré stepped into the room, a set of keys dangling useless from his hand. His eyes scanned the empty doorframe only briefly, as if endeavouring to avoid the fact that there had been a solid, iron-bound door there only a short while ago.

"My Lord," Uré murmured, pulling the attention of the Protector towards him. From the other end of the room, the Protector looked his way. Uré resisted a sharp intake of breath. Only last night, he had seen the Protector bundled into a cart and taken away to the city, his face lacerated and his eye socket spilling profligate amounts of blood. Even in his most optimistic assessments, Uré considered it likely that it would be some weeks, if at all, before he would see the Protector in the Keep again. Yet, against all expectation, here he was. That same blood still caked the Protector's face but it was dried and black, staining his face in the flickering light with a wraith's gaunt, shadowed visage. Where there was an eye before, however, there was now a puckered, pink swathe of scar tissue, pulling the skin around it tight and distorting the Protector's features. The one good eye looked wild. Stretched, tense lines etched every movement of the Protector's frame. Whatever Uré did here, he knew he must step carefully. Uré had walked the parapets earlier, gleefully anticipating his control of the Keep once he could bring the troublesome Hetar into line. He had seen the Protector's wounds and believed them mortal. So much so that he had not believed the Guard at first when advised that the Protector had returned, yet he could not deny his own eyes. Uré tried to put his fear aside and strode purposefully towards him.

"Where is she?" The Protector demanded as he approached, flinging his arms wide as if to encompass the whole of Morlyn in his query. Straw dust flew as he strode towards the hole where the door once stood and Uré now stood, watching his approach with increasing concern. Practically screaming with rage, as if Uré was directly responsible for his pain, the Protector came to a halt suddenly, stopping a finger-length from Uré's face, shouting directly into it. "What have you done with her?"

For one of the few times in his life, Uré was truly afraid. He had no answer for his Lord, who was clearly not in his own mind. Other than knowing the Protector had been questioning a Witch the evening before when the fire broke out, Uré wasn't even sure who the 'she' was he was talking about. In a surreal, detached part of his mind, even while trying to frame an answer, Uré noted that the puckered skin covering the Protector's ruined eye was laced with veins, pulsing with dark blood.

Steeling himself, Uré tried to calm his voice and survive the encounter. Dissembling would be of no use here, Uré felt intuitively. The only thing he could do was say what he knew, and deflect the Protector's focus to others. Let the Protector's rage come down on shoulders other than Uré's.

"M'Lord," he mumbled, taking just a half step backward to gain himself some semblance of distance. The Protector allowed him the luxury, though his eye remained fixed on his House Master. Unnervingly, the Protector seemed to be mumbling under his breath in a language that Uré didn't recognise. Uré continued, having more and more trouble getting the words out. "The Witch that was here last night escaped in the chaos of the fire. Our minds have been focused on the blaze itself and rescuing what we could of the Keep rather than escaped prisoners, but I've had a tracker out since last night to follow her!"

Uré blurted out what he knew, not knowing if it would suffice or if it would save him. He could feel the air in the cell growing colder, though there was no reason for it to be doing so. The light of the torches seemed to be failing as well. With every word he spoke, his breath ran out. He seemed unable to replenish each syllable.

"The tracker hasn't returned, m'Lord. We are awaiting his word!" Uré gasped in the suddenly frigid atmosphere, his voice rising to a squeak, his throat closing over as he tried to release the last of the information. "The Guard on the servant's gate was killed, m'Lord!"

The Protector stared a moment longer, holding Uré's gaze. That pronouncement was interesting, for if the Witch escaped that way, she must have had help. For a moment the air was still, as if a decision was being made, then the light flowed back into the room. Suddenly, the pressure eased and Uré gasped in relief.

As if nothing had occurred, the Protector spun on his heel, resuming his search of the room. Behind him, Uré put a hand on the cool stone of the wall to balance himself.

"Is the Great Hall still of use?" the Protector asked as he moved about the room.

Surprised at the normality of the question, the House Master rallied somewhat. "It is, m'Lord," Uré pronounced with a little more confidence, pleased the conversation was moving on as the warmth flowed back into his bones. "What do you require?"

The Protector looked back towards Uré, his one eye blinking somehow all the more disturbing. "Get ten of our best Guard and three trackers in the Great Hall immediately. Have horses prepared for all including myself," he ordered perfunctorily. "We ride within the hour."

"As you request, m'Lord," Uré said as he bowed low, even though the Protector was paying no attention to him now. Taking the cue, Uré gratefully took a few steps towards the doorway, carefully avoiding a prolonged glance at the ruined, twisted remains of the iron hinges. He disappeared into the corridor, took a deep breath to recover himself fully, then took off up the corridor, robes flying behind him. If the Protector wanted to leave the Keep, Uré would certainly do all he could to hasten that event!

The Protector remained in the cell for a short while before giving up. The knife wasn't here. Cursing in frustration, he left to organise the chase. Possessions often held echoes of the owner and, with the knife, the Protector may have been able to glean more about this girl that would have been of benefit. No matter, he thought, as he passed through the empty doorway to make his way back to the upper Keep. His trackers were the best in the land. He would find her the hard way, and make her pay all the more for his trouble.

Within the hour, all in the Keep were well aware that the Protector had returned, and all were afraid. Clearly there were unnatural forces at work here, and only those who were to travel with him were anything but pleased to know the Protector would soon be leaving again.

Having questioned those who were at the Keep the night before in detail, the Protector had hints but frustratingly few facts about what had occurred. No one had seen the witch leave and no one knew how the fire had started, though there were questions about a sandy-haired boy who had been replenishing the wood stores. He had, very conveniently the Protector thought, also vanished. Uré, the fool, had let the wench who knew anything about him die before finding out that the boy had not returned home and had

211

apparently disappeared too. No believer in coincidence, The Protector considered that he would happily give his other eye if one did not have something to do with the other!

Now aware of them both, the Protector was comfortable he could deal with both the witch and the boy. All he had to do was find them.

One other item bothered him considerably, however, for he had taken the time to also examine the body of the Guard who was killed. The bolt that had taken his life was a clean, professional shot. Two children were one thing, but that bolt meant they were being assisted by someone who was far more of a threat. He had been advised that the tracks of three people had been found winding through the woods next to the Keep and down to the road towards The Spine, which meant they would likely be tracking them into woods or the hills beyond. Neither were ideal environments for tracking someone who could pick people off at a distance with a crossbow.

Never a patient man and far less so now, the Protector resisted the urge to stay and gather more information. Every moment's delay meant his quarry was further away, so there was no time to lose.

With the briefest of discussion, the Protector gathered his Guard and took to the road in the mid-afternoon light. Setting a brisk pace, the Protector's trackers loped ahead of the heavy fall of the horses' hooves on the hard-packed road. Heads low, they scanned the ground carefully, looking for entrances to the forest where their quarry may have taken to the trees.

Chapter 22 - Matriarch

News of the Protector's return spread through Morlyn faster than the fire had spread in the Keep the previous evening. Many prayers were raised to gods and spirits for protection, and the Abbey was soon inundated with supplicants seeking surety that their souls were safe. Few believed there was anything good about the Protector's miraculous recovery.

Wilmen, who had passed the night in the Abbey rather than risk returning to the Chandler's, which may be watched by now, was with Egan when there was a soft, respectful knock at the door to his study.

"Enter," said Egan, reaching for his water as Otho, Egan's assistant, entered with a bow of his head. A sober, balding man in his late thirties, Otho had a look of disorganisation that was misleading. Wilmen was well aware that Otho had a sharp mind with a memory for detail that Egan relied on heavily to maintain the day-to-day routines and function of the Abbey.

"Abbot. Lady Wilmen," Otho greeted them formally as he entered the room, continuing on as Egan nodded in welcome. "There is news of some concern I believe you should be aware of." In typical fashion, Otho concisely recounted the facts as he knew them. "Morlyn is unsettled. As you know, the Protector was grievously harmed during the blaze at the Keep and was taken to the healer here in the city for what all believed was his final journey." A frown creased his brow and he seemed to be puzzled by the news himself. "It appears, however, that his wounds were not as severe as first assumed. Indeed, the Protector himself appeared at the gates of the Keep on horseback, alive and well, though in a dishevelled state of mind and appearance."

As one, Egan and Wilmen sat forward, dumbfounded as Otho summarised his clipped account.

"It is not known how this has happened, but the rumour of witchcraft is rife and people are afraid. They are turning to the Abbey for support and assurance." As if this were as simple as asking if the Abbot would like some tea for himself and his guest, Otho queried succinctly, "What would you like me to tell them?"

213

Egan glanced at Wilmen, who just looked back, equally shocked. If Otho were making some kind of jest, the point clearly eluded them both. Turning back to Otho, Egan ignored his question and pressed for more.

"Alive and well you say, Otho? Both Wilmen and I saw his wounds and would consider any recovery, let alone one so swift and complete, a highly unlikely consequence!" Egan had difficulty keeping his voice level and framing the right questions. "How is it that you came by this news? Do you really think it true, or is it just market gossip that has run amok?"

"If it is just gossip I would be surprised, Abbot," Otho answered implacably. "The Guard themselves are troubled and talking of the Protector's return with some fear." Almost as an afterthought, Otho added, "While his reappearance at the Keep seems to be true, I am not convinced as to his state. Some say he was covered in blood. Other reports name him horribly disfigured with just one staring eye. I have heard enough – and there are enough people at the gates and in the chapel begging for sanctuary from evil – to lend weight to the story, Abbot. Whether the latter stories are wild fancies or based in fact, I cannot say."

Otho fell silent once more, awaiting the Abbot's direction.

Glancing once more at Wilmen, who looked as if she might throw up on his floor, Egan calmed himself to deal with the immediate problem at hand.

"Thank you, Otho. I cannot deny that this is strange news, yet our people must be our first consideration. To calm them, please have the monks gather those within and tell them I will hold a service at noon to ask the gods for their guidance. To those outside, let them know that there will be another service each hour while the day lasts for those who still seek comfort." Egan paused. "For the rest, Otho, please take it in hand and organise whatever else you deem fitting. While there may be alarm at present, I'm sure there's a reasonable explanation for what has occurred, and I have other pressing matters to attend to with Lady Wilmen for the moment."

If Egan's dismissal bothered Otho at all, he showed no sign of it. With typical passivity, Otho simply accepted his Abbot's directive and moved to meet his will. "As you wish, Abbot, I will see to it at once." Turning the handle of the door to exit, he bid Wilmen farewell with a nod of his head, then left the room.

Egan turned to her. "Well, Wilmen. What think you of this turn of events?" Wilmen's eyes came up to greet Egan's. "Do you think it can be true?"

Wilmen took just a moment more to answer, clearing her throat and sitting forward on the soft cushions, arms resting on her knees. Her fingers clenched and unclenched together, as if striving to take hold of something they could not grasp. "I know not, my friend, but truly I cannot see any way in which this is good news." Wilmen shook her head, trusting Otho's information but unable to understand it. "Egan." She spoke softly, carefully, as if her words themselves might betray her. "If this is true, then the Protector has lost all caution and control. You saw his wounds and know as surely as I he should not have lasted the night, let alone appeared at the Keep this morning in any way other than carted on a bier." Locking eyes with Egan, she finished with a tremor in her voice. "The Protector has called on dark powers to aid him in this. We have suspected him capable of such for quite some time, but never has he shown his hand so clearly. Something has happened to alter the game, Egan, and I fear it is Alaena!"

Wilmen surged to her feet, worry warring with anger on her face. With no word from Tag, and only her gem shining bright to assure them that Alaena was still alive, Wilmen and Egan had fretted away the morning awaiting news, unsure how to act or where to direct any action they took if they did. Wilmen felt her frayed nerves unravelling.

Stamping her foot, Wilmen swivelled to face Egan directly, aware that time to hope that an option would present itself had run out. At the very least, they needed to confirm the Protector had indeed returned to the Keep, and learn what they could of his intent. Once they knew that, they could plan their next step.

Before Wilmen could take a breath, Egan started speaking, obviously thinking the same thing. "We have to know what is going on at the Keep, Wilmen," he said as calmly as he could. "I agree, this appears to be dire news indeed, but let us understand it before we act and show our own hand, perhaps too soon! We need someone at the Keep."

Wilmen folded her arms and took to pacing, thinking hard as Egan continued.

"I cannot go. I have the Abbey to consider here and services to hold. You were at the Keep last night, and I don't think it wise for you to be at the gates once more, lest someone wonder about your interest there. If there were others we could trust to avoid putting the Council at risk I would suggest that, but the stakes now are too high. Rogan has rarely been seen there so won't arouse suspicion, and we can summon him quickly. What think you?"

Wilmen turned once more, absently scuffing the rug beneath her. An overwhelming feeling of impotence assailed her, knowing there were things to be done but not knowing what they were. Ultimately, she could only agree with Egan for the moment, but her need would not be satisfied with this meagre activity. While there were other priorities and many other things to consider, Wilmen's mind was occupied with Alaena. Where was she? Had she escaped the Keep safely? Was Tag with her, or was she on her own and in more danger? These questions circled her thoughts continuously and would not be put to rest. The only real hope she had came from the gem and the light that blazed from it. If she didn't have that, then Wilmen may well have folded into despair by now.

Thinking of the gem, she paused, a dangerous idea occurring to her. She halted, considering, then realised in the silence around her that Egan was waiting for an answer.

"Forgive me, Egan. I am disturbed." Sighing in frustration, she added needlessly, "I wish we had a clearer path!" Aware that Egan may balk at her suggestion, Wilmen decided there and then to act on her instinct. "Of course, my friend, your plan has merit. We need an understanding of matters at the Keep before embarking on our next step. Rogan is a good choice; I will summon him while you attend to matters here. Then I may rest, as it may be a while before we have another!"

Interpreting Wilmen's assent on face value, Egan nodded in agreement. He himself had too much on his mind to consider alternatives in any case.

"As you suggest, Wilmen. Let us meet back here after the first Service and talk more. Perhaps Rogan can bring us news by then and we can plan with more surety."

Standing, Egan paused before making for the door, concern for Wilmen etching his face. He moved to her and gently placed his hand on hers, feeling the raised glyphs on her ring under his fingers. Allowing the touch to convey his care for her, Egan attempted to calm Wilmen's concerns.

"We have come this far, my friend," he said with feeling. "Now that events have started to move quickly, fear not. We will not falter or fail, and in the end the Light will prevail."

Wilmen's eyes softened as she turned her hand upwards, entwining her fingers with his. Egan's eyes were full of emotion as he shared her pain and her hope.

"Be strong, Sister, for the Light shines in the world once more and great days are upon us!"

Wilmen, overcome with feeling, leaned forward and bestowed a gentle kiss on Egan's cheek. Stepping back, she wiped a tear from her eye, smiling tenderly at the man with whom she had nurtured and protected Alaena with from the day she had come to them. "May it be so, my friend, for there is but a single Light shining in a world of dark, and we cannot let it fade!"

With no more to be said, they shared strength a moment more before allowing their hands to part and drop to their sides.

Wilmen moved on to find Otho and ask that Rogan be called to the Abbey, as Egan returned to the Abbey's offices to prepare his sermons.

It took little time to find Otho before Wilmen retired to her rooms, aware that Rogan would arrive shortly. For what she had planned, it would be enough.

Wilmen's room was plain and undecorated, as befitted the modest demeanour of the Abbey, with a small bed, a cupboard and writing table the only furnishings. A window at the far end of the room opened onto the Abbey gardens, allowing plentiful light into the room creating an environment conducive to easy contemplation.

Unfortunately, little in Wilmen's mind could be deemed peaceful or introspective. Her mind awhirl with emotion and concern, Wilmen took care to close the heavy door behind her and take a breath, before moving to the desk and reaching to the back of the drawer fitted snugly within it. Her hand closed around the intricately carved box within to draw it forth, then she placed it in her lap as she sat at the single austere but functional chair before it.

Not expecting otherwise, but nonetheless relieved to see it, light blazed forth as soon as her trembling fingers pushed the lid of the box back. Within, the topaz continued to shine without pause or concern. Until now, Wilmen had not lifted the Star from its resting place. She had been content to simply watch the light shine from the incandescent depths of the stone and be assured, by this singular display of intent, that hope remained in the world.

Tentatively, her fingers touched the gem. A tingling met her contact, but no heat and no other indication that power lay there to be tapped. Lifting the stone forth, Wilmen brought it to her face, staring within, transfixed.

While consistent, the light was anything but settled. It swirled, spun and eddied within the heart of the stone, contained yet marvellously unencumbered, as if an infinity of possibilities existed within the heart of the fire.

Aware that time ran against her, Wilmen pulled her gaze back. The enthralling play of power within the stone was entrancing, and she needed to move herself back from the intoxicating allure to do what she wanted to do.

Maintaining the distance she achieved, while still feeling connected to the stone, Wilmen gave herself up to her objective.

"Alaena," she whispered into the gem. "My love. My hope. Are you there?"

Nothing happened, and everything happened.

Still well aware that she sat in a nondescript room of an Abbey in lower Morlyn, Wilmen experienced a momentary swell of disorientation as she felt something shift in her mind. A greater reality opened to her, and she saw lines of light and flows of power that were beyond her understanding. She felt a connectivity to the world that dwarfed the entirety of her previous experience.

The glimpse was fleeting, however, and the moment of perpetuity she experienced through the connection with the Star resolved in an infinity of fleeting moments to a calm, green space. A space with trees and stone and root that was so normal that Wilmen's mind reeled.

"Mother?"

The inquiry was so innocent, so full of love and warmth that Wilmen's breath stopped for a moment. It was all she could do to maintain her focus and hold back tears. The voice was so dear, so preciously cherished, that Wilmen's soul trembled at the contact.

"Alaena?" she ventured. "My dear?"

In all her life, Alaena had never referred to Wilmen as her mother, though in word, deed and love Wilmen had considered herself no other. If she had any doubt that it was truly Alaena, however, it was obliterated by the familiarity of the voice, the underlying closeness of the bond she held with Alaena. Before she had even phrased the question and the answer came back, Wilmen knew.

"Yes, Mother, I am here," Alaena's voice echoed in her head. "I am in the forest to the north of Morlyn with friends, and all is well."

The directness of the answer didn't help. So many questions tumbled through Wilmen's mind that she had difficulty framing the next. *How? Who?* For one of the first times in her life, Wilmen did not know how to respond.

Alaena's familiar laugh and spirit resonated through the link, allowing Wilmen a moment to recover herself.

"Mother. At last I have you at a loss for words, it seems!" Alaena's humour was a balm for Wilmen's frayed composure. For a moment, Wilmen wondered why Ala seemed unconcerned that they were communicating this way. Then it occurred to her that if Wilmen had the stone, what was Alaena using?

While Wilmen pondered, Alaena continued as if they were discussing the orders to be made today over the kitchen table at the Chandler's in Morlyn. "As I'm sure you know, I have fled the Keep, though I could not have done it alone. I am with Tag and Rince, both of whom played a part in my escape."

The mention of Tag brought Wilmen back to the present, allowing her to think more clearly. Pushing questions of Alaena's flight and this impossible communication away, she focused on her immediate concerns. "I thank the Light that you are safe, Ala dear, and I don't doubt Tag will keep you safe. Where are you bound though, for I will come to you as soon as a horse can carry me!"

"No, Mother, do not seek to find us," Alaena ordered.

Her frank response took Wilmen by surprise. Alaena had never been forceful, let alone compelling. Now, however, her tone was decisive and her message entirely clear. Wilmen was taken aback.

"We have taken to the forest rather than draw enquiring eyes, and Tag is covering our tracks as we move deeper in. It will take us some days to traverse the depths before we can start our ascent into the mountains. We will doubtless be pursued from the Keep, for our departure was hardly a discreet affair!"

Unable to contain an exclamation, Wilmen allowed a little incredulity to show. "Hardly discreet! Ala! The Keep has been razed by fire and we thought the Protector dead, yet we hear now that he has been miraculously restored! Not only is he apparently whole and hale once more but has returned to the Keep to re-join his Guard!"

In some way, communicating this way allowed an interaction on a deeper, emotional level. Though leagues apart, Wilmen could feel Alaena's essential mood in a way she never had before. While words were involved, Wilmen knew they were communicating at a level above – or perhaps it was better described as *outside* – the mere articulation of vocabulary.

At mention of the Protector, both anger and fear resonated through the link, along with something else Wilmen had difficulty defining and aligning with Alaena. If it had a name, perhaps it would be judgement?

"The Protector healed and returned to the Keep?" Ala mused. "Yes, Wilmen, would it were that he had died, yet the man has a dark power that he wields without morals. It does not surprise me that a simple knife wound would not see the end of him."

Before Wilmen even had a chance to ask how Alaena knew the Protector was wounded by a blade, or why she showed no surprise at the fire at the Keep, Ala's tone turned brisk again. Decisive once more.

"Mother, this news unsettles me. I will speak with Tag to advise him that pursuit is likely soon and it will be relentless. The Protector's return to the Keep is far more likely to be driven by a desire to find me than to see to repairs. Revenge will drive him now more than anything else, and it will push him to extremes. Do not use the stone again unless in dire need, Mother. I feel that there is danger in this as well, and I do not know how deep the Protector's power runs. Keep the stone close, and I will contact you again when we reach the mountains if I can."

The light in the stone didn't fade or alter, but somehow Wilmen knew Alaena had gone. "Ala?" she queried tentatively, with no reply, no sense of the connection that had been there between them. "Ala?" she ventured once more, embarrassed to hear the quaver in her own voice. No response came and Wilmen felt childlike, holding a toy in her hand that she realised she had no idea how to use. Lazily, light spiralled in the gem, spraying her palm with gentle, vibrant surety of power and promise to be realised. Clearly, the old Power was at play here and Ala was the key, but what it really meant and how to make the most of this gift, Wilmen knew not for now.

If Wilmen took anything from the strange liaison, it was Ala's words reverberating in her mind. Spoken with such unaccustomed authority that Wilmen spent some time trying to align it with her understanding of Alaena herself. "Do not seek to find us," Alaena had said clearly and, indeed, with authority.

Closing her fist around the stone, Wilmen suddenly felt old beyond her years. She had spent so long raising and nurturing Alaena that she had barely accepted the fact that Alaena was becoming a woman now. Even so, to think that Alaena had transcended herself already to find true power of her own was something Wilmen had difficulty accepting, yet the short conversation just passed allowed no other conclusion. Alaena had come into power somewhere, somehow, and was taking control of her own destiny and path in the world. Whether this boded well or ill Wilmen knew not, but her Ala was no longer a pawn in the game to be cast aside.

Sitting alone in her room in the Abbey, Wilmen pulled her cloak tighter about her shoulders, wishing fervently that the fears circling her soul were as easy to keep at bay as the evening chill. Looking down, she again unclenched her fist, allowing the light of the gem to shine free. Swirling eddies of colour bathed the room once more, reflecting and refracting off tears that lay unnoticed on Wilmen's cheeks.

Staring down into the depths of the gem, Wilmen resisted the urge to speak to Alaena once more. Alaena had said there was danger there, and though Wilmen didn't understand how or why, she trusted that Ala had spoken truly. Before standing, wiping her face and readying herself to find Egan and somehow try to convey to him the meaning if not the means of this unexpected communication, Wilmen held the gem close to her chest and pushed *"I love you"* into the heart of the stone with all her soul, hoping somehow that the emotion if not the words would reach her precious Ala as she made her way north.

A short while later, Wilmen composed herself and left the room in search of Egan with a look of contentment and contemplative calmness on her otherwise steady features. Whether it was reality or imaginative desire, she could still hear the warmth of Alaena's faint response in her head, delivered as if on the wind.

I love you too, Mother.

Chapter 23 - Warrior-Smith of Ald

The afternoon was interminable. Spending her time between her own chamber, resisting the urge to examine the gem over and over again, and Egan's formal chambers awaiting him to finish services, Wilmen felt she might go mad from the inactivity. During the afternoon, she heard of the party of Guard and trackers that the Protector had formed and ridden at speed from the Keep towards the mountains earlier that day. Knowing there was only one likely reason for the Protector to hunt with such haste only served to increase Wilmen s worry and apprehension.

At last, services were due to end. Wilmen returned to Egan's chambers to plan their next steps. To her dismay, Egan was not alone.

"Sister Tria," Egan began when he entered and saw her waiting. "Allow me to introduce Darven Ross, a Warrior-Smith from Ald, who has travelled with little rest since evening yesterday to speak with the Abbey."

Turning his attention to the man accompanying him, Egan continued. "Warrior-Smith, this is Sister Tria, who is in our confidence. Any message you have for me can be shared with her, for I value her counsel on matters of import such as those you must bear."

The monk stepped aside as Darven entered the room. As he entered, Wilmen noted the burly shoulders and was reminded of the custom in Ald. All men were titled 'Warrior' as their first moniker, as swordsmanship was central to life in Ald. The second part of the title referred to their trade. This man was young, perhaps around twenty years old, Wilmen guessed. By the size of his chest and shoulders he had spent several years already working the hammer and forge.

Noting the eagerness on his face accompanied by the travel-stained garb, Wilmen recognised a man that would have little interest in pleasantries.

Waving a hand in welcome, Egan gestured towards the chairs and table. "Please, Darven, Sister Tria and I have some important matters of Abbey business to discuss so we can spare only a short while for you. Sit for a moment and tell us in what way may we be of assistance?"

"Lord Abbot," Darven began even as they took their seats. Had he not had such a serious look on his face, Egan may have chuckled at his youthful enthusiasm.

Egan did however take the time to hold up a hand quickly and correct the appellation. "Please, I am no one's lord!" he said kindly. "If I may call you Darven, then, should it suit you, I am simply Abbot."

Darven Ross nodded as if this were immaterial. "Yes, Abbot, thank you," he responded quickly before moving onto his point.

"I bring welcome and tidings from Orindum, son of Ikartan, Prince of Ald!" Darven began formally before stealing a sideways glance at the woman in the room with them, whose name he had not registered when Egan first spoke. The woman appeared to be paying polite attention but seemed distracted. Darven paused, glancing uncomfortably between the two, unsure as to how to convey the importance of the issues at hand. Clearly, they were inappropriate to be shared with womenfolk, yet Darven wished to cause no offence. "Abbot," he began directly. "This concerns the word of Keziah." Even as he spoke, he sensed the change in the room. Both Egan and the woman had fixed him with their full attention at mention of the Prophet of Ald. Delicately, Darven leaned towards Egan and ventured a suggestion. "Perhaps, Abbot, we could discuss matters of such import privately?" Turning a condescending glance towards Wilmen, he nodded once before turning a solemn countenance back to address Egan in a low voice he felt both conciliatory and persuasive. "I fear your companion here may not appreciate their gravity."

The response he received was not the one he sought.

For a moment Egan's eyes registered confusion, as if he didn't quite understand the point that Darven was making, then a frown creased his broad forehead as Darven's point became clear. The woman herself, as women were want to do in Darven's experience, became immediately emotional.

"How *dare* you!" she began, the enraged expression on her face a precursor to a tirade.

Before she could go further, however, Egan held up a hand and spoke in low, serious tones.

"That day will come, When Prince's Stone awakes and calls out bright."

Silence descended on the room for a few heavy moments following the opening lines of Keziah's Prophecy. Darven's eyes were alight; Wilmen's were daggers directed towards Darven. Egan continued.

"I will forgive the insult afforded to my companion, Darven, as I hope will she, if you assure us both that it will not be repeated." Egan indicated Wilmen with a nod of his head. "Sister Tria here has my absolute confidence, and I will assure you in return that she is more than capable of 'appreciating the gravity' of anything you may wish to bring before us." Not waiting for an answer, for they had no time to banter what he considered the ridiculous preconceptions of the male population of Ald, Egan brought the discussion back to the topic at hand. "Forgive my directness, Warrior-Smith, but as I mentioned, Sister Tria and I have other pressing business to consider. Are we correct in assuming that the Prince's stone is indeed awake, and that Orindum now seeks the Appointed One?"

Darven shifted in his chair. This was not going as he had anticipated. He had expected to be hailed as the bearer of grand news, which would lead to a search for the Appointed One, wherever he may be. Instead, Darven was being challenged to validate an assumption that this was in fact the case. He was also disconcerted, the matter of the inclusion of a woman in discussions such as these aside, that the Abbot would speak so informally of both the Stone and his Prince. Endeavouring to re-establish the importance of his mission, Darven attempted to highlight his purpose to give the Abbot and his companion some understanding of the momentous importance of his quest.

"*Prince* Orindum," Darven began, accentuating the title, "has indeed sent out riders, of which I am proud to be one! We are to seek out the Appointed One, wherever he may be, and bring him to Ald where he may learn and where we may guide him in his quest to overcome the Beast, in whatever form that may take!"

If Darven expected a fanfare, or at least some indication of appreciation of the importance of the task he had undertaken, he was again sorely disappointed. Egan merely nodded as if Darven had commented on the weather.

"Yes, Darven," Egan said, accompanied by another of those sidelong glances towards his companion. "Sister Tria and I had assumed much of this from our knowledge of the Prophecy, and from our study of other writings in the libraries here in Morlyn and at Ald when we have had the opportunity to visit."

Egan paused while Darven digested this information. Egan and his companion had studied the matter of the Stone and the Appointed One?

"Tell me, Darven," Egan continued after a moment, carefully avoiding the fact that all they had read of Ald histories and prophecy assumed that the Appointed One would be male. "Where will you seek the Appointed? How will you know if you have found the one you seek?" Leaning forward to accentuate his final question, Egan fixed Darven with a direct stare. "Lastly and perhaps most importantly, Darven. What will you do if the Appointed does not want to accompany you back to Ald?"

Many people who met Darven and spoke with him saw only his size which, he readily admitted, was considerable even by the burly standards of your average Smith. Any assumption that brawn and brain were not found together did not hold true with Darven, however. While he would never call himself a scholar, Darven had taken to reading and writing at an early age. His propensity to absorb knowledge and engage in some degree of philosophical conversation with his mentors were one reason he had been selected and trained as a rider, should occasion arise, in the first place. It was Egan's turn, therefore, to be surprised by Darven's considered response.

"I am most pleased to hear you have spent time in our library, Abbot. That being the case though, your questions seem strange. There are many tomes that talk to the time of upheaval and unrest that will accompany the rise of the Appointed. Rumours of the beginnings of such times have already reached Ald and surrounding lands. I had little time to seek further information on the road, but from mutterings even in the corridors of the Abbey in my short time here, I gather that Morlyn itself has of late experienced the beginnings of unrest!"

Warming to his subject, the young man leaned forward to continue. Muscles rippled in his arms as they took the weight of his torso against his knees. Grey-blue eyes engaged Egan as directly as Egan's pale green had fixed on Darven earlier.

"As to how I will find him, Abbot. Aside from informing you of the Stone's awakening, I am hoping you can help me or might know of something. In times such as these, the populace will bring their fears and concerns to the Abbey, seeking solace and assurance. If there is any place where I could find information about such things, it would be here, would it not?"

Rather than answering straight away, Egan gave the woman another sideways glance, forcing Darven to reassess the situation here again. Did this woman actually hold an important post here in Morlyn? While females in Ald were never in positions of power, Darven had read and been taught that this was not always the case elsewhere. Perhaps now was not the time to press. If Egan and this woman were willing to share their knowledge, then perhaps they could help each other. If they were not forthcoming, then he would learn more of this later one way or another. In Darven's mind, only one thing was sure: He would never be diverted from his quest, and he would find the Appointed. If some were disinclined to assist, then he would find others more aligned to his objectives.

"Lord Abbot," Darven continued, reverting to the more formal address. "When I find the Appointed, I assure you I will not need to force him to return to Ald with me. My message is simple. We wish to help, and in Ald he will have access to all the considerable resources we can supply from men and arms to knowledge and mystic support. Once I explain this and ensure him of our absolute support, what reason would he have not to travel back with me?"

The sheer innocence in Darven's eyes as he stated this last question almost as a fact moved Egan. Here was a man dedicated to his cause, which was something Egan could respect. Though perhaps misguided in a few worldly ways, Darven's words rang with compassion and enthusiasm for his quest. Egan had absolutely no intention of telling Darven that the Appointed One he sought was, to all appearances now, a sixteen-year-old girl who was currently deep in the forests to the north of Morlyn in the company of only a peasant boy and an assassin, all of whom were fleeing a madman who only the previous evening had very likely called on evil powers to bring himself back from the brink of death. No. That was information to be held tightly from this Darven Ross, at least for the time being.

Egan would not lie, of course, but could point Darven in a general direction that would give himself and Wilmen a day's grace to control the situation before they had to deal with Darven once more.

"Darven Ross," Egan responded at last, returning the formality. "I wish you all success, then, for these are indeed testing times. As you surmise, dark deeds and tidings are all the rumour, and we at the Abbey see more and more souls in need of spiritual succour in these days than ever before." He settled back in his chair, encompassing Wilmen in the discussion. "Sister Tria and I have been discussing events at the Keep recently that you may not be aware of, but are very much of the type of unrest of which you speak!"

For the next few minutes, Egan gave Darven the details of the fire and the destruction of the Keep that had the populace disquieted. He finished with a description of the Protector as Egan had last seen him at the healer's in the city. Egan had believed The Protector's wounds to be mortal, though rumour had it today that the Protector had survived the night. Perhaps, Egan suggested to Darven in closing, that his best place to start if he were looking for momentous events, would be the Keep itself.

"In any case, Darven," Egan said as he concluded his tale. "I'm sure you are weary from your travels. I fear our rooms at the Abbey are somewhat sparse in terms of accommodation, so you may prefer an inn in the city, but you are welcome to bide here as long as you wish until you are ready to move on. Shall I arrange for a room for you?

Even before Egan had finished his tale of the destruction of the Keep, Darven became aware that as much was being omitted from the tale as was being shared. That being the case, Darven realised questioning further would gain him no value. One of the lessons that had been pressed into him over and over by his mentors was that if, in the pursuit of his quest, he found people dissembling, then they had information that would be of use. With that in mind, Darven asked a polite question or two, then thanked Egan for his hospitality and excused himself, stating a need for a bath, hot food and an ale to wash away the dust from the road at a nearby inn.

Before leaving he also apologised to Sister Tria for any offence, citing a difference in custom as the cause rather than any intent to cause discomfort, before Otho was called to see him on his way.

***

Once the door had closed behind Darven and the heavy fall of his boots faded away, Wilmen leapt to her feet. "Of all the condescending, superior, contemptuous men I have had the misfortune to meet, that man outclasses them all!" she spat, kicking furniture aside as she attempted to pace the cluttered room. Spinning back to Egan, she continued to vent, spreading her arms wide for added effect. "Did you see? He barely even glanced at me the whole time he was in the room! It was as if I wasn't there! Light burn me!" she swore, vexed beyond civility. "It was all I could do not to slap him and tell him to go back to Ald where he was wanted!" Wilmen, completing her stomping circuit of the room, found herself back where she had started and, with nowhere else to go, flopped back down to her seat.

"Wilmen," Egan began cautiously, his face half smile, half serious. "I understand your frustration, and honestly I am not sure how you even contained yourself while he spoke. I applaud you for doing

230

so though, for he was an interesting character and one I expect we haven't heard the last of! If nothing else, it is good to know Ald's position, for we suspected that if this time ever came, they would not sit back and wait for their Appointed One to come to them."

Wilmen nodded, aware that she had allowed Darven's ludicrous assumptions to distract her from what was important here. Taking a deep breath, she pushed her anger down. "Indeed, Egan," she nodded in agreement. "Let's put Darven Ross and the concerns of Ald to one side for now and decide how best to get help to Tag and Alaena."

Within the hour, organised by the efficient Otho, Wilmen was leading her horse into the laneway behind the Abbey. Her saddlebags bulged with rations and her travel cloak lay on her shoulders. Secreted away in the cloak lay a small bag of coin for use at need on the road, a spare knife and, tucked away safely in an inner pocket, her precious Star. While reluctant to do so, Wilmen had replaced the onyx container she had kept it in for all these years with a small silk bag to make it easier to carry as well as rendering it less conspicuous in her cloak.

In the alley, Rogan waited impatiently, standing beside a horse as impressive in size as Rogan was in bulk. Standing some eighteen hands high, it looked able to carry three people with little difficulty, though Wilmen suspected even this beast would tire if pressed to carry Rogan himself for some distance.

"Sister," Rogan growled, his voice reminding Wilmen of boulders grinding together. "What urgency drives us today? A messenger came from the Abbey, advising I meet you here ready to ride as soon as I could, which I have done." Looking around, Rogan lowered his voice to a dull rumble and leaned over Wilmen to ensure their conversation was not overheard. Wilmen felt a mountain was leaning towards her and resisted the urge to back away. "Does this have to do with the Star and the Appointed?"

Wilmen nodded, eager to set off but aware that Rogan needed some inkling of their purpose.

"Alaena has escaped the Keep," Wilmen explained in a low voice filled with urgency. "She and Tag have fled into the woods with the Protector and his Guard in pursuit." Rogan's eyes widened as the story unfolded. "They are a day ahead of us at least, but I know for the moment that they are safe." Wilmen hesitated. She could tell Rogan of the strange conversation she had with Alaena through the Star, but that would take too long. Placing a slender hand on Rogan's massive arm, Wilmen's eyes conveyed her urgency. "We need to be on the road, Rogan. While Tag and Alaena are on foot, the Protector is mounted The sooner we can find them, the sooner we can offer aid."

She finished quickly. "Let us talk more as we ride, Rogan, for there is indeed no time to be lost. We travel first for Fyr, then on through the forest towards the mountains as far as needs be."

With that, Wilmen gathered the reins of her horse and mounted smoothly, settling into her saddle as she checked her belongings were secure. Rogan frowned briefly, both discomforted and concerned by Wilmen's message. Regardless, the need to get on the road was apparent, so Rogan shrugged his broad shoulders and accepted that the rest of the story would come on the road.

Rogan mounted with less grace, partly because of his size and partly to accommodate the scabbard of the great sword he had belted around his girth. Finally he settled in with a grunt, his steed huffing and pulling at the reins before taking a few steps to get accustomed to the weight of its rider.

Pressing heels to flanks, they made their way slowly out of the alleyway and into the streets of Morlyn, turning south and picking up pace as they left the centre of the city behind.

So intent were they on their objective ahead, neither looked back to notice the lone rider that tracked their path through the city from a distance. As Wilmen and Rogan entered the woods and picked up pace, the rider took the same road as well, though dropping back even further to maintain a good distance between them.

Though his mount was yet to recover fully from the ride to Morlyn, Darven Ross coaxed it into a reluctant canter as the woman he followed from the Abbey and her gargantuan companion urged their own horses to a run. Whatever had these two racing into the woods even as the sun dropped down towards the horizon and an evening gloom settled onto the path before them, Darven Ross would know of it and be sure to take any action necessary to serve the wishes of his city and his Prince.

Chapter 24 - Birthright

"You promised to tell me of Wilmen and how you came to be at the gate to meet us, Tag," Alaena said softly from behind. "Now seems as good a time as ever, don't you think?"

Tag, Rince and Alaena had been making their way south since leaving the clearing mid-morning, keeping well within the trees and away from the road. At the outset, Tag had taken the lead with Alaena following and Rince trailing at the rear, still struggling with weariness from the events of the past few days but recovering quickly. Even had he not, Rince was determined that, with Alaena seemingly in perfect health as she made her way through the forest and with Tag striding forward as if nothing could tire him, he would not be the one to slow them down. As the day passed and they delved deeper into the woods though, they found fewer and fewer tracks and game trails to follow. More and more often, Tag was forced to lead the trio around obstacles that stood in their way. Going was slow.

With Alaena's question, Tag stopped dead. It was passing mid-afternoon on the day following their escape from the Keep. No one ever accused Tag of talking too much. After a full night and most of this day travelling with little rest between and only the more impenetrable depths of the forest to await them, Tag was even less inclined than he usually would be to take time out for a social chat.

Alaena came to a stop as Tag turned, with Rince close behind. Rince didn't know why they had stopped, but he immediately found himself a nearby stone on which to sit and rest. Whatever they were discussing, Rince didn't care. As long as it meant he had a moment to catch his breath, he was more than happy for them to talk as long as they liked.

"Alaena," Tag said, remaining calm. "I am more than happy to honour my promise to you at a later time, but I will save my breath for the track if you don't mind. Unless you'd like to clear the way for us instead while I walk behind?" he added a little sardonically.

Alaena thought for a moment. "Yes, Tag, you're right. Wilmen's story can wait. We must make better time," she said seriously, taking the assassin by surprise once more.

Stepping towards him, Alaena put a hand gently on Tag's arm to secure his attention. Leaning close, she lowered her voice so that Rince wouldn't hear. "I am not entirely sure how, Tag, but a short while ago as we walked, I heard Wilmen calling me. We spoke briefly." Alaena's smooth brow crinkled for a moment as she tried to describe what had happened, but her clear grey eyes sparkled as she recalled the experience. "It was very strange. It was a little like talking across an ocean while standing next to each other at the same time."

Alaena shook her head. She felt that understanding would come, and this wasn't the point. "In any case, Tag, Wilmen tells me the Protector lives. After what we've done to him and his Keep, we will very likely be pursued soon, if we are not already!"

Staring at Alaena as if she had just turned a strange shade of blue, Tag didn't know what question to ask first. If there was anything life had taught him though, it was to stay focused when challenges presented themselves and to deal with the important issues first. In his profession, those issues were usually the ones that were the difference between living and dying.

"The Protector lives!" Tag hissed, stroking the pommel of the dagger protruding from his belt. "Now that is poor news," he breathed quietly. He took a glance at Alaena, who watched him as if she were awaiting an answer, then over to Rince who was sitting resting his head on his arms nearby, then back to Alaena.

"I had hoped it were otherwise from the tale that Rince told me, but if he lives then I could not agree more, we must make better time!" Without considering anything further but the need to flee as fast as they could, Tag started to turn away. "You help Rince to his feet and aid him in keeping up, and I will see if I can find a faster path."

"No, Tag," Alaena said, pulling him back towards her before he could take a step away. "You help Rince. I will lead the way."

With that, Alaena dropped her hand from Tag's arm and stepped past him onto the track. Even had he wanted to, Tag may have had difficulty resisting. Alaena's very demeanour now was one of confidence and command, and he felt for a moment as if his feet had been rooted to the earth when she had so unequivocally said 'no'.

In moments, Alaena was moving away and Tag's moment passed. In his lithe fashion, he moved quickly to Rince and helped him to his feet. Rince rubbed his eyes and glanced around as if he'd just arrived. "Come, boy," Tag said kindly but firmly. "It seems our companion is sick of waiting for us, so we'd best hurry to keep up!"

Shrugging off a strong desire to lie down and sleep, Rince moved the direction Tag indicated, for Alaena had already disappeared into the trees and they had to rush to catch up.

For the next two hours or so, until the late afternoon light started to fade, the small party moved through the wood. They travelled close together, for Tag had no desire to let Alaena out of his sight, and it seemed that as long as Rince was near Alaena, he would keep walking after her until his legs fell off.

When they started moving again, Tag assumed Alaena had simply come across a track out of luck, for the branches and bowls that had seemed to bar their way every step earlier on in the day were no longer an impediment. The ground they walked on remained clear, allowing them to move at a much greater pace than before. It didn't take long, however, for Tag to start to wonder at what exactly was occurring here. Not only did their path remain devoid of obstacles to tear at them or bar their way, it also travelled in a reasonably direct line south, which happened to be exactly the direction they wanted to travel.

There was no talking as they walked, though every now and then a sound of humming wafted towards Tag from Alaena, who occasionally reached out to touch leaf or bush as she passed. At times, Tag was sure she was nodding to them with a smile tugging at her lips as though meeting an old friend. Glancing backwards, Tag felt a tingle of fear, which was an emotion he had not experienced in many years. The forest in front might be a clear path as they moved forwards, but behind it seemed to close in as a wall of green where no path had ever been.

While Tag believed in Power and the Light, he believed in no God. As he walked, Tag had to wonder, though. If ever a person could experience something holy, it would be walking through the green like this, with light filtering through the thick canopy above to guide their way in speckled, yellow-green patterns as the forest opened a way around the young girl and her companions as they moved.

Tag estimated, to his continued amazement, that they were travelling at a pace very much as they would at a walk on the road itself, which skirted the western edge of the forest from the north of Morlyn and through smaller villages until it met the mountains known as The Spine. At that point, a single pass connected the northern lands of the King to the southern realms.

As dusk approached, Tag began to think about where they were and when they might camp, for they could not march all night. It was difficult to tell with no points of reference within the confines of the forest, but Tag considered carefully. Their forced march last night escaping the Keep took them most of the way to Fyr, a little over four leagues from Morlyn until they left the road. Once in the forest, they had rested and made little progress from that point until Alaena had taken the lead and, for all that Tag could tell, somehow come to an agreement with the forest to grant them easy passage. Even as he walked, Tag felt the peace that seemed to imbue their surroundings as they passed.

He allowed them to walk for a while longer before realising the last of the light was fading. Unless they wanted to light a fire and announce their position through either the light of the flames or the smell of the smoke, he knew they had to stop soon. Even with their path apparently straight and clear before them, Tag had no desire to bumble into the depths of the Wytharn Wood in pitch blackness.

"Alaena! We should stop before full dark," he called. "Can you see a place to wait out the night?" In the preternatural silence of the woods around them, he felt like he was shouting even as he kept his voice to a soft call. He could see both Alaena and Rince, now shadows on the path before him, slow and stop.

Alaena's gentle voice drifted back to him. "We have only a little further to go, Tag, do not worry. We are almost there!"

Almost there? Tag thought. *Almost where?* By his best calculation, he figured they had traversed perhaps one-quarter of the wood, with the most difficult terrain yet to be encountered, though it seemed that was the least of their problems for the moment. In any case, they needed rest, and even with the best of paths it was safer to travel in the light than risk stepping into a hole and breaking an ankle along the way.

Tag stepped forward to lay a hand on Rince's shoulder and reach out for Alaena, who was already turning away to move on.

"Wait, Alaena!" Tag felt as though he were losing his grip on the situation. There were too many things here that he didn't know or understand. Alaena turned back and he thought he could see a slight smile on her face in the gloom. In frustration, he begged, "please. At least tell me what is happening so I can help keep you safe. What do you mean 'we are almost there'? Almost where?"

Alaena's head cocked to one side at the question as if pondering. Rince simply looked from one to the other, as if waiting to see if he should sit and have another rest of if he should stay ready to move on once more.

"You know, Tag," Alaena said before Rince could decide which to do, "I don't really know. I just feel that something important is about to happen and we shouldn't tarry. Trust me in this and we will know soon!"

Alaena spoke with such surety that Tag had no argument. If the trees around them and the growth underfoot did her bidding, then who was he to argue with her intent?

Hefting his pack from his back, Tag let go of Rince long enough to pull forth a small, shuttered bullseye lantern, along with flint and steel. "As you say, then, Alaena, just for a short while. At least wait one moment so we can have a little light as we move so none of us knock ourselves out on a low hanging bough."

238

Quickly, Tag knelt to the ground and pulled forth a wick and small, sealed oil reservoir. Moving deftly despite the lack of light, for Tag had done this many times before in dark places, the wick was loaded and lit with a few quick strikes of the flint. Once settled back in the lantern, a beam of light shone through a glass window at the front, which Tag reduced even further through the use of a small shutter. When ready to go, only a small pool of light showed on the ground before them. It was enough to light their way but would not be seen by prying eyes any distance into the woods either side of them.

Lifting the light enough to weakly illuminate Alaena's face for a moment, Tag could see her nod then turn and begin the trek once more. Keeping closer now, he kept the light down to show only the path and the feet of Rince and Alaena before him while they moved step by step, deeper and deeper into the Wood.

***

Focusing on the ground and their path for a while, Tag paid little attention to the surroundings of the small party. Step followed drowsy step as the unchanging ground moved beneath their feet. Tag wasn't sure when it happened, but there was a point sometime later in the night when he realised that he was standing alone with Rince in the middle of the path. It was difficult to remember, but Tag was sure that something or someone was missing.

Even as he tried to focus and work out what it was, Rince gently folded to the ground beside him to lie in the small pool of light from the lantern Tag was still holding, though he was unsure why. Even as he heard Rince's breath deepen in sleep, Tag made one more effort to fight the exhaustion overwhelming him.

Shaking his head, he almost lost hold of the lantern, which was starting to feel impossibly heavy. Kneeling down, Tag placed the lantern next to them both, noticing how the ground felt impossibly soft through his trousers. Placing both hands down, he smiled through his stupor. The earth under his hands felt like gentle fingers caressing all his hurts. No longer even considering resistance, Tag lay down alongside Rince in bliss, falling into a

239

deep, dreamless sleep as the foliage wrapped round them like cocoons to keep them warm.

Alaena didn't register when she left her companions behind, only focused on what was before her. She had stopped thinking about Rince and Tag some time ago. With each step she took, a tangible sense of anticipation and awareness built within and around her. Alaena could feel the forest holding its breath. The stones and earth around and under her stilled themselves even further in anticipation of a momentous event. Mostly though, she could feel an ache and a yearning waiting some way into the trees before her that she approached without trepidation, for she knew without the need for explanation that her arrival, at this time and in this place, was right.

The clearing Alaena stepped into was perhaps twenty paces across, making it feel spacious after her long walk with forest pressing in on either side. It took a moment for her to realise she could see clearly at last too. The canopy above was open to the sky, allowing moon and starlight to gently wash the clearing with an pale silver light.

Alaena stopped. There was no sound. The trees were still and none of the usual noises of the wood intruded, though she had no time to consider such oddities. Her focus was entirely occupied by what was standing motionless in the centre of the clearing.

It was vaguely man-shaped. The ethereal light allowed her to see clearly that it had a head, torso and unusually long arms and legs, though Alaena could see no eyes or any other distinguishing features. Somehow, the creature had the aspect of stone. It was facing and staring – if an eyeless creature could stare – directly at Alaena.

Several moments passed as Alaena took this in, unsure what to do. The creature remained eerily motionless. After a short while she wondered if she was mistaken and if this was indeed just a piece of stone that had vaguely human shape. Perhaps her first assumption that it was anything more was just a trick of the moonlight, though that did not explain the strange yearning emanating from the shape that flooded her heightened senses.

240

Just as she decided to step forward to examine it more closely, its head bowed, stony chin touching its rocky chest in one smooth motion. In the same movement, its strange appendages folded forward until it knelt on one knee to the ground.

"Lightwielder."

The heavy voice, laced with the same yearning projecting from the creature, came without warning and spoke directly to her mind. Alaena jumped in surprise.

"I have been waiting a long time to meet you."

Alaena paused again, unsure. Briefly, the temptation to just turn around and flee this strange situation leapt into her mind, but she dismissed it immediately. She had come too far and there was no turning back now unless it was into the arms of the Protector once more. Curiosity also played a part in staying her flight. She had never heard the term, but when the creature referred to her as Lightwielder, a thrill of recognition had run down her spine.

Alaena wanted to know more.

On one knee, the creature looked even more like a strange stone in the midst of the clearing, granite bathed in silver under the stars. Was it alive, Alaena wondered, or was it somehow actually a stone animated? Curiously committed, Alaena took a tentative step forward in the deafening silence of the area. Immediately, the creature's head lifted. The blunted, featureless form of the head stared so directly at her it was unsettling. So many questions crowded Alaena's mind she had difficulty sorting her thoughts.

Her first words were direct. Still just one step into the clearing, Alaena asked bluntly, "What do you want?"

Immediately, she regretted the words, concerned not only that she was being rude to this strange being but also because, spoken aloud, the utterance sounded like a strident shout in the eerie silence that surrounded her.

If the creature were offended or otherwise perturbed, she could not tell. It waited a moment as the silence settled once more, then

241

as smoothly as quicksilver, regained its feet. As if pondering the question, its head tilted to one side, giving it a truly human aspect for the first time to Alaena's eyes.

Again, the words came into Alaena's mind. This time, a sense of anticipation accompanied the longing undercurrent.

"It would be far easier to show you than to tell you, Lightwielder," the voice came to her calmly. *"If you are willing, come forward and you will know all."*

Deep in the preternaturally silent forest, in a clearing bathed in the silver light of the stars, the creature extended one misshapen arm, beckoning her forward with a clubbed, stony hand. Alaena felt like she was standing on an island in the midst of a frozen ocean. Fear warred with excitement, and she knew turning away, if indeed she really could, would be a decision she would regret for the rest of her life.

Some five steps away now, the creature stood statue-still. It did not move as she took the first step, nor the second, though she felt its strange emotions swell as she closed the distance between them. It exuded a trembling sense of ancient anticipation that was palpable. Another step and another, then with nervous trepidation, Alaena extended her hand towards the creature's outstretched limb. Inches now separated them, the passionate sensations now flowing towards Alaena so tangible that she felt like crying, running and laughing all at the same time.

Finally, their fingertips touched. Alaena slid her hand into what passed as the palm of the creature before her. It was cool and smooth, like the surface of a pebble just pulled from the river. At her touch, the aching need she had been feeling changed abruptly to an overwhelming feeling of relief and release. The hand of the creature closed around hers and she heard words in her mind before the world overturned. *"Be at peace, Lightwielder, for my gifts pass to the one so Appointed, at last!"*

How long Alaena spent locked in communion in that strange, silent space, she could not say. When she became aware of her surroundings once more, she remained standing in the clearing, arm outstretched. It felt as though only a moment had passed, yet the first rays of the sun had already broached the trees and were shining down into the clearing, glistening like gold on fresh growth all around her.

Before her, the strange being was nowhere to be seen. Instead, on a bed of fresh grass and vines where it had stood, two items lay gleaming in the early morning light.

Kneeling, Alaena looked carefully. The first was a sword, plain but beautifully made. In the back of her mind she recognised it, but she paid it little heed, for her eyes were drawn immediately to the other. It was a bracelet of a kind, but one which called to her very being. Wrought in spiral waves of gold, the band was about the width of two fingers and set about with topaz, emerald and diamond. Between each gem a small symbol of the sun was set at the crest of each wave in brighter, yellow gold. Unable to resist even if she wanted to, Alaena reached out to close her fingers around it. A tingling, welcoming sensation accompanied the touch. It was surprisingly light and felt intimately familiar to Alaena, though she had never set eyes on it before. Even as she considered it, the knowledge came to her, sending a shiver down her spine. This, she knew, had once belonged to Simcha, the Matriarch of the Temple of Eternal Light. Lifting it higher, Alaena watched the play of light through the gems and glistening off the gold. Turning it this way and that as she stood, Alaena was mesmerised. The metal and the gems absorbed, refracted and reflected light like nothing she had ever seen. It was almost like the bracelet was alive, rejoicing in the light that bathed its multi-faceted surfaces.

Holding her breath in anticipation, Alaena straightened the fingers of her left hand, ready to slip the bracelet on. Even as she prepared to do so, Alaena wondered if she had the right to wear such a thing herself? Even as she posed the question to herself, she knew the answer. This precious thing had been bestowed on her by people who had given their lives to see it delivered into her hands. To do anything other than accept the gift would be to spurn their memories, many of which still tumbled in the background of Alaena's mind, sorting themselves one by one.

Confident of this fact at least, Alaena closed her eyes, pushed the bracelet onto her arm and accepted her legacy.

If she had expected thunderous shocks of power, Alaena was disappointed. Once on, the bracelet seemed to have no weight. Opening her eyes again she watched it seem to shrink, fitting her wrist snugly as she let her breath out slowly and smiled. The power it held shimmered like the object itself but, unlike the gold and gems which made it up, its inherent force simmered just below the surface. Rather than being ostentatious or overt, it held its potency ready to be called upon at need.

Curious, Alaena considered testing her ability to tap the well of might she could feel it contained, but sense prevailed as she called herself back to the present. She remained alone, deep in the woods with pursuit not far behind. She needed to find Tag and Rince and tell them what had happened, then move on with the journey she had accepted.

Once more, erudition presented itself. She needed to find her friends, but she knew now that there were far better ways to do so than just shout their names at the top of her voice and hope that they could hear and answer.

Kneeling again, still avoiding the sword that lay near for the moment, Alaena brushed the growth at her feet with her hand. She was rewarded with a tingling sensation that seemed to float between where her fingers touched the earth and where the bracelet rested snugly on her wrist. Intrigued, Alaena splayed her fingers out wide, then carefully pressed her hand down on the earth, much as she had done on the stone at the Fields after Scruff had died.

Immediately, her senses expanded. She could feel the forest. The water running near and the rocks over which it ran were palpable to her, as were the myriad of creatures that sat quietly nearby, wary of the power they could feel near their nooks and nests. Looking around in wonder, Alaena realised the trees were no longer an impediment to her field of vision as she saw with more than her eyes. She could sense Tag and Rince lying asleep on the forest floor, some way down the track behind her. Two foxes were sniffing the air curiously a short way further into the forest, wondering if the human scents they smelt were a threat or something to be investigated.

Eager to test her newfound powers, Alaena knelt fully then leaned forward to press her left arm down into the earth as well. The bracelet on her wrist shifted a little, spraying reflections as she focused, feeling both foreign and strangely familiar at the same time. Extending her senses, Alaena felt only a momentary thrill of freedom and potential before alarm rang through her awareness. She pulled back, snatching her hands from the ground into fists as a small bead of sweat formed on her brow.

Shields. Somewhere in the back of her mind, the knowledge she had gained told her that power of this kind must not be wielded unprepared and unprotected. There were great dangers in doing so, and beings who could tear her mind apart in an instant if they found her as she tried.

Forcing away the visions of taloned beasts that her new memories brought terrifyingly to her mind, Alaena reached for the sword at last, laying her right hand tentatively on the hilt before lifting it carefully from the ground. Once more, knowledge flooded her mind. This was Al'Tahal's sword. The Swordmaster of the Northern Palace and the love of Simcha's heart.

Much as Alaena wanted to explore this further, she lowered the weapon for a moment, thinking hard. In the moment she had spread her awareness, she had felt the Protector. He was leagues away and not likely to reach them this day, but he was coming. She couldn't feel him personally from this distance, but she had felt a black, poisonous power that she knew to be his within the forest to the north. It infected the Wood around it with malice, and with her enhanced senses, she needed to expend no power to feel it radiating towards her. They needed to move.

Backtracking quickly, Alaena found her two companions lying peacefully, cradled by leaf and vine that had grown around them while they slept. Much of the knowledge that had come to her in the night was still a mystery, but some essential understandings were already coming through to her mind. By altering her perception to see with her mind rather than just her eyes, Alaena could see rings of colours surrounding her friends lying before her. Even as she focused on her companions, she recalled from another memory that the same talent could be applied to any living thing. Should she wish, Alaena knew without ever having practiced the art that she could look at a tree and know if it was hale or rotten inside.

Shaking her head, she allowed herself a quick smile. If every new thing she had learned was going to have so many branches, then she had a long road ahead of her indeed!

Bringing herself back to the present, Alaena focused her mind. Though she had never done this before, it felt second nature to her. As Simcha had done so many times so long ago, Alaena stitched Shields across her awareness, using the lines of light visible to her mind as she engaged her craft and focused on her companions lying before her. Lanes, Alaena recalled absently. The lines of light were called Lanes.

Shaking her head to dispel the distraction of knowledge once more, Alaena refocused on her companions and the task at hand. Rince radiated an aura of peace and contentment, blissfully ignorant of what Alaena feared were dark times to come.

Tag, lying so close, was a far more complex conundrum of auras. He was dedicated and fierce but there was also a grey, untrusting edge buried deep in his soul. Shunning faith or forgiveness in others, he held his feeling close. Alaena also found herself surprisingly relieved to see that there was no hate or evil. Tag would keep himself a mystery to the world as much as he could, but he would never betray another and never betray his principles. Alaena still hadn't discussed how Tag had happened to be at the gate to the Keep only two nights ago to make their final escape possible, but Alaena now knew she could trust him. The rest would come.

Wishing she had more time to explore this new awareness, she sighed. Now was not the time.

"Wake." Gently, she prodded the minds of her two companions.

Rince came awake slowly, stretching luxuriously on the carpet of green growth. As his eyes opened, his first sight was of Alaena standing over him and he smiled. Tag likewise took a few moments to wake. As soon as awareness touched him though, his

246

eyes flew open and he sprang to one knee, instinctively drawing a dagger from his boot in the same fluid motion. His glance up and down the path took in Alaena standing before him and Rince lying next to him, as he clearly tried to understand what had happened and why it appeared he had been sleeping in the middle of a path in the depths of the wood.

"Peace, Tag," Alaena said quietly, drawing his attention to her. "Much has happened this night, but we are all safe and whole for the moment." Smiling slyly, she couldn't resist adding, "Though had I known you were quite so prone to fall asleep so readily, perhaps we might have found ourselves a more reliable guide through the woods?"

If Tag heard the humour or appreciated Alaena's attempt at levity, it was not evident. Instead, he gradually gained his feet, staring at Alaena as if seeing her for the first time. The girl that had accompanied him for the past two days still stood before him, starkly different.

Before he could tackle the conundrum of how he could possibly have fallen asleep for what appeared to be the entire night, he focused first on the obvious as he returned his blade to the sheath sewn carefully into his boot.

A band of gold, fashioned to resemble waves with small representations of the sun at the crest of each swell, sat snugly on Alaena's left wrist. The band was encrusted with gems that Tag considered would likely be worth a King's ransom. In her right hand, she casually held a blade such that Tag had never seen. Rapier thin and as long as his arm, it would appear plain to the untrained eye. To Tag's expert eye however, the early light glinted off a weapon superbly crafted that would be deadly when wielded by the right hand.

Uncharacteristically nonplussed, for clearly Alaena's night had not passed as uneventfully as his own, Tag ventured carefully.

"Much indeed, girl," he said gruffly. Indicating the bracelet and sword with a nod of his head, he continued. "Who knew, for example, that you could find both a jeweller and a swordsmith with such superlative skills this deep in the wood and at night. What's more, who would be willing to gift such treasures to a wanderer within?"

Raising his eyes to Alaena's face once more, Tag hesitated before continuing. The sounds of the wood were the only noise intruding on the silence as he paused. Alaena's eyes were curiously different. They had not changed colour or even shape so much as depth. That tingle ran down Tag's back once more to lodge at the base of his spine. Like no one had before, he felt like Alaena was looking into his very soul.

Thrust once more into the unusual situation of feeling like he had no control of events or understanding of what was going on around him, Tag cleared his throat and started again.

"Alaena," he phrased carefully. It was the first time Tag had called her by name. Calling her 'girl' now just didn't feel right. Cursing his hesitation and wondering how he suddenly felt so childish, he asked simply, "What happened last night?"

Rince looked from Alaena to Tag, understanding little. The gold band encircling Alaena's wrist was beautiful, and he thought the blade looked fine as well, but he too had too many other questions of which the bracelet and sword were just one.

Alaena was watching them both and seemed to be considering Tag's question before answering. As with so many other things happening, her response was unexpected. Even as Rince wondered if he should say something now, the filtered light around him seemed to dim and a voice spoke inside his head. He could feel Alaena's presence there, as if she were holding him close. Somehow Tag was there too, and yet not.

Frightened at first, for too many things were occurring that he did not understand, Rince recoiled in his mind. Immediately, Alaena's presence surrounded him, radiating peace and love. *"Fear not, my friend. You have given much for me these past few days. I will not allow you to come to harm."* The resistance Rince felt faded away in an overwhelming rush of trust. Obviously, there was no need to fear. In a moment he forgot that he was even worried and relaxed completely, waiting for whatever may happen.

"Thank you, Rince," the voice came to his mind. Smiling, Rince replied in kind, saying somehow without words that she needed to thank him not, for he loved her and would follow wherever she led. The words in his mind seemed to echo out into a void. Rince wondered vaguely in his lassitude whether Alaena even heard them, or even now if he had said them.

"You are safe, Tag. Fear not." Still connected, Rince heard the words clearly, though they were not directed at him now. It was Alaena's voice, but the words were spoken as though they were uttered quietly on the other side of a very thin wall. Rince smiled even wider. He had already learned to love Alaena and trust her with his life. Tag was old and overly cautious but could still learn, Rince was sure.

With detached ambivalence, Rince felt Tag's emotions flow through this strange link. Tag wasn't afraid, he was full of cold calculation. The ice in him resisted, hardened by long years of isolation and distrust. Grudgingly though, it thawed as Alaena's gentle urging unwound the complex caution that had allowed Tag to survive as long as he had.

Against the ocean of Alaena's will, Rince eventually felt Tag's resistance crumble. The wall between them evaporated, and Rince felt their conscious thoughts meld together in this strange, empty space. Through his fog of contented lethargy, Rince smiled once more. With lessons like this, perhaps Tag would learn even faster than Rince thought he would.

After eternal moments of shared consciousness, Alaena's presence modulated. As though another being joined their communion, her voice rang out once more. Rather than the deep, sonorous voice from before, this was a lighter feminine tone. It made one think of laughter and light.

In their mind's eyes, Alaena appeared once more as she spoke, the bracelet on her arm still held up before her. Rince's blue eyes widened, aglow with reflected, rainbow light. Alaena's soft face took on an alien, elongated appearance, bathed in matching reflections. Gold and yellow-white light washed through the waves of the bracelet's spiral design. The gems set within sparkled green, blue and ochre with light of their own, bright counterpoints at the crest of the golden waves. Her voice modulated once more, this time taking broader tones and strange, archaic inflections of speech.

"This be the Bracelet of Simcha, last and most holy Matriarch of the Temple of Eternal Light. As companion and abettor to Hor'yn, Arch-Mage, together they gave their lives to save the world until such time as I, the Appointed, should come to free them of the burden they accepted to save the world."

Despite the ethereal tranquillity of their state, a deep sorrow reached through the words to touch the souls of Rince and Tag. The memories behind Alaena's voice were proud, but they were also profoundly grieved. Rince, with little in his experience to help him understand the emotions he felt, simply bowed his head as tears gathered in his eyes.

Tag, with a life of ruthless passion lived so far, experienced the loss as profoundly as if he were living it himself. His very soul yearned to help and forgive and heal. Mostly, however, he understood the yearning for an end. For closure. Though aching to drop to his knees and sob, he stood firm as the emotions buffeted him. Whatever came, whatever sacrifice was required, he would do it to see this through to an end.

As quickly as it came, the other voice faded and melded into Alaena's own. In her clear, light voice, Alaena spoke quietly, her words absorbed into the deep forest that surrounded them. Lowering her arm, the bracelet's light faded green, blue and white into the tangled mat of vine at their feet. *"Now bequeathed,"* Alaena said with a conviction tinged with sorrow's echo, *"this Bracelet is mine to wield in this age, for while Fire burned all in the Dark days, so the Light will come once more."*

For an eternal second, all was still. It was as though the Wood had taken a breath and was reluctant to release it, such was the solemnity of the moment.

Without fanfare, the moment passed. Once more, they were merely three companions standing on a forest track in the depths of the wood, while the wind gently ruffled the leaves about them in the filtered, early morning light.

Rince, blinking as if just awake, awkwardly brushed tears from his cheeks as he glanced tentatively around, peering at the forest as if to validate he was still where he thought he was, before looking back once more to Alaena with eyes full of wonder.

Tag regained awareness of his surroundings quickly but paid little attention to them. His emotions still in turmoil, Tag realised he was clenching his teeth with all his nerves on edge, eager for action. After a moment, he realised his fingers were hurting and he looked down to see his knuckles white on the hilt of his dagger, clenching the worn leather binding like it was his only hold on hope. Teeth or fist, he wasn't sure how to unclench either or even sure if he should.

Alaena came back to herself quickly, though it was clear to her already that what 'herself' was the previous day and what it was now were vastly different things. It wasn't just an awareness of being different. In that respect, Alaena knew things now that others only dreamed of glimpsing, and she was privy to knowledge of the dark days that had long been lost. What was strange to Alaena was the recognition that she was now a different person. Shaking her head, Alaena allowed herself a small smile before setting herself to the task she now knew lay before her: she must get to the mountains. But first there was the practical matter of her new sword. She could hardly go traipsing through the woods waving the blade of Al'Tahal around like a machete! Fortunately, her new knowledge was more than up to the task.

In short order, Alaena had crafted a makeshift sheath for the sword, wrapped around with some cloth from her backpack and secured around her waist comfortably with a short length of cord.

When she was done, she looked up to see Tag staring at her like he'd never seen her before. "Tag?" Alaena enquired gently. "What is it?"

Tag almost jumped when addressed, such was his discomfiture. He felt like his mind was full of sod. She was standing before him obviously expecting a response, but he couldn't recall what the question was. If only his teeth and fingers would stop hurting, perhaps he could concentrate again.

"Tag," Alaena repeated after a few moments. Stepping forward, she placed a soft hand on his clenched fist and caught his gaze with hers. Again, the now familiar voice spoke in his mind, pushing his fears away. Finally, his last defences crumbled. Tag's jaw unlocked and he loosened his grip on the dagger, though he kept his arm high simply so he would not lose contact with Alaena's hand. A tear welled in his eye as Alaena smiled before him, nodding in understanding.

Falling to one knee at last Tag bent his head in supplication and put his hands to the forest floor. "At last, you have come!" he said simply. Shaking his head, he commented almost to himself, "I did not think it would be in my time."

Looking up, Tag closed his fist once more, this time lifting it to his heart rather than dropping it to his blade. Overcome with emotion, Tag committed himself to wherever the journey might take him. "Appointed," he began formally. "That you are here now is both a joy and a sorrow. While I am no scholar, in terms of the latter all prophecies of this age speak of death and upheaval to come with your presence. I am fearful, then, of what is to come, and what your arrival represents."

Tag paused for a moment, letting the words float into the brooding depths of the forest. Alaera, prompted by Tag's words, could see through the mind's eye of her new memories the desecration of the land that led to the last desperate, defiant act of Simcha and Hor'yn. She could still feel the echoes of their Word of Command resonating through the depths of the Earth beneath her feet.

Fortunately, Tag continued quickly, allowing Alaena to pull her thoughts away from the overwhelming fear and desperation that led to such actions before contemplating whether she would have the courage to do the same should she find herself in the same position.

"For the former, though," Tag continued bluntly, "those same Prophecies also say that you represent our only hope. Without you, we will all surely perish!"

Again, the gravity of his words invoked visions of demons and death, with bodies strewn across landscapes blasted by fire and blanketed by ash. Once more, Alaena had to pull herself forcibly back to the present as Tag concluded.

Looking fervently into her eyes, Tag committed himself to her purpose. "If by my life or my death I may serve you, Appointed, I will do so. From this moment on, I am yours to command and will follow wherever you may go, should you have me."

Completing one of the lengthiest soliloquies of his life thus far, Tag once more bowed his head, awaiting the acceptance or rejection of his offer of service. What he
really expected to hear or feel he wasn't sure, but the words that came from the Appointed in response to his oath filled Tag with elation.

"Your offer of service is accepted, Tag. In accepting your fealty, know that I accept both your loyalty and your life. We are now bound together in the Light on our soul paths from this point forward. In return for your service, I will honour your commitment and do all in my power to keep you safe, that we may both find peace at the end of the road. Stand now, that we may walk this road together from this point on!"

Finally, Tag raised his head to see Alaena's hand outstretched before him. On her wrist, the bracelet glowed warm in the light filtering down from the forest canopy. Brushing his hands free of dirt, uncharacteristically conscious of the fact that he hadn't bathed for some days now, Tag took her hand at last and smiled as he gained his feet.

Rince just looked from one to the other as they stood there, aware that something important had just happened but, just as importantly, that he was hungry. Somehow now just didn't seem the right time to ask about food, though, so he shifted uncertainly on his feet, wondering what to say.

Glancing at Rince for a moment too, Alaena's smile stayed as she asked Tag, "Night is coming so we should not tarry, but perhaps something else from your bag would be a good idea too, lest Rince fall behind from lack of sustenance?"

A short while later, with immediate cravings sated by some cold rations from Tag's satchel, Alaena turned and led the way forward into the darkening Wood, skirting the road southward directly towards the mountain, Rince and Tag following close behind. They moved quietly, each occupied with their own thoughts. The path on which they trod remained clear of obstacles and travelled straight as an arrow through the wood, heading directly for the mountains.

Tag, bringing up the rear, could not resist looking over his shoulder regularly, unable to decide if he was starting to enjoy or remained eerily discomforted that the path behind them disappeared into a tangle of tree, root and vine as they walked.

Chapter 25 - Pursuit

Even as Alaena, Rince and Tag resumed their trek through the depths of the Wood towards the mountain, Wilmen and Rogan's steeds entered the northern end of the forest at a run. Small animals scattered in alarm from the immediate vicinity as the heavy, pounding footfalls of Rogan's massive beast echoed deep into the trees.

As soon as they entered the cover of the trees, Wilmen's concern grew. They had left too late in the day. The light was failing. The moment she and Rogan had entered the Wood, gloom shrouded them. They had perhaps an hour's ride before darkness fell completely, at which point it would be too dangerous for both steed and riders to push the horses to anything more than a steady walk. In silent agreement, Wilmen and Rogan spurred their horses to a greater pace, eager to cover as much ground as possible before the light failed completely.

Keeping a good distance between them, Darven matched pace, well aware of the risk they were taking and growing ever more curious as to what might drive the woman and her gargantuan companion to risk the darkening road at such a pace. One sardonically amusing thought he did entertain while he leaned forward to press his mount for more speed was that at least, with the noise the huge man's beast was making, he did not have to be concerned about losing his quarry!

In contrast to Darven's mood, the Protector became more and more discontent as he travelled deeper into the Wood.

Having set out from the Keep early in the afternoon, two trackers had gone ahead as instructed, to find traces of the Witch and her accomplice, a boy with sandy brown hair. In a cloud of sooty dust, they had raced out of the Keep, down to the mountain road that led into the Wood with all haste, while the Protector's more heavily laden contingent kept their beasts to a fast walk, awaiting news before picking up their own pace.

By the time the Protector's party reached the edge of the tree line, one of the trackers came back up the road at a gallop to meet them, reining his beast in tightly and turning it roughly to match pace next to the Protector in order to report as they continued to move. Clearly pleased to be able to deliver good news, the tracker somewhat breathlessly reported to the Protector that they had found the point at which the group they sought had left the road, only a short way into the Wood. Even now the other tracker was following that path, leaving a clear trail for the Protector's group to follow behind.

Glancing quickly, the tracker scanned the pale features of the Protector in the filtered afternoon light, looking for his reaction. The patch meant he couldn't see what had happened to that side of his face, but even the dim light couldn't hide the puckered scar that tracked deep across the Protector's forehead. While not regularly in his company, the tracker had attended the Gathering only days before in Morlyn where the Protector had spoken. The tracker would swear there had been no wound then, let alone a healed scar. What he was seeing confirmed all the rumours that had been rife within the Keep for the last day or so. Something unnatural had occurred here. A thrill of fear travelled down the tracker's neck. Suddenly, he wished he was anywhere else but even remotely near this man.

The Protector chose that moment to glance sideways. The tracker held his breath, unreasonably afraid, for he had more news to deliver. He had expected the Protector to be pleased with his initial report, but if the fact that they had found the trail so quickly was met with disdain or displeasure, how would the next piece of information be taken? Still, there was nothing to it but to go on, so he spoke quickly, eager to end this strange conversation.

"I can take you straight there, m'Lord," the tracker continued, "but you should know also that there were three tracks leading into the woods, not two as we were told!"

This time, the Protector turned his head fully to stare straight at the tracker with his good eye. The stare, framed by the Protector's broken, twisted face, was full of malice, and it took all the courage the man had not to kick heel to his horse and bolt away down the track there and then.

"There were two smaller prints of children as we expected to find, m'Lord, but another heavier track was with them. It was a man's print, m'Lord, so it seems there are three we seek, not two as we thought!"

The Protector, to the tracker's eternal gratitude, simply nodded when receiving this report, already aware that the two children had not escaped alone.

Taking the party by surprise, the Protector said no more. Instead, he urged his horse forward, eager to chase down his prey now they had the trail. The tracker and the hand of Guard left behind spurred their horses, urging the beasts to a run to catch the Protector and lead them after a few more minutes to the trail into the Wood where Alaena, Rince and Tag had first left the road.

A short while later, the party found themselves in a small clearing not far into the Wood where the ground was covered by a tangled web of vines that looked very much like new growth. Nearby, a stream bubbled. On a fallen log at the other side of the clearing, the other tracker leapt to his feet as the party trampled through, crushing the new growth and sending a smell of fresh sap into the air.

The Protector stepped forward to face the man directly. He wasted no time with niceties. "Where are they?" he demanded, frowning.

The unfortunate tracker was unable to say. With fear in his voice, he assured the Protector he had inspected every inch of the clearing. There were three obvious tracks leading into the clearing, but none leading out. There were no discernible paths, other than the one they had used to enter, going in or out of the clearing either. It was as though they had reached this place and flown away, the tracker said, unable to explain it any other way.

A few of the Guard signed themselves against evil at this point, reminding themselves in low voices that the girl they were chasing was a witch. Perhaps she had indeed cast dark magic here and whisked herself away on the wind.

The Protector paid little attention to these mumblings. Dismissing the tracker as useless, he wandered the clearing, extending his senses as much as he dared into the forest to understand what had happened here. There was magic, most certainly. Old magic.

For the first time, the Protector felt the thrill of the chase. He had been looking forward to finding the girl and gutting her slowly as he took her for himself, but had not considered that a challenge. Her Master, however – for the man that had arranged her freedom could be none less than that if he was capable of this kind of conjury – represented another challenge entirely.

To take a soul like that, the Protector thought, would be his greatest feat to date. He could almost taste the power flowing into his being. For reasons none of his Guard or the trackers with him understood, the Protector turned suddenly, pointing into the Wood to the south, directly towards the mountain.

At a certain point, the Protector had felt it. A residual trail of power, leading straight as an arrow into the depths of the wood. Somehow, the Sorcerer had led his companions through the Wood where no paths seemed to exist. The Protector did not need a path however, for the direction was clear. Explaining nothing, he had led his confused men back to the road, mounted and taken off at a gallop to the south, the rest of his party scrambling into their saddles to follow, praying for their souls as the trees flashed by on either side of them.

So it was that, as the afternoon light started to fade and gloom enveloped the road, the Protector and his Guard found themselves some distance past Fyr and well on the way to Taram, the last village before the road started to climb into the mountains towards the Wytharn Pass. The Protector, seemingly possessed, had pushed the party relentlessly since taking off at mad speed earlier in the afternoon. The Wood had passed as a blur for his exhausted party, yet there seemed no end to the Protector's mad flight.

As swiftly as it had started, the headlong dash towards the mountains ended. With only a few leagues left to cover before the road started its climb into the haunches of the mountain, the Protector slowed his pace. His party, while relieved that they were no longer likely to break their necks galloping along a road in the dark, watched nervously as the increasingly dim figure of the Protector peered intently into the woods to his left. Much as they tried, none of his companions could see or hear what held his attention, for they could see little past the line of trees immediately before them. Hopes that some may have had for continuing a while longer to the inn at Tyr were dashed when the Protector pulled his horse to a halt and leapt from the saddle. No sooner did his feet touch the ground, the Protector ordered torches lit and stomped over to the edge of the road, staring once more into the wood.

With every man in the party eager to avoid the Protector's wrath, no time was wasted. In moments, all had dismounted. Packs were flung open, and flasks of oil pulled forth to douse the ends of dead branches lying nearby that blazed into light quickly with flint and steel. With no other apparent option, the horses were tethered to roots and low branches to stop them straying. Soon after, the small group was gathered and ready to move. The Protector, who had remained with his back to them staring into the trees as preparations were made, finally turned. The still vivid wound across his forehead had the appearance of blood in the red glow of the torchlight. For a few heavy beats of their hearts, only the sound of the crackling wood of the torches broke the silence of the deep wood.

"We hunt a witch tonight, men."

Hardened to battle as many of his party were, more than a few jumped and surreptitiously signed themselves against evil. The Protector's voice grated with emotion, anger warring with eagerness in his tone.

"Loosen your weapons, be alert and stay close," he continued, his one dark eye moving purposefully from man to man in the flickering light, assessing their resolve. Dishevelled against the backdrop of a forest made even darker and more foreboding behind the pool of light cast by the torches, those he viewed thought, very privately, that the Protector looked like a figure from a nightmare.

Without taking a torch for himself and with no further comment, the Protector pulled his own sword from its sheath, turned and stepped purposefully from the path into the trees. Nervous glances passing between them and torches held high, the rest of his party followed suit, leaving the horses behind as they followed their Protector into the gloom.

Chapter 26 - First Blood

Alaena slowed, then stopped entirely. Rince, immediately behind her, came to a halt as well, glancing back quizzically over his shoulder at Tag, who shrugged and lifted the small lantern he had to light their way, to see if he could tell what had captured Alaena's attention.

Her slender hand reached out to touch a branch that bordered their strange path, head cocked as if listening. Staring at her still in wonder, Tag again felt a protective love flood his being. Perhaps this is what it is like to be a father, he wondered, then chuckled at himself. These were musings that only yesterday he never would have thought to experience.

Dropping her hand after a short while, she turned to them with a strange mix of sadness and anger in her eyes. "The Protector and his Guard are here," she said without preamble, gesturing vaguely to her left.

Tag's hand leapt immediately to his sword, as if fearing they would leap upon them from the trees at any moment. Rince just peered around, alarm etching his features.

"Fear not," Alaena said quietly, calming them both. "They are some way from us yet, and the Wood will deal with the Guard." Frowning, Alaena seemed to consider, turning to look at the path ahead and behind. "We could outpace them without difficulty, but the Protector is a problem best dealt with now rather than later," she decided, appearing to think aloud. "Come, there is a place not far ahead that will suffice."

With that, Alaena turned and resumed their trek at a faster pace. The path continued straight and clear. Tag no longer checked behind but instead scanned from side to side, frustrated that his light penetrated only a few feet into the trees before being consumed by the Wood. Rarely had he felt so vulnerable in his life, yet he could think of nothing to do other than to trust and follow this strange woman along this unworldly path in the depths of the Wood as the night deepened and enemies approached.

Soon the path led naturally to a small clearing. Tag, at a nod from Alaena, opened the shuttered lantern enough to illuminate an area a few dozen spaces across, where rock from the mountain's roots showed through, leaving a flat, clear space in the centre.

Allowing no time for discussion, Alaena spoke quietly, her voice again taking on that strange, almost alien lilt. Pointing to the far side of the area, she ordered, "The two of you wait in the trees. Stay out of sight and stay quiet, for this is a battle I will wage alone."

"Ala!" Rince said, speaking up for the first time since dark had fallen fully. "What do you mean? I don't understand any of this!" His voice raised a little, venting frustration. "If the Protector is coming, then we must fight him together, surely!" Brave beyond his years, Rince set hands on hips and took a stance of defiance. "I will not let you face him alone, Ala. We have come this far and cannot lose you now!"

Looking fondly at the boy, Alaena smiled gently. For a moment, the girl he knew shone through. "No, Rince," she said kindly but firmly. "You will doubtless help in future, but this is a fight that I am now, even considering Tag's undoubted skill with the blade, best equipped to deal with."

Glancing eastward towards the road once more, Alaena cut short any discussion. When she turned her face back, her features and tone brooked no further argument. "Go." she ordered. "Take shelter in the trees, for he is almost upon us."

Not waiting for a response, Alaena turned quickly and made her way to the rock in the centre of the clearing. There she stood facing into the forest, legs braced slightly apart and head bowed, either in prayer or in readiness.

Tag, unclear as to what was happening but wise enough to understand an order when it was given, took Rince's arm and pulled him away. A shiver ran down his spine as he dragged Rince across the area and into the trees, extinguishing his lantern as he went, for he had heard the final words Alaena breathed in that alien tone as she moved.

Taking a position well protected but giving a direct view into the clearing, Tag knelt, pulling Rince down beside him. Not wanting to be distracted by pointless banter, he quieted Rince's protestations with a hand on his shoulder, pointing towards Alaena. With the lantern dark now, their eyes adjusted quickly. Though there was no moon, starlight washed the area in an ethereal light, outlining Alaena's slim form perfectly as she stood motionless on the granite beneath her. Arms by her side, she looked both indomitable and desperately vulnerable for a moment, standing alone under the stars, bathed in silver light.

No, Tag thought to himself. *Definitely not vulnerable.* While her sword remained on the loop of leather by her side, the bracelet on her wrist spoke otherwise. The gems encircling it glowed subtly green, red and gold. The words Alaena had uttered as she moved to the rock a few moments before came back to him, and Tag hunkered down lower, keeping a hand on Rince to ensure the boy did nothing unwise.

Uncommonly nervous, Tag played Alaena's words back and forth in his mind. Tumbling meanings around in his thoughts, he wondered what they meant. *"This ends now,"* Alaena had whispered. What was going to end, Tag wondered, and how would it end? Shaking his head, he almost smiled to himself, though the curl of his lip in the dark hinted more at sarcasm than humour. Such questions were for scholars, not assassins, he chided himself gently. That said, what kind of assassin sat behind a rock in the middle of the night in the depths of the strangest Wood he had ever seen, playing nursemaid to a boy on the orders of a girl who was apparently going to protect them both from the murderous Protector and his Guard? The sardonic curl to his lip stretched further in the dark as he considered the irony.

Tag's musings were cut short and his thoughts returned to the immediate situation as sounds floated out to them from the dark. Crashing, cursing and the snapping of twigs and branches intruded on the silence as something forced its way through the foliage and undergrowth, finally breaking free to stand on the other side of the clearing, panting.

Bathed in starlight, which accentuated his atrocious state, the Protector was a sight to behold.

Clothing in tatters and bleeding from many cuts and abrasions, the Protector halted, breathing heavily. His ruined face appeared all the more hideous as the silver light of the night sky etched out trails of blood, the puckered skin of his eye socket and half-healed scars in macabre detail. Since leaving the road, he and his party had forced their way through the Wood, which at times had felt impenetrable. Along the way, his party had dwindled one by one. Root, vine and limb had cut them off from each other, disorienting all bar the Protector himself who, guided by the beacon of power only he could feel radiating from within the trees, stayed true to his course.

When the last torch had gone and the lost cries of his companions faded behind him, the Protector had flailed on through the dark, falling many times over root and vine only to regain his feet and have thorns and branches tear at him in the dark as he blundered on, blind to all except his objective.

"You!" he snarled at last, facing Alaena. The exclamation hung in the air as an accusation.

The Protector had expected another, but there was no doubting the power emanating from this girl. He could feel it and taste it in his twisted being. His mouth almost watered, lewdly savouring the pleasure and strength he would gain from taking her soul.

His hand grasped for his sword, but his fingers closed on air. Somewhere between the road and here, the Protector's weapon had slipped from its sheath or fallen from his grasp, lost. Undeterred and with the superlative confidence that accompanied his towering ego, the Protector simply smirked. He would not be using a sword to have his revenge on this upstart girl, in any case. He only needed a hand about her throat, then all she had would be his.

Somewhere in the back of his mind, a shred of sanity was calling out a warning. This was not the same girl who had quailed in his dungeons less than a day ago. There was power here, and there was danger for him. Pushed long past restraint and with the memory of steel embedded in his eye still fresh, the Protector

263

threw caution to the wind and let the bile in his soul free to wreak his revenge.

His twisted smile still in place, the Protector wasted no time. Unclenching his fists, the necromancer raised arms to the heavens, scribing black symbols in the air as he mouthed guttural incantations. As if a veil had been pulled across the sky and stars above, the clearing darkened. Like projections of the gloom that descended, tendrils of caustic magic snaked from the Protector's outstretched hands, burning through the air towards Alaena, eager to possess her. The ground trembled and even the trees around them seemed to lean back, finding the evil loosed in their midst abhorrent. Tag and Rince both remained rooted to the spot, unable to tear their eyes from the venomous vines of necrotic malevolence that writhed their way towards their precious Alaena.

For a moment, Alaena quailed. She knew nothing of Power such as this. Her mind went blank, panic threatening to overwhelm her. There was evil in this man before her. She felt it in her bones. Alaena could still smell the Protector's vile breath as he pressed his body against hers in his dungeon while he ripped her clothes away and described in succinct detail just how he was going to violate her body and mind. If the man was evil, the black conjuration writhing its way towards her came from the basest parts of his soul. It radiated a prodigiously malicious intent and if Alaena let it touch her, as t would in moments, she knew all would be undone.

Strangely, it was the thought of Rince that broke Alaena from her lethargic state. Raising her head, Alaena stared into the blackness and found her courage. For her to die at the hands of this vile man was one thing; the thought of Rince in his hands though, that could never be permitted.

While Alaena herself had little personal experience with magic, her new knowledge made it clear that there was power at hand and, at this point, she had no other options. As the Protector's incantation reached a fevered pitch and the blackness reared to swallow her whole, Alaena lifted her head. Releasing herself to the outcome, her calm, clear voice cut through all fear.

"No," she stated evenly, raising her eyes to encompass the extent of the evil that surrounded her. "This will not be."

Turning her thoughts inward, Alaena reached for Simcha's bracelet in her mind. It responded immediately, charged with latent force. Rather than seeking to commune with it as she had before, however, remembrance and recognition dawned as she made the connection. Like the Lanes, Simcha's bracelet was not an object of power in itself. Intimately, she knew that now. Rather, it was a conduit. It connected the user with the true source of Power that lay beneath. Experiencing a thrill of anticipatory trepidation, Alaena drove her awareness through the bracelet in her mind and down into the Earth beneath her feet, beseeching aid.

For the first time in an age, through the mind and will of Alaena, the bracelet of the Temple of Light communed with the Earth. Together and in perfect unison, they bestowed their Power to the Appointed.

Potential flooded Alaena's being as the Lanes opened fully in her awareness for the first time. Instantly, lines of silver light sprang into her perception from root, rock, tree and sky. All were ready to answer her call and her command. Rocked with the enormity of the response, Alaena steadied herself on her feet. While such a prodigious stream of force could not be absorbed by the untrained mind, Alaena immediately grasped and managed the flow, realising as she did that Simcha's knowledge was unfolding in her mind at the same time, teaching her both caution and care in the use of such force, even as it flowed into, through and around her being. Stunned with the beauty and raw grace of the power she now understood lay all around her, Alaena rejoiced in the unfettered supremacy of her will. Her bracelet responded in kind. Blazing forth with argent strength, she felt it as a part of her being, filling her with surety and unrestrained might.

At last, Alaena knew what she must do. With a simple thought, a stinging net of shields sprang into place around her mind, keeping the blackness at bay as she gazed at the Protector through the morass of his conjuration. His twisted features were approaching apoplexy and his remaining eye was bulging with blood as he strove to complete his spell and his domination of Alaena. Feeling her resist now, his efforts became more frenzied and desperate, but her defences were far beyond what the meagre minds he had overwhelmed in the past could muster. With her shields set, Alaena shifted her mind to channel Power. It flowed from the Earth without pause or restraint, and Alaena let the bracelet continue to guide her in her work as her conjuration took shape like an old friend.

The spell came to her quickly as the blackness engulfed her, futilely seeking entrance to her mind.

Untouched in the maelstrom and revelling in her power, Alaena completed her spell and brought down her will.

Lightning convulsed in the clearing. Coruscating coils of power cauterised the air, shredding the Protector's spell in a heartbeat. The concussive release of force threw Rince and Tag backwards to the ground as they shielded their eyes from blinding light that crackled through the air and illuminated the area like the sun. Simultaneously, like long fingers sprouting from the earth, root and vine erupted from the ground around the Protector. Writhing up his body, thick, verdant growth encased his legs and torso before reaching for his arms and head. Suddenly terrified and striving to respond while his body became mummified by living wood, the Protector endeavoured to conjure a defence but found his mind as locked as his body was imprisoned by the impossible.

As suddenly as it had begun, the prolific display of power ended and starlight reclaimed the clearing. By the time their eyes had adjusted once more, Tag and Rince could see that Alaena had made her way across to stand before the Protector and his living prison.

She stood a moment before him, gathering her breath as she surveyed her handiwork. Alaena could see no part of the Protector's body other than portions of his ruined face and his one eye that stared at her madly. A mumbling came from within his wooden prison, but Alaena made no attempt to understand the words. Finally, she spoke. Her voice carried clearly to Tag and Rince across the tranquil calm that now descended on the area.

"You are an evil man, Protector, and I deem you fallen," Alaena pronounced. "I cannot return the souls you have taken or undo the grief you have effected in your life, but I can see to it that you will no longer cause harm in this world."

Pausing, Alaena wondered for a moment if she should allow him the opportunity to speak. Testing with her senses, she decided against it. Anger and hate still radiated from his being. There would be no contrition, and there was no hope for penitence for this man.

Formally then, and without further consideration, she concluded her judgement.

"May Light return where you have extinguished it, and may Earth rejoice at your end."

If the Protector had any last words, he either did not or could not utter them. In any case, the memory of his end would never leave the minds of Rince or Tag for as long as they lived.

With no further words, Alaena raised her right hand, palm upwards, then bowed her head and closed her hand to a fist. Between one breath and the next, the root and vine encasing the Protector shuddered, then coiled closed and twisted tight, crushing him as effortlessly as one might crush an insect beneath a boot. The sound of bones snapping lasted only a moment, but the verdure continued to twist and tighten until it merged into one and all trace of the Protector was gone.

When dawn came, the morning light would show a new tree standing oddly out of place in a clearing deep in the Wood. Though it would grow and then die in its time, no one who ever saw it could say what kind of wood it was or why it never seeded to produce another of its kind.

Chapter 27 - Aftermath

The party of three came together somberly. Alaena, thoughts still humming from her first real use of Power, moved slowly back to stand on the rock once more. Weariness of both body and mind threatened to overwhelm her briefly, but with her feet touching the stone directly again, she drew strength from the Earth, reviving her body a little while giving time for her mind to adjust to what she had just done. As she did so, Tag and Rince tentatively stepped out from the trees and moved towards her.

First to break the silence that blanketed the area in the aftermath of her battle with the Protector, Rince enquired carefully, his voice tinged with concern. "Ala?" he ventured, taking another step towards her. "Ala?" he repeated a little louder when there was no response.

Finally, Alaena dragged her gaze from the ground beneath her to look at Rince and Tag. A small smile creased her face before she spoke. "Fear not, my dear friends. I will be fine," she said quietly, glancing back at the tree where the Protector had once stood. "Perhaps I overdid it, but at least I recall now some of what I might be capable of," she mused almost to herself. Shaking herself free of some of her lethargy, she looked back and smiled once more. "A little rest is all I need, and perhaps some time to think ..."

Alaena got no further before Rince ran forward with a cry of relief to wrap his arms around her. When Alaena returned his exuberant embrace, Rince wasn't sure whether to laugh or cry.

Pulling him close, Alaena recalled the moment fighting against the Protector when she realised what mattered most to her. Emotion welled in her and she closed her eyes, holding Rince even tighter for a moment as she regained control of her tattered emotions.

Still channelling power, Alaena's enhanced senses could feel the strength of the emotions running through the boy as they held each other close. Strangely, as she held his body close to hers, Alaena realised that their time was not yet here. Somehow Alanea could feel that they, Alanea and Rince, were not yet complete. At fifteen, Rince was still very much a boy while she, at seventeen, held feelings far more mature and complex than he did, even without the wisdom, knowledge and power imparted to her this past day.

No, Alaena thought. *Someday perhaps, but not yet.*

"Ah Rince," she said aloud and a little self-consciously as she disentangled herself from his embrace to step back and look fondly into the sparking joy reflected in his eyes. "If ever I find myself absorbed in retrospect, it is good to know you will always be there to remind me of myself!"

Reluctantly releasing his hands, she turned her thoughts to Tag, who stood a few feet further back, unsure what to say or do. He and the others who believed in the Light had always talked of the Appointed to come, but thinking and seeing were two entirely different things. For a moment he questioned what use he could possibly be to one so unquestionably potent, but he already knew the answer to that question. As much use as he could be, as long as his body held breath and strength to do so.

"Appointed," Tag said simply, bowing low. "We have waited and hoped, but it is an honour beyond description to be here with you as you are revealed." Overcome with emotion and with realised hope, Tag knelt to one knee in homage, something he never thought he would do. Looking at the Appointed with wonder and starlight reflected in his sharp gaze, he concluded simply but with typical directness: "Now the Protector is no more, what do we do next?"

The question was loaded with possibility and apprehension, for Tag knew well that the prophecies spoke of the Appointed as the key to saving the world. While the Protector was an evil that Tag was glad to see eradicated, he was hardly a threat of that magnitude. With the Appointed revealed, it was only the beginning, and Tag was unsure if the Appointed, who was still young in years if not in power, was even aware herself of what might come.

"Indeed Tag," Alaena responded, dropping her hands from Rince's shoulder and glancing around the Wood as if to satisfy herself that the immediate danger had passed. "'What next' is indeed an excellent question." Her tone was sombre, but her gentle smile remained in place as she glanced back at Tag.

"Come, my friend!" she said buoyantly. "That is more than enough bowing and kneeling for this night, I assure you!" Stepping towards Tag, she held out her hand for his.

Still on one knee, Tag hesitated a moment, staring at her outstretched hand. The one she offered was her right and the bracelet, quiescent now, encircled her wrist like a statement of sovereignty. It represented a force that was beyond him, and after what he had just witnessed of the power it could unleash, the sight of it hanging before him on the Appointed's slender wrist transfixed him.

Alaena saw his reaction and grinned. She leaned her hand slightly closer, curling her fingers playfully. "Come, Tag. There is nothing to fear here for those who are with me in the Light!"

The movement broke the moment and Tag, embarrassed by his reaction, looked up quickly to see Alaena's eyes twinkling with amusement. Sheepishly, he took the proffered hand in his and stood, disengaging the contact quickly to brush himself down and hide his discomfiture.

"Well!" Rince said from behind them with an echo of his typical boyish bravado returning. "I would certainly like an answer to the question, even if Tag here seems to be having trouble finding the words!" Stepping closer to join them both, he finished the thought. "Where will we go now, Ala? Can we return to Morlyn, do you think?"

At that, Alaena's features turned serious again. There was so much Rince didn't know and, while she might hold all the power in the world, she was not ready yet to talk about what she knew and what was to come.

"Soon, Rince, very soon, but first I must rest. In any case, the others won't be here for some time yet, so let us sleep a while and recover ourselves while we can. We have done well this day and, where opportunity presents, a traveller will never neglect a soft bed, don't you think?"

Forestalling further questions, Alaena chose an area on the far side of the clearing from where the Protector had met his demise. Shields bristled into place around her mind automatically as she opened it once more to the Lanes. Instantly, the Earth responded. A lush growth of grassy cover sprouted forth, rapidly weaving itself into a thick bed that carpeted the rich earth below.

Rince grinned widely, accepting the miracle before him as just another of the amazing things it appeared Alaena could do now. Tag, bemused, just shook his head in wonder as he watched Alaena walk over to the area and place her hand on the ground. "Thank you," she said simply to no one in particular, then laid down and closed her eyes, falling quickly into a deep sleep.

Silence descended on the clearing, broken only by the quiet whisper of a breeze returning to pass through the trees. Creatures within, sensing danger had passed, began to move once more. Tag and Rince just stood, staring at Alaena for a while. Words seemed insufficient and unnecessary to both, even if either could think of something to say that would even attempt to encapsulate their feelings about the events that had just transpired.

Eventually, in silent agreement and with no sensible alternative presenting itself, they moved to join her. They lowered themselves protectively to the grass on either side of Alaena. The ground was lush, and the grass smelled like a promise.

Before they too succumbed to slumber, Rince rolled over and said in a sleepy voice, "Tag?"

"Yes, Rince?" Tag responded with equal lethargy.

"Who was Ala talking about? Who else is coming?"

Tag tried to ponder for a moment all the possibilities of who or what might appear in what remained of this extraordinary night out of the depths of the Wood to meet with the Appointed, but it was too much for the state of his somnambulant thought.

"I have no idea, Rince," he said plainly. "I have absolutely no idea."

Soon after, the three were alone with their dreams as the trees watched and the earth cradled them.

Interlude 10 - Change

In the depths of the Wood, where the Appointed and her companions lay embraced by the Earth, a leaden silence hung heavy in the air. The lethargic atmosphere persisted for some time after The Protector had fallen.

The forest itself, as always, seemed untouched and unaffected. In the hearts of the trees though, change took place.

This one moment of human affray amongst all they had seen would have passed entirely unnoticed, had it not been for the human child. The Power she carried was recognised. It was honoured and respected here.

Quietly and peacefully, with the imperceptible patience that had seen tree, root and rock survive the ages, the forest rejoiced.

To the far north in the wood, a ranger's wife breathed a pensive sigh of relief. The babe she rocked in her arms had refused to quiet and she was nearing despair, for the child had been inconsolable for much of the afternoon now. Without warning, the child calmed. Looking down at its face, the woman watched, amazed, as the child's distress faded with a few final whimpers to a contented gurgle, before snuggling to her breast to sleep.

Leagues to the east, an apprentice cut wood for his smith's furnace just within the edge of the forest. Sweat stood out on his brow as he worked, muscled arms and axe splitting logs with single, precise blows. This was a practical man, rarely given to flights of fancy, yet even as he hefted the blade for another blow, a thrum of perception ran through him. Holding back the blow, the apprentice turned to look deeper into the forest, wonder touching his gaze. A sense of absolute peace descended on him, and the axe fell from his work-worn fingers to thump on the ground, unnoticed as he stared into the depths of the wood, a gentle smile on his face.

Some distance to the south, deep within The Spine that separated the northern lands of Morlyn and Tyr from the southern lands of the King, Vetren lay lost and witless on the floor in his mountain tomb. Once Demon Prince, the dim scales of his torso pressed hard against the pitted granite of his prison. Around him, a revolving sphere of silver-threaded power, the Holding had spun unchanged for what his broken mind believed was forever. For a while longer he lay staring, his dull eye barely open. Somewhere in the drifting madness, change registered. His slitted eyelids trembled open a fraction more and, for the first time in many years, his eyes focused. Fear touched his soul, for hope was beyond him now and this was likely just another madness sent by the sorcerers to add to his torment.

He watched for a while, supine in a puddle of his own drool and excrement, wondering if the end had come at last and hoping it would all be over soon.

Lost to time and with no way of knowing how long he had stared, Vetren's hopelessness once more overwhelmed him and he gave in to despair. As he had some many times since his mind had gone, he simply closed his eyes and began to sob. This change meant nothing. There was no escape. He would lie here entombed until the mountain itself came down upon him. Somewhere in his broken mind, he wondered if even the weight of the earth itself would be enough to break through the Holding to crush the life out of him at last.

Uninterested and unaffected by Vetren's suffering, the Holding continued to spin around him. Rather than being bathed in silver light now, however, the cavern in which he was imprisoned glowed with another hue. For the silver trails and spindles of power that spun around the Demon had transmuted to gold, blazing with renewed power and a promise of the sun.

Chapter 28 - Reunion

Wilmen and Rogan had travelled most of the night at a painfully slow pace. Each had a lantern that helped light the way but, fearful of alerting the Protector and his Guard who they knew were somewhere ahead, they kept their flames low and shuttered. In many places, the road kept the trees back from overhanging their route, allowing illumination from the night sky in to supplement their own meagre light and maintain a moderately brisk pace. In just as many areas though, boughs and branches, thick with leafy growth, obscured the sky and rendered their way to little more than a tunnel of inky blackness. In these places they plodded along slowly, the small pools of light cast by their lanterns forcing them to nothing more than a slow walk.

Darven Ross, ever more curious as he trailed the pair through the forest, kept a safe distance. The lights from their lanterns, though they kept them low, were the only illumination on the road. It was a simple matter to stay back while being sure that he would not lose them. Even where the road turned and weaved through the wood and the light disappeared momentarily, the heavy thud of the hooves of the horse that carried the giant of a man accompanying the woman from the Abbey echoed deep into the Wood, and was assurance that he remained on their path and a convenient cover for any noise his own light mount might create as it picked its way along the road in the dark.

Around midnight, the pair reached Fyr, passing through without pause. Darven hesitated as he approached the village, holding his mount back in the dark of the trees, considering. Fyr consisted of little more than a row of wooden houses and an inn set by the road. At this hour all was quiet and dark, bar the two dim figures who soon disappeared from sight into the woods at the other end of the village.

Darven hesitated in the shadow, unrewarded. No inquisitive soul ventured forth to investigate or even show any interest in the two that had passed by in the night. No light flickered, nor did any shade pull back from a window, as far as Darven could discern. When enough time had passed to satisfy him that he was alone in tracking this unusual pair through the Wytharn Wood in the depths of night, Darven gently nudged his horse into motion. Keeping his senses alert, Darven Ross passed through with his head bowed low before being swallowed by the Wood on the other side without incident.

When the gloom enveloped him once more, Darven was tempted to kick his horse to a canter. He had no wish to lose the pair now. As he considered a quicker pace, his training at the Temple of Ald came back to him.

"Haste is the enemy of order," was just one of the tenets that he had learned at Ald that applied here. Sure enough, keeping his mount to a gentle, steady pace, the echo of the hooves of the giant's horse eventually came to him through the Wood first, followed shortly by glimpses of light flicking through the trees.

Swallowing a knot of tension, Darven allowed himself to relax once more in the saddle, keeping a good distance between himself and the two he tracked. It had been a long ride from Ald, and it seemed he would be in the saddle for a while yet, for these two showed no inclination to stop anytime soon. Weariness settled in Darven's bones, but despite this, a smile creased his visage. Many riders had set out from Ald to all points of the compass. Though he had travelled long and far, it was clear to Darven that something uncommon was happening here. Women and giants did not just take to the woods for night-long rides without reason!

Perhaps it would lead to naught, but he had difficulty believing that would be the outcome here. Darven had seen the Prince's light before setting off on his quest. He had studied the Prophecies of the Appointed and accepted that if he, Darven Ross, had breath to serve the Appointed in whatever way possible, then he would do so without hesitation. Darven had learnt at a very young age that his own life was little compared to that which the Appointed could bring to the world. If the Appointed required anything of him, then Darven would give all he had to deliver.

Grimly, Darven set his teeth and urged his mount to a faster walk, trailing the firefly glimpses of lantern light through the Wood. Shifting once more in the saddle, Darven settled in for the journey, wherever it may take him.

***

276

With only a few hours until dawn, Wilmen was approaching despair.

Talking quietly with Rogan as they travelled, she had exhausted all options. Rogan understood the mechanics of keeping the Appointed safe and protecting her from harm, but Wilmen knew he did not agree there was an absolute need to keep her safe above all else. To Wilmen, Alaena was infinitely precious. There was nothing more important or immediately exquisite than Alaena, both for what she represented for the Light and, on a very personal level, for what she meant to Wilmen. Rogan, on the other hand, was yet to be convinced that Alaena was actually the Appointed. He appeared to accept Wilmen's story, but he had kept his opinion as to what he believed that meant in reserve. They had all been living with the stories and prophecies of the Appointed for so long, Wilmen understood that scepticism was likely until he could see for himself.

Lifting herself in the saddle, Wilmen winced. It had been a long time since she had spent an appreciable time on a horse, and her bones were getting too old for this kind of thing. Putting discomfort out of mind, Wilmen squinted into the darkness ahead as they pressed on. Now was not the time to let a few aches and pains distract her. As it had for the last several hours, the road continued to lead into a tunnel of blackness. With her eyes failing her, Wilmen continued to listen as best she could, but riding next to the heavy clop of Rogan's steed, the odd sound she heard from the Wood gave no indication that their trek would end soon. The path ahead remained unknown, and Wilmen's structured mind would remain commensurately uncomfortable until she knew what they faced.

The pair continued on, conversing little now. Aside from the fact that Rogan sat several hands higher than Wilmen, making conversation difficult in any case, both knew that dawn approached and a decision had to be made. With more light they would make much better ground, so pressing on would seem sensible. They were both weary as well, however, so perhaps an hour or two's rest would be the wisest choice, lest they come upon the Protector and his Guard unrested and unprepared for what might transpire.

After negotiating another bend in the road, Wilmen and Rogan both stiffened, wary. Their lanterns lit shapes and movement ahead. If they had come across the Guard themselves, then it was already too late to avoid being seen.

Wilmen lifted her lantern higher to see better. Taking in a quick breath, she glanced up at Rogan, who expelled a deep rolling breath before returning her glance with a similarly quizzical look on his face. Pulling their steeds to a halt, they risked a little more light, unshuttering their lanterns to better illuminate the area. There, loosely tethered to trees on either side of the road, were nine horses quietly grazing on the foliage nearby. Their heads lifted and turned towards the light, eyes reflecting the flickering flame of the lanterns in the dark.

Whispering – for where there were horses, it was likely their riders were not too far away – Wilmen looked up at Rogan and asked, "What do you make of this, my friend?" Glancing back at the unlikely sight, Wilmen mused uncomfortably. "Nine horses with the tack of the Keep, including, if I am not mistaken, the Protector's horse as well!" She inclined her head towards the great roan that the Protector usually rode. She had kept her voice low but couldn't disguise a tremor of fear in her tone. This might be a trap, and nine armed men might be about to leap on them from the shadows!

Rogan, ever practical and implacable, merely grunted as he shifted his weight, moving to dismount. "Let us see more so we may understand this, Wilmen," he said as his bulk settled to the earth. Rogan's horse shifted a few steps sideways, very likely pleased to have the weight lifted from its back for a while. He held his lantern high as Wilmen nodded and dragged her cloak aside to clear her legs, then dismounted as well.

"Look, Wilmen," Rogan rumbled as he moved to the closest beast, lantern still held high. "These horses have been here awhile, for the earth nearby is bare. They have been tied here, foraging, for some time I believe."

Putting his hand to the flank of the nearest horse, he stroked its coat, pondering aloud. "The beast is also dry and the coat is cool."

Rogan rumbled his assessment. "I would say it has not been ridden for a few hours at least, perhaps more!"

Wilmen calmed a little as she processed the implications of Rogan's words. "Then," she began, mind working hard as she turned to the trees and stared into the dark before them, "they came this far and had to take to the trees at need, for what else would drive them to leave their horses here unattended?" She shook her head, her concern returning, but now it was for Alaena rather than herself. Alaena was in the middle of those woods somewhere.

"Indeed, Wilmen." Rogan's voice came to her from a little way away.

Ending her brief contemplation of the dark, Wilmen turned to find that Rogan had moved a short way further along the road, where some of the other horses were tethered. He was holding his lantern high and peering into the trees.

"Here," he said bluntly. Next to the road, broken twigs and trampled undergrowth showed clearly where the group had taken to the Woods. They had certainly taken no precaution to conceal their tracks, for the path beaten in was clear.

Though he lifted his lantern high, the shuttered light penetrated only a few yards into the gloom. It was apparent that the Protector's party had entered at this point, but where the path led remained shrouded in the darkness of the trees beyond. Grunting with dissatisfaction, Rogan reached up with his left hand to pull the shutter of his lantern back to allow more light to shine out. It helped little. The extra light simply showed that the path continued into the trees before the shadows swallowed the meagre illumination.

While Rogan swung the lantern back and forth, trying without success to glean more of the situation, Wilmen accepted the reality of what was required here without further pause.

"Gather your things, Rogan," she said curtly, turning back to move to her horse and retrieve her saddlebags. "We leave the road here."

Rogan, lowing his lantern, gave one more look into the Wood as if willing it to give up its secrets, then shrugged. It appeared the leisurely part of their journey was done and it was time to take to foot.

Wasting no more time, they stuffed their pockets with rations and slung a length of rope, along with a waterskin each, across their shoulders. Rogan thought for a moment about leaving his sword behind, for it was a large and heavy weapon to carry on a trek through the depths of the Wood. In the light of the lantern he'd placed on the ground while taking what he needed from his saddlebags, however, he glanced around the horses of the Protector and his Guard grazing contentedly on the foliage by the side of the road. *No*, Rogan decided quickly. *I am large and heavy too*, he thought with a chuckle. *My sword would not abandon me, so why should I abandon him?* Besides, Rogan considered more seriously, the sword was something he was more than likely to need. He secured it properly in its sheath on a wide leather belt at his waist and patted it contentedly. Its weight was comforting.

Wilmen, for her own part, kept only her knife at her waist as a weapon. After rolling up her cloak, she pushed it firmly into her bag as well. There would be no point wearing it to catch on every twig, branch and bough along their way. Feeling as ready as she thought possible, Wilmen turned to find Rogan standing by the path, looking into the shadows as if he could discern threat from afar.

Rogan turned to her also the lantern light he held high casting eerie shadows over his rotund features. Smiling grimly, he gestured wide with his hand and a shallow bow. "M'Lady," he quipped lightly, very much at odds with the situation at hand. "After you."

Checking her dagger once more to ensure it was secure about her waist, Wilmen took a breath and stepped into the forest. Rogan followed and shortly after, both had disappeared from sight, swallowed by the Wood.

***

Darven Ross, perplexed, watched from a distance. He was too far away to hear what they were saying, but close enough to make out their movements in the light of the lanterns they carried. It was clear to him from the actions of the woman and her huge companion that they had not expected to find a veritable herd of horses tethered by the side of the road in the dead of night some leagues from the nearest village. Though he understood none of this and was starting to wonder if following these two into the depths of the Wytharn Wood in the deep of night would further his quest to find the Appointed, he could not deny that this was all very unusual.

Darven permitted himself a wry smile. Unusual was certainly what he was looking for! Only one thing was clear when the two finally finished their investigation of the area and left the road to take off into the wood. Obviously, the party who had left their horses here earlier had taken to the wood, and these two were tracking them. Well, Darven thought to himself, it would not be hard to track the trackers. Perhaps, given all the interest in the Wood and what was within, what he sought would be there as well.

Soon after, Darven entered the Wood at the same point to continue his pursuit.

So it was that, even as the moon above passed the zenith and tracked its way down towards the horizon, a steed bearing the brand of the Princedom of Ald stood with two bearing the mark of the Abbey of Morlyn and yet more showing the livery of the Protectorate Keep of the same city in a group by the side of the road in the middle of the wood in the late hours of the night. Any traveller to come by in the early hours of the morning would certainly have a puzzle to unravel here.

For the beasts themselves, each looked at the other briefly, then bowed their heads to graze, sublimely uninterested in anything but the fresh growth at their feet.

With eerie ease, Wilmen and Rogan – as well as Darven still tracking them from a distance – made their way into the depths of the wood without hindrance or obstacle. Had they had to hack their way through the Wood to find their path, then they may well have spent a day or more making their way. Had they encountered resistance or worse from the Guard whose horses with their own they left far behind on the Morlyn road, then their trek may have been much longer indeed, if it had continued at all. Travelling silently, for a strange, otherworldly calmness permeated the air, Wilmen and Rogan found the way straight and uncluttered. It was as if the Wood were making way for them, welcoming them into its heart.

Unable to say why, Wilmen's spirits lifted with every step she took. They had travelled all night, yet she found weariness leaving her body more than settling in as she walked.

Though traipsing through a Wood in the early hours of the morning was hardly his preferred activity, Rogan found himself smiling for no reason at all as he put one foot in front of the other, feeling the Wood draw him inward. After a while, he found himself touching the trees and brushing the leaves of bushes with his hand as he passed by, something he hadn't taken the time or had the inclination to do since he was a child.

Darven Ross was discomforted, mainly because he knew he should be wary. There were dangers about him he knew nothing of. Despite this, Darven found himself curbing the desire to simply run forward to join the woman and her gargantuan companion to enjoy their company as they walked. Shaking his head, it occurred to him that he might very well be enraptured or under a spell. Again, caution sounded a warning in his mind at the possibility, but soon after the thought drifted on as quickly as it had come, replaced by a pleasant musing as to whether or not he, the woman and the giant might one day be friends.

In this way the hours passed for each. None of the three stopped to consider the strange path they were on that seemed to lead them with uncanny ease directly into the heart of the Wood. Nor did they look curiously up to wonder at the trees above, which seemed to part just enough at the point of the path they were on to let enough light through to ensure that they neither tripped nor stumbled as they walked.

By the time they reached the clearing and stopped in amazement, Wilmen and Rogan felt well rested and at peace. Daylight had started to creep into the sky above, and the wide clear area they stepped into from the path was bathed in an early morning glow of freshness and the promise of new growth.

Taking a moment to absorb the scene before them, they both breathed a sigh of relief to see Alaena, Tag and Rince stretched out on the ground on the far side of the clearing, apparently whole and hale. Neither expressed surprise when Darven Ross appeared from the wood to stand next to them shortly after, smiling sheepishly as a child might if he had just done something he shouldn't but knew he wouldn't be chastised for it. It just seemed right to the three of them that they were all there.

Each did take a moment more to examine the strange tree that stood nearby, for it felt wrong to them and they had never seen one of its kind. They had no time to explore this curiosity, however, for Alaena's voice rang out across the clearing.

"Welcome, friends!" she said with a smile, sitting up and stretching her arms to the sky as she did so. "It is good to see you here on this beautiful morning!"

Without waiting for a reply, Alaena gained her feet in one lithe and graceful movement and moved across the clearing towards them as Tag and Rince slowly roused too, taking longer to wake from their deep slumber.

Stopping first before Wilmen, who had tears of joy in her eyes, Alaena took her trembling hands and squeezed them gently. "Mother," she said tenderly, holding Wilmen's gaze with hers. "I understand it all now, and I thank you for all you have done."

Overwhelmed with emotion, Wilmen finally threw her arms around Alaena. "Ala, my dear," she said, hugging her tight as Alaena returned the embrace warmly. "You are safe and you are well. It is all that I hoped for!"

They held their embrace for a while more. Then, sooner than Wilmen wanted, Alaena pulled herself away gently. "It warms my heart also, Mother, to see you here whole and hale," she said fondly. "Yet there are more important things to tend to than our reunion for the moment."

Turning towards Rogan, Alaena motioned one hand towards the towering bulk of the man standing next to her. "I have yet to meet your companions formally, Wilmen," she continued, tilting her head up to consider his features. "Yet this gentleman would be hard to forget! You are Rogan, if I recall correctly from your occasional visits to the Chandler's, yes?"

Alaena smiled, and Rogan bowed forward to return the greeting. When he spoke, his voice was deep and full of echoes. "I am glad you remember me, little one. Rogan Elmest at your service," he rumbled, touching a hand to his forehead in respect. "It is good to meet you properly after all this time. I must say though …" Here Rogan paused to survey the Wood around them, before returning his focus to Alaena and continuing with a chuckle, "If you had asked me some time back, I would have bet a barrel of my best ale that it would not be first thing in the morning in the middle of the Wytharn Wood!"

"Indeed, Rogan," Alaena said, her lip curled in slight amusement at the understatement. "I expect that, for all of us, things are not now what we expected them to be even a short while ago."

Turning then to Darven, Alaena's eyes narrowed a little as she assessed the solid little figure. She could sense the man's passion and essential integrity, so she did not fear for herself or her companions, but his motives were unclear.

Fortunately, Darven took any questions away as soon as he spoke. Feeling deflated to find just a boy and a girl and an old man at the end of his efforts this night, Darven spoke directly. It now seemed apparent that he had made a mistake, and it was likely that these people weren't able to help him. If so, he'd best start the trek back to his horse before thieves found it on the road and he became stranded. Before that happened though, he wanted to understand what this strange group were doing in the Wood and if they could help him on his quest to find the Appointed in some way before he moved on.

Taking a step towards Alaena as she turned her attention to him, Darven stood with legs apart and hands on hips. The pose he adopted was almost a challenge to anyone to deny the legitimacy of his quest. "I am Darven Ross, Warrior-Smith and a Rider of

Ald!" he stated boldly, the titles announced as if they were royalty. "I have been sent by my Prince, whose Stone blazed forth its Light not two nights past, on a quest to find the Appointed! I am to bring him to Ald, where together he and our Prince will save the world for us all!"

If Darven hoped for some exclamation or startled astonishment from the group at his bold pronouncement, he could not have been more disappointed. If anything, the woman and her huge companion actually frowned. The girl standing before him, to whom all seemed to be deferring, simply raised an eyebrow. The other two just shared a glance between them, then returned their attention to the exchange.

Annoyed at the lack of response, Darven paused for a moment. He had hoped to impress upon them the importance of his quest and elicit any aid they might give, but clearly his message was lost on them. Perhaps, as commoners, such concepts were beyond them and he needed another tack.

"I can see that you do not appreciate the importance of my quest," Darven said as kindly as he could, scanning the group. The two women he dismissed immediately, for they knew little of anything bar bearing children and gossip. The boy looked like a peasant and equally below his consideration. The older man looked withdrawn, though he sensed a threat in his stance that Darven could not quite place. In any case, for his purposes he settled his attention on the enormous man in the group as the one most likely to understand and appreciate the urgency of his quest.

Darven took a step towards him, then fixed him with an intent gaze. The man seemed surprised to be singled out for attention, raising an inquisitive eyebrow at Darven after a surreptitious glance at the woman next to him once more. Lowering his voice, Darven adopted the gravelly tone of the Priests of Ald, whose voices filled the recesses of his mind. They had recited the Prince's Passage of the Prophecies of Ald to him at morning prayers every day of his life.

The words floated eerily around the clearing in the early morning calm as Darven recited the precious words to the stranger, hoping for some spark of recognition.

That day will come
When Prince's Stone
Awakes and calls out bright.

Man's peril now
Awakes in step
And Power returns to sight.

Come forth, stout men
And heed the call
Look North and South and East.

The Appointed One,
Whose hand will heal,
Must never heed the Beast.

Allowing a moment for the import of the words to sink in, Darven scanned the serious face of the man to whom he had addressed the recital. "I seek the Appointed, my friend," he said with pleading urgency in his voice. "Can you help me?"

Once again Darven was forced to reconsider his position, for the man simply lifted a hand as if in helpless supplication, then nodded his head towards the older woman at his side, deferring to her once more. Frustrated, for he had little time to waste with the prattling of women, Darven endeavoured to maintain his calm and returned his attention to her. For reasons that escaped him, the woman was appraising him with a critical eye and looked displeased. What was her name, anyway? Darven pondered briefly. The Abbot in Morlyn had introduced her as Sister something, he recalled, but it was unimportant at the time and the name had slipped his mind.

Sighing, the woman spoke with contained emotion, which Darven could understand. She very likely would much prefer to be at home in her kitchen than traipsing around with what he could only assume was her extended family in the woods, after all.

"Unlike those in Ald who pay little attention to people and events outside their own domain, well do we know the words of the Prophets of Ald, Darven, Warrior-Smith," she stated bluntly.

Wilmen used the formal address purposefully and with some grim satisfaction, well aware that women in Ald were not permitted without permission in special circumstances to refer to men by their titles. She resisted the urge to slap the man across the face to shock the look of disdain and disinterest off his features as he looked at her.

Deciding that their best path was simply to be rid of him, Wilmen endeavoured to dispel any interest he may have with them. "We have nothing to do with the Appointed in your Prophecies, Rider of Ald." Indicating Alaena, Rince and Tag, Wilmen concluded quickly, hoping Darven would simply move along. "I am sorry you have wasted your time, but my friend and I were simply coming to find my daughter and her friends, who were lost in the woods."

At this, Darven's eyes narrowed. This was clearly a fabrication, which rang warning bells in his mind. As another regular lesson with the Priests of Ald taught: "Where there is deception, there is a truth that must be told." He glanced to the woman's companion once more, seeing nothing useful or informative in the bland expression that blanketed his fat features. Anger began to build in Darven, for he did not appreciate his time or his attention being wasted by this clearly deceitful woman. Before he could voice a retort, however, a gentle voice behind him interrupted.

"Let us not dismiss him in haste, Mother," the girl said quietly.

Swivelling quickly on his heel, Darven stared at her, feeling discomforted. Despite his desire to maintain it, he could feel his anger dissipating as she continued, her gaze catching his. He felt he couldn't look away even if he wanted to.

"Why do you seek the Appointed, Darven?" she queried gently as a strange peace settled on his soul. "Why does your Prince need the Appointed in Ald, when the work to be done lies elsewhere?"

Deep in his mind, Darven was aware that something strange was happening to him. His desire to answer this girl and please her was unreasonably strong. While he would never lie, for his Priests' teachings made it clear that all deceit led to the damnation of the soul, he would normally be telling her that she should leave such questions and concerns to men rather than be occupying herself with such things. Instead, the answers practically leapt from his tongue. The pleasure he felt from unburdening himself to this girl was almost physical.

"Why would we seek the Appointed?" Darven queried rhetorically. "Better to ask that In these times of peril, why would we not?" He returned the question with rapidly escalating enthusiasm. "The verses I quoted are known as the Prince's Passage of the Prophecies of Ald, but in full they are a lengthy tome indeed!" Adopting a quieter tone of conspiratorial exchange, Darven leaned closer to what he felt now was his confidante, his initial intent to dismiss her question entirely subsumed by an overwhelming desire to convey his message to her in full.

Placing a hand on her arm, Darven spoke fervently. The action did not go unnoticed by Tag, who moved quickly but unobtrusively. As the Warrior-Smith talked with increasing animation, Tag circled behind the two while his hand moved under his cloak. In mere moments, he had the comforting surety of his most trusted knife in his hand and he stood within striking distance of the Rider. Should Darven's passion move his hand to his sword rather than just stay in his voice, Tag would ensure that it was the last move the Warrior-Smith ever made.

For some time, Darven spoke. None of the party asked questions while he spoke of Ald, his Prince, the Prophecies within the Keziah Codex or the Appointed, for Darven needed no prompting. Indeed, as far as the others around them could tell, Darven seemed as eager as anyone had ever been to divulge all he could to the slim girl who stood before him listening intently. They heard of fearsome beasts with tails, talons and horns that were to come. According to the Prophecies of Ald, they would extinguish all life on Earth unless the Appointed were to save them. They heard of fire and ruin and desecration on scale unimagined that the Prophets foretold, lest the Appointed stood forth and oppose the destruction. They heard of a darkness the colour of the blackest blood consuming the sun, lest the Appointed stand forth and ensure the Light endured. Finally, Darven explained that Ald, with full knowledge of the Prophecies, had taken upon itself to find the Appointed when he was revealed through the Prince's Stone, and to bring him to Ald so that they could lend all their resources through the Prince to the Appointed. Together, they would plan and act to save the world.

At last, Darven ran short of words. For a few moments, he seemed to struggle, as though there was more to say but he didn't know what it was.

"Thank you, Darven Warrior-Smith," Alaena said quietly, pulling her arm back a little and allowing Darven's hand to fall away.

With the contact broken, Darven seemed to come back to himself, starting with surprise at the extent of the information he had just given out to these strangers. Most of it was never to be spoken of outside Ald and even within Ald, much of the knowledge reserved for the Riders and their Priests and no others. Taking a step backward, Darven choked back a biting retort as his face burned crimson with shame. "How?" he spluttered, unable in his distress to frame an appropriate question. Suspicion closed over his features as his shaking hand found the hilt of his sword.

As the muscles bunched in Darven's solid arms to pull the weapon free, a blur of movement from behind had Tag's knife at his throat before Darven's sword had barely begun to clear its sheath.

"Careful, Warrior-Smith," Tag whispered close, threat edging his tone. Resting his other hand on the top of Darven's sword, he pushed gently as he continued. "Let us not have any blood drawn here this morning, for if you are indeed committed to the Appointed as your prophecies and your Prince command you to be, then all our feet follow the same path."

Looking from Tag, whose grey eyes scanned Darven's face looking for signs of intent, to Alaena and back again, Darven calmed. He had misjudged the old man whose steady hand now had a knife to his throat and unequivocal threat in his eyes. Slowly, Darven forced himself to relax and allowed his sword to return fully to its sheath. His mind ordered itself once more. By the time the blade settled home and Tag pulled the knife back just a little, Darven was able to frame his question better.

Releasing the hilt and gently raising his hands to show his acquiescence, Darven turned his attention to the girl once more.

"So what will you do with me now, girl?" he enquired with an edge of anger and fear in his voice. To his knowledge, there was only one answer for what had just happened. It also explained why a female appeared to be leading this strange group through the Wood.

Taking a step back even as he realised that escape was unlikely, Darven spoke boldly, for he would never allow fear to dictate his actions.

"I take you as a Witch, girl, for your touch has clearly ensorcelled me!" he spat accusingly. "Why, now I think on it, perhaps I have been under your spell for some time, for it feels like as soon as I entered this Wood I have been drawn here for your dark purpose!"

Drawing himself up, Darven scanned the group once more and planted his feet apart, ready for whatever might come. He at least knew he had acted without reproach, even if the Priests would chastise him for his betrayal.

"Do what you will, Witch," Darven stated with sullen finality. "I have nothing more to say and nothing more to give, so finish with me or allow me to go!"

"Ah, Darven," she said with an echo of sadness in her voice that surprised him. "What irony there is that you are not the only one to falsely accuse me of Witchcraft these past few days." Tilting her head to one side, she looked at him carefully while she continued. "Did your Priests of Ald, in all their teachings, so imbue you with such a clouded perception of the world that you can consider no alternative other than, as a woman, I must be a Witch to have so ensnared you?" she asked curiously. "Is there no other option that you may want to consider before condemning me as evil?"

Darven frowned. He was entirely out of his depth here but did not understand why. He also had no idea what the girl was talking about. What other possibility was there than Witchcraft for what he had just experienced? Without understanding the question he was being asked and unsure what answers would suffice, Darven chose silence instead. Standing his ground, Darven folded his arms and just stared sullenly at Alaena, then around the rest of this strange party, not sure where the conversation would go next.

For a short while, silence descended on the clearing. Other than the sounds of birds and insects waking to go about their day in the early morning light, no one said a word.

Alaena let the moment stretch until it was obvious Darven was not going to engage in further debate on the topic of Witches or otherwise, then looked to Wilmen, who glanced back with a querulous look as if to say, "What do we do now?"

Alaena's brow furrowed as she pondered her options, then a small smile crossed her features as she glanced down at the cloak Wilmen had folded across her arm.

Turning back to Darven, Alaena once more addressed the stoic Warrior-Smith, who wore a look of adamant dislike for all that was transpiring here.

"Darven," she began carefully. "First, allow me to introduce myself, for our conversation thus far has prohibited such civility. My name is Alaena, daughter of Wilmen who, amongst other things, is the Chandler of Morlyn." Glancing toward Wilmen, Alaena permitted herself a wry smile before returning her attention to Darven.

"While I find your opinions and thoughts on the matter of Witches, the Appointed and women in general largely inaccurate as well as somewhat offensive, Warrior-Smith, it is not for me to endeavour to undo a lifetime's teachings in a moment for you here."

Darven's expression changed little, but his eyes bored into Alaena's as if trying to understand her intent this time, at least.

"Clearly you are undecided regarding our intent, your purpose and our association from this point. Perhaps," Alaena continued with a slightly mischievous smile touching her lips, "it would help if you could discuss the matter with your Prince before deciding on your next step?"

At this, Darven's head jerked and he could not hold the hope from his face. He wanted nothing more than to be away from this strange place and this strange group of people so he could regroup and decide what to do to further his quest. While he had no intent to return to Ald at this point, he would certainly not be lying to say that a conversation with Prince Orindum would be of benefit, and if that meant an opportunity to leave, Darven would certainly take it.

"I thank you, Alaena" Darven addressed her lamely. "I would find it most beneficial to talk over what has happened here with my Prince, if I have the leave of you and your … friends … to depart?" he posited hopefully.

Once again, Darven was discomposed by Alaena's unexpected response. To his delicately phrased question, the girl simply laughed. It was not a mean or snide chuckle by any means. In fact, it sounded light and free and without malice at all.

"No, Darven, I do apologise for misleading you!" she exclaimed with some amusement. "I did not mean to say you should go to your Prince now to discuss it, for that would take days, would it not?" she queried unnecessarily. Growing serious, the girl took a step towards him and locked her gaze with his. "What I meant was, would it help if you could discuss this situation with your Prince here and now?"

Alaena paused for effect, letting the question sink in as Darven looked even more confused, then glanced around the clearing as if he expected Prince Orindum to step from the very trees before him, before Alaena's movement drew his eyes back to her.

Quietly and calmly, Alaena stepped to one side and approached Wilmen, who also gave her an unsure look. Was this going to be the norm from now on? Wilmen wondered. Alaena was going to just do the unexpected now? Wilmen started to speak but Alaena shook her head, indicating she should stay silent. To Wilmen's surprise, Alaena gently reached for the cloak that hung over Wilmen's arm. Holding it up, Alaena shook it out, allowing the cloak to unfold fully before reaching to the inside pocket, drawing forth the slim, silk pouch that lay secreted within.

Alarmed, Wilmen reached for Alaena's arm to warn her, hold her back from revealing the Star that lay within, but Alaena simply smiled and patted the hand that reached for her gently. "Peace, Mother," she whispered close. "The risk taken here will be worth the reward. One must also show trust in order to earn it."

Gaping, Wilmen tried to mouth words to argue, but Alaena simply turned back towards Darven, working at the string that kept the pouch closed to pull it open. Rogan, equally surprised but amused enough at Wilmen's discomfiture to enjoy what was unfolding, nudged Wilmen companionably in the side.

"Best close your mouth, Wilmen," he chuckled in a low whisper that sounded like suppressed thunder rolling. "You look like one of the fish on the Morlyn Docks gasping for its last breath!" he joked with another nudge.

Wilmen, both embarrassed and annoyed, did not deign to respond other than snapping her mouth closed, folding her arms back around the cloak Alaena had returned and staring at Alaena once more, who had worked the pouch open now.

Standing before Darven, Alaena lifted her left hand and held it palm upwards as she upended the pouch before Darven. As she did so, Wilmen noticed the strange bracelet on Alaena's right wrist. Wilmen had never seen it before and would have taken considerably more interest had not the Star fallen free of the pouch to land in Alaena's hand for everyone to see.

Of them all, Darven's reaction was the most profound. The gem landed lightly in Alaena's palm and, from the moment it came free of the pouch, all eyes were transfixed by the glistening, glimmering light shining forth from the heart of the gem. Darven stepped back at first, hand reaching for something to hold him steady as he absorbed what he was seeing. Then, with astonishment giving way to overpowering wonder, he carefully stepped forward once more to gaze closely at the gem. Finally, as Alaena held the Star steady before him, he raised his eyes to meet hers.

Nodding as if to substantiate what Darven's eyes were telling him was impossible according to the teachings of the Priests of Ald, for it was gospel that the Prince's Star was unique in the world,

Alaena whispered, "Orindum!" as she placed her slender hand on his arm, holding his steady

Darven jumped in shock, gasping, for Orindum was the name of Darven's Prince. As Alaena tightened her grip on his arm to ensure he did not break away from her, Darven was ashamed to recall he had given away Orindum's name to Alaena in his inexplicable outpouring of information to her only a short while ago.

If Darven was shocked at the name, he almost swooned a moment later, for the voice of his beloved Prince filled his head in a strange, hollow way, as though they were standing next to each other talking in a hall full of echoes.

"Who addresses me with such familiarity?" the voice in Darven's head demanded. *"Where are you? Show yourself!"* The last was clearly a command, and Darven ached to obey. In his bewildered state, Darven faltered and Alaena spoke before he could frame any words.

"Orindum, Prince of Ald." Like Orindum's voice, Alaena's filled his mind. It was the strangest thing in the world to Darven, to be looking at the girl whose mouth didn't move but to hear her words so clearly in the cavernous space in his head. His fear and shock passing, Darven looked to her slender hand on her arm, to the shining Star in her other hand, then back to her eyes, which now appeared unfocused as her words continued in his mind.

"Forgive my intrusion on your thoughts, and likewise my inability to appear in person to you, Prince, for I am many leagues away in the depths of the Wytharn Wood."

Alaena paused for a moment, but there was no response. Surprise, consternation and confusion all resonated through the link to Alaena, but patience and caution accompanied them. *Good,* Alaena thought. At least this Orindum was wise enough to listen before reacting. Without preamble, Alaena came to the point.

"My name is Alaena, and I am here with your Rider, the Warrior-Smith Darven Ross." Here Alaena could sense his surprise over

the link, but still the Prince remained careful, allowing Alaena to continue without interruption.

"Darven tells me you have sent your Riders to find the Appointed, Prince of Ald. Though Darven himself remains to be convinced, allow me to say that I am the one you seek! I would meet with you one day, but there is a task to be finished before I come to Ald, and it would assist me greatly to have Darven accompany me to achieve this end. Do you grant him your leave to fulfil this task before he returns to Ald?"

The void remained quiet for several seconds once Alaena finished her pronouncement. Darven felt a thrill of achievement flood his being as Alaena announced herself; he could feel the truth of her words through the bond of mind that they shared. When the Prince finally responded, Darven's relief was profound.

"Alaena," the Prince's voice pronounced carefully, quietly. *"I have kept the Star of Ald with me since its light awoke some two days past now to ensure it remained safe as I deemed it precious!"* His incredulity was palpable through the link. *"Never did I dream it might lead to this, though, for I feel the truth of your words even though I understand not how I can even hear you through the gem."*

"Indeed, Prince," Alaena responded. Her voice resonated with strength and surety. *"There are a great many things that will be new to the world soon, though unlike this one, I fear much of what is to come, as your Prophecies foretell."*

"I feel the truth of what you say, Alaena, and my heart sways me to trust even though, but perhaps in part because, your voice comes impossibly to my mind," the Prince answered after another short pause. *"If you are indeed the Appointed, then Darven and all the resources of my city are at your disposal, for our purpose since Keziah penned the first prophecies has been to learn and then prepare for your coming."*

There was another pause in which both Alaena and Darven could feel the Prince thinking. Alaena exuded patience over the link, while Darven oozed discomfort. He felt like a child listening at the door to a conversation not meant for his ears.

"Perhaps, Alaena, you could make your way to Ald before undertaking this other task?" the Prince ventured carefully. *"Should the Light will it, it would be my honour to welcome you to the city as our long-awaited Appointed."*

There was no subterfuge in the Prince's proposal, but Alaena could sense his prevarication. His offer to honour her within the city of Ald would only be on condition of his being satisfied that she was indeed the Appointed. If he decided not, then he would likely opt to imprison Alaena for her falsehood. Either way, Alaena had neither the time nor the patience to banter words with Prince Orindum.

"My Lord," Alaena began politely before moving straight to the point. *"As I have said, I have a task to complete before I contemplate any other action. I will likely come to Ald to meet with you and plan at some point, but for the moment I require only one thing of you."* She paused, feeling surprise and suppressed offence resonate through the link. The Prince was unlikely to have had anyone, let alone a woman, require anything of him of late, Alaena suspected.

"I would prefer Darven Ross accompany myself and my party to complete this task, but I will not ask it of him without your consent as his liege Lord." Before he could answer, Alaena added, *"If nothing else, my Lord, the task would likely allow Darven to decide either way if I am indeed the Appointed that Ald seeks, or not. Would that in itself not make the journey worthwhile for him and for yourself?"*

Somehow both Darven and the Prince sensed the presence of a coy smile on Alaena's lips through the void.

With the answer came a sense of resignation. The Prince was already out of his depth talking to someone through his Star, and Alaena was not offering a choice. She knew the answer he would give before he framed it in their minds.

"Very well, Alaena. Darven may travel with you as long as he deems it appropriate to his quest to find the Appointed, but I would ask for two conditions in return," the Prince conceded graciously.

Well used to political games from his dealings with the Priests and other factions of power in Ald, the Prince expected reciprocity for his own concession granted.

To his surprise and consternation, Alaena was in no mood for further discussion.

"Prince Orindum," she began, forestalling the Prince's next words. *"Forgive my directness, but your conditions are irrelevant to me and we have already taken up too much time talking. Based on your words, Darven knows he can join us or return to Ald as he wishes and I will leave that decision to him."* Alaena sensed Orindum's objection and quelled it immediately. "Farewell, Orindum," she stated abruptly, sending both understanding and finality through the link. There would be no further discussion on this. *"Should the Light allow, I will see you in Ald after the task before me now is done."*

With that, Alaena closed her hand over the stone, severing the link.

***

Far away in his tower in Ald, Prince Orindum sat in silence. He stared at the light that continued to swirl in fascinating spirals within the gem in the palm of his hand while chewing on his bottom lip, as he often did when vexed.

The woman he had spoken with both fascinated and frightened him. Her surety and rectitude were imprinted on his mind. Strangely, he had felt Darven there too, though he had not spoken. Perhaps he chose not to, or perhaps he could not, but his presence during the conversation was tangible.

Darven's situation was, though, the last thing on his mind now. A woman? If anyone had suggested the ludicrous notion that the Appointed could possibly be female before this, he would have scoffed and suggested they needed to familiarise themselves better with the Prophecies or visit a Healer to check the soundness of their mind. Even so, he had felt with absolute surety through the link Alaena had established that all she said was true. Perhaps he had been ensorcelled and she really was a witch.

Even as he considered that far more likely possibility though, his mind kept telling him otherwise.

If it were true, how would she be accepted by the Priests and the populace of Ald? Could he accept such a thing himself, when all their teachings and the society of Ald placed females on little higher status in society than servants? Such a notion turned all they knew from the Prophecies and, for that matter, all on which the society of Ald itself was based, completely on end.

In his musings, Orindum considered speaking to the gem to see if he could re-establish contact with Alaena and Darven, but even as the thought occurred to h m, he closed his long fingers over the stone as he shook his head. The sense of finality he had experienced when Alaena had finished the conversation so abruptly was clear and complete. Be it Alaena the Appointed they had waited for so long, or a charlatan claiming the title for the status it would bring, she clearly had power of a kind not seen in this world for hundreds of years. Before risking the ire of someone like that, Orindum would consult the Priests and the Prophecies once more to seek guidance and council.

It was still some time before Orindum gained his feet and he left the tower. His step was slow and thoughtful as he crossed the rugs scattered across the stone floor of his study, making for the stairs. As he closed the door behind him, he still gripped the gem tightly in his palm. His fingers glowed gold through his clasped fist as he descended slowly at first, then took to the corridors of the palace at a run.

Chapter 29 - Sacrifice

Collapsing her spell, Alaena took a steady breath.

It was strange, she thought. The use of her powers were entirely alien to her, yet somehow so familiar. Even as she brought her awareness back to the clearing in the Wood, other spells and incantations floated tantalisingly close in her memories, along with visions of a world past. Somehow these coexisted with Alaena's recent years without conflict. She could recall growing up in the Chandler's with Wilmen and Rince a part of her life as readily as she could recall the halls of the Temple of Light where Simcha herself held power as Matriarch in happy days when all was learning and love, then the later days, after the demons had come, when all came to destruction, desolation and loss.

A few moments later, Alaena was looking at the faces around her. Concern warred with curiosity on Wilmen's face. Rince's blue eyes, as always, sparkled with unquenchable optimism. Rogan's aspect was hidden from view in the voluminous folds of his face, but his spirit radiated inquisitiveness. He understood little and wanted to know what was going on here. Tag emanated wonder and steadfast loyalty, for he had given himself in service to Alaena now, and nothing would ever undermine that vow. Finally settling her eyes on Darven, Alaena saw doubt and disbelief sparring with hope and possibility. While the education that Wilmen had given Alaena had been concerned with far more routine matters than the Prophecies of Ald, the summary Darven had offered with Alaena's subtle prompting made it clear that the last thing anyone in Ald expected was that the Appointed would be female, let alone a girl yet to come into womanhood.

For these few moments, there was no sound in the Wood other than a light breeze ruffling the leaves of the trees. With none of the party other than Darven being aware of what had just transpired, all felt it better to wait for another to speak rather than break the silence themselves.

Finally Alaena spoke, addressing Darven first. "Warrior-Smith," she said softly, kindly. "You have a choice to make now, but I would ask you hold your answer a short while longer, for this is something everyone needs to understand before they too decide whether or not to journey with me."

Noticing Darven's gaze still on the gem in her palm, Alaena smiled and closed her hand over it before she carefully returned the stone to its pouch. She would have to remember that in these times, things such as this were a source of fascination and distraction for people, rather than being commonplace as they were in the time of Simcha when the Temple of Light served the land.

Alaena's comment made little sense to the others, but it appeared Darven understood, for he nodded slowly as the stone slipped back into the pouch and Alaena returned it to Wilmen with a cryptic smile. "Thank you, Mother. I should not need this again for some time, if you could please keep it safe."

Nodding dumbly, Wilmen looked at Alaena with a feeling of helplessness as she accepted the pouch back and tucked it back safely into her cloak. She felt uncomfortably sure that there were far too many things going on that she didn't understand. The difficulty was, she had so many questions, Wilmen wasn't even sure where to start.

"Ala, my dear," she began. Avoiding the banality of a question like, "Are you well?" Wilmen opted for what seemed a simpler query. Indicating Alaena's wrist, Wilmen endeavoured to keep her voice light as she asked, "That bracelet is beautiful. Where did it come from?"

If Wilmen expected a response as simple as "I found it in the Wood," then she was sorely disappointed. Alaena's response shocked Wilmen to her core as long-awaited hope welled in her being.

"This?" she asked, lifting her arm to admire the gems on the bracelet as they caught the early morning light that filtered through the trees. "This bracelet, the symbol of the Order of Light, belongs to Simcha, Last Matriarch of the Temple of Eternal Light in the city of Radiance that once was the crown of the Southern Realms," Alaena pronounced in a formal tone. Looking at her companions, she finished simply, "It was given to me to carry on as Appointed, for Simcha's work is not yet done."

For a moment it appeared she would continue, but first Alaena bade them all to sit. There was much to say.

"Come, friends," she said softly, turning and making her way to the other side of the clearing where the grass was soft and the air was cool. "Let us break our fast here, for I have a task to do and would not ask any of you to accompany me without understanding the risks we would face."

Shortly, rations were retrieved from packs and all were comfortable, eyes riveted on Alaena who sat on a nearby stone. Somehow, Wilmen thought as she gazed at the girl she had known so long, something had changed. She looked the same, but her eyes had a depth to them that Wilmen had not seen before. Once again, Wilmen's eyes fell to the bracelet on Alaena's wrist as Alaena readied herself to talk. *Yes,* Wilmen thought to herself with butterflies in her stomach. *This is where it all begins.*

"I do not know how long ago it was," Alaena started, her quiet voice floating across the clearing and melting into the Wood, "but it was before the Desecration that the Prophecies of Ald refer to, and it was beautiful."

Eyes becoming distant, Alaena spoke as though she were reliving the memories, not just telling them what she knew. Wilmen's heart filled with love and wonder as she watched.

Lifting her arms skyward, Alaena's eyes scanned the heavens for a moment, then returned to encompass the trees encircling them and the earth beneath them. "All around us, in lines of Light above and in every root and rock beneath, Power lies at the ready. In the world of old, all knew this and rejoiced in it, for the Light and the Earth together were a boon to all peoples, and the world knew peace and beauty because of it." Alaena's gaze returned to the group, and each felt a thrill of awe as her eyes engaged each.

"In all the world, there were three places of distinction and learning. The first was the Northern Palace, also known as Seawatch, for it occupied the promontory northernmost in this land, some forty leagues to the north of where we sit now. There, Menlos ruled for many years as a kind and beneficent King, loved

301

by all those who served him. The second was the Earth Temple, homed in the very mountains we approach to our south now, and where the Order of Earth was based, overseen by Hor'yn, Arch-Mage of his Order. A proud man and bold, Hor'yn was a Master of his craft." Alaena shook her head as memories flooded through her mind. "Hor'yn was capable of what people even then considered miracles of magic, yet he built the Order on his principles of love for all things living on and in the earth."

Here, Alaena paused and sorrow touched her face. "Finally," she continued softly, "there was the Temple of Light. Here, we dedicated ourselves to understanding the Light and the Lanes of Power, and how to use them to best serve humanity."

Wilmen glanced around to the others, all of whom seemed to be transfixed by the story that Alaena wove. Had anyone noticed that Alaena had shifted from saying 'they' to speaking of these long-dead people as 'we'?

"Together," Alaena continued, "we three oversaw a prosperity and a golden age for all peoples of this land. There was nothing the Earth could not supply or the Light could not provide to meet the needs of our people, all governed under the fair and righteous hand of Menlos."

Alaena stopped for a moment. A haunted look settled on her features, and fear touched her eyes. She gripped the rock beneath her as if to anchor herself against a coming storm. When she spoke again, her voice took on an alien lilt, as if her memories and the past lives she described had become real in her mind. Wilmen resisted the urge to reach out and comfort her Ala, so real was the fear in her eyes.

"Alas, it was by our very gifts that we were undone!" The cry, though coming from Alaena, was entirely alien to Wilmen now. Even Alaena's features as they creased with grief and loss remembered were not her own. It was Simcha speaking to them now.

"We did not know! How could we know?" Simcha demanded of the empty air of her past. "Travelling on the Light, they came. Demons! Red-scaled and taloned monstrous beasts whose only desires were to rend, maim and devour. We, who had in our confidence and haughty presumptions that we were masters of all, learned far too late that the Light is just Power. It can be used just as easily by good as it could be by evil.

"Oh, the devastation that followed as we learned to fight and to protect ourselves left us all but undone! Had not Menlos ordered us to refuge in the Earth Temple, this world might indeed be the run of demon hordes today, for everything above ground was razed by flocks of demon spawn in their paroxysm of devastation.

"For a year or more we held our ground in the Earth, where Hor'yn's power was absolute, while outside, above ground, everyone and everything perished. We learned to shield ourselves from the minds of the demons and we learned to fight, for while there is great healing power in the Earth as we knew, there is also staggering potential for destruction for those that can channel such Power."

Tears welled in Simcha's cat-like eyes and rolled down her cheeks as she recalled the horror of those days.

"Many a time we thought we should gather what armies and Power we had within the Mountain and take the attack to the demons themselves. After all, were we not charged with the protection of the land? Could we in all faith stay hiding in our holes beneath the Earth and let all others die?"

Simcha's hands spread in supplication, as if still seeking an answer to that question today.

"This was the question Menlos put to Hor'yn and I many a time at council, for he felt the death of every one of his subjects keenly. When first we considered an offensive, we knew it would be suicide to try. As precious days and weeks passed though, we began to see hope. Slowly those demons that ventured close to the temple were pushed back and killed, though it took a dreadful toll on those faithful to the Light and to the Earth. Menlos led many of the raids on the demon encampments, until he himself was killed and consumed by one of the Despised."

Wiping her eyes, Simcha's voice modulated. Now strength and fortitude began to sound through. "It was there that the battle finally turned. Al'tahal, Sword Master of the Northern Palace, took the place of Menlos to lead our defence, and our strategies formed. Between Al'tahal, Hor'yn and I, we held a slim hope. Al'tahal believed that if we could lure the demons into our temple within the mountain rather than fight them on open ground, humanity might yet survive."

Shaking her head as she continued, it was difficult for the party to tell if Alaena thought Al'tahal mad or a mastermind.

"Al'tahal's plan was in one sense brilliant but in another it invited ruin, for it was a final and desperate gambit. The winner took all and the other lost all, for it meant us feigning weakness and opening our defences to invite the enemy within!

"The battle was immense, and had we not been within our own walls, it would have been ruinous. The demon hordes overran our halls with fire and fear and hate as soon as they saw us defenceless, and we responded with the same, for they had taken everything from us. All we had left was the bottomless pit of our revulsion and detestation for the pain they had brought us. The few hundred faithful left in the temple fought bravely, and for a while it looked like we might prevail after all, for the demon numbers were dwindling fast under the concerted forces of Earth and Light. Alas!"

The cry, so raw with emotion, made them all jump.

"At the end, even as hope clenched our hearts, a final surprise awaited us! The leader of the demon horde entered as the battle was turning and brought his powers to bear." Alaena swallowed around a knot in her throat. Simcha's memories in her mind were difficult to relive.

"We had not fought such a one before, though we did not know why. Perhaps they prefer to leave such dirty work as the subjugation and elimination of a world to their underlings. In any case, when he realised that his hold on this world was slipping, the Demon Prince entered the fray directly. His Power was ..." Simcha paused, shuddering in recollection before one word struggled free of her dry lips:

"Unthinkable."

Again, she swallowed, struggling to find the words.

"His name was Vetren, and all trembled before him. Standing twice as tall and wide as a man, his long jowls dripped venom and his mien was fearsome to behold. We thought ourselves Masters of the Art, but Vetren wrenched Light from the air in scorching bolts of Power that ripped through both human and demon spawn as easily as a man might tear paper with a knife. The monster seemed to reap pleasure just from the act of killing, regardless of who or what might be the subject of his rage.

"Again and again, we retreated. All fell around us as Vetren pursued us deeper and deeper into the mountain, taunting us with his depraved desires. His great, taloned feet scored grooves into the polished stone floors of the temple. If it had been one or other of us alone in the fight, then all would have been lost. But even Vetren, the Demon Prince himself, was unable to penetrate the combined power of Shields weaved by the Arch-Mage and the Matriarch of the Temples of Earth and Eternal Light!

"Finally," she said quietly, pride warring with desolation in her eyes, "we could run no further. Together, Al'tahal, Hor'yn and I had fled into the depths of the mountain, into a cavern with no discernible escape. I urged Hor'yn to open a passage in the rock so we could continue our flight, but we all knew that Vetren would follow and that there would be no respite. It was there and then that Hor'yn shook his head. He took my hand and put his other on the shoulder of Al'tahal as he laid out his final, desperate ploy."

For a moment, Simcha seemed to come back to the present. With the saddest of eyes that reflected a millennia of regret, she looked at each of the party sitting mesmerised by her story. Her words then were pleading, almost beseeching, as if begging for validation of their decision.

"What were we to do?" Alaena implored each of them. Her hands reached towards them, grasping air as the part of her that was

Simcha recalled the agony of the decision. "We could not allow Vetren to leave the Mountain, for if we three together could not contain him, then whatever was left of the world outside would be his for the taking! Yet he was just too strong. Too powerful. We could not raise spells to kill him without risking our Shields, yet even with the combined strength of Hor'yn and myself, our Shields trembled under the ferocity and might of Vetren's assault!"

Taking a deep breath, Simcha closed her eyes to complete the tale.

"Here," she said, "it was the Mastery of Hor'yn that both saved and doomed us all. He had realised during our flight that if our Shields could keep Vetren out and away from us, then they could also ensnare the Demon Prince and keep him from causing further harm. We could weave a Holding, Hor'yn explained as the sounds of the Demon approaching our final sanctuary grew louder. A physical net of Shields around Vetren that would trap him!

"Even as my hope welled, Hor'yn then made clear the single flaw in his plan: the Holding would work, but it would not last. As long as we lived, the spell would survive with us and the Demon would be secure. When any of us passed though, then the Holding would break and the Demon Prince would be free once more. The only way to truly ensure his capture until such time as he could be destroyed was to weave our own life forces into the Holding so that, while it would mean trapping ourselves in the net, Vetren would never again be free to vent his rage and loathing on the world.

"As Hor'yn outlined his desperate plan, the howls and curses of the Demon grew in volume. Dust fell from the roof of the cavern with the pounding of his weight along the tunnels through which we had fled. With moments to spare we agreed, for we were the last defence of the Earth and if that meant committing our souls to its protection for an eternity, then so be it."

Simcha's alien features were pale now, her lips trembling as she recalled the last moments.

"When he entered the cavern, Vetren was even more terrifying. In such close proximity, the heat from his body burned our skin and made us want to flee for our lives. Huge and slavering with hate as he was, it was all we could do to hold our composure. Even so, brave Al'tahal stood his ground before the Demon Prince. For one precious moment, as the Sword Master's unflinching presence before him made Vetren pause in surprise, his attention diverted enough to allow Hor'yn and I to reverse our Shields to form the Holding."

Shaking her head, Simcha clasped her hands together to stop them from trembling.

"Its rage was terrible," she said with wide eyes. "Never before had I witnessed such base ferocity as the Demon Prince displayed when he realised what we had done to him."

Staring at each of the party before her without really seeing them, Simcha described how the mountain itself shook with the virulence of the force that Vetren expended in the extremity of his rage. Trapped within a stinging net of Shields that formed a Holding to contain him, Vetren's wrath was as complete as it was impotent.

At this point, Simcha's head bowed and she fell as silent as the Wood surrounding them. The party members, reluctant to disturb the preternatural stillness, sat with their thoughts until she stirred once more.

Finally, her head raised again and she looked carefully around the party, as if assessing the impact of her tale. To Wilmen's considerable relief, Alaena's features were fully human once more and her voice was again her own.

Concluding her tale, Alaena described how Hor'yn and Simcha melded might and knowledge as they gave up their physical existence to form a sentinel which would be charged to return both Simcha's bracelet and Al'tahal's sword to the Appointed when the time was right.

"So you see," Alaena finished gently, fully herself once more, "I have accepted Simcha's bracelet and the task she and Hor'yn set down all those years ago. I will journey to the Earth Temple within the Mountain and delve deep to find what has become of the

Demon Prince after all this time. If it is still alive, I will find a way to kill it."

Pushing her bracelet purposefully up her wrist and adjusting the sword at her side, Alaera stood and surveyed the five sitting dumbstruck on the ground before her before she finished. "Who will join me?"

Chapter 30 - Earth Temple

The sun had cleared the trees and mid-morning passed before those that were to travel with Alaena set off.

After many questions, Wilmen had made it clear that, if she had to, she would accompany Ala to the gates of this demon's hell to see her safe. Rince and Tag merely nodded to each other, then looked expectantly at Alaena, their faces making it clear that their intention was to stay with her until the end as well.

Rogan, though he expressed a desire to go, left to make his way back to the road and the horses quickly enough when Wilmen suggested he return to the Abbey to inform Egan what had transpired here.

Darven Ross took more time to agree, though there was no doubt in his mind at the outset that he would travel with Alaena. A lifetime of indoctrination by the Priests of Ald was eating at his mind as he battled with the thought that the Appointed was a female. He had been taught since birth that to be born male was a privilege he should respect and be thankful for. Even the Prophecies themselves confirmed it was a man who would arise with powers such as the Appointed was foretold to control. How could a female even hope to harness such might and the responsibility that came with it, Darven wondered. In the end, Darven told himself he would travel with Alaena and her companions for as long as it took to see the truth of it for himself either way, for he could not dislodge the strange conversation with the Prince that he had been party to from his mind. If she was not the Appointed, then she was a dangerous conjurer who Ald needed to guard against. Perhaps her goal was even to disrupt his search and prevent him from finding the Appointed himself, for the Prophecies also told of dark forces that would resist the rise of the Appointed on this world when he arose.

It was all Darven could do to maintain his scepticism, however, when as they set off, Alaena gestured and spoke to the trees around them. The hairs on his neck tingled as Power thrummed in the air. To his amazement, the trees seemed to sway, then part slightly. Boughs untangled themselves and scrub leaned aside, opening a path through the forest before them, heading straight as an arrow shot to the south. Shaking his head, Darven hitched his bag higher on his shoulder and checked his sword belt was secure before taking a deep breath and setting off into the relative gloom of the trees once more. Despite his misgivings and mistrust, Darven could not help feeling a tingle of apprehensive anticipation as he took to the path with these strangers, for at the end of this journey there might be a demon waiting for them.

The journey south to reach the foothills of the mountain could only be described as surreally pleasant. Alaena and Wilmen headed up the small party, talking quietly as they walked. The older man called Tag took the rear of the group, leaving Darven and Rince in the centre. Darven found Rince talkative but shallow, with no appreciation or understanding of the wider world that those in Ald took for granted. Soon Darven gave up on the possibility of learning more than Rince thought the world of Alaena, and moved closer to the two women in front of him to better hear their conversation, his ears pricked by mention of the demon once more.

"As I said before, Wilmen, I am not sure," Alaena was saying. "Simcha's memories and the knowledge I was given end with Vetren's capture. The Demons came in the twentieth year of the rule of Menlos. Hor'yn, Simcha and Al'tahal captured him some two years after that, but how long ago that was I can only guess."

Looking around thoughtfully as she spoke, Alaena considered the question more fully. "I can only guess that hundreds of years have passed, for my memories of the Earth when the Despised were at last overcome are filled with little but fire, death and destruction. The forest around us was razed, as was much of the life that flourished before, yet all have regrown and once more the land is peopled.

"As to Vetren himself, none of us know how long a Demon lives, so I cannot say if he still survives in the Holding created for him or if, should we be able to find passage into the depths of the Temple after all this time, we will simply find a corpse lying within."

It was some hours before the trees started to thin. Here the foothills of the Mountain began, and their breathing became heavier as they started their ascent.

Though summer still held sway in Morlyn and the rest of the Southern Realms, the air at this altitude felt cold and thin. They had climbed for most of the day and reached an area where the rock stubbled ground flattened a little, allowing their tired feet a moment's rest from scrabbling for purchase. Looking around, the party saw nothing to raise their spirits. Everything was dry and barren. Even the rocks themselves looked whiter than those lower down the mountain, reflecting memory of ice, snow and bone.

***

Rince, rubbing his arms to warm himself as Alaena paused once more to scan the area, looked sideways at Tag.

"Well, Tag," he said with a wry smile curling his dry lips, "at least we didn't try to do this in Winter!"

Receiving just a grunt from Tag in return, Rince tried no more and turned to see what Alaena was doing. Though Rince would have preferred to keep moving, as the activity kept him warmer, Alaena was stopping more and more often as they ascended. Finally, Alaena help up a slender hand to bring them all to a halt.

Curious, Rince stepped forward a little more to look, for something didn't seem right here. Alaena's attention seemed to be focused on a flat slab of rock embedded in what appeared to be an even larger slab of rock set vertically in the side of the mountain. The strange thing, Rince realised, was that the smaller slab and the larger one it was set in were entirely different kinds of stone. How that could be, this far up the mountainside, Rince was unable to answer, but clearly it wasn't natural.

His interest piqued, Rince was about to take another step forwards when he felt a hand on his shoulder. "Wait, boy," Tag breathed into his ear. "I think our climb is ended."

Wilmen and Darven, came up beside them both, exchanging querulous looks.

The four unlikely companions stood side by side, watching with fascination as the Appointed scanned the area carefully, then took a step forward to examine the rock before her.

After a moment, Alaena glanced over her shoulder to her companions with a small smile touching her face. Wilmen's heart nearly broke. The look she gave them held so much of Alaena's beloved face yet was so unfamiliar at the same time. The moment passed, and Alaena turned back to the rock slab before her while Wilmen sighed in heartfelt loss. Her beloved daughter was both hers forever and could never be hers again.

For long moments, nothing more happened. Alaena stood with her back to her four companions, apparently contemplating the stone before her. Rince shifted from one foot to another as Darven clenched and unclenched his fist around the hilt of his sword as if the action could unlock the tension that was building around the moment.

Tag, impassive, simply waited as he kept his steadying hand on Rince's shoulder to keep the boy from doing anything rash. Something was happening here. Despite his outward demeanour of calm disinterest, his soul was afire as he watched the set of the Appointed's shoulders. The thrill that washed over him as Alaena moved was palpable. With no spectacle or ceremony, the Appointed simply stepped forward and placed her hands on the stone slab and bowed her head in concentration.

Later, Tag couldn't describe exactly what had happened. Perhaps because the transition was so abrupt, he simply didn't have enough memory to describe it.

Between one moment and the next, the dark granite slab upon which the Appointed placed her hands transformed. In one moment, it was merely another worn stone set in the side of the mountain. The next it was a beautifully formed edifice of such splendour that the party was left speechless. Darven, so overcome, simply dropped to one knee in homage. Never had he seen anything so truly remarkable.

Pillars of a deep black stone that they didn't recognise framed each side of a magnificent tableau of opalescent tracery, set in a massive sheet of polished granite. The entire stone was flawless. It looked like it had been carved and set by master stonemasons only days before, such was its sheen and unmarred beauty. The design, expertly utilising differing facets of the stone to express the joy of the earth in black, silver and grey, reflected the rays of the sun, spiralling and spinning across a joyous landscape that depicted life and shouted out love for all things living. It was impossible to look upon it and not be moved.

Without turning, Alaena called to them. Tinged with sad joy, her words came to them from a time lost now to all memory but hers.

"Behold! The Fourth Door!" Though still Alaena's voice, the alien lilt was strong now as it echoed against the door amongst the stones of the mountain. "Here did the Maidens of the Light come to greet the Sun at dawn and to farewell Her at dusk, then dance into the night to revel in the stars themselves, whose Light holds power of their own."

Turning, Alaena faced her companions once more. They stood silent as she completed the movement, enthralled. Disquiet tingled through each of them. Though Alaena's face and body were unchanged as they observed her, it was clear to each of them that it was not Alaena looking back. Standing before the magnificent doorway that had appeared from nowhere, Alaena's eyes glowed yellow in the afternoon light as she scanned the slopes, the sky and the horizon. Wind up the mountain tossed her dark hair and ruffled her clothes as if in welcoming play. Though the bracelet she wore was quiescent, Alaena's stance spoke of a power and surety that did not belong to the girl Rince knew or the young woman that Wilmen had raised.

Without really understanding why, Wilmen reached out and placed an arm around Rince's shoulder. Unresisting, he let Wilmen pull him close so they might both take comfort in the touch. Tag, standing alone as always, simply bowed his head in homage. He had already committed himself to her and needed no further prompting. Darven Ross, already on one knee before her, bowed his head. After a lifetime of teaching that males were the superior sex in all ways, his mind still struggled with such deference to a female, yet what he had heard her say and seen her do since he had met her forced him to question all he knew. Surely someone with such power, even if female, was at least worthy of respect, if not of fealty. The Prophecies spoke of the Appointed coming in the Light to save the world. Whether or not this Alaena was the one he still doubted, but Darven had seen enough to at least decide that for the moment, where she went, he would follow.

Long moments passed as Alaena examined the world around her. Finally, her gaze returned to the group standing silent before her. She looked at each in turn as one might assess a stranger. The disquiet in their hearts turning to trepidation, Wilmen held Rince closer. For a moment she wondered if her Alaena were gone and if Simcha had claimed dominance of her soul, for there was no love or even recognition in the look those alien eyes passed over her as she stood, heart in her throat.

At last, the feeling passed. Abruptly, much as the slab of rock before them had inexplicably become an intricately carved edifice between one moment and the next, Alaena returned to them. The cast of her eyes lost their strange glow and her look focused once more on her friends before her. As if only just realising herself that something strange had occurred, a small smile tugged at the corner of her mouth.

"It appears", Alaena smirked with some understatement as she straightened the gold bracelet on her wrist and smoothed back her hair a little self-consciously, "that Simcha and I are getting to know each other better!"

Pulling away from Wilmen gently, Rince took a tentative step forward. It wasn't clear to anyone if he was hesitant to step towards Alaena or if the imposing bulk of the door immediately behind her slowed his step.

"Ala," he queried gently, taking another step in her direction as concern for his friend overcame caution. "Are you all right?"

Even as Alaena started to nod and reassure him, Rince's curiosity overcame him. Sweeping one hand at the door as the other swept an errant lock of hair back from his face, he asked the question on everyone's minds.

"What is this, Ala? Did you make it? Is this how we get into the Mountain?"

Turning back to the door, Alaena sighed. For a moment, Rince thought she wasn't going to answer.

"Much has changed since I last stood here," Alaena began suddenly, turning back to address them directly. Shaking her head, she corrected herself quickly. "Since Simcha last stood here."

Sighing with memory, Alaena explained. "There are seven doors to the Temple of Earth. The first and seventh, at the beginning and end of this range of mountain, are the main entrances. Each door leads to a different part of the Temple." Laying a hand on the black stone, Alaena ran her fingers over the intricate carvings with fond memory. "This is the Fourth Door, named Althir, which leads to the Hall of Reflection. Though this is beautiful and a work worthy of admiration in its own right, it pales against the first and seventh gates. I hope that we will have the chance to see them again as well, one day."

Glancing at the sun, which was dropping quickly to the horizon, Alaena closed off the conversation, for she had no desire to spend the night on the side of a mountain when comfort and sustenance, she hoped, awaited only a short way away.

Turning away once more, Alaena gazed at the door, marvelling at its beauty. "You asked me, Rince, if I made this? Alas, though I wish I could make claim to such skill, I am not such an artisan! This door was made by the stone masons of the Earth Temple by order of Menlos over a thousand years ago. When the Demons came though, we could not have such obvious indications of the home of our Power displayed for all to see, for they would have overwhelmed us at the outset. Thus, we spelled covers for them so that each door would appear simply as a stone slab to any observer other than those who knew what they were looking at."

Turning one last time, Alaena saw their faces and raised one hand to forestall more questions.

"Peace, my friends," she said patiently. "All can come later, but for now we have had a long climb and we have yet to see if the way into the Temple still remains."

With that, Alaena wasted no more time. She placed her hand on the door once more, this time pressing her palm to the image of the Sun that dominated the centre of the design. For a moment nothing happened. Then, accompanied by a low murmur from Alaena, the Sun image began to glow, pulsing to the sound of her voice. Slowly, Alaena's voice increased in cadence and pitch, matching the pulse of the light emanating from the image. Between one moment and the next, Alaena's bracelet sparked to life, each gem around it flashing with the same glow as the sun image on the stone.

Instantly, the door transformed. It did not slide aside, grate apart or grind back in some way as the others had expected. Instead, it became strangely translucent. The design that gave it its beauty was still there to see, for traces of light spiralled across the detail of the surface, lazily following the designs set in relief in the stone. The stone itself, however, turned from a deep ochre black to a pearly transparent grey that, even in the fading light, the party could clearly see through. On the other side of the door, a dark passage led directly into the mountain.

"Come, my friends," Alaena beckoned, gathering her breath after the effort of opening the portal. Turning her head for a moment, she gave them a satisfied smile and said confidently, "The Way is open still!"

Alaena turned back and simply stepped forward into the stone. Her body passed through without pause or apparent obstruction. In a moment, viewed through the vague grey haze of what was the door and the sparkling lights that shone within and upon it, the dumbstruck party could all see Alaena standing on the other side beckoning them forwards.

Again, Tag was the first to respond. Pulling his cloak around him, as if wanting to ensure that the light leather didn't catch on anything as he moved through, he stepped forward the dozen paces required to approach the Door. Pausing only for a moment to put his hand forward, Tag swallowed quickly and pushed his body into motion, focusing on the Appointed who stood on the other side of this strange construct waiting patiently. Every instinct screeched at him to pause, for surely he was about to walk into a solid object, but he had not come this far to turn back now. As Alaena had done, his hand, then the rest of his body shifted through the shrouded barrier as he stepped forward. Stepping out the other side, Tag felt like he had walked through a film of water without somehow getting wet.

Darven Ross was quick to follow, then Rince and Wilmen stepped through, blinking when they emerged as if surprised that no harm had come to them.

Excitement tinging her tone, Alaena spoke as she bowed formally at the waist and swept one arm from the doorway and on into the tunnel. "Welcome, my friends, to the Earth Temple! Would that we were here in happier days, but I hope that when our task is done I can show you some of the marvels we wrought when Earth and Light flourished!"

Looking at each as her initial mood turned sombre, Alaena seemed unaware that she was referring to herself and Simcha as one now.

"In any case," she continued as a firm rectitude crept into her tone, "we will come to that in time. For the moment, let us attend to the task at hand."

Alaena lifted both her hands towards the roof of the rough rock entryway that surrounded them. At first, it appeared to the party that the sky outside was brightening, for the light permeating the pellucid door seemed to become stronger. Soon it was apparent though that, impossibly, the very rock around them began to glow. Looking down the tunnel, the darkness disappeared as though lamps were set inside the walls for as far as they could see.

"Come," Alaena urged, taking off at a fast walk down the tunnel. The others followed quickly, eager not to be left behind in this strange place. Awestruck, they stared about themselves as they walked, marvelling at the light that surrounded them.

Only Tag, taking the rear as always, looked back. He wasn't sure whether to smile because it was unlikely now that they would be followed, or frown as no path of retreat now lay open. The Fourth Door or Althir as Alaena called it, had returned to cold, black stone. It appeared, thought Tag sombrely as he loosened his cloak once more, adjusted his pack and checked his knives, that the only way out now was forward.

Looking in her element, Alaena paced ahead with long, purposeful strides. Her attention seemed focused only on the corridor before her and their destination. The rest of the party followed behind, staring about them with reverence. Even Rince, usually buoyant and full of optimism, was subdued. In his experience, rock didn't glow and one didn't just walk through solid rock. Staying close to Wilmen, he walked as near as he could to the centre of the corridor, keeping the walls to either side of him as far away as he could.

Darven Ross was particularly perturbed. For a while he stared hard at Alaena's back, as if by sheer willpower he would suddenly come to understand what was going on here. Darven had always considered himself an apt pupil of the Prophecies and had dedicated himself to his studies. The day he had been named a Rider of Ald was one of the proudest of his life, being testament to and reward for the diligence he had shown to learn and understand the messages that the Prophets had left them.

The Prophecies had certainly foretold the coming of the Appointed, who had the power to save the world. They had also made it clear that the Earth and the Light were powers to be respected, which the Priests honoured on a daily basis in the temples of Ald.

All his life though, based on those teachings, Darven Ross had understood that the Appointed was a figure that would work with Ald to help aid the world from a coming disaster. It would not be Ald that would be at the beck and call of the Appointed, as this Alaena clearly appeared to think it would be. There was also no mention of a Menlos or a city under the mountain where the stone of the walls glowed with a light of their own to guide the way. There were no tales of trees that moved to make paths for those that might wish to traverse a wood quickly or, Darven looked around quickly and suppressed a shudder, of tunnels that, like the paths in the wood, seemed to be bored through the rock directly into the heart of the mountain.

No, Darven Ross thought as he stared once more at Alaena's back. There must be more answers than this! He quickened his pace.

"Appointed."

They had been walking in silence for some time. The rock around them, quite apart from its unnerving glow, appeared to be a natural formation to Darven Ross with only one exception. As far as he could tell, it burrowed as straight as an arrow might fly directly down and into the heart of the mountain. As honest as he was to admit to himself that he knew little of mountain caves and their formation, he was equally sure they did not travel in straight lines!

"Appointed!" he repeated a little louder. Determined to understand some of the impossibilities he was witnessing, Darven had quickened his pace to come alongside Alaena, who was striding with determination in every step down the unlikely passageway.

Without pausing in her step, Alaena gave Darven a sideways glance before swivelling her head to look forward once more. Had Darven been any less stoic of character, he might have ended his attempt to converse with the Appointed there and then. Her fleeting glance had been full of otherworldly implication and golden glow. *It is only the light reflecting from the walls,* Darven told himself as he gulped back a desire to flee.

"Appointed," he stated one last time, aware at least this time that she heard him. "May I ask where we are and where we go, for though we follow you without question, I would at least prefer to endeavour to prepare for what we may encounter!"

"Be still, Warrior-Smith," Alaena responded calmly, though with palpable authority. Her pace down the corridor continued unabated and the stocky Darven struggled to keep up. "Soon, you will see where the path takes us. It is many years since I last trod these halls, though, strange as it is to say, I have never left the Temple!"

Feeling rebuked as might a child, Darven ran out of words and fell back a few paces, his face troubled and his stare falling back to the walls around him.

During the few times in his youth that Darven had ventured underground, he had found it oppressive. Though the confined space and the weight of the earth around and above him did not suit his spirit, for Darven would much rather be walking under stars and sky than earth and rock, there was another side to this. Darven Ross simply did not like the dark. He had grown up with stories and Prophecies that talked only of demons and desecration, to whom death and darkness were the closest of companions. To Darven, only a fool would delve into the earth to seek the perils that hid in the depths, yet here he was, following a near stranger further down into the earth than he had ever been before, seeking the very demons he had been raised to fear.

With the light around him though, strange as it was, Darven Ross was able to maintain his courage. If power such as this existed in the world, then perhaps this Alaena, whether or not she was the Appointed spoken of in the prophecies, could save them yet.

Step after hurried step, Darven Ross and the rest of the party followed the Appointed. He did not know how long they had walked, for time lost all meaning in this preternaturally illuminated corridor. On and on it went at a gentle, downward slope. After a time, Darven found the very directness of it unnerving. It was unnatural that, despite walking for what felt like a day or more, they had encountered not so much as even a bend in the corridor, let alone a turn. There were no side corridors, no doors and no break to the monotony. The corridor was taking them into the depths of his fears.

At last, Darven Ross pulled himself to a halt. Contrary to all expectation, it seemed that the interminable corridor had come to an end. Not a few hundred paces from where they stood, the lighted corridor ended and darkness, black as the heart of the mountain, lay beyond. In Darven's mind, salvation lay in moving from the dark into a place of light, yet the Appointed strode ahead, apparently oblivious to the fact that she would soon be swallowed in darkness.

Rince and Wilmen passed Darven by shortly after, with Wilmen leaning heavily on Rince's arm after the long trek. Each gave him a strange look as they walked by, but did not stop to ask why he was standing dumbstruck here in the corridor when it appeared that they had at last reached their objective. Perhaps they had no breath left to spare for the question or, like him, understood so little of what they were doing there that too many questions battered their minds to frame a single one coherently.

"It is imposing, is it not?" The voice came from right next to him, making Darven Ross start in shock. The old man stood beside him, looking at the walls of the tunnel about. To Darven's eye, he appeared irritatingly fresh despite the long trek down and into the mountain. Unable to frame a response in words, Darven Ross simply shook his head and turned his head back to stare at Alaena, who had almost reached the end of the corridor with Rince and Wilmen close on her heels.

Shrugging, Tag stepped forward as well, leaving Darven Ross to watch for a moment, aware that the further Tag moved away from him, the more alone he was in this strange place. Shortly after, Darven found his legs and doubled his pace down the corridor to catch them all up.

By the time he joined them again, he could see that the light emanating from the tunnel walls illuminated enough to show that a space of some kind lay beyond, though detail was tantalisingly lacking. In contrast to the plain stone floor of the corridor they'd traversed to this point, the floor beyond the tunnel's end seemed to be tiled, though the exact design was difficult to discern, obscured as it was by a fine layer of dust.

None of the party spoke. Alaena stood on the border of the darkness beyond and the light of the tunnel around them, facing the foreboding blackness.

For a time, Alaena's companions waited, watching. Unlike Alaena, who stood like a statue staring into the unknowable dark, Rince fidgeted while Wilmen shifted her weight from one leg to the other, easing her tired bones. Darven Ross peered intently into the depth of the darkness before them, his hand clenched tightly on his sword, wondering what awaited them in the blackness. Of the group, only Tag stood as still as Alaena, for his faith in her was absolute and his only thought was to wonder at what this amazing girl would do next. He stared into the darkness with her as if redemption awaited him in its depths.

Finally, Alaena lifted her left arm, the bracelet on her wrist glimmering yellow gold and in the filtered light from the tunnel behind her.

"*Illum*," she pronounced softly, succinctly, as she cupped her hand before her. The eyes of everyone in the party watched her with avid anticipation.

With her expelled breath, a small ball of incandescent light filled her hand, like a dozen fireflies had suddenly converged in her palm. Flickering briefly, the light waxed and waned before stabilising to a bright pinpoint of light hovering just above Alaena's outstretched hand.

"*Ciel*," Alaena breathed, lifting her hand as she did so. The ball of light followed her hand as she moved. At the extent of her reach, Alaena pulled her hand back, but this time the ball did not follow. It continued upward, like a firefly set free, into the darkness before them.

Though bright in its core, little illumination escaped the conjured light. It appeared to be floating upward, a pinpoint of hope ascending to a dark, limitless void. Straining eyes, sore feet forgotten, none in the party could discern any boundary to the space in which the light travelled. Finally, perhaps a hundred feet from where they stood with Alaena's conjuration now a star in a backdrop of nothingness, something changed. High up and far away, a rough-hewn ceiling of yellow stone glistened back a jealously guarded reflection.

Frowning, Wilmen tilted her head to one side, trying to make sense of what she was seeing. So far away, detail could not be discerned, yet Wilmen could see lines and patterns set in the rock far above them. At last, Alaena smiled as the rest drew a breath in awe, for no sooner than Alaena's light touched the ceiling far above than the cavern before them lit up. Like a roaring blaze started with a single spark, Alaena's light touched the ceiling and spread quickly, as if the rock itself were fuel to the fire. Far above them, an intricate tracery of granite set into the roof blazed into light, shedding illumination on that which had not been seen for over a thousand years.

The thrill of unexpected magic died quickly though as their eyes took in what they saw. The cavern was enormous. Easily a hundred paces wide and perhaps twice that in length, a thousand years of dust covered everything. Even the millennia of detritus though, could not cover the scale of the devastation that had befallen this place. Upturned legs of tables and chairs that had been blasted aside poked silently up from the floor, stout legs splintered like matchwood. Great rents scored the floor and walls as if the core of a lightning storm had loosed itself in the confines of the great hall, tremendous bolts leaving long torn scars in the rock wherever it had struck.

Wilmen, who knew of the legends of Light and Power that their practitioners once commanded, was shocked to her core. Her eyes tracked a single trench that had scored a line across more than half the floor. It appeared to have melted the very stone where it struck, leaving a deep rent in the polished surface to the point where floor met wall, then ran up the wall as well to almost three times her height. Wilmen found herself wondering how anything and anyone could control forces of such intensity. What kind of creature, she wondered, could conjure anything potent enough to melt stone? How was it possible to harness, let alone direct such stupendous might? Apprehensively pondering these sober thoughts, Wilmen finished scanning the area before her gaze returned to Alaena's back.

Alaena's head was bowed. Her hair was hanging loose and her shoulders were set in a manner Wilmen didn't recognise. Somehow, though Alaena's features faced away from her, Wilmen felt it spoke of anger. A tingle ran down Wilmen's spine as the truth came to her. A few feet in front of Wilmen, where the uncanny corridor joined the cavernous hall, stood one of the beings who had not only battled such power but had, somehow, contrived to capture the being that wielded it. Perhaps after all,

Wilmen thought as she held onto hope, this was not a moment to fear what had passed, but one to rejoice in what might yet be.

Taking a step forward, holding up a hand to stay Rince as he started to move with her, Wilmen approached Alaena carefully, trying to keep her breathing slow and her nerves calm. Coming to stand next to her, Wilmen reached out tentatively, intending to take Alaena's hand in hers as she had so many times in the past when one or the other of them needed comfort. This time was strangely different though, and Wilmen withdrew her fingers before making contact with Alaena. Instead, Wilmen sighed and endeavoured to break the silence that hung heavy on them all.

"What is this place, Ala?" Wilmen enquired gently as she once more surveyed the area. Through the dust and destruction, the myriad of lights sparkling above them reflected on grand patterns of inlaid stonework on the walls. These, along with beautifully carved columns that still supported the roof far above them spoke of the grandeur of this Hall. "Would that I could see it in all its glory, for it must have been magnificent!" She turned her head towards Alaena as she finished, hoping to engage her in conversation and understand what she was feeling. At the words, Alaena's face lifted and turned. Once more, Wilmen felt distinct discomfort as she again looked at Alaena, only to see a stranger standing before her instead.

"Magnificent?" The words came from Alaena's mouth, but the voice was not hers. Alaena looked curiously at Wilmen for a moment, as one might glance at someone who looked remarkably like someone you knew well, but the interest was fleeting. Wilmen felt a palpable relief when Alaena's alien stare returned to survey the space. "Indeed it was." she responded quietly. "This was and is the Hall of Reverence, where the voices of those who gave their lives to the Light came together to hail Earth and Light and share their love in song. It was beautiful and grand in itself, yet it is only the smallest hall of several that lie east from here, deeper into the mountain."

Discomforted by even this small interaction and thinking she had finished speaking, Wilmen was tempted to step back or away from Alaena. To her surprise though, Alaena continued. "It was here that Hor'yn, Al'tahal and I fled at the last," she said solemnly. "It is the wrath of the Demon Lord you see about you as he pursued us from here into the tunnels beyond."

As Alaena spoke, Rince, Tag and Darven Ross moved forward too, each touched in their own way by her words, which echoed about the cavernous chamber as she described the fight and flight that had taken place here a millennium past.

"It is strange to me," Alaena stated abruptly. The inflection in her voice extended her consonants and brought a regal lilt to her monologue. "Here I stand in what appears to me to be an ancient ruin, yet I feel that only yesterday did we three fight for our very lives in this same place!"

Alaena stepped forwards suddenly, making the others start in surprise. Striding out into the Hall, her feet kicked up small eddies of dust as she moved, boots on the stone floor echoing strangely, dust damping the sound. The rest of the party exchanged helpless looks before moving to follow.

Being careful to avoid pieces of splintered furniture and the great gouges burnt into the floor, they followed Alaena as she picked her way to the far western end of the Hall where an irregular opening approximately the height of a man and wide enough to step through with ease cut through the wall. Strangely, the edges of the hole weren't burnt or charred like the other damage in the Hall. Instead, these were relatively smooth, as if the stone had simply evaporated away rather than been melted through. Wilmen, Rince and Darven Ross stayed close to Alaena, peering into the hole in the wall to try to see what was beyond. Tag, bringing up the rear once more, focused his attention on the area around where they stood, studying it with interest.

Immediately beneath where everyone stood, Tag could see that the floor and the wall before them were unmarked. At quite a circular line, some ten paces out in each direction from where the strange opening punctured the western wall of the Hall, the floor and wall was burnt and scarred, as though an attack of particular ferocity had taken place here.

Alaena moved forward to place her hand on the stone at the edge of the hole in the wall. Simcha's memories flooded her mind. "Here

Hor'yn wove and held our last defence in the Temple before I opened this route for our escape into the tunnels." She paused a moment in contemplation, then, speaking as if to herself, she said, "Would that there had been another path, but we were at our extremity. Besides, who could have known the darkness and death that this road would bring to the world?"

For a moment more, Alaena stood as still as the stone all about her as she contemplated the darkness of the opening before them. Her companions, at a loss for what to say or do next, shivered a little in the coolness of the underground cavern, awaiting Alaena's next move.

"We will need Light," Alaena declared suddenly, without turning. "Your Stone, Mother." The words were not a question. They were equally a statement and a demand.

For a moment no one moved before Wilmen realised Alaena was referring to her and the gem she carried. Quickly, Wilmen fumbled in her pockets, strangely unnerved and fearful as she sought the bag amongst the pockets and folds of her cloak. It was with almost physical relief that her hand finally closed on the leather case and pulled it forth.

Looking down at the carved lid as she levered it open, Wilmen let out a breath she was unaware she was holding. All was well. Within, the gem pulsed slowly and lazily with light, just as it had these past weeks since Alaena's awakening. As scintillatingly interesting as it was in the depths of the jewel, however, Wilmen did not understand Alaena's request. This was hardly sufficient light to guide the party for a venture into the depths of the mountain.

Looking up as Alaena turned, Wilmen cautiously proffered the case and the gem within it to her. Once again, the alien cast of Alaena's eyes and face sent a shiver of trepidation down Wilmen's spine. The feline aspect of her gaze was even more pronounced as Alaena stared into the depths of the gem, smiling in satisfaction.

"Wake, my friend," she whispered as her long fingers plucked the stone from its silken rest. "You, like myself, have slumbered far too long!"

With that, Alaena held the gem high. "*Enradi!*" she whispered into the air as she closed her fist about the Stone.

Wilmen, Rince, Darven and Tag simply stared at Alaena's hand, held aloft against the backdrop of the centuries old wall frescos. In between breaths that plumed steam in the cold air, Alaena's hand started to glow from within as though she held a piece of the sun concealed in her hand. When she lowered her arm and opened her hand, each of them shaded their eyes, for within the gem blazed forth a yellow-white light that cast a brilliance that lit up the walls and floor for several yards in each direction.

Now, Alaena's eyes glowed that same yellow as she looked up from the gem with a satisfied smile on her feline features.

"Rince," the strange voice said from Alaena's mouth. Her eyes fixed Rince's as he raised them to hers with an intensity that he strove to but could not match. "Stay close to me and keep the Light high."

Rince, nodding dumbly, hesitated with trepidation as he started to hold his hand forth, palm up and open.

"Fear not, my friend," the alien voice soothed. "The Light will not harm you unless you mean it ill!"

Not entirely comforted, Rince pushed back his fear and trusted in his friend, though she seemed very strange to him now. Either way, he would make sure he allowed no harm to come to the gem.

Delicately, Alaena placed it in his hand as Rince flinched, expecting to feel some kind of sensation from the blazing jewel. Instead, it felt cool and smooth to his touch as he closed two fingers on it and held it up to guide their way.

"Good Smith," Alaena said next, turning to Darven Ross, "have your sword at the ready, for I know what we left but I do not know

327

what we will encounter today. We may have need of your strength."

As she glanced behind Darven Ross to Tag, he felt her eyes assessing him keenly. "Guard our path and watch the dark places, Assassin," Alaena stated baldly. "For the Light may not shine on all things we might meet."

Tag, putting aside his discomfort at being so addressed, for no one still alive had named him assassin to his face, bowed stiffly from the waist. "As you wish, Chosen," he said carefully, choosing Alaena's title rather than her name. The soul behind the eyes of the woman who stared into his now had no resemblance to the exhausted girl he had met not even a sevenday past outside the gates of the Protectorate Keep.

Before Alaena had completed her turn back to the hole in the wall to step through, Tag had loosed his cape and drawn a thin, razor-sharp and evilly curved stiletto to hand. As Rince stepped through to follow, holding the gem high like a beacon of faith, and Darven Ross prepared to step through after, Tag turned briefly to take a long, last look at the cathedral-like space of the Hall of Reverence behind him. *Well,* Tag thought, *if I do not see the like of this again in this life, let it be said that an assassin stood for the Light on the last of his days.*

With that, he stepped through to follow the silhouettes of Wilmen and Darven Ross between the bobbing Light that Rince held high, as they followed the Appointed into the mountain in search of a Demon.

Chapter 31 - Demon Prince

To Wilmen, the journey through the tunnels of the mountain was a tortuous expedition. After the long trek through the Wood and into the Mountain to reach the Seventh Chamber itself, Wilmen had hoped that their journey was at an end.

Delving ever downward into the bowels of the earth, the uneven passage twisted and turned upon itself like a maddened serpent. Often the way split left or right. Other cavities and passages appeared off to the side of the path they trod too, yet Alaena's lead never wavered. At every point, turn and intersection, her purposeful step took one path or the other without hesitation, as though the memory of the way was burned into her mind. For the rest, the light Rince held aloft was a blessing. Often, they found themselves scrambling over rock and rubble that had broken away from wall or roof, making them stumble and bruise their already battered feet. At other points, which unnervingly confirmed their path was true, the gut rock of the Mountain was burned black and scarred, much as the walls of the chamber above them was. Clearly, the battle between the Demon and the three who fled a thousand or more years ago had continued unabated through these subterranean warrens.

At one of these points, Wilmen dragged her hand across the stone, looking with wonder at the soot that stained her fingers. Was it really possible that the damage done to this rock was ages old and, more wonder as Wilmen watched the light continue to distance from her, was the creature that defended such attack the one and the same that now led them through the same passageways into the Earth?

As time dragged on and Wilmen, struggling to sustain the pace, found herself unsure as to whether it was day or night outside, or whether she might ever see the sky again. At some point though, she realised that the light was changing. The gem that Rince held aloft still shone like a promise against the shadows but Wilmen, looking down more and more often as she forced one foot in front of the other, noted that the shadows around her were less distinct, shrouded as they were by an illumination more silver than the yellow-gold of the gem.

Wearily, Wilmen raised her head, keeping one scraped and scarred hand on the rock wall beside her as she continued to trek forwards, wondering what new challenge was before them now, only to be jolted suddenly to a halt by a hand behind her, pulling her backwards with surprising force.

"Take care, Wilmen," Tag breathed into her ear from just behind. "It would be a pity to have come all this way only to render yourself senseless when we have at last arrived at our destination, would you not agree?"

If there was sarcasm in the voice, it was lost to Wilmen, for the scene before overrode all other considerations. Tag had grabbed her collar and jerked her backward to stop her cracking her head upon the upper edge of a jagged hole that pierced a stone wall before them.

Alaena, Rince and Darven had already stepped through into the chamber she could see beyond and were spreading out in the area, staring avidly. Wilmen, bending carefully as her back complained, followed them through with Tag close behind. Rince slowly lowered his arm. The light he carried was no longer required.

Finally, all the party stood within the chamber, staring. They were so deep in the mountain that the very air around them felt the oppressive weight of it, but none had time for any other thought than that which dominated their senses. Before them was an impossibility even for the mind of Wilmen, who had thought that she was at last starting to understand some of the power of the Light.

The chamber itself was unique. The rock making up the corridors they had passed through to reach this place had been of various types. Deep yellows in sandstone swathes of rock dominated, threaded through with seams of black slate, speckled shale with grey-flecked granite that looked like bones compressed in the earth becoming more and more prevalent as they moved deeper and deeper into the Earth. In this place though, it was impossible to tell. The walls were blackened, cracked and charred as though the sun itself had exploded within, melting the walls in part and rendering the rest unrecognisable.

Even this was secondary, though, to the source of light within the space that drew all their eyes. In the centre of the black cavern hung a sphere comprised of luminescent Light. Crackling with threads of silver and blue power that crawled across the surface, its topmost pole reached twice the height of Tag, whose dagger hung forgotten in his hand for the moment as he gazed dumbstruck at the radiant impossibility that existed before him. The lower portion appeared to be embedded into the granite floor of the cavern itself. What was within was difficult to tell through the brightness of the living, sparkling surface of Light.

Such was the spectacle before them, the party found themselves transfixed. The sphere wasn't just bright; it appeared alive. Writhing cords of dazzling power scythed and gyrated endlessly across and around the surface of the sphere. In her mesmerised state, Wilmen wondered fleetingly if this might be what bolts of lightning would look like if somehow they could be captured and brought into one place for perpetual display.

Alaena's movement broke the spell. As she turned to them, her face fell into silhouette as the light from the sphere behind her cast her features into shade, rendering them unreadable. Staring at the shadow of Alaena's face, Wilmen could not suppress a gasp of surprise as weariness left her bones. This was it, whatever 'it' was. Sensing Rince tense beside her, Wilmen gently and carefully reached out her hand, placing it firmly on his arm as a warning. Now was not the time for impulsive action.

Though the rest of Alaena's features were shrouded in shadow, her eyes were clear to all of them, for their depths glowed a golden hue that shone through an entirely alien aspect.

In the charged, flickering half-light, Alaena's features appeared downcast. Her voice was low, subjugated by the ceaseless crackle of the cascades of light that crawled across the surface of the sphere behind her. Alaena's companions strained to hear.

"Last time I was here, I thought we came to die, for our enemy was stronger than even our worst imaginings. Many died so that we might reach this point, and my soul still feels the yearning for the many lives lost so that we might prevail, yet prevail we did!"

331

Alaena's voice strengthened as she spoke, steel entering her tone to overcome the incessant noise that permeated every corner of the chamber.

Raising her head to survey them directly, Alaena's feline eyes glowed gold against the coruscating argent-silver backdrop as she announced. "So it is that I, Simcha, First Matriarch of the Temple of Light, stand here at last with Alaena, Appointed and Chosen of our Order, to finish what was started so long ago!" she declared suddenly, passionately.

Quickly, as if the last thousand years waiting could not condone another second's delay, Alaena's unearthly gaze shifted to Tag and Darven Ross. "Assassin, Warrior," she addressed them with authority that brooked no question. Glancing briefly over her shoulder to the construct blazing with power a few paces behind her as if there was even a remote chance that the two she commanded could comprehend it, her order fell to one word. "Defend," she stated baldly before her gaze moved on to Wilmen and Rince.

Tag and Darven Ross, commanded but feeling entirely unprepared, took a few nervous steps forward. Drawing forth his sword, Darven moved to the right and approached the circular ball of power licking his lips as Tag, wicked knives appearing in each hand from the folds of his cloak, moved to the left, his eyes tracking bristling coils of power that curled white with energy. Weapons at the ready and with both for the first time in many a year feeling entirely unequal to the task they had been set, each squinted to see within while trying to maintain as much distance as they could from the blazing sphere of energy.

Tag and Darven Ross already forgotten, Simcha, channelling through Alaena, turned back to encompass Wilmen and Rince in her gaze. Strangely she smiled before speaking as the construct behind her continued to blaze forth unrelenting force. Extending her arms, she held her hands out, one to each.

"Come, my friends," she urged, beckoning each with her eyes to take her hand. "What three began, three must finish."

Wilmen and Rince glanced at each other, shifting their weight nervously from foot to foot. Like Tag and Darven Ross, they found the sheer scale of power demonstrated here beyond them, yet there seemed no option but to see it through.

Wilmen's discomfiture stemmed from a realisation of ignorance. Until just a few days ago, Wilmen had believed she had some grasp of the possibilities of the power of the Light, but what she had seen since then and what blazed before her in an apparent perpetuity of potency dwarfed even the grandest flights of her imagination. Rince was unsettled in equal but opposite measure. While the concept of magic was not unknown, his limited experience placed it alongside tricksters at the tourney who made coins disappear from their hands only to turn up in another pocket, or behind his ear.

Ultimately with no more than the innocence of love and unquestioning trust guiding his movement, Rince looked into Alaena's eyes and reached out with his left hand to take Alaena's right while his very bones trembled.

Even as Alaena's fingers closed on his, Wilmen stepped up beside him and placed her right hand in Alaena's left for, as Alaena's mother, how could she do otherwise?

With the touch of their hands, a connection was established that transcended the physical. Neither Wilmen nor Rince could see it, but a palpable sense of something greater felt suddenly tantalisingly close, like standing on one side of a door that, with just a turn of the handle, would open up a vista unlike any other they had seen before.

"What occurs now," Alaena's voice rang in their minds with Simcha's strange accents twisting the words, *"will change you, but will not harm you. In accepting this without bond or inducement, you will free two of Earth's greatest defenders from many years of a bondage that they embraced willingly for the sake of all life on this planet."*

The words came smoothly, reassuringly as Alaena moved slowly to one side, drawing Wilmen and Rince with her across the rough stone floor of the cavern.

Unnoticed, Tag and Darven Ross had taken opposite sides of the blazing sphere, watching the lightning crawl unnervingly around the circular form while wiping sweaty palms regularly to keep weapons at the ready against whatever might transpire next.

Tag, who had taken the side of the sphere closest to Alaena, Wilmen and Rince, glanced their way every few moments, unable to predict what might happen next.

Eyes still locked with Alaena's, the words flowed once more into Wilmen and Rince's minds. Despite the noisome, staccato crackling of the wildfire light echoing like splinters off the rock all around them, they were as smooth and clear as if they were all standing together and speaking in a sealed room.

"The choice is simple but it must be yours and yours alone. Tell me. Do you accede?"

Wilmen felt Rince agree immediately. Without words, his commitment was made, and Wilmen understood that it was irrevocable. The sense of anticipation that had been building since Alaena took her hand crested towards a crescendo. A smile wafted across Alaena's lips beneath the alien aspect of her eyes. The door in Wilmen's mind she had imagined earlier, behind which a great unknown stood waiting, shifted minutely, ready to crash open.

Fear and mistrust warred with Wilmen's desire to comply. She understood nothing of what was happening here any more than she understood what would happen if she too agreed to what this Simcha so obviously desired and was asking her to do. Wilmen's essential strength of mind required more.

"Ala?" Wilmen queried timidly, loosening but not yet dropping her hand from Alaena's for the moment. Wilmen somehow knew she had encapsulated a world of concern, caution and care in the feeling that accompanied Alaena's name.

The alien eyes tilted as if trying to recall the name. For a moment the noise, the light and the unknown became too much for Wilmen to bear. Briefly, she squeezed her eyes closed, tears welling as she tried to shut this impossibility out and think.

"*Mother.*"

The voice still came to Wilmen's mind, but it was her dear Ala's voice, true and clear. Wilmen's eyes flew open, shocked. Choking back a sob, she looked into Alaena's eyes which, for the first time since they had entered this mountain, were entirely her own.

"*Mother,*" Alaena repeated, squeezing Wilmen's hand to emphasise her words and her passion. "*I know you are weary, and I know you are scared, but I understand it all now.*" With both hands occupied, Alaena indicated the cavern and the impossible sphere behind her with a flick of her head as she continued, becoming more the girl Wilmen had raised and loved as her own with each word. "*Only a week ago we were making candles together,*" Alaena quipped with a familiar smile, "*yet here we are now before powers that the world had all but forgotten.*"

Her black hair swaying, reflecting blue and white bursts of light from the sphere behind her as she shook her head, Alaena's features adopted a grim set. "*Would that we could step back but that is not possible now, Mother,*" she began. "*There is much more to explain than just this Holding, but if you trust me just a little longer, you will understand everything. The world is in peril and, if you will, we can take the first step in the Light to set us on a path to save it once more.*"

Finally, Alaena asked the question again, coming to Wilmen's mind in her own words and with all the love they shared within it.

"*Do you accede, Mother?*"

Aware that her only alternative was to walk away and abandon them all, Wilmen acquiesced. What else could she do in any case, when her daughter asked? "*Yes, Ala. If this is what we must do in the Light, then let it be done. I accede.*" she responded formally.

Instantly, a surge of relief and a wave of anticipation flowed between them.

Surprised, Wilmen felt Alaena pull her hand forward and watched her glance downwards. Following her gaze, Wilmen realised they were standing next to a pedestal that appeared to flow straight from the floor to form a flat surface over which Alaena positioned their hands before letting them go so she could gently slide the bracelet from her wrist.

That done and reaching for Wilmen and Rince again, Alaena placed their two hands and both of her own on the wide band of the bracelet, surrounding it completely. The gold felt heavy and cool under their touch. The gems set in it, quiescent for the moment, were smooth bumps against their fingers.

Wilmen watched then as Alaena's hands, her hands, Rince's hands and the bracelet they held all slowly descended towards the surface of the pedestal.

The moment before they touched, Wilmen glanced back up to Alaena's face. Reflected in the crazed bursts of light from the Holding nearby, Alaena's features were wholly alien now. Her eyes glowed the colour of the golden band they all held. Simcha's concentration was fiercely focused. It was too late to change their course now. Calmly, Wilmen shut her eyes once more, resigning herself to whatever was to come.

Behind the dark of her eyelids, the blistering bursts of light from the Holding shone through as, through her hands, Wilmen felt the metal of the band connect with the granite pedestal at last.

For the briefest instant, Wilmen and Rince experienced eternity as the bracelet in their hands burst into light, then it was done.

In that moment, their minds felt the bracelet link to the pedestal and through it, to the Earth itself. Lines of Light appeared in their minds as their perceptions expanded, extending far beyond the small planet on which they stood, making them aware of how small they were in the creation of all things under the Light. A tumultuously heady song of power and freedom thrummed through their souls as Wilmen and Rince opened their eyes to see the cavern awash with light from the gems in the bracelet that were blazing like the sun in the cavern. Red, green and yellow gold from the gems joined the blue-white blaze of the Holding, forming a cacophony of colour that drowned all senses in the depths of the mountain.

Closing her eyes again, Wilmen wondered at the clarity of her thoughts. Such an experience should have overwhelmed her, yet the very fact that she could ponder why her mind was not already lost with the scale of what she was seeing and experiencing was revealing. Using the unexpected lucidity of her thoughts, she turned her perceptions inward to consider this. Immediately, Wilmen felt Alaena's warm presence and Simcha's colder but yet more comprehensive consciousness surrounding her. With a consideration that felt as detached as watching someone in a race rather than participating in it, Wilmen surmised that Simcha, through Alaena, was protecting her.

No, Wilmen then realised through her enhanced perception. It was more than that. The sounds she could hear were words and enchantments, woven into and around the pulsing lines of Light that surrounded them. While she didn't know what the final work would be, Wilmen could feel Simcha and Alaena pulling strands of light out of the ether, knitting them with the skill of master weavers, though on a scale that encompassed the stars themselves.

As the tapestry of the spell they were weaving neared completion, other sounds intruded. The whine of the Holding changed pitch, escalating up to the limit of human hearing. Through her physical eyes, Wilmen saw Tag and Darven crumple to the ground, weapons discarded as they pressed their hands to their ears in pain. Dispassionately dismissing them, Wilmen closed her eyes once more, understanding now that they would have to fend for themselves.

Returning once more to the shared awareness of her mind, Wilmen realised that Simcha and Alaena's conjuration was approaching its zenith. The threads were gathered and tied. Lines of light pulsed power into a central construct of the work where its purpose would be met. The whine of the Holding peaked at an ear-splitting shriek as a web of splintered cracks spread across the roof and walls of the cavern.

Finally, a Word was spoken that shook Wilmen to the core. She could not articulate it and her mind was unable to encompass it.

The force of authority it carried and demanded was absolute. If there was anything in the world she knew, or in the universe of Light that Wilmen had just witnessed capable of conjuring and commanding such power, it could only be called a God.

With that, darkness engulfed them all.

***

Wilmen's consciousness returned to the sound of growling. Disoriented, she wondered for a moment whether she had been struck blind, for she was in utter darkness. She was lying on a cold stone floor and her head hurt, but she could not recall falling.

"Ala?" she whispered timidly, unwilling to draw the attention of whatever lurked nearby. Reaching left for Ala's hand, she felt only more cold stone. Reaching right, patting the floor to feel her way, Wilmen recoiled for a moment as she touched something soft. "Rince?" she queried softly, feeling her way back and finding his hand lying unresponsive on the stone next to her.

"Your friend is well, Wilmen, as is your dear Appointed."

The voice was again within her head and had the same strange lilt that Simcha's had when Wilmen spoke with her, but this felt decidedly different to the conversations she had had with Simcha, or Alaena for that matter, in this manner thus far. In those conversations, their voices had come to her from outside her mind. This voice spoke to her in a far more personal, intimate manner. It wasn't just speaking to her mind; it was *in* her mind. Further, it was a male voice.

Fearful, Wilmen chose not to respond. In the dark, she could hear things moving. The growling nearby adopted a lower tone. It sounded neither animal nor human. It was somehow more threatening than either. Wilmen did not want to find the source, and she was even more sure that she did not want it to find her. Urgently, Wilmen shook Rince's hand, hoping against all hope that he would wake.

"*Wilmen.*" The voice spoke more forcefully. It was uncomfortably close, disconcertingly intimate. "*I wish you no further distress, but we need light.*"

In the darkness, Wilmen nodded dumbly. That made sense. They could do nothing but wait for that rumbling, snarling something to find them if she sat here like an idiot in the dark. Wilmen waited, for she had no stone or flint, let alone any other way to start a fire. Surely this strange man who spoke inside her head would have a way.

"*No, Wilmen.*" The voice spoke kindly, gently. Wilmen felt as though he were adopting a tone he might take with a child. "*You have what you need to do this. Clear your mind of all else and call the Light. It will answer your need!*"

"*Call the Light?*" Wilmen thought in return, discomforted. "*I've been praying to the Light for most of my life and it has blessed me with great comfort, but it is I who serve the Light, not the Light that serves me!*"

The voice responded immediately. Its tone carried an urgency that had not been there before. Wilmen also felt quite plainly a sense of trepidation.

"*Your old life is past, Wilmen, for good or for ill. Search your mind and it will come. Quickly now,*" the voice urged, "*for with the Holding brought down, time now runs against us!*"

The Holding is down? Wilmen thought obliquely. *What does that mean?* Having asked the question rhetorically in her mind, she certainly had no expectation of an answer, yet as soon as she framed the question, she knew the answer. Simcha, Hor'yn and Al'tahal together had led Vetren, Prince of Demons, to this place. At their extremity and at great cost, they had created the Holding around him to seal him in a tomb of light until such time as the Appointed could come to free them all and see an end to the demon once and for all.

A chill went through Wilmen's soul as her memories unfolded in full and the truth dawned. She did not just remember the facts of the final battle with Vetren; she could recall every detail of the fight and see it in her mind, for it was the last thing that Hor'yn had done before committing his soul to the Holding until such time as he himself could be freed.

All this flashed through her mind in moments. It took only a second longer for Wilmen to confirm what she now understood.

"*Hor'yn?*" Wilmen asked timidly.

The low, sonorous voice responded immediately. "*Indeed, Wilmen, it is I, Hor'yn, Arch-Mage of the Order of Earth, returned to this world from our long vigil, thanks to you and your companions.*"

Even as Wilmen thought, yes, she already knew this, the undercurrent of concern that accompanied her awareness of Hor'yn with her resolved itself. Of course they needed light. With the Holding dispelled, Vetren was free!

Feeling Hor'yn rejoice as she stood and reached for her power, Wilmen opened her mind and engaged her legacy.

Stitching shields across her conjuration as naturally as she breathed, Wilmen drew enough power to bring a small ball of incandescent flame into existence. For a moment, Wilmen shared the feeling in her mind as Hor'yn exulted in the feel of power flowing through them once more. The fire floated in the air just before her, sustained by her will without effort.

With a gesture of her hand and a flick of her consciousness, the flame moved a few feet away, expanding and enlarging as it travelled. Moments later, the cavern was illuminated in an eerie yellow-white glow. Glancing down quickly, Wilmen assessed the immediate area.

To her right, Rince sat upright, shaking his head. He was very likely having the same conversation with Al'tahal as she had just experienced with Hor'yn, for Wilmen was aware now that just as she had become the host of Hor'yn to bring him back to this world, so Al'tahal would return with Rince.

Before her, Alaena lay unconscious on the stone. Wilmen extending her senses. Through Hor'yn's Art, Wilmen could see that that Alaena would recover, but she would need time after the expenditure of so much energy. Such things were not done without cost, as Hor'yn and now Wilmen were both well aware.

Clasped tightly in Alaena's hand, Wilmen saw Simcha's bracelet, now quiescent. A thrill went through her as more memories flooded her mind. Taking a moment more, Wilmen looked closer. Still wrapped in cloth, Al'tahal's sword was here, lying by Alaena's side where she had fallen.

Satisfied all was as it should be, Wilmen lifted her gaze to take in the cavern, feeding more power to her flame to bring light to the far corners of the area. What she saw chilled her to the bone. Memories flooded her mind as clearly as if they had occurred moments rather than millennia before.

On the far side of the area, the Demon Prince was gaining its feet. Head swivelling and sniffing the air suspiciously, perhaps wondering if this was another cruel trick of its captors, it was extending its talons and reaching out tentatively to where the Holding had been. Slowly, Wilmen could see, it was coming to the realisation that it was free.

"Al'Tahal." Wilmen spoke with low urgency, not taking her gaze from the scene on the other side of the cavern. Somehow it did not unnerve her to hear Hor'yn's clipped accent threaded through her words. "Your sword," she stated succinctly.

Glancing down for a moment in the dim light, Wilmen saw Rince's gaze land on Al'tahal's sword lying before him. Stepping around Alaena, who still lay unconscious on the floor, Wilmen started to move forward even as Rince, with a strange smile on his face, bent to retrieve the weapon.

Forty paces away from Wilmen, Tag and Darven Ross trod warily in the conjured light. Weapons in hand, held in white-knuckled grips like tokens of defiance, they assessed the abomination before them. Standing some seven feet tall, Vetren towered over the humans.

Pushing away a tremor of fear, for their battle to contain the Demon an age ago was Hor'yn's most recent memory, Wilmen called out a warning as the demon's lips pulled back, baring its fangs. A guttural, grating growl echoed in the cavern as the beast stepped forward, gaining confidence in its freedom. The demon appeared unsteady, but Hor'yn's memories screamed through her mind, urging caution. It was a master of subterfuge and, though doubtless weakened, remained a fearsome foe.

For a moment, Vetren's gaze left the humans before him to look towards Wilmen. Her fear deepened. Vetren's red eyes glowed like a disease in the yellow light, and his gaze held nothing but madness and hate. There was no sanity reflected in that fleeting glance. The Demon was a formidable enough foe even while sane. If madness had taken him, Wilmen wondered if they had just come here to die again after all.

Needlessly, Wilmen called a warning to Tag and Darven Ross as the Demon's attention swung back to the humans immediately before him. Even as another spell formed in Wilmen's mind, Vetren struck.

With explosive violence, the Demon lashed out at Tag and Darven Ross. Dulled and blackened with age but still deadly, Vetren's talons whistled through the heated air of the cavern. Black spit and old venom sprayed from his maw as he screamed a millennia of rage from within his haze of insanity. Pivoting his prodigious bulk to lend strength to the blow, the force behind Vetren's movement was massive.

Saved only by his agility and a lifetime of experience of knife play in close quarters, Tag leapt clear as the claws whistled past his face with ferocious intent. Darven Ross, positioned to Tag's right, gripped his sword tighter and watched as the Demon moved. Transfixed for a moment but clear of the deadly reach, Darven readied himself to attack. The Demon was too large, Darven realised with a flash of perception. It had committed itself to the blow and lost its opportunity to strike this time around. Once the momentum of its mad lunge carried it past him, the side of the beast would be exposed.

One moment more he waited to time his thrust, then, even as he tensed to strike, Darven Ross realised his error. The Demon hadn't miscalculated. Its talons could not reach him, but they were not the only weapon it commanded. As the Demon came around, its long, scaled and spiked tail scythed through the air behind it. The thickness of Darven's leg, the appendage whipped around like the arm of a catapult set free. With no time to react, Darven Ross took the impact in his midsection. Bones cracked across his ribcage as his armour crumpled and gave way like wet parchment. Lifted from his feet by the force of the blow, Darven Ross sailed through the air to crash heavily into the far wall of the chamber. For a moment his body hung against the blackened wall, sword clattering to the ground as his hands went limp before he crumpled to the floor, blood seeping from his mouth.

In the maelstrom of his mind, Vetren had long ago lost the capacity for lucid thought. All that existed in his twisted, broken soul now was a base emotion of hate and an overriding desire for destruction. The deep, essential and visceral satisfaction Vetren obtained by striking down one of the creatures who stood before him at last touched the depths of his broken being and defined what he was now, for there was nothing else left to him. Vetren had at last tasted blood and death again and elation filled his existence. Now, more violence was required. Much more.

Completing his circle, Vetren came back to face the other human immediately before him. Salivating, he growled low and took a step forward. The first satisfied a very small part of his need for violence. The second would begin to sate his hunger as well, which was immense.

Ten paces away from where Vetren advanced on Tag, Wilmen loosed her conjury. Shaped like cords of Light, the spell speared towards the Demon, knitting together as it flew and spreading forth like a net to entrap Vetren's mind, for Hor'yn most feared that Vetren would recall his magic and doom them all before those with weapons could bring him down.

Like Darven Ross, Hor'yn realised he had miscalculated. Trying to form the spell around Vetren's mind was like trying to catch smoke in the wind. All intelligent thought and ability was gone, and with nothing to anchor itself on, the spell had no grounding.

Harmlessly, it dissipated. The effort was not without reward however, for it made Hor'yn realise quickly that Vetren himself was without magic. The reason was not obvious, but Hor'yn had neither the time nor inclination to ponder how this might have occurred. The only thing that mattered was the realisation that the Demon, without magic, was more vulnerable now than he had ever been before.

As Wilmen gathered her thoughts through Hor'yn's memories to ready her next conjuration, Tag steadied himself. Consciously taking a moment to breathe, he contemplated the horror advancing on him. Tag, used to being taller than most, stood barely as high as its chest. Aware that the wall close behind him gave him little further room for retreat, Tag chose to distract rather than attack outright. It was clear he was not going to win this fight by with a contest of brawn, but resorting to subterfuge might gain him a few extra moments of life.

Forcing himself to relax, Tag drew himself up to his full height, flicking the knife in his right hand with practiced nonchalance into the air. As it travelled upward, the polished surface of the wickedly sharp blade spun quickly, catching the Light from Wilmen's globe and drawing the eye of the Demon for a precious moment.

As the blade reached the topmost point of its arc, Tag lashed out with his left hand. The dagger there flew with pinpoint precision for the monster's neck with all the urgency of Tag's fear propelling it, striking home even as Tag's first dagger returned to his hand.

Tag's offensive bid was flawless. Had it been any other being, the creature would have gone down clutching at its throat as blood poured forth. A Demon Prince, however, is like no other. The knife slammed home in Vetren's throat but could not penetrate the overlapping scales that covered the thick, red sinew of his neck. Nicking only a chip from the natural armour of the beast, the point skidded across Vetren's neck before its momentum carried it off into the darkness behind.

Affronted even more past reason that the pathetic creature before it had dared to attack, Vetren advanced a final step and lifted its enormous arm to strike. Madness and hate filled the red-gold haze in his eyes. Tag, pressed now against the wall behind him with nowhere further to retreat, raised his remaining dagger in a futile gesture of defiance. If this was how it was to end for him, at least he would go down fighting at the last.

Courage, or perhaps pride, forced Tag to keep his eyes open and brace himself as the beast brought its fist down like an anvil to crush him beneath it. Even as he did so, a blur of silver streaked across his vision. Moments later, a roar of pain erupted from the Demon as its face contorted in agony. Tag, instead of a blow that crushed his skull to pulp, felt hot, black blood spray across his face, arms and chest.

Wiping the sticky, burning liquid from his eyes frantically so he could see once more, Tag heard an alien yet strangely familiar voice nearby.

"My companion is not yours this day, Demon." the voice stated clearly.

If Tag could have cheered without fearing the Demon's blood that covered his face would leak into his mouth, he would have. The tone of the voice was low, steady and sure of itself as it continued.

"You have been freed only to greet your long-awaited demise."

At last Tag cleared his vision enough to see. Vetren had staggered back. Still yowling in pain, his right arm was severed at the elbow and lay twitching on the ground nearby. Before him, Tag saw a sight that made him wonder if perhaps the Demon's blood had driven him from his mind, for standing between himself and the Demon Prince was Rince. As if to confirm this vision, Rince swivelled his gaze quickly from the Demon to Tag, nodding as if to say "all is well." Unnervingly, Rince's eyes had a feline cast and glowed yellow in the dim light of the cave.

In his hand, Rince held the blade that Alaena had found in the wood with her bracelet. Tag had thought it a superlative weapon at the time but clearly even that assessment was understated, for now along the entire length of the blade, etched runes pulsed with Light.

Turning back to the Demon, Rince advanced a pace while Tag watched both the swordsman and his sword in amazement. Gone was the lanky, unsure boy. Now Rince moved with a practiced, deadly balance. His hand held the enchanted weapon with familiarity and a comfortable surety that came only with many years of experience. Waving it with deceptive casualness towards the beast, Rince took one more step forward, kicking the severed limb aside with intended indifference as he moved. The Demon retreated in step while its blood continued to flow, forming black pools on the black granite of the cavern floor.

Even as he wondered if Rince was going to finish it there and then, Tag saw his head turn towards Wilmen for a brief moment. His feline eyes blinked once in the reflected light of his sword before he took a quick, sure step back. Even as Tag wondered what this meant, Wilmen loosed her second spell.

Taking her chance while she could, this conjuration was devoid of caution or subtlety. With Vetren's unshielded mind in tatters, there was no longer a need for a measured approach. Reaching to the depths of Hor'yn's Mastery, Wilmen gathered Power of frightening intensity. Within the lattice of the spell in her mind, the Lanes opened as she called forth Light, spun it to a focus with steel precision, then launched it at the beast.

Dazzling and overwhelming white force banished shadow from every crevice and corner of the cavern as the area exploded with brilliance. From Wilmen's outstretched hands, spears of untrammelled argent power surged forth. Rending the air with fearsome force, they slammed without mercy or pity into the body of the Demon Prince. Instinctively shielding their eyes from the blast, Rince and Tag's hair sizzled and curled in the heat as Vetren's bulk was blasted off his feet before them by the force of the onslaught.

Scales melting from the intensity of the blaze as he crashed to the floor, Vetren's form glowed vivid red as Light burned through him from inside to out.

Finally, the spell gave out and darkness took them all.

***

For a few moments, nothing moved. No one spoke. While everyone's eyes adjusted to the relative gloom again, it felt like time itself toyed with stasis. Slowly, as a sickly smell of burned flesh permeated the air, they started to move.

Rince was the first to move, turning to Tag with his familiar grin in place, though it was oddly distorted by his rounded, cat-like gaze. Flicking his wrist upward, Rince touched the hilt of his sword to his forehead in a formal salute towards Tag, then swept it downward, affecting a small bow as he did so. The runes, still glowing, left patterns of Light across Tag's sight as the blade moved. "My friend," Rince said quietly, his voice still tinged with alien overtones. "It is good to see you whole, for of all living on this world, it is only we few in the room who have faced this one and lived to tell the tale!"

Tag, at a loss for words, was spared the need to answer. Wilmen, who had made her way carefully to where Darven Ross had fallen, was kneeling beside him, and she exclaimed loudly.

"Al'tahal!" she called, commanding. The tenor of her voice matched Rince's lilt. "Rouse Simcha! The Warrior-Smith has life in him yet!"

At that, Rince's head came up and graced Tag with a quick, uncharacteristic grin. "It appears, my friend, that you are not the only one to be blessed by the Light today!" he said with apparent merriment, before moving swiftly and surely across the cavern to where Alaena lay still unmoving on the stone.

Stopping at her side, Rince took a moment to survey Alaena. Lying prone, her dark hair covered most of her face where she had fallen.

"Simcha, my love." In the quiet of the cavern, his words travelled clearly to Tag, who remained rooted to the spot, still not entirely sure how it was that he still drew breath. "Your face is unfamiliar to me now, yet I feel your Light shine still and my heart rejoices for it!"

Kneeling quickly, he pushed Alaena's hair gently back before cupping her head in his left hand and lifting it gently from the stone. With his other hand he reversed his grip on his sword then leaned close, touching the exposed hilt to the bracelet still secure in her grip. "Come, my love. Join me once more!" he urged her.

Slowly, surely, Tag watched the scene unfold like a dream. Without warning, Alaena's bracelet came to life, the gems around it gradually glowing stronger, brighter, to match the pulsing runes running up and down the weapon.

"Yes, dear heart. I am here," Rince said, his attention focused intently on Alaena, his face just inches from hers.

With barely a transition from one breath to the next, Alaena opened her eyes and smiled. Even from this distance, Tag could see the unearthly glow of her eyes matching Rince's.

"Al'tahal," she breathed, raising her free hand to touch his arm tenderly. "Is it done, at last?"

"Indeed, Simcha," Rince responded as she sat up. The sword in his hand and the bracelet on Alaena's wrist continued to pulse dully, still charged with latent Power. "The Beast is dead. We are at last free of it, thanks to you, though our reunion must hold a moment longer," he added, gently taking Alaena's hand away from his face as he turned towards where Wilmen still knelt, tending to Darven Ross. "Our battle to subdue the Demon was not without cost." He held his arm out to help her stand as he finished. "One of our companions has fallen and needs the help only you can give."

Tag recalled the sickening crunch of metal tearing and bone snapping as the Demon's tail had scythed into Darven. A veteran of many a fight, Tag knew that it was a miracle that the Warrior-Smith's heart still beat at all. Unless Alaena could work another wonder, then Darven Ross would not be with them much longer. Watching her lean wearily on Rince's arm and rest her head on his shoulder as they made their way past the debris strewn across the cavern floor to join Wilmen, Tag moved to join them, wondering if she even had the strength to try.

By the time Tag approached, Alaena, Wilmen and Rince, as he knew them, were kneeling around Darven Ross. Wilmen had brought her Light to hover over them and Tag watched it suspiciously for a moment before accepting it as just another implausibility on this day of impossibilities. Tag's heart fell as he looked down at the stocky Rider of Ald in the yellow-white light.

Wilmen had removed the Warrior-Smith's armour and laid it carefully to one side. His chest and abdomen were a mass of blood. Splintered bone protruded through his broken frame in multiple places. Even with his faith and belief in Alaena, Tag resigned himself to the fact that they would be leaving this mountain one fewer than when they entered.

"My friends, even were I not so weary, such hurt would press me hard. We will need to do this together."

Without waiting for them to acquiesce, or perhaps they did so in their minds for all Tag knew, Alaena gently slipped her bracelet onto her wrist once more, then reached out to take Wilmen's right hand in her left and Rince's left hand in her right. As if performing a rite shared many times, Wilmen placed two fingers of her left hand to her chest and bowed her head while Rince pressed the hilt of his sword to his heart with his right like a promise.

In the silence of the cavern, Tag held his breath. The weight of the mountain above him was oppressive, and after all that had happened, he held back an inappropriate and entirely uncharacteristic urge to giggle. He had to be in a dream, for none of this could possibly be real.

With no warning, Tag jumped as, simultaneously, Alaena's bracelet, Wilmen's light and the runes on Rince's sword flared. Once more, the cavern was bathed in illumination, though it was entirely unlike the blaze of Wilmen's earlier conjuring that had killed the Demon. That power was devastating and absolutely destructive. The Light this time, though still bright enough to make him narrow his eyes to see, was warm. It pulsed with a beneficent radiance that made Tag stand taller. The smell of Earth and the wonder of Light filled his senses as he looked on transfixed.

Finally, Alaena lowered their hands with hers, locked together like a tryst to hover just above Darven Ross's ruined chest. As Alaena held them there, no words were spoken, yet Tag could feel the change in the air. The atmosphere became more urgent, more intent. Soon after, Tag realised the colour of the light pulsing from globe, bracelet and sword alike were beginning to change, modulating from white to yellow to gold to brown, then cycling through once more, faster and faster as Alaena began to quietly chant.

The words were too low to hear, but their cadence increased in pace with the cycling light as the three bent their heads lower in concentration or prayer or desperation, Tag could not tell which.

Finally, when the kaleicoscopic colours of the light melded together so much that Tag could no longer distinguish one colour from the other and Alaena's voice became a continuous flow of sound, she reached an end. For a long moment, the Light stilled, blazing in the air above them all while preternatural silence again filled the area. Finally, Alaena shifted, lowering their hands as one to Darven Ross's chest. As they touched his ruptured flesh, Alaena spoke a final time. The raw, commanding power of her words made Tag, standing close and captivated by the sight, catch his breath and stagger to stay on his feet.

"By the Light," her voice intoned in an entirely alien timbre. "So Be It."

Light erupted once more, but this time the source was Darven Ross. In white-gold radiance, his body blazed like a blessing as power flooded his being.

Just as quickly, the dazzling display faded, leaving Tag blinking like an owl in the dark to see as his eyes adjusted once more. Wilmen's globe, now returned to a low ebb, finally showed Tag all he needed to see. At first glance, after all this, it appeared Darven Ross had indeed been beyond help. Blood still covered his unmoving form in an atrocious volume of loss that no body could survive. As Alaena leaned back with a weary sigh, releasing Wilmen and Rince's hands as she did so, Tag looked closer. While blood still covered his form, Tag realised that the shattered stumps of bone were no longer visible. Further, his skin appeared smooth under the mess that covered him.

Even before Tag had a chance to exclaim his wonder, Darven Ross coughed once and opened his eyes to see Wilmen's globe of Light hovering above him still, shedding its steady radiance.

Glancing around, Darven saw Alaena, Wilmen and Rince, with Tag standing behind them, smiling wearily at him. Feeling entirely exhausted and utterly rested at the same time without fully understanding why, Darven Ross chose to simply lie where he was for the moment and smile back.

Interlude 11 - Emissaries

The days and weeks following the defeat of Vetren were full of emotion for all the companions.

By mutual, unspoken agreement, the party had not dallied in the cavern where the Demon had finally been killed. They spoke few words and placed no tokens to mark where Vetren's blackened husk was left to lay. Making their way back up through the Mountain, they returned to the Hall of Reverence where Alaena, drawing on her powers once more, sealed the hole in the wall that led to the tunnels so that no one would venture there again.

With that done, following Alaena's lead, they moved eastward through wide, dusty corridors to other, larger Halls that made up the Temple of Earth. As she had done when they first entered the Temple, Alaena lit each Hall with conjured Light as they passed from one space to another.

Tag and Darven Ross walked together but said little, overawed as they were by the scale and majesty of the spaces they traversed, while Alaena, Wilmen and Rince paused frequently to touch an object here or comment there on a past memory that Simcha, Hor'yn and Al'tahal shared. More often than not, their words were full of sorrow and painful reminiscence, for many they had known had died in defence of these Halls. Scarred walls, testament to the destructive powers loosed in the Temple during the final retreat, lined their path and bones lay scattered throughout, covered in dust and decay.

At last, they came to the largest and grandest Hall of all. It was unscarred, for Simcha, Hor'yn and Al'tahal had begun their fight and flight from Vetren deeper in the Temple, and it was here that Tag and Darven Ross truly understood the scale and grandeur that was the Temple of Earth.

Turning as they entered, Alaena broke the silence. "This is the Hall of Menlos, so named for the King of the Northern Realms who brought prosperity and peace to the lands," she said quietly. The alien overtones were gone and her features were her own, yet she spoke with calm authority and assurance.

"It is an empty place now and Light has not shone here for many a year, but now we have a chance to rebuild what once was.

"Behold!" Alaena exclaimed as she raised her arms. "We return victorious!"

"*Erit Lux!*" she cried as her bracelet blazed into life and Power thrummed in the air.

A moment later, Tag and Darven Ross gasped involuntarily, while Alaena, Rince and Wilmen smiled like conquerors. Far above their heads, quartz stalactites pulsed as if waking, then, as one, flared to life with brilliance. At the same time, the veins of quartz set into the marble floor woke in unison, patterning the floor underfoot with living designs of sun, stars and earth.

In moments, the entire chamber was illuminated with clean, white light that lifted the soul.

The immense circular space was breathtaking. Smooth rock walls displaying alternating layers of dark basalt, golden sandstone and a prominence of silver-grey granite reached up to a domed ceiling easily one hundred spans above them where the quartz stalactites shone white. The floor itself, easily half a thousand paces in diameter seen through a fine layer of dust, was polished marble inlaid with quartz matching the stalactites above.

Finally, Alaena turned to them all once more. Stepping to Rince to take his hand in hers, she gave a smile as she addressed them all.

"Here we stand, my friends, on the cusp of a new era. There is much work to do!"

"Warrior-Smith," she said, addressing Darven Ross directly, "after we have rested, I will show you the way to the First Door. It opens to passes through the mountain by which I would ask you to make your way back to Ald. Tell your Prince that the Appointed has come and Light returns to the world. Take with you my request for an audience with him, yourself as my emissary and any others of his retinue he may wish to bring to join us in the Temple so that we may discuss our paths from here."

As Darven Ross nodded his acquiescence with a broad smile on his face, Alaena turned to Tag.

"Assassin," she started, a semblance of her old grin flickering on her face. "First, we are going to have to find another title for you, as I suspect your prior profession may be behind you now!" Like Darven Ross, Tag simply smiled. "If you would, my friend, return to Morlyn's Abbey and ask the Abbot if he would be so kind to visit us as well. I expect he will be pleased to hear of events and eager to join us in our efforts to rebuild what was lost."

Lastly, without letting go of Rince's hand, Alaena turned and held her other out for Wilmen to take. With that, the Appointed and Matriarch of the Temple of Light, the Arch-Mage of the Order of Earth and the Sword Master of the Northern Palace stood once more together and began to make plans for the renewal of the Earth.

Interlude 12 - Dominion

Patience was a learned and often valued commodity in an immortal. In Kahu Pyra's opinion, as Demon Overlord of the Arkris and Guardian of the First Key, it was an attribute of worth only to lesser beings.

Since Vetren had first visited his dreams, Kahu had lusted after the world he had discovered. The minions he had put to uncovering all they could of the missing Demon Prince had delivered information that regularly filled both his mind and body with craving. This world teemed with such an abundance of life and resource that Arkris, backed by the power of the First Key, could rise to even greater heights.

Such power combined with the First Key consumed the Overlord's mind. There were many days where he sat upon his throne and pondered little else.

With a painful and possibly prolonged death the reward for any delay, Kahu's minions had ample incentive to deliver the information he sought. They did not fail him, though a few died regardless at and by the hand of their overlord's whim as they delivered their reports.

The planet Vetren had discovered was indeed a rich prize for one willing to undertake the endeavour but the sun it orbited was many light years away. It would take years to prepare such an expedition, and a number more for a starship to make the journey there using the Power of the Lanes before the abundant resources of the planet could be commanded and consumed.

With little further consideration and no consultation, for his word was Law to the Arkris, Kahu Pyra ordered construction of the ship to begin immediately. To sate himself in the meantime, he pondered his plans to bring blood, death and destruction to the Earth.

It could be such a pleasure, he thought absently as he considered disembowelling the underling who had brought him an entirely unsatisfactory meal, that he thought it likely he might lead the expedition personally.

www.ingramcontent.com/pod-product-compliance
Lightning Source LLC
Chambersburg PA
CBHW050322200626
46810CB00022B/28